Between men and women
there is no friendship possible.
There is passion, enmity, worship, love,
but no friendship.

~ Oscar Wilde

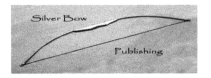

THE OTHER HOUSE

by

Uriel Buitrago

Silver Bow
Publishing

720 Sixth Street, Unit # 5
New Westminster, BC
CANADA   V3L-3C5

Title: The Other House
Author: Uriel Buitrago
Publisher: Silver Bow Publishing
Cover Art: "Integer GXOy45" painting © Candice James
Layout and Design: Candice James
Editor: Candice James

NOTE: This Book is a work of fiction. Names, characters, institutions, places, and events are either the product of the author's imagination or used fictitiously. Any resemblance to actual persons – living or dead – events, or locales is entirely coincidental

ISBN: 9781774032138 book
ISBN: 9781774032145 e book
© Silver Bow Publishing

Library and Archives Canada Cataloguing in Publication

Title: The other house / by Uriel Buitrago.
Names: Buitrago, Uriel, author.
Identifiers: Canadiana (print) 20220235678 | Canadiana (ebook) 20220235724 | ISBN 9781774032138
   (softcover) | ISBN 9781774032145 (EPUB)
Classification: LCC PS3602.U42 O85 2022 | DDC 813/.6—dc23

The Other House

to

Elena Iriarte
who had the patience to read my first story
a long time ago...

The Other House

Five in the Morning

Chapter 1

Three knocks on the wall woke her up early in the morning. Different from the ones she was used to when he wanted his medicine or when he needed to go the bathroom, the knocks were so weak that they seemed to come from a very remote place. She reached for her slippers under the bed, slipped into them, then went to his room.

"Tell me I am wrong," she said taking his hand. She turned on the lamp on the little table and then she realized Joe was dead. "You can't die without answering my question." She kept talking. She just wanted to confirm her suspicion that Joe, her husband who lived with another woman, was actually involved in the murder of Antonio. It was a question that had tormented her for all those years. And it was the reason she had promised her daughters to take care of their father during this past year; she hoped he would confess the truth.

She turned off the lamp and opened the curtains. She also opened the window to ventilate his bedroom, and before leaving, she covered his face. In that year Joe lived in her house, she had contemplated the idea that when he died, she would never give the news to Rose, the other woman. She had no connection with her, only that they had shared the same man for many years. So, in her mind, she felt she had certain rights for taking care of him during his illness.

She thought about the decisions she had come to. First, she would make sure his funeral was in the pavilion of the veterans, with a ceremony and military protocol. Then, as he had wished, she would bury him close to the fallen soldiers in the war. She picked up the phone and called Sarah, her daughter, to tell her what had happened.

"Your dad died a few minutes ago," she said. She also told her daughter they needed to discuss some family matters before his burial. Her daughter cried, and she said a few words of comfort then hung up the phone and went to the kitchen. She turned on the coffee maker as she did every day and absentmindedly prepared two cups. She took down, from the shelf, all the little jars of medicine, with tiny writing that explained the kind of medication and how each should be administrated. Then she collected medical formulas, biopsy tests, and doctor's diagnoses that had accumulated throughout that year. She piled everything on the dining table, and then put all of it in the trash.

She followed the same routine every day, only today she started a few hours earlier. She moistened a cloth with wood lotion and proceeded to buff and make the piano shinier and then went upstairs shining the handrails as she climbed the staircase. She then descended, sweeping the stairs, and when she reached the living room, she looked at Joe's bedroom and saw his bare feet. She had never seen them before and hardly remembered any of his body features. During those ten years she lived with Joe, she only saw him naked a few times but did not recall any particular or peculiar trait on his body. She covered his feet with the blanket and closed the door of the room.

Almost at eleven, her three daughters arrived, Sarah the oldest, Linda, and Rosario. After a few warm greetings and hugs, Emily turned to the girls.

"Before you go into his bedroom, I want to ask you a favor," she fidgeted a bit. "I took care of him for all of this year, and therefore I have some rights."

"Explain yourself, mom," said Sarah.

"I do not want *her* to know about his death."

"Mother, don't you think it's too late to hold those grievances?"

"I'm his wife," Emily replied.

"And she is the mother of his son."

"If she wants to know, let her come to find out."

"Oh, Mother! "We've already decided she needs to know."

The family conversation was over. Emily called the funeral home to arrange Joe's funeral and then she sat by the window. She saw Sarah crossing Oak Street.

Before entering the courtyard of Rose's house, Sarah stopped on a small bridge surrounded by lilacs, bamboo stems, and some overgrown bushes that were the signal of an abandoned place. She looked at the house. It had nothing to attract the attention of anyone who passed by except for the column of smoke that rose from the chimney. The oak planted in the courtyard stood like the only authority that guarded the house. Sarah also looked at the small park space her father built when they were little so she and her sisters could play with their autistic brother. She noticed the space had lost the wooden tunnel, and the iron spider they once rode on was hidden under the grass. The carousel with its faded colors was tilted to the side and one of the seats of the swing moved back and forth as the wind rushed through the park. Whoever passed by the other house on Oak Street wouldn't believe that children's shouting had once cheered the street in the afternoons so long ago.

Chapter 2

When they first met, Joe was twenty-four years old and Emily was just seventeen. The town then was in a state of chaos. It was one of those forgotten places that nobody knew existed. It was a town condemned to ostracism by a journalist from the New York Times who reported a massacre that occurred there in 1932. That event was like a curse that changed the town's name and its fate. Little York, its former name, was changed for No-town by the same journalist, just to remind the nation that it never existed. The town was then invaded by mobsters from Kansas City, St. Louis, and Chicago. Their presence was like invasive cancer that took over No-town. They took over the offices of the Municipal Building and the mayor's office.

Benjamin Crompton the First made his way to the mayor's office elected by an *ad hoc* City Council whose members were his comrades. Since then, the members of the City Council were appointed by Crompton the First and they re-elected him; a circle that kept operating for more than seventy years. It was a period of negligence and nepotism because Crompton the First passed the office on to his son Ben Crompton the Second, and he passed it on to Ben Crompton the Third. No-town became an allegory, a joke, a frustrating dream for those who were the founders, among them, Emily's great-grandmother. No-town was, as an intellectual said: "the land of the unreasonable where Frank Kafka might've gotten his inspiration to write *The Trial*."

So, Emily lived in No-town. When she was ten years old, she lived in the big house that her great-grandma Marie built after she sold her bank to Crompton the First. Emily lived with her parents John and Maggie, her aunts Katherine, Jennifer and Lisa, and her uncle Mark. All of them Maggie's siblings. Her uncle Mark was called JR or Mark Junior to distinguish him from their grandfather whose name was also Mark.

The house was the same since the time her great-grandmother Marie built it and Emily had good memories of her childhood there. The house was large, with many rooms, an attic, and a balcony in the back, where her aunts held their gatherings every afternoon when the hot days allowed it. It had two patios, one in the front and a large backyard with many oaks and a very well-maintained lawn. The backyard had, for a long time, very regular visitors on summer days. These were not the young men of the town who were at the age to get married; instead, they were cats that appeared in the backyard at the beginning of May; when the days became hot.

The cats came out of the forest and were docile. They would lie on the stairwell of the entrance or climb on the low branches of the oaks. It was unknown why they only came to that particular backyard and not to the ones of the other houses. The phenomenon was known in the town, and the house was notorious, not for parties, but for the cats, so much so that it was known as *'the house of the cats'*.

Emily's aunts gave little importance to this situation. It was not a problem for them to find the cats on the balcony or in their rooms. Whenever they left the house, they had to scare them to make their way out.

Her aunts did not work, nor had they gone to college, because they lived on the inheritance left by Marie, their grandmother. Besides their beauty, none had any skill or talent. The only one who had some talent was her Aunt Katherine, who played the piano occasionally, and she was affectionate and fun with her. She was the aunt Emily admired, but Katherine traveled often and was not home much. The other aunts, Jennifer and Lisa, were reserved and had bad tempers. Jennifer had a loud laugh, while Lisa was shy. Lisa had many secrets that she rarely shared with her sisters. When she did, the three, including Maggie ended up disgusted, yelling and calling each other names. When Maggie got married, discussions about Lisa's secrets took a back seat. In addition to her secrets, it was said that Lisa liked mature men.

Her three aunts lamented that the town had a brothel. Their nights of loneliness, and the inability to have male company whenever they needed it, was because of its existence. If it had been up to them, they would have eliminated the brothel from the map. Her Uncle Mark, on the other hand, said that Colton, (the name of the brothel), was heaven. Uncle Mark was lazy, slept late, and went to Colton at night.

Her Uncle Mark was kind to Emily even though he blatantly told stories from Colton at lunchtime. Maggie scolded him or asked him not to tell the stories when little Emily was around. But he often forgot those recommendations. He brought her surprises that made her happy: a dark-eyed doll, a music box, a small guitar, and so many gifts that she put in perfect order on the mantelpiece in her room.

Those were the times when Emily was happy. She played in the yard with the cats and in the house across the street lived a couple that her aunts said was strange because the woman had prominent breasts and the man had a terrifying appearance with his large ears and small face. The woman wore red lipstick and very tight tops that made her breasts more visible, all of this combined with her voluptuous walk, attracted the attention of men and had her husband be on the verge of constant jealousy.

But those explosive moments of this man did not remain for long and ended when he made peace in bed with his woman. It was noisy lovemaking, yelling profanities at each other that altered the peaceful afternoons in the neighborhood. Afterward, for a few days, the woman dressed as an old lady from the mid-twenties in long gowns that covered her body from neck to foot with no neckline. But that seriousness and good lady posture finished when she caught her husband cheating again with the prostitutes in Colton. Then, again as an act of revenge, she dressed up provocatively to go to the grocery store or found different sorts of excuses to go anywhere to provoke his jealous behavior.

The man had the habit of sitting on the porch with his denture prostheses in one hand and a glass of water in the other. He washed them in plain sight of those who passed along Oak Street. He was a terror to the children because he looked like a demon without the prosthesis. The skin on his cheeks became stuck to his cheekbones and his face underwent a sudden transformation, making his ears more prominent and his head smaller, like an elf from those scary children's books. He purposely removed his dentures from his mouth when children walked home from school. Sometimes when boys and girls passed in groups, they called him nicknames: "Hello devil," "hello Quasimodo," or "hello monster." But, when they passed alone, they ran without looking at the house.

The couple had a girl whose name was Tandy, about two years younger than Emily. Although her aunts forbade it, Emily became friends with Tandy. She did not care what they said about her parents, nor the teasing of the children as they passed by. They played every day after school.

Running parallel to Oak Street was a stream of clean water in which they went shoeless and walked up or down looking, for aquatic insects and tadpoles that they put in a jar. They sat on the bridge in front of the house and with their feet in the water they talked.

"You're my best friend," Tandy said. "I don't have friends at school, and sometimes they call me the daughter of the devil."

"I'll never call you that."

"You're very good," she said." I am a crazy girl, very crazy. I don't know, but something in my head doesn't work."

"Bah, you're not crazy."

"Have you seen the devil?" Tandy asked.

"No, I've not."

"My mother says that all men are the devil."

"My father is not the devil."

"Your father does not go there?"

"Where?" Emily raised her eyebrows quizzically.

"To that place."

"What place are you talking about?" Emily was growing visibly uncomfortable.

"That place where those women are, the bad women!"

"My father does not go there, he is good."

Tandy clasped her hands together, swished her feet in the water, and stared into the stream, "Mine goes almost every night, and that's why he fights with my mom."

"Uncle Mark always goes there," said Emily, "but he is good."

"Ah, then he's a good devil," Tandy said, and both laughed. They played until Aunt Katherine called her for her piano lessons.

When her Aunt Katherine was traveling, she played all afternoon. In the evenings, she practiced what her aunt had taught her. Emily liked to play the piano and enjoyed practicing the lessons she learned from her aunt. She had learned to read the notes of some classical pieces, and she played "Moonlight" and "For Elise" by memory. During the break at school, Emily would go to the music room without anyone noticing and play the piano. Afraid that someone would discover her, she played the keys softly so people in the halls would not hear the music.

Emily did it many times until one day, Mrs. Carter, the music instructor, entered. Scared, Emily apologized to Mrs. Carter. When she was going to leave, almost running, the instructor ordered Emily to return to the piano and play what she was playing. Amazed by Emily's skills, the teacher asked her to attend her lessons and piano practices. From that day forward, the two were not only instructor and student but friends. When Emily turned twelve, she was a master of the piano. She was the first on the list in the musical presentations and invited to interpret the musical backgrounds for the plays in the school theater.

And then, the moment came when Aunt Katherine had nothing more to teach her, but Emily still admired her. Katherine was joyful and had energy, and she looked like Glinda in the movie "The Wizard of Oz", and for that reason, Emily asked her one day, *"aunt, are you an actress?"* And her aunt laughed.

No one at home knew the reasons for Aunt Katherine's trips, nor did anyone ask her because they were living in their own world. When Emily was little, she invented the story that her aunt went to distant cities to play the piano with very large orchestras. Then, over the years, the story ceased to be an invention because she came to believe it was true. She told Tandy her aunt was a very famous pianist and lived with that fictionalized belief for some time.

Katherine was the only aunt that had a closet with lots of clothes, and her room always remained locked when she was traveling. On one occasion, Emily turned the knob and the door opened. Her aunt had left without locking it. She entered and closed the door behind her. There were so many things to look at, but the first impact was the scent of the room that smelled like her aunt, the sweet aroma of roses she would always remember. She was curious to open the dresser drawers, the tables on each side of her bed, she wanted to look at her closet, to put on her dresses and shoes. But the desire to lie down in her bed was stronger than her mere curiosity. She took off her shoes and laid down and thought: *"When I grow up, I will be like my Aunt Katherine, beautiful, intelligent, and a pianist."*

When she left Katherine's room, she forgot to close the door and that was a big mistake. The consequences derived from that simple error were enormous and significantly affected Katherine, her favorite aunt, for whom she would have sacrificed her life.

Her Aunt Lisa, the bitter one, went into the room when she saw the door open. Lisa, with that devious curiosity that characterized her, found the love letters Katherine had received from a man and read them all. So, she came to learn that Katherine had traveled the world with someone. But the trips of her sister with a lover were not what Lisa had expected to find. She learned in the letters the man was married with children, and he lived in New York.

The same night Lisa read the letters Katherine arrived home. The next morning, everyone sat down at the dining table for breakfast; her father John, Mark, her three aunts, and her mother who was in charge of the kitchen and the house.

"How was the trip?" asked John. No one ever asked her questions about her travels, nor had she expected John, her brother-in-law, would ask her about her trip.

"I was in southern Italy."

"Sicily?" John insisted.

"Cinque Terre," said Katherine.

"Were you alone?" Lisa asked.

"Yes, as always," Katherine answered.

"Liar," said Lisa.

Everyone was silent for a long moment.

"Nobody in my thirty-two years of existence has called me a liar." Katherine broke the silence

"You're a liar," Lisa said again.

"You are haughty."

"Oh, yes, what would you call it? My secret? My everything? My life? What about my married lover?" Lisa said mockingly. "Poor thing, you have to wait until the wife gives him permission to..."

"Enough!" Katherine shouted.

"Well, the next time you disappear, do not leave your door open."

"I never leave the door open, and if it was, you don't have the right to enter."

It was when Emily felt a blow somewhere in her body. It was a very painful blow. She was not even disappointed to discover her aunt was not a famous pianist who was going to play the piano with big orchestras all over the world. She felt pain in her heart when she saw her aunt helpless, defeated, and about to cry.

"At least my secrets do not include any member of the family," continued Katherine drying her tears.

"Explain yourself," Maggie asked.

"Nothing sister, time will reveal it," said Katherine as she stood up and went up to her room.

Nothing extraordinary happened during the rest of the day, but everyone avoided looking each other in the eyes. The conversations were short, and everyone had an excuse to lock themselves in their rooms. Nobody answered the phone nor came out of their bedroom to take their meals. Uncle Mark went to Colton earlier than usual.

The next day Katherine announced that she was leaving forever without telling anybody where she was going. She spent the morning packing two large suitcases and when she was about to leave, Maggie came in and locked the door.

"What did you mean when you mentioned the word *secrets*?" She asked her sister.

"Nothing," Katherine answered after a long pause.

"I suspect you know something," insisted Maggie.

Katherine, trying to ignore her sister's words, went to the closets and searched to make sure she didn't leave anything behind.

"Do you know anything I need to know?" Maggie asked again.

"Sister," said Katherine, "leave this house with your husband and daughter as soon as you can."

"Why?"

"Just do it."

When it was ten on the big clock in the living room, Katherine left saying goodbye to Maggie and her niece but nobody else. That afternoon, Emily's parents told Mark that they were going to live in another house. The reasons for which her parents made that decision also remained secret, although they hinted that the environment was not good for Emily, who was at the age when she should have exemplary images to emulate and not that of her aunts. But that was not the motive, and Emily did not get to know it until much later when she was married and with children.

They moved to another house a few blocks up Oak Street. The communication with her aunts Jennifer and Lisa was almost nil because when Emily's parents left, it was on very bad terms; Maggie heard some sporadic news from her sisters when she went to the store and happened to meet one of them. It was Uncle Mark who often came to see Emily, but neither Jennifer nor Lisa had any intention to forget the past and so didn't come to visit their niece.

The house was small but big enough for the family. It had a large patio and a porch covered with a screen where they could sit and chat. It was such a safe and pleasant environment. Her parents were never happier, and she was the center of all their attention. She went to school in good spirits every day and stayed to practice the piano under the direction of Mrs. Carter until dusk.

Chapter 3

One day Mark came to tell them that he was leaving the town. He wanted to live in a big city where other winds blew. He said to his brother-in-law, John, that he was fed up with the town, with the Mayor, with Colton, and, above all, he was very tired of his sisters. The house had become a place where his sisters invited people, talked about useless things, gossip; meetings that ended in parties every night until dawn. He was disgusted with Jennifer and Lisa because he thought they were squandering the inheritance left by Marie, Emily's great-grandmother. The two women were spending it on those parties without any control, cashing checks anytime and whenever they wanted to.

When Mark decided to leave town, he thought about his niece and went to the bank in St. Louis to cash a check. It was a considerable amount of money that he put on the dining table, dividing it into two equal parts. "This money is for Emily's education," her uncle said and kept the other half. Satisfied with his decision, he said he was leaving town that night, but he did not tell them where he was going. He was so disgusted with his sisters, that he left without saying goodbye to them.

It was also a sad farewell for Emily, more than it was with her Aunt Katherine. She went to school with a feeling of loneliness and the sensation that something was missing. During a break, she passed by Mrs. Carter's office. As always, her instructor had the radio on and a sad piece was playing, but that morning Mrs. Carter was happy.

"I have good news," she said. The director of the Music Department from a university in St. Louis had written her a letter asking for students with a talent for music. She had thought about Emily.

"Although you have some years left to finish high school, I've decided to begin your preparation immediately," she said.

Mrs. Carter started that day by writing a response to the Department's director; a letter describing her student, her skills, the ability to adapt to new challenges, and, above all, her personality that she defined as one of the sweetest in her classroom. To ensure the director had a favorable response, Mrs. Carter had Emily record a piano piece by Chopin that she added to the letter. The answer came a week later, and Mrs. Carter waited for Emily to read it. The response was favorable and emphasized that Emily had her place secured in the Department by the time she was done with high school.

Emily gave the news to her parents, and they were very happy. They had the money Uncle Mark had left for her education under the mattress, and they decided to open an account at a bank in the nearest town, but time went by, and they procrastinated until they forgot about it. To make matters worse, Maggie had a bad habit of buying things, even if they were not useful. Maggie had the same tendency as her sisters, to spend money and pretend she was rich. She donated a sum of money to a foundation of dubious reputation dedicated to protecting wild cats, only with the idea of her name appearing on a list of philanthropists in a local magazine of mediocre presentation. Neither her husband nor her daughter knew about that donation.

And then, what they were not expecting, happened. Maggie started to feel sick, a hereditary condition affecting her pancreas. They spent the last resources on the diagnosis, some medicines, and a few days of hospitalization that resulted in nothing. Her illness advanced, and it seemed she must have been suffering from the illness for a long time because neither the medicine nor the radiotherapy sessions helped her. The doctors had given her one last hope, a new treatment still in a state of trial. It was costly because it required extensive and delicate professional care and scientific observation. And there was another, even more, serious problem; the side effects; if she survived, they were expected to be devastating and the chances of successful recovery were low.

* * *

John Fletcher went to let Jennifer and Lisa know about Maggie's illness. Upon entering the front yard, he noticed the abandonment of the place. The grass had grown, the house had lost some tiles, and a branch of the oaks had fallen off, opening a large hole in the roof. The cats had taken over the backyard and there were many. He saw through the windows that the house was empty and at the stage of abandonment; he concluded that his sisters-in-law had been long gone.

Father and daughter came to inspect the house later. They had contemplated the idea of bringing Maggie to live in the house now that her sisters were no longer living there. The house where they currently lived was small and Maggie needed a spacious and comfortable room to spend her last days as all her ancestors before her had been able to do.

When they opened the door, they saw that the cats had invaded the house. They were everywhere, in the kitchen, living room, and the bedrooms of the second floor. The first thing they did was to take them out of the house. Despite the abandonment, all of their belongings were still there: the glassware on the shelves, the Chinese porcelain in the cupboards, the family portraits in the room from the first generation to the last, the dining table and the chairs, everything was perfectly protected from dust and the cats, because her aunts had covered all the furniture with blankets and sheets.

Her father went up to the second floor with a notebook in his hand, writing down what was missing and what needed to be repaired. He had to take care of the hole made by the large branch of the oak that fell on the roof and he'd have to replace the tiles the wind had damaged.

The repair and cleaning of the house took several days. Later when they started moving to the house, they discovered the cats had come back. They caught them and released them in a forest away from the house, but the cats returned later. They closed the doors and blocked the chimney to prevent them from getting inside, but it did not help. John made a thorough inspection of the entire house with the idea of finding the holes through which they entered, but he couldn't find any.

Maggie died one year later.

The death of Emily's mother marked many changes. Her father found a job in a factory where he worked in an isolated room with three workers. The room was dark and the machines operated by the three workers made a lot of noise. He was placed there with the promise of promotion after a short period, but he realized that promise was just an illusion and it was simply a matter of luck for anybody to get out of that isolation and be placed anywhere in the factory which had much better working conditions. But that was the only job he could find and he needed the money for daily expenses.

Emily felt, at sixteen, life had given her the responsibility of a grown-up, as the woman of the house, and that meant taking over all the chores, including caring for her father. When her dad came home from work, she prepared for him the bathtub with hot water, clean clothes, and dinner. She took his dirty uniform and put it in the washing machine for the next day.

"How was your day?" She asked.

"It was okay."

Sometimes when he arrived, Emily looked at his face faded by the smoke.

"It is getting me," he said. "This dirt is getting in my lungs." As always, she went to the kitchen, poured hot water into a ewer and gave it to him with a clean towel.

***

Emily did not know the whereabouts of her aunts. It hurt her so much, that lack of love from her Aunt Katherine, from whom she had expected affection and some compassion. It was unforgivable what had happened to Katherine but time passed, and she forgot about her favorite aunt. She did not have a fond memory of her other aunts, the only things she could recall were Jennifer's boisterous laugh and Lisa's sour temper, nothing an adolescent on the verge of being a woman would learn from.

From her uncle Mark, she learned that he lived in Philadelphia. He was in contact with a young woman, thirty years younger from Guatemala whom he wanted to marry. Emily had enjoyed some correspondence with him for a few months until he stopped writing. Although she kept writing to him, he did not respond to her letters. She kept the hope that one day he would come to town and visit them.

Chapter 4

Emily took over the responsibilities of the house as a mature woman. She cleaned the house on weekends, prepared the meals, made the coffee every morning, and placed a cup on the dining table for her dad before leaving for the high school. Now that she had the piano available just for herself, Emily practiced with great dedication. Since receiving the letter from the director of the Music Department, she had counted the years before finishing school, and now had just one more to go. During that year, Mrs. Carter thought about having her in public performances and was busy finding music festivals in the state for Emily to perform at.

Emily's dream was to be a pianist, and she would overcome all obstacles in her way. One afternoon she told her father she was going to play the piano on the day Ben Crompton the Third celebrated his first year as a mayor of the town.

"I don't like it," said her father. "Wherever that man shows up, there are problems."

John Fletcher had heard in the factory that Crompton liked young girls, and when he heard his daughter would be playing the piano in the presence of the Mayor, John became worried.

When the day of the Mayor's celebration finally came, there was noise everywhere, but curiously, there were no people in the streets. While the noise could be heard, nobody was able to determine its source. Those who were curious about it believed it came from the patios of the houses and so they thought it was everything but a celebration. It was a sign of disagreement, discomfort, and protest. For a moment, it was so loud, like a riot on the verge of breaking out at any time. The only thing sure was that people complained about Ben Crompton the Third the same way people did in the past about his father and grandfather. There were expectations or hope that somebody would put an end to the corrupt hegemony of the Cromptons. Although nobody said it explicitly, all knew that killing the Mayor was the only solution to the problem.

That afternoon when Emily came back from her presentation she was upset. She did not want to tell her dad in detail about what had happened but gave him a slight overview of the incident. The Mayor came to the stage to thank her for the performance and had given her an effusive hug in which he touched her breasts. In response, she called him '*shitty mayor*', a quiet exclamation that nobody heard, but the Mayor did and replied to her: '*you will pay for it, little pretty bitch*'. She would not play the piano again in any public presentation, anywhere if the Mayor showed up.

John Fletcher thought the Mayor's threat to his daughter was not serious, but he was wrong. It all started a few days later after that incident. It began in the oddest way, when he and Emily least expected it and without being able to foresee the consequences.

One morning the phone rang and when John answered, the call was cut off. It started that way; phone calls every morning that made John believe it was the Mayor. He thought the Mayor intended to know when he was at home and when not; in other words, the Mayor was targeting Emily. He gave his daughter some instructions such as locking the doors, lowering the curtains, not opening the door to anyone, or leaving the house, even if there was an extenuating need, just get on the school bus and go to school. He had also considered purchasing a weapon for his daughter to defend herself. He pulled the baseball bats out from under the bed and put them in strategic points in the house.

When he returned from work, he asked his daughter, "has he called?"

"No," she replied.

Days passed by, and then one afternoon after returning from school, Emily forgot to close the door. The cats came in without making much noise. Emily sat down to play the piano when she suddenly sensed somebody was looking at her. She turned in her seat and, in the doorway, saw a tall man with broad shoulders that eclipsed the sunlight. The man was young and resembled those heroes from the comic cartoons, with a square jaw and a lock of black hair on his forehead. He wore tight jeans and a white T-shirt with the slogan *Make Love, Not War.*

"I was guided by the cats," the man said.

Nervous, Emily stood up, thinking the man was sent by the Mayor and asked him to leave.

"They told me to walk down Oak Street until I found the cats," the man said ignoring her. "By away, my name is Joe Romano. I'm looking for Mr. Fletcher," he said somewhat menacingly.

"He is taking a nap," she lied. The man looked at the cats that kept coming down from the second floor and crowded in the living room.

"What a coincidence," he said. "I dreamed about killing cats last night."

"You can come back later when he is awake," she said.

The man left without further words. When her father came back at night, Emily was nervous. She had not taken the cats out because she felt safer with them in the room. She told him that a man had come looking for him.

"Did he say his name?"

"He said his name was Joe Romano."

"What did he look like?"

"Tall and had Dick Tracy's smile."

Her father's smile vanished into a serious grimace. In addition to the calls, a man was searching for him. The man not only knew he frequented the hairdresser, but now he knew where he lived too. At the hairdressing place, he was told a man had come many times and asked for John's whereabouts and then left without leaving any message. The hairdressers reassured him that, judging by his attitude, the man did not represent any danger. Except for the cartoonlike description provided by his daughter, he knew nothing about that man. Everything was a mystery. The calls in the mornings and the mysterious man were worrisome. He thought that he may have been sent by the Mayor. Emily could see her father looked concerned and seemed somewhat scared.

She heard him getting up at midnight and walking in his room until dawn. He did not drink the coffee she prepared, and in the afternoon, she found the cup untouched in the same place.

John was also depressed at work thinking he would never be promoted from that nasty room, yet he had hope. He was hoping one day the supervisor would come to the room to give him the good news of a promotion. And one morning, John had not finished wearing his protective helmet and mask when the supervisor showed up at the door. He called him out of the room because the noise and dust produced by the machines were unbearable. They walked a few meters away from the room and sat down on a pile of little blocks of steel. The supervisor came to tell him bad news, he wasn't going to be promoted.

"First of all, I want you to know it is not my decision," the supervisor said.

"The Manager?"

"It came from above."

"The Mayor?"

23

"You know John, I'm your friend. They did not pay attention to my reasons for promoting you."

"What reasons did you give them?"

"I gave them many: your age was one of them."

"So, I must continue in this hell."

"I'm afraid so, John; it's not my decision. If it depended on me, I would have promoted you immediately." The supervisor was apologetic and avoided John's sight. He scratched his head and then adjusted his helmet as if he were about to undertake a mission that required all his determination. "I am so sorry, John. Keep yourself safe and keep hoping."

A thick cloud of dust that struggled with the wind came through the door of the room. It was as if the wind were trying to push the cloud back into the room, but it managed to squeeze into the courtyard.

The "Room," as everyone called it, was attached to the back of the building and had no communication with any of the sections of the factory. It was an isolated place built with a purpose, but nobody knew exactly what it was. It appeared to be one of those remnant locations from the slavery era that survived and was used by the coal mine at the beginning, when Crompton the First was around. There were different names and nicknames workers applied to the Room, among them, 'the training Room', used by the high ranked employees. This name, however, didn't describe the actual use, nor the characteristics of the Room. Others, perhaps more optimistic, called it 'heaven', and by the way they sarcastically said it, anybody could infer something terrible had happened to them when they were there, and when they were luckily promoted, then it became 'Thank God I'm out of there' or 'Thank heaven I was promoted.'

The finalized product in the Room did not have any use nor was it a necessary part of the whole process in the factory. It was a bright piece of steel that looked like a kids' toy, like a little animal with no shape, a little elephant that seemed like all the animals of the jungle. John used to call it with the names of the different animals. It was a good description because the finalized piece had all incorporated, but nobody could identify any of those animals. He repeated the names in his mind to forget the itching sensation on his skin and in his lungs, nose, and eyes; in other words, to forget where he was. The process of polishing the steel bars raised a thick cloud, hot and heavy, that slipped through the filters of the mask, reaching the nose and lungs.

The three workers, including John, piled the metal pieces at the entrance of the Room. Anytime they did, they removed the mask and took a deep breath before returning to their machines. The next day when they came back to work, the pile was gone and another one of raw bars of steels was there. It was said that the polished figures of steel were taken somewhere and melted into the bars that were then brought back again to the Room. Whether that useless and meaningless cycle was real or not, did not matter much because it was part of the unlikely events in No-Town, a town where the improbable occurred, like the Caribbean town of Macondo, but the difference was, that in Macondo, things were magic, but in the town, weird and incredible.

Chapter 5

One morning John had an excessive cough and went out into the yard. There, leaning against the wall, was a tall man with a thick folder under his arm.

"Mr. Fletcher, finally," he said.

"How do you know my name?"

"Everyone knows your name," he replied.

"So, are you the man who is looking for me?"

"Yes, I am." He introduced himself as Joe Romano from Chicago.

"You have the name of a boxing fighter," John said.

"I'm afraid you think I'm here on behalf of the Mayor?"

"Yes."

"Well, you are right. I've called and searched for you for almost one month."

The reasons why he was looking for John were, of course, a dirty move the Mayor had made on Joe Romano who had a small distributor deposit for office items in Chicago. It was a business he had built with the savings from five years of hard work in a coal mine in South Carolina. It was located in a prosperous suburb with a population of active emigrants who owned offices and other businesses. One day, Joe Romano received a call in which he was asked to serve as a supplier for the Mayor's offices in a town somewhere in the South. The proposal couldn't be more tempting, but when Joe had a map in his hands to look for the town, he couldn't remember its name. He remembered it sounded weird, and he found a spot that he was sure was the town. The offer was so big that he thought it was his gold mine that he estimated was about three hundred miles away. Joe went to meet in person with the person who had called him. This person was Benjamin Crompton the Third who, for a year, had taken over the office as Mayor. The nicknames of liar, quarrelsome, defrauder and defector, and all the others that people used to call the Mayor were unknown by Joe, who innocently accepted the proposal with no guarantees, other than the honor of his words.

In one single trip, Joe supplied the tools and items needed in the offices of the municipal building, but he never got paid. His small deposit lost all its support, and he had debts to take care of, rent that needed to be paid monthly, and salaries for his four employees. After calling the Mayor many times and confident that he wasn't going to get an answer, Joe went to his office. But the Mayor was good at playing tricks and with his resentment against John, he told Joe Romano that John Fletcher was the official in charge of making the payments for the municipal offices. That was why he started looking for John.

"You owe me three hundred thousand dollars," Joe went straight to the point.

"What?" John shouted.

"You owe me three hundred thousand dollars."

"Am I dreaming a nightmare or what is this?" John started coughing.

Joe had a folder with receipts, invoices, and notarial records showing the legality of the documents. Joe showed him the receipts, one-by-one, for the items he had sold to Crompton, with duplicates and notary stamps and the letterhead of his small deposit. Finally, he showed the documents with which he closed his business in Chicago and the one that stated that he was John Fletcher's creditor. He got this last document in the collections department at the Mayor's office.

John took the document and looked at it to ensure that the name was his.

"I am so sorry but that is not me; there may be another John Fletcher." He said.

"I'm bankrupt and in debt." Joe took a deep breath. He closed the folder and leaned against the wall again. He looked thoughtful and hopeless as if he had lost everything. He looked away at some undefined spot in the backyard then took his pack of cigarettes and offered one to Fletcher.

"No, thanks, the dust I breathe in daily is enough" John replied.

"Crompton is a bastard," said Joe.

"I do not have a single tie to the Mayor," Fletcher said.

"Just now I realized his game," Joe said.

"What are you going to do?"

"I'm going to kill him."

"Don't even think about it, he'll have all his dogs on you." Fletcher put on his mask and helmet. He did not want to listen to the man's plans that could cause him more problems. "They must be looking for you by now" he warned him.

"I am not going to kill him; it's going to be worse than that."

***

John didn't hear from him for almost a month. Then, one morning, John Fletcher saw from the distance that the Room was on fire. *'Son-of-a-bitch!'* Fletcher exclaimed. He suspected that Joe had set fire to the room. The firefighters tried to extinguish the flames that rose from the rubble. They had knocked down the front wall to access the Room, and with axes and electric saws, cut the wooden crossbars resisting the flames. The flames had entered through a skylight opening a large hole in the main wall that separated the Room from the factory. There were men up in the factory's roof who tried to cover the hole, slowly and without interruption as if it were a job to which they were accustomed to every day. They were perhaps the only ones in the whole factory who were aware of the fire, although judging by the fact that they never looked down, they didn't have communication with the firefighters nor the men of the Room. The machines inside, covered by smoke, had their pulleys and pistons in place. In a corner, the pile of polished steel bars coated with ashes had lost their unidentifiable animal shape and looked like the raw ones waiting for their transformation process to start over again. The men who worked with Fletcher approached when they saw him arrive.

"I don't know if this is the end of hell," one of them said.

"It is," said John. "Don't you think it's better that way?"

Chapter 6

The first thing John did when he returned home was to see how much cash he had under the mattress; one bill of 50 dollars, two of 10, and three of 5, in total of $85 was all he had left from the money Mark had given them. With that, he could buy some food that would be enough for a week. And after that, they would have to rely on whatever came along. He did not think of good providence for help as any Christian might. Fletcher was a good man by conviction, not because he expected divine providence to reward his good behavior. In a town where finding a job required licking Crompton's hand, Fletcher was lost. He would never find another job. He had no alternatives. Surviving would require some luck, but Fletcher did not have it. There was nothing he could do. His biggest worry was his daughter.

There was, in the town, a small grocery store whose owner was friendly and helpful to John. He paid the owner a little debt with the 85 dollars and bought some groceries. Whenever he saw the refrigerator had only scant groceries left, he returned to the store to ask the owner for more credit. And so, it went until one day, the owner denied him the credit.

"I'll pay you everything no matter what I have to do," Fletcher said.

"You do not have a job, John, how are you going to pay me?"

At this time of events in the Fletcher household, Emily had been practicing one of the hardest movements by Chopin. She was on a mission to reach the level of perfection for a concert that Mrs. Carter wanted to take her to; a concert performed by young talents from all over the state. Emily practiced until late that night. John went to his room and closed the door to block out the music. He didn't want to think about selling the piano which would be like cutting her wings or crippling her fingers. However, he had no other solution. He thought about it every night and cursed the Mayor and Joe.

He also damned his dead wife who had valuable jewelry that she donated to the Wildcat Protective Foundation. That was a time when the word *prevention* was not in the family's vocabulary. It was a time when there was plenty of money to spend and squander. But that was the past, and there was nothing else to do now but sell the piano.

Without telling Emily about his decision, John sold it. The new owners came in the morning and loaded it into a truck. When she came back from school, she didn't see the piano. She knew then things were bad and did not believe him when her father said the piano was in the repair shop. She was sad. She locked herself in her room and did not leave until the next day to go to school.

"I'm sorry you had to sell the piano," the barber repeated every time John went to the barbershop to have his hair cut or his mustache trimmed. It was a comment that did not need an answer, and he avoided it as he cleared his throat or looked at the photographs on the wall. The barber wrote down in a book the debt of fifty cents for each shave, knowing John would never pay him. On one occasion, Fletcher entered the barbershop more depressed than usual. He sat down in the chair and waited silently for the barber to put the towel around his neck and apply the shaving foam. He grabbed the *National Geographic* magazine and saw on the front page a photograph of a six-year-old girl who had lost her legs. The girl had lost her legs stepping on a mine in Crimea. She and her four brothers had lost their parents in the war, but the girl was strong and she had a dream; she wanted to be a doctor to help people. When John finished reading the story, he felt his problems were nothing compared to those of that girl. That story gave him courage.

Fletcher tore off the page with the girl's picture, folded it several times into a small square which he kept in the pocket of his shirt. He left the barbershop optimistic, suddenly feeling that nothing wrong was going on in his life.

"*Everything is okay,*" he exclaimed. It was a splendid day; he rubbed his hands and touched the photograph of the girl in the pocket. He looked down Broadway Street at the building where the piano was supposed to be for sale. The building stood out among the others because it had a big guitar above the door. He walked over and identified Emily's piano in a corner. It had a tag with a "sold" sign and curious, John asked who bought it.

"It is confidential," said the seller. "But I can tell you, the piano is a donation. Whoever bought it is donating it."

When Emily came from school, he told her about the piano. She asked him not to remind her about it because Mrs. Rita Carter was upset about the whole situation. Her instructor had thought about doing rifles, selling small pieces of art such as paintings, porcelains, anything with some value that kids in the school could donate to get the money to get the piano back to Emily. Now, hearing from her dad that it was already sold, things became more difficult, and Emily felt helpless. She wouldn't tell Mrs. Carter about it, and she would just surrender to resignation.

Days went by, and one afternoon, John heard a truck backing up that slowly entered the driveway and stopped next to the door. John stepped out of the house wondering if it was another surprise from the Mayor delivered to his home. The truck's driver asked for Emily.

"I'm her dad," said John.

"Well, in that case, you tell us where we can put the piano."

"This may be a mistake," said John.

The driver opened a folder he had in his hand to verify the address and name.

"This is what I was given," the driver handed the folder to John. It contained the right address, and his daughter's name was correct except for her last name which was Smith and not Fletcher. "And you may want to look at the buyer's name, just to make sure" the driver pointed at the bottom of the document where John saw a note that said *a donation for Miss Emily Smith from JR*.

"Son-of-a-bitch," John said quietly.

The driver and his assistants unloaded the piano and placed it in the same spot where it was before. When Emily returned that afternoon, she saw the piano and couldn't hide her emotion. Her father had left the folder with the documents on top of the piano and she, curious also saw that JR was her benefactor.

"Oh God!" she said, also quietly.

Father and daughter were conscious then, that JR had donated the piano, but both did not say anything. Each had a different name attached to those initials, a name that neither John nor Emily aimed to say or confess to the other. Moreover, they were wrong.

For John, JR was Mark, Emily's uncle and he believed it was his brother-in-law who signed as Junior to surprise his niece. For Emily, it was Joe Romano, and she never told her father about it. But JR was neither, it was Mrs. Rita Carter, Emily's piano teacher, whose complete first name was Jean Rita and she sometimes signed as JR, but Emily didn't know that.

It was strange that Emily thought Joe Romano was her benefactor. She had seen him a couple of times walking down Broadway and on one occasion their eyes met and both said hi to each other. Why did she think he was the benefactor? It was a mystery she couldn't explain. She never did know Mrs. Carter was her real benefactor.

Chapter 7

The same day they met outside of the Room; Joe went again to Crompton's office. After several hours of waiting for the Mayor, he sent one of his comrades with a threatening message. Crompton still insisted that John Fletcher was his creditor and he didn't want to see Joe anymore, with a warning that next time he would be in trouble.

Joe had to close his business in Chicago, bankrupt and without hope of recovering his money, he thought to take revenge on Crompton. He was thinking about a vengeance that would truly make him pay.

He moved into a house on Oak Street across from where Emily's friend Tandy had lived. The house, which needed urgent repairs to be somewhat habitable, was behind some oaks that made it invisible; the perfect spot Joe wanted, a place that blended into the background and was unnoticeable. Then later, he changed his appearance. He let his beard grow, not too short or too long so it would call attention to himself. He had an appearance that enabled him to camouflage easily among the townspeople. It worked perfectly.

John did not know Joe was living across the street until he saw him getting out of his car, an old Cadillac. John gave his daughter some recommendations and forbade her from speaking to Joe Romano.

Whenever his desperation was unbearable, John had the folded page of the *National Geographic* with the photo of his heroine who gave him relief after touching the little bump in the pocket of his shirt. The girl in the photograph, sitting next to her brothers, looking at the camera as if nothing had happened, encouraged him to live.

When he changed clothes, he made sure to put the paper in the pocket of the clean shirt. He begged in the grocery store, and he made some good friends in the barbershop who once in a while surprised him with an envelope with some money inside.

***

Meanwhile across the street, Joe planned his revenge. He went incognito to Colton where he met Rose, a beautiful prostitute with an angelic face and the body of a goddess. She was a prostitute for exhibition only because nobody had permission to touch nor dare approach Rose. Most of the permanent costumers would have paid any amount of money for one night with her, some with the intention of making her their mistress; that would have represented, for her, lots of money and a stable future. She had never gone to bed with any of the men since she arrived at the brothel from Ukraine, and people speculated she was still a virgin. Joe was the only man in the brothel who had pursued her, and she was the only one to whom Joe confessed his idea of revenge against the Mayor. The secret was well-kept with Rose because, despite her intelligence, she was antisocial; that sort of woman who was educated and knew who she was. She did not communicate well with people, not because of language barriers, it was just her way; living in silence.

Rose served as an accomplice in Joe's plans. She gave him information on the days when the Mayor came to the brothel, whom he went to bed with (always the same prostitute), the time they went to sleep and the room they slept in. She also informed Joe about the make, color, and model of Crompton's car, his perfume that masked the smell of a sedentary man, and she also provided irrelevant information such as his obsessive behavior regarding his bad breath that he tried to control using bottles of Listerine every day.

Joe learned everything: the name of the mayor's wife, his children, what they ate at breakfast, lunch, and dinner. In summary, after gathering this information, his enemy was easy prey, and Joe felt he had Crompton the Third in his hands.

He could kill him, but that would be a one-day revenge. Joe wanted a vengeance that would hurt Crompton for his whole life, like those duels of the Middle Ages, when one of the opponents received a sword mark on the face; an indelible scar that reminded the victorious one of his sweet victory and earned the defeated one public mockery and humiliation. That was what Joe wanted. Breaking a leg, cutting off a hand, an ear, bursting an eye, putting a mark on his forehead or crippling him, any of those marks would've made his revenge sweet.

The plan was like this: Rose would supplant the prostitute who slept with the Mayor, and she would leave the door unlocked. Before she started to take off her clothes, Joe would come to the room and he would hit him on his head so the mayor would lose consciousness, and that was all. Then, after his revenge was finished as he had thought, he would flee to California with Rose.

They decided on carrying out their plan on a stormy night, and they had to wait for many days.

**

One evening, Joe heard thunder in the distance.

"Finally," he exclaimed.

From the south came dark clouds obscuring the afternoon. He packed a few things in a bag, the ones necessary for the escape: a flashlight, a knife, a bottle of whiskey, and a few other things. Then he sat down to wait. When he heard a few taps on the door, Joe thought it was the wind that might be knocking on an eave of the house, but he listened and the taps came again. He took out the gun from the bag and went to open the door. Standing at the door was Emily.

"I came, breaking my dad's rules, to thank you," she said.

"I don't know what you are talking about," Joe replied.

"The piano, I know it was you."

"No, miss, I do not know what you're talking about," he repeated.

"Well, it's fine, someday I'll pay you back."

It was a very short dialogue, and her presence was like a curse, a blessing, a mixture of everything: bad luck, an incantation, any riddle was useful to explain what happened that day and what started then, marked their lives forever. Emily crossed that day on his path as he did in her dreams.

Later, when he saw it was midnight and the storm was about to begin, Joe came out with the bag on his shoulder, ready to meet Rose for his revenge, but he looked towards Emily's house. He saw the light in the window, and instead of getting into the Cadillac, he went to her house. He leaned into the window and saw her in the chair playing the piano. She wore a transparent white nightgown that showed her shoulders and the roundness of her hips. He did not remember how long he was at the window, but he desired her and thought about pursuing her. One step away was the door with the knob gleaming on each flash of lighting. Joe wondered if it was unlocked. He did not try to find out. He returned home, smoked a cigarette, and then emptied the bag on the table. He opened the bottle of whiskey and took a long sip he swished it in his mouth then spat the liquid on the floor. He forgot Rose and his revenge against the Mayor.

The next morning, he saw John Fletcher getting ready to remove a branch from one of the oaks the wind had knocked over onto the roof. It was a large and long branch, a difficult task to take down for one man and much more for John who was old. Joe went to help him.

"I don't need your help," said John.

"Oh, yes you do!" Replied Joe.

"The last thing I need from you is your help."

"And the last thing I need is to see my neighbor being killed by that branch."

"No, I don't want your help."

"It's a big branch and you can't remove it yourself," Joe insisted and before John said anything, he climbed the ladder with the ropes to secure the branch. John kept silence and, wondering who that man was, conceded to work with his neighbor.

Joe laid strings from one side to another, from the house to the trees, with extensions and safety knots, to do the job safely. In all of this initial operation, John was just an observer, but he eventually ended up helping Joe. They made sure when cutting it from the tree, the branch, given its size, would not do any more damage to the house. When everything was ready, Joe put on the harnesses, secured himself to one of the ropes, and climbed up very carefully, with the chainsaw on his back, to the point where the branch joined the tree. He managed to cut it, and it went down to the patio with no further damage to the house.

When Joe was about to get down from the heights, Emily came out of the house. She looked up at the tree and, for a second, she imagined Joe falling from the heights. And it happened, as though she had a psychic power or the ability to alter the ordinary course of things. She saw him fly through the air and fall backward into a pile of dry leaves.

The leaves saved him from certain death but rendered him unconscious. The noise of the impact caught the attention of her father who had begun to cut the branch into pieces. Her dad came to help him while she remained anchored in the door on the verge of screaming. They took him to the emergency room. The doctors, after some X-rays and auscultations, recommended stillness and rest for a few days.

Emily couldn't get rid of the feeling of guilt. On the mornings when she left for school, she saw the lonely house and thought about Joe Romano. In the afternoons when she returned, she thought again about him. After a few days, she could no longer stand that feeling and went to visit him, disobeying her father's mandate. The door was unlocked and she entered. The house was a total mess. Joe had the note *"do not disturb"* on the door of the only room. An unnecessary warning because nobody else lived in the house. Avoiding making any noise that might interrupt his rest and recovery, she began to clean the floor, organize the kitchen, wash the windows, and scratch off the nicotine marks on the old furniture. There were, on the table, some dollar bills and keys for the Cadillac. She took the money and the keys and went to the store to buy food, enough to supply the refrigerator. She supplied the bathroom with toothpaste, hand and body soap, shaving foam, and an electric shaver. Before she left, she wrote a thank-you note for the piano. A few days later, she brought food she had prepared for him and left it on his table. And one afternoon, after her father left for the barbershop and after she completed her school homework, Emily went to see Joe.

Eleven twenty

She remembered then, as she was by the window waiting for the ambulance, that distant afternoon thirty-five years ago when his hand seemed to come out of nowhere, like an extension of the house dragging her inside. She barely realized it was dark in the living room as he lifted her in his arms. She asked him to lock the door because she was afraid her dad would come at any moment, searching for her...

Chapter 8

...He made love to her all afternoon.

When she returned home, she filled the tub with hot water, put one foot in and then the other, slowly; then she laid down until her entire body was submerged. She remained that way up to the moment, she felt her lungs were going to explode.

She had always associated her life with music, for example, the happy moments with Mozart, the moments of rebellion with Beethoven, but that afternoon she played Liszt's "Inferno" because she had a whirlwind confusion of feelings. She felt the encounter was marvelous, but at the same time, she was afraid this feeling was going to overcome her dreams of being a pianist.

The next day, when she returned from school, she went directly to his house and at the door Joe was waiting for her; his warm hand, the same darkness in the living room, the same smell of sweat that filled the house began to be familiar, even though at first it had seemed the most unpleasant of all the smells.

And many afternoons went by that way. He made love to her in the twilight and got her pregnant with their first child. Also, in the twilight, she asked him if he frequented Colton, and he responded 'no'.

At school, she made her way through the crowd of teenagers but now she felt older than the other girls. During the piano lessons with Mrs. Carter, she thought about Joe. She was distracted while practicing Chopin's nocturnes and it was an eternity until three o'clock when the bell signaled the end of the day. Mrs. Carter, who knew her very well, as if she were her daughter, realized the changes in Emily. She asked Emily if she was pregnant.

It was in the middle of winter when she had the first symptoms of her pregnancy. She still had three months to finish her senior year; by then, some changes had happened in her life. She was no longer the teenager she had been. It was as if, in that short period, she had exhausted all experiences. In some ways, she felt emptiness. On the other hand, her dad asked many questions that she answered always preventing any displeasure or disagreement with him.

Mrs. Carter helped her to get around the problems at a time when the word *pregnancy* was prohibited in the curricula and corridors of schools across the nation. And it was much more difficult in a town with as many contradictions like the one that had a church on every block and at the same time a famous brothel and a corrupt mayor that she had snubbed. A pregnant adolescent, unmarried, and still in high school would be the gossip in social circles and for the teenage girls who talked about the Bible and Colton and grown-up gossip. She also would've been given an exemplary punishment that could include public humiliation, harassment, and dismissal from school.

Joe asked her to marry him, but Emily said no.

"There is no other way out," he insisted.

"And my father?"

"Leave it to me."

Joe came one afternoon. He had shaved and dressed like a gentleman; hair combed back, like a Hollywood movie star, a well-outlined mustache that gave him a few more years and a little seriousness. Her father opened the door and asked him to come in.

Emily did not know what to do. She thought to go to the kitchen and prepare lemonade, but she wanted to disappear or lock herself in her room. Suddenly, Joe called her.

"Emily, sit next to me." He spoke as if she were already his wife, and obediently she followed his command. Joe took her hand.

"Mr. Fletcher," he said with a firm voice, "your daughter is pregnant."

John stood up thoughtfully; his face went from calm to angry. He put his hand in his shirt pocket and felt the little bump of the paper to cheer himself up and face his future son-in-law. John took a deep breath.

"I lost my job because of you; the fridge is empty because of you and now the story that you got my daughter pregnant?"

"I am responsible for your daughter's pregnancy, but I am not responsible for you losing your job," Joe replied.

"Then who burned the Room?"

"I didn't."

"The Mayor?"

"Whoever it was did you a favor."

"What?"

"As you heard it, your health was in danger." They kept silent for a moment.

"Crompton, bastard," exclaimed John.

"I also despise him, but he's not the motive of my visit."

"To what do I owe this honor?" John asked with sarcasm.

"I'm going to marry your daughter."

"Son-of-bitch," Fletcher screamed.

There was a long silence. Without asking her, they closed the conversation after agreeing on the date of the marriage. It was going to be a simple ceremony, without guests and no honeymoon.

The wedding was in a Catholic church in the outskirts of the town; a poor church compared to the others that were large and had painted walls and domes on the ceilings. The church was also old, nobody came to the Masses. Pigeons and swallows nested where the beams joined to support the roof. The priest, presided with the same enthusiasm he would do for the services in a funeral ceremony, and without preambles. He went directly to read two passages of the Old Testament; one from Corinthians and the other from Ephesians. When he read in Corinthians that *the man is the head of the woman,* Emily felt a chill all over her body. When they left the church, it was a hot sunny afternoon, the traffic light changed from red to green, the cars stopped, and people passed by on the street; it was as if nothing had happened. But when she entered Joe's house, she felt deep emptiness. Joe instructed her to prepare lemonade for him and his father-in-law while both sat down in the living room. She was Joe's wife, and he was her head, just as the priest commanded in the church.

***

A few days later, when she was barely getting used to the idea of being married, Joe gave her a big surprise. He had enrolled in the army and was leaving for the Vietnam War. She, who had thought that resignation was the only way to get around in her marriage, locked herself in the room and cried.

"You forgot you have a baby on its way and a wife that wants you here, not in the grave," John said surprised.

Joe had no reply. A few days later, he took the train to Chicago and had to wait for some hours in that city until the general command in Hanoi gave the green light to board the plane to Vietnam.

Emily moved back to live with her father because she needed his companionship and couldn't stand her loneliness. She had thought about her marriage and also had many questions.

Right after he left for Vietnam, she started to wonder if he loved her. But if she loved him was the question that bothered her the most, not because of the question itself, but because she didn't know the answer. Then, a few weeks later she received a letter from Joe. It was on May 15, 1960, her birthday.

Two handwritten pages about the war, comments on how he felt, the hardships, but no words of endearment, neither "*I am missing you*", nor "*I think about you always.*" Nothing like that, and worst of all, he didn't remember her birthday. The letter answered her question and she thought of being the wife that awaits her husband's return, and thoughts of recreating the moments of love upon his return vanished all of a sudden.

The letters kept coming every two weeks and Emily put them on the piano next to the one from the director of the Department of Music. However, Emily had an unpleasant sensation: the fear that one day soldiers commissioned by the army would knock on the door with the sad news of Joe's death.

She went to sleep late at night after watching the news with her father. In the morning, after she prepared the coffee, she sat down in the living room to watch the news again. Some news channels said the American troops totaled 125,000 men while others, such as the BBC estimated the number of 180,000.

"What an unnecessary waste of money," her dad complained. John, disgusted by the news, turned the TV off and left the living room and she then turned it back on.

In August of the same year, an American command launched the first offensive on the communist enclave in the Batangan Peninsula, whose objective was to measure the forces of the communists and at the same time to intimidate them. The attack was devastating because it had destroyed pagodas and rice plantations and killed hundreds of farmers. The American Marines declared the attack a total success and planned other offensives towards the north.

The American generals appeared on television smiling, smoking cigars, and that image contrasted with the protests against the war in the streets of New York, Washington, and Los Angeles.

The generals were proud of the triumphs of their troops and did not spare the praises addressed to their soldiers. On the other side, the enemies did the same: General Thanh said the Liberation Forces could defeat the American troops on the battlefield. The TV news showed the bodies of the North Vietnamese on the beaches of the Batangan Peninsula, floating in the sea, and funeral ceremonies of American soldiers killed in combat. Emily thought about Joe and suffered while the letters kept coming and she continued to put them on the piano without reading them.

She never wrote back to him even though she had a lot to tell him. For example, the happy end of a painful birth and the name she chose to call his daughter. Joe did not know anything about that, and when he came on leave a year later, he was pleasantly surprised; his daughter was six months old.

"Her name is Sarah," she said when he walked to the crib.

"Sarah? Why you did not call her Maggie," said Joe with the army bag on his shoulders.

"Maggie, like my mother?"

"Yes," he said.

"It's an old woman's name."

Joe had called his child "he" in his letters, as if he were certain that it was going to be a boy. "He," he wrote, "will go to school and be a professional," "he" will have more luck and live in another town, in a big city and will play baseball. He was so sure that upon his return, he would find out his child was a boy; so, during that year in Vietnam, he bought miniature soldiers, airplanes, and warships. When he saw his daughter in the crib, Joe took her in his arms and looked at her for a long time.

"Why didn't you answer my letters? Why didn't you tell me my child was a girl? Why didn't you tell me about her birth? Why, why?"

"I was overwhelmed by the news and couldn't write letters to a dead soldier," she ventured to say, but those were not the words that she wanted to say. Joe laughed aloud at Emily's answer, a sarcastic laugh that made his daughter cry and drew the attention of his father-in-law who came out of his room.

"What's going on?" Fletcher asked.

"Nothing," said Joe, "just that I find out now that my child is a girl, because my wife didn't answer my letters."

The breakfast was frugal, toast with butter and black coffee. It was a breakfast of a low-income family, that of a family that had an empty fridge, and counted coins to go to the store to buy two or three items of food. His father-in-law got some bills and coins out of his pocket that he put on the dining table.

"It's not enough," John said. "We can't get a bottle of milk for that money."

"I brought some home," said Joe.

He took an envelope from his military bag and handed it to John. He opened the envelope, and he couldn't believe his eyes, several rolls of bills of different denominations, five of 100-dollar bills, 10 rolls of 50-dollar bills, and many more rolls of 20- dollar bills

"It's a lot of money," John exclaimed.

"They are savings."

"Army salary?" John asked sarcastically.

"No, they're just savings," said Joe.

"I do not know how you got that money, but my gut feelings say it's bad."

"Father, enough!" exclaimed Emily.

"That money smells bad."

"It's money, and we need it," said Emily.

"I'd rather die of hunger before using his dirty money," John said, pushing the envelope away.

"I need it, I have a daughter to feed, and I won't let her die of hunger, whether it's dirty or not," Emily took the envelope.

"I risked my life for that money, John," for the first time he did not call his father-in-law Mr. Fletcher.

"How many did you have to kill, Joe?"

"I have killed nobody; well, yes, but it was not my intention."

"Sniper with a salary."

"Neither assassin nor sniper nor defector, just a lucky player," said Joe.

Emily interrupted the dialogue, arguing that the finances of the family were too terrible for squeamishness. And the origin of the money was the least of her concerns, as long as it was enough to sustain the family.

That same morning, Emily counted the money again, it was enough to cover the expenses of the family for a long time. She took the reins of the house and went to the grocery store to pay the debt but left the credit open in case she needed it in the future. She bought clothes and toys for her daughter and filled the fridge with groceries and bought herself a silky dress with flowers and a pair of fashionable shoes.

It was not a salary of a soldier, of course. She never asked him what he did or how he made that money. What mattered to her was that she would never be worried again about such problems. Her father had initially shamed her for accepting the money, but when he saw abundant food on the table, he forgot about his complaints.

Chapter 9

He had made the money playing Russian roulette in a suburb of Hanoi. He started one weekend when he was looking for a place to play poker and accidentally found a hiding place in a dirty and smelly neighborhood of Hanoi. Joe initially had no knowledge of the game. From the barracks, he witnessed the whole ritual: the preparation of the players who risked their lives, speaking in their native language some words that could be a goodbye, a prayer, or simply a plea; the

screams, and the flow of money like a river without control, the nauseating smell; and the bad breath of people, the opaque light, the death; the total excitement.

All that tragic chaos held something extraordinary, such an irresistible attraction that he did not think twice to put his name on the list of the players. It was life or death, and it was getting rich in a second or dying in the same period. The game was not determined by turns; but by the amount of money the gamblers bet, time by time, that encouraged the players to take the gun. It was a strange excitement, sickening, and inexplicable, exclusive in very few humans, whose emotions are controlled not by the brain, but perhaps by adrenaline. At the time of his turn, when the screams exploded again, Joe walked to a wooden platform that swayed in the air to the table where a gun waited for him and his opponent. The table was long and had two chairs, one on each side. There was a punch bowl with water, rags, and soap to clean the blood. Then, his opponent appeared, an 18-year-old boy who should have been in college rather than playing that game.

The young man sat at the front with an attitude that seemed ready to undertake a long conversation. He said some phrases on his tongue and then stared at the table. A third man joined them, he put a blindfold over his eyes and then inserted a bullet in the gun cylinder and rotated it, producing a rattling sound.

Joe discovered in that precise moment when one sets out to die, the mind is blank and it is the adrenaline that determines everything.

Some humans like himself are equipped by nature with the ability to perceive extraordinary events, even more so in those instances when survival is the only desire. For a second those humans become super-humans because they manage to perceive everything, even the most remote sound, like owls in the night. Joe had that super-human ability because his hearing was perfect, a momentary saving skill perhaps, or at least it was for him, that he could hear the tick of the gun cylinder when after spinning, it stopped and the bullet, was not in the exact position to fire.

The third man with the bandage around his eyes put the gun on the table and gave a bow as a sign that the game started. Joe knew by the noise, that he was safe if he took the first place and asked for more money. He took the gun and directed its muzzle against his temple, then pulled the trigger. What he heard was total silence, and then a sudden explosion of cheers and yelling. The third man took the gun and rotated the cylinder for the second round, and again Joe didn't hear the tick and asked for more money for him to take the gun and more money was bet. Joe did the same once more and the screams and curses and excitement suddenly burst. He was rich at that moment. The third man blindfolded set the cylinder to spin again, and it was when Joe heard the tick of the bullet in position, the sound he learned that night was the sound that saved him. The players gambled more money in the game, but Joe did not take the gun, the young man did.

He always remembered that scene when the young man bent his body on the table slowly, with nobility, like a pigeon of colorless plumage that turns its neck and dies. All of those who died before his eyes after that night playing Russian roulette; bent their neck and then their torso as if they fell into a trance from which they never woke.

Joe never told anybody about this ability he had, but he became famous overnight in the secret circles of Hanoi. Famous in an anonymous environment where he was called the "American" or the "Nagoi dannog mayman" or "The Lucky Man." How he made so much money was when he did not hear the tick, he bet everything and tempted the crowd to gamble more.

Chapter 10

He brought money home to his family and felt some satisfaction. In all that time in the army, Joe fulfilled his obligations with responsibility. He was disciplined and could be a professional soldier, but he did not have that in his plans. He was in the war because he wanted to be there and for no other reason.

On his second stint in Vietnam, he had an appointment set up upon his return where he was going to make much more money than he had made in his previous deployment. He was going to confront a man from the Viet Cong with the same fate, someone who had survived all odds playing roulette. Like Joe, the man had a psychological fixation on danger. The only difference was he had been in the game for a long time, a veteran with luck. Without tricks or super-human skills, the man was coming to challenge him, and Joe had a month of psychological preparation for the challenge even though he was sure the *tick-sound* was not going to fail him. For those doubts that sometimes assailed him, Joe thought of his wife and his child.

Joe survived the man from Viet Cong and won much more money than he had on his previous bets.

When he finally returned from military service, he brought enough money to support his family, but it wasn't for Emily. When she realized that he didn't bring as much money he had on the previous visit, she got upset. Joe, on the other hand, found another surprise; he was a father for the second time, and like Sarah, his wife did not tell him about the pregnancy, nor her decision to call her Linda. It was an unpleasant welcome for Joe, no words of endearment and happiness upon his return. Right after she counted the money, she told him that he had to find a job because the household finances had become as terrible as before.

The third pregnancy was not welcome. Emily, who in other circumstances would have been patient with Joe, protested, claiming reasons that Joe never accepted. She complained that her pregnancies were complicated and the laboring painful, that her body was not meant to have more children.

By then the relationship between the two was not perfect, it was just normal. One of those relationships where both parties get used to living together despite the contradictions. She went to bed early while Joe stayed with Sarah, playing in the living room until late at night. Love in bed was a simple act. Most of the time she avoided it with the argument that the baby in her belly protested when he made love to her.

Time passed and they came to realize that sustaining a stable marriage required much more than patience and tolerance, but neither admitted there were problems. It was only a matter of time, and the birth of their third child marked the beginning of major problems they couldn't ignore. It started with the name they were going to give the newborn. Emily wanted to call her Katherine, because she had brown eyes and was brunette like her favorite aunt.

"We'll finish calling her Cat," said Joe, "just like cats."

Joe wanted to call his child Carina because he thought she looked like his grandmother. Emily protested because that name, besides having no meaning, wasn't familiar to her. Who entered to settle in the situation was John who started calling his granddaughter Rosario.

"She is a brunette and will be a damn beautiful Spaniard," he said. "Like those *ballerinas* on stage."

Emily did not speak to Joe for several days, but her displeasure did not end there. Their relationship had reached a point where the two avoided each other as often as possible. Three long months passed before Joe found a job in a nearby town. The job demanded physical work, and that was what he wanted. He worked the morning shift in the maintenance department of a company that produced appliances. The factory was new and large and had an ambitious plan to meet the demands of the Mississippi Valley and part of the eastern states.

He got up at six in the morning, turned on the radio, and listen to the news, while Emily cooked breakfast. Joe prepared his lunchbox for work, a sandwich made of smoked ham, two leaves of lettuce, cheese, and bread. He always carried the same lunch completing it with orange juice and an apple. At three o'clock in the afternoon, he returned home, took a shower and a nap until five o'clock when he got up to watch baseball games on television, and at seven o'clock sat down to have dinner with his daughters and father-in-law. Emily joined them at the table and sometimes she participated in the conversation.

"Bob Gibson had a good race," said Joe.

"It's going to be a season out of the ordinary, the record of the year, Joe."

"We're still in the middle of the season, it's a long way off, John."

"Yes, you're right, son-in-law."

Emily listened to the conversation between her father and husband. She took the dishes from the dinner table to the kitchen and appeared later with black coffee and some cookies for all. She sat Rosario on her lap and, in a cup, she had cold milk for her daughter. Emily moistened pieces of the cookies in the milk and gave it to the girl, who ate with appetite. Father and husband watched the scene in silence. Joe went to the living room to watch TV.

"I do not understand his attitude," said Emily.

"What are you talking about, daughter?"

"That attitude, as if he were *la prima donna*."

"Remember that he is a veteran of war."

"And what about that?"

"Don't you understand, daughter? Life is nothing. It is that simple for those who return from the war," said her father.

"That's exactly what I hate about him. That he acts like he doesn't care about anything."

"Besides, the man wants a son."

"How do you know?"

"Every man wants a son."

"How easy it is to say that."

"And I want a grandson."

Emily kept silent and, upset, put Rosario in the crib, then went to see her other daughters.

***

When the baseball season was over, Joe had a lot of free time. On the slow summer afternoons, Joe woke up from his nap and went with Sarah on his shoulders to the ice cream parlor. Then, when Linda turned two, he took both in the Cadillac and bought them ice cream. That was a routine he did for almost two years, and then, for no apparent reason, stopped doing it.

One year later, he realized the house needed painting. That idea led him to prepare a list of activities that kept him busy every afternoon for some time. The idea was not that of a husband who tries to improve the home where his family lives, but that of a man who was struggling with boredom. He made an elaborate list that included cutting the grass once or twice a week even if there were times it was unnecessary. He also included changing the broken tiles, cutting the branches of the oaks, cleaning the attic, and many other activities that made a long list. Just as he finished it, he felt the cats pass between his legs and wrote on the list: take care of the cats in capital letters and quotation marks. Then he hung the list on one side of the fridge.

The list had nothing of interest in particular for Emily, except at the end was "CARING FOR THE CATS." That caught her attention. The next day when she saw him getting ready to begin the activities, she asked him about the cats.

"They need the care they deserve," he replied.

"What *care* are you talking about?"

"I explained it to you in the damned letters."

"Fucking damned letters," she said in low voice.

During those days when he risked his life playing Russian roulette, he had seen, on the streets of Hanoi, children with big heads who looked like Martians with small eyes and no eyebrows, a little mouth that seemed to release a silent scream; and a bulging forehead, exaggeratedly big that looked like it was going to explode. The disease was so common that it seemed to go unnoticed by the Vietnamese themselves.

On the other hand, the American soldiers were stunned and dropped a dollar or a penny to the mothers. Joe was curious to know the causes of the illness and one day as he was going to the barracks to play Russian roulette, he visited a local hospital. The disease was Hydrocephalus, according to doctors, or Toxoplasmosis, according to the pathologists. The first name referred to the disproportionate growth of the head caused by the accumulation of water in the brain, explained one doctor. The doctor tried to make himself clear, using the same words he would've used to explain to the mothers whose children suffered the disease. The second name referred to the cause, a tiny parasite, smaller than a pinhead, called *Toxoplasma* that lives in the intestines of cats. The parasite passes on to pregnant women, explained the doctor when they manipulated the fecal matter of cats. This was the primary cause of the disease and the source of paranoia that Joe started to feel when he recalled that his wife was pregnant and surrounded by cats.

From the moment he heard all this from the doctor, Joe started to have nightmares and wrote his wife a letter or two every week, warning her about the danger of living with cats. He explained to her the potential risk for his child, the description of the disease, exactly what the doctor said, and sent the letters urgently. Since he did not receive an answer from his wife, he decided to come to make sure of the situation himself. That was why when he had arrived, without greeting his wife, he went straight to the cradle to examine his daughter Sarah. He touched her head, looked at her eyes, and as almost every woman does when she sees her baby for the first time, he also looked at her hands. His concern was such that many days after being sure that Sarah was a normal child, he continued to watch her and did the same when his other daughters were born. His worries continued until the day he wrote in the list *"take care of the cats."*

He gave her an explanation when she asked him about that activity on the list. The answer did not make any sense to her.

"The girls are normal," she ventured.

"Yes, but you never know."

"What are you insinuating? Are you telling me that you are planning to get me pregnant again? That will never happen," she said adamantly.

Chapter 11

One morning, she was preparing breakfast when she heard Linda crying on the second floor. Emily ran up the stairs to her room. Looking out the window, Linda was crying inconsolably, watching the dead cats in the backyard. Emily felt a twinge in her chest. She remembered the list that Joe had hanging on the fridge and went to the kitchen immediately: "Taking care of the cats" had a mark as an accomplished activity. She lied to her daughters, inventing a story. Ensuring that no one outside the family knew about it, she forbade them to comment on the matter at school.

She thought Joe was crazy. He had been thorough with the activities to such an extent that, if he discovered an imperfection, no matter how small, he would start over. For example, a stain on a wall was a reason to repaint it. Seeing him wearing his boots, turning the machine on, and cutting the grass when it barely showed over the surface, was a bad sign for Emily. Her husband was crazy and was driving her crazy. She did not want to rush to conclusions but had thought about it many times. She talked him into swearing on the name of his daughters and for the dignity and honor of the family, that he would never kill more cats.

He kept the promise for a few months. In that elapse of time, things seemed to return to normal, although he continued with the maintenance of the house with the same thoroughness. He climbed the trees to cut the branches, carrying the tools at his back and without any protection that would save him from a possible fall. Emily lowered the curtains and concentrated on the chores of the kitchen. If he did fall, she didn't want to witness it. She prepared lemonade with ice and sweetened it with wild honey. She served the lemonade when he came in, helped him take off his boots and the overalls that she put in the washing machine to have them ready for the next day. She had dinner always served at seven, and everyone sat at the table.

Although nobody mentioned Joe's activities and the slaughtering of the cats, it felt like something ominous was about to happen.

In that period when everything seemed to follow a normal course like that of any family, Emily had a little peace of mind. She thought she was happy, but it was an incomplete happiness. She assumed the role of the wife and thought it was not as despicable, nor was it similar to what she heard from her aunts who talked about their friends, most of them wives who, if they were not complaining about their husbands, they were voicing their annoyance and frustrations over their husband's ineffectiveness in everything, especially in bed. She heard them say some of those frustrated women read erotic novels and desired the husband of their neighbor; that such and such woman, without finding how to relieve the pressure of her desires, had become addicted to pills to cure anxiety and depression. Emily compared herself to all of them and saw the chances of falling into a situation like that were not so remote. Deep inside, she felt something was not right; that she was like a bird in a cage.

She wanted to be a woman in love, that of a lover, and in the years that she had been married, she had been partially satisfied but deep inside, she wanted more. She was still a young woman, beautiful and healthy, with an attractive body and despite the three births, her libido evolved and needed attention.

She lived with a man who, despite his vitality, made love to her only with the idea of having children. But still she prepared for the intimate moments by wearing lingerie, lace stockings, and corsets. Elegant and sensual pieces and striking makeup to surprise him, but Joe turned off the light as soon as he came into the room. If he made love to her, it was in the dark. She accepted things as they were and accepted the wishes of her husband to have another child.

After several attempts, Emily got pregnant and demanded he promise that it would be the last, even if it was a girl and Joe accepted her demand. That was a time when the two spoke of the new child every day. Sarah, Linda and to a lesser extent Rosario, participated in the conversation; they planned the future of the baby and waited for the moment of its birth with much anticipation.

A few cats survived the massacre and ventured to come inside the house. Joe, now that he knew Emily was pregnant, cleaned their feces every day, scrubbed the stains with soap and water and then alcohol, until he eliminated all traces of debris. He swept under the furniture, sofa, beds, under the rugs and did not let his daughter Sarah help with the cleanup.

He did the repair work in the house when necessary and spent his free time watching television and taking care of Emily. He was very dedicated in those first months of her pregnancy; he also helped with the housework. He washed the clothes, dried them in the machine, and separated them for his daughters and wife.

Emily, on the other hand, was not sure that the unexpected changes were going to last forever and had doubts. The truth was, she had a premonition something was going to happen and things would go back to how they used to be.

One afternoon, when she returned from the store with her daughters, she heard metallic sounds in the second floor. Emily went upstairs and found Joe sitting on a bench, looking at the floor with a gun pointed at his temples. He had the last issue of *Time* magazine on the nightstand with war headlines and he still had his work overalls on. It seemed like a nightmare, but it was so real she felt nauseous and ran downstairs to the bathroom. She closed the door preventing her daughters from hearing her cry.

She became sick from her nerves, started to tremble at the slightest noise, the bustle of the cats at night woke her up, and so she sat on the bed crying. The smell of cat feces bothered her too. The smell of the food at meals also made her nauseous. Any routine event caused her panic.

Joe blamed the sickness of his wife on the cats and one night he got up to kill them. Emily heard the shots, and the weeping and sobs of her daughters worsened the situation. Early in the morning Emily felt a sudden pain in her abdomen and Joe had to rush her to the hospital. The symptoms were those of a miscarriage and the doctors predicted the causes as urethral infection and stress.

It was an event of unpredictable consequences; however, neither she nor Joe mentioned the miscarriage in their short and sporadic conversations. During her convalescence, he was as diligent as before, but there was always the feeling that things were not going well and they both knew it.

After recovering, she continued with her routine as the woman of the house. However, she felt the need for a change in her life. The change had to be radical from her role as a mother and wife; it had to be a complete revamp of her personal character. At thirty-five, she needed to reaffirm her sense of self. She started giving importance to the comments she heard when she went to the store for groceries, comments on people's private lives, even if they were trivialities. She was afraid people would talk about her husband after the scandal of the cat massacres. She asked her daughters, and they gave her the bad news: kids in the school called them the "daughters of the cat-killer." Emily was furious, but her fury was not because of the nickname, it was because of Joe.

Emily was not recovering from her stress, and her father recommended a visit to the psychologist. A few days before he had seen the office sign of a psychologist on Broadway; Emily couldn't believe there was one in town, so she went to see for herself.

The office did not have the appearance of a real office, nothing to indicate the presence of a professional, except for a diploma from the University of Chicago, as the only decoration on the wall and an old yellowish reproduction of van Gogh's *Starry Night*. An old desk with books on evolutionary and comparative psychology and a shelf crowded with magazines of the American Society of Psychology completed the office. The psychologist, a beardless young man with long hair, stood up when he saw her coming in.

"You are my first patient, miss," he greeted her.

"Mrs." Emily corrected.

"Today is my first day as a professional psychologist," he said enthusiastically.

The session began as a regular dialogue in which she unknowingly ended up confessing everything: her three never planned pregnancies, her intimate life, which in other circumstances she would have refused to tell. In a few seconds, she was in the hands of the young psychologist. She told him about her husband, how she met him and his desire to go to war. The psychologist came to know everything without her having the slightest hesitation in confessing her fantasies, dreams, frustrations, disappointments, follies, desires, everything as if he had complete power over her psyche.

He recommended therapy for couples; an idea she rejected up front since Joe would never submit to an exercise like that. He also recommended a job to occupy her mind and force her to stay away from the environment that caused her stress. Dedicating her free time to community service as a volunteer in a beneficiary club or congregation was also on the list. The psychologist mentioned an association of ladies in the town who were dedicated to the protection of animals. Emily let out an uncontrollable laugh that became a silent cry that surprised the psychologist.

"That therapy is not applicable," she said. "Part of my husband's madness is killing cats, and that is the cause of my stress."

Eleven twenty-five

She heard Linda and Rosario cleaning and dusting in Joe's room. They talked, but their voices were indistinguishable. They sounded the same. The girls, as she kept calling them after so many years, couldn't agree if it was better to close the curtains in their dad's room because the sun was intense at that moment or just leave them as is. They had emptied the dresser drawers onto the floor and separated all kinds of objects, keychains and boxes with cufflinks and minutiae they thought had some value and placed them in an urn.

"He wore these cufflinks with his white shirt to go to Colton," said Linda.

They had found an almanac with lines, circles, and phrases. The calendar of the year 1998 had the days of the week marked with the phrases: Monday, day of getting up late; Tuesday, the same; Wednesday the same; Thursday beginning of Friday; Friday, make Emily's life bitter; Saturday, escape from her reach and count the money, then spend it at the Sunday yard sale; Sunday, disappear all day.

"Oh Dad!" exclaimed Rosario...

Chapter 12

...It was not so easy to close the last chapter of her ten years of marriage. If she was to make an inventory, the only thing she could rescue from her past was her daughters. She adored them and was willing to give her life for them if necessary. Although none resembled her; Sarah, for example, was tall and blonde with a beautiful face and a clear forehead. Linda, different, volatile, with traits that predicted an angelical beauty, was the daughter who could give her heaven or hell. The youngest, Rosario was sweet, funny, restless and was perhaps the one that reminded her of her own childhood. They turned her life around, gave her joy in spite of everything, and would keep her alive and help her overcome the difficult moments that were to come.

One night she heard Joe's footsteps coming toward the bedroom, and so she pretended she was asleep. She sensed his body odor, a mix of the cologne he wore and hair gel. But that smell didn't irritate her as much as the sound of the gun on the night table. He sat on the bed and touched her shoulders, trying to wake her up, but she kept her eyes closed. He asked why she had not read his letters from Vietnam. He spoke in a monologue, without a beginning or an end. He voiced a summary of his years in Vietnam, things she already knew. He was on the verge of confessing he had been unfaithful to her with the prostitutes in Hanoi but didn't.

Joe said in a broken voice, "I went to the post office with the hope of finding your letters."

She did not say anything, nor did she open her eyes, but she did feel a slight sense of triumph. And those were the only words he said to her for a very long time.

From then on, he was frugal with the money he provided for the support of the house. He gave her money in an envelope for his daughters every month. From that night forward, Joe slept in the room his father-in-law had occupied before he moved to another house on the outskirts of town.

* * *

Emily subscribed to all the fashion magazines which she read avidly with the idea of improving her appearance and with the intention of making Joe jealous. New fashion trends caught her eye over and above Hollywood gossip. She was convinced a change in her character would come in handy at her age. She could have turned to her intellect, become wise and intimidating, but she chose the easiest and most effective way and that was vanity. She began to take care of her fingernails and toenails, using red or dark tones of polish, and she wore shoes, open in the front so Joe could see her toes. She used these and other tactics she learned in the magazine. She wore makeup following fashionable styles: the romantic, the cavalier, sensual and provocative styles.

Part of her vanity was smoking. She had never smoked but learned and adorned the act of smoking with poses, gestures, and attitudes, all learned from the old movie stars. The way she held the cigarette in her lips could provoke lascivious looks from anyone who saw her. But Joe remained indifferent.

Veteran's Day came, and for the first time since his return, Joe wanted to celebrate it. He made plans to go to the celebration with his daughters. It was a plan he didn't tell Emily about, so it was a surprise for her. She was not invited. He woke up his daughters and helped the youngest to get dressed. He was wearing a casual suit and a Red Sox baseball cap and when Emily saw him in his mismatched attire she felt a kind of disgust. But, as always, he didn't pay attention to her and didn't say good morning either before leaving with his daughters.

After they left, she sat down to play the piano. The wind came through the open door, stirring the curtains in the room. It was going to be a frigid winter, according to the news. The wind picked up and scattered the letters on the piano that Joe had sent to her from Vietnam. For a moment, she was curious to read them, but she held back. Even after the cat massacres and his confession about the way he had made money in Hanoi, she did not want to know anything more about his stories. She gathered the letters in a package and put them in a box where they remained until the day of his death. The letter she had written the director of the Department of Music and never sent, had descended on the sofa; and the first thing that came to her mind was using it against him. The envelope had her name as the sender but did not have a recipient. That alone could catch his attention, more so if she put it on an open place easy to see.

The situation reached the point where the two openly avoided each other. If she heard his voice in the dining room, she went straight to her bedroom or to the kitchen. The same thing happened with Joe. For their daughters, their parents' estrangement eventually became normal, as normal as going to school.

The news that Emily found a job in a tailor-shop was not well received by Joe, who gave her all kinds of reasons for abandoning the idea. Joe said her daughters needed her, and she had household responsibilities as a mother and wife. But she had thought about it for a long time and didn't want to give up on the idea. She was going to work at a tailor-shop; she felt the job would give her security and restore her self-esteem.

Chapter 13

The tailor-shop was on a lonely street among old buildings in the downtown area. It had a small sign on the facade of the building with the name *'Wagner's Tailoring'*. It specialized in fancy attire. The shop exhibited elegant garments and made custom dresses for women, and the prices were expensive.

The owner was an intimate friend of Ben Crompton the Third, whose wife came in from time to time to order a custom designed dress. The owner's name was Sir von Wagner, a German immigrant who suffered frequent headaches. He had been diagnosed with a disproportionate expansion in a superficial brain artery at a hospital in Chicago; but he never took it seriously, claiming lack of time and being a German of good ancestry.

As a good capitalist, he paid more attention to the finances of his business than to the maintenance of the building; it was cold, dimly lit inside and on the walls rose spots of lichen that in winter became white like a layer of snow.

Sir von Wagner promised fumigations of fungicide, but it was a promise never fulfilled and the jungle of mushrooms and lichens continued to climb the walls. As for the salaries of his employees, he occasionally, tried to make up for the problem with bonuses that most of the time were below what the labor laws recommended. And the holidays at the end of the year were sometimes priced individually with each employee, those who were excellent as well as being good workers got the usual vacation and those who did not make the grade received one or two days less, without any right of recompense because his answer was that there were too many people in town without jobs and everyone was easily replaceable.

Emily worked in the sewing section with a woman named Camille who had a detective degree from an academy in New York. Camille worked as a detective for a while then resigned, and ended up in No-town with her boyfriend with whom she broke up when she caught him visiting Colton. She taught Emily how to sew, and put the thread in the intricate system of the sewing machine, and how to pedal without losing the rhythm.

They became friends and sometimes went to a small cafe when they left the tailor-shop. They drank a cold tea or a cappuccino, and talked. Emily ended up telling her everything about her private life, the problems in her marriage, her artistic frustration, and the decision to accept her destiny with stoicism. And Camille told Emily about her life, a past full of love affairs that made her blush, some of which a modest woman wouldn't tell. But those afternoons in the cafe that had opened its doors just days ago, took her away from Joe and that was what she wanted.

Camille was a woman of contradictions and her variable temper would surprise Emily later.

* * *

When Emily received her first paycheck, she bought elegant dresses, fashionable shoes and an expensive make-up kit. She went to the shops in a nearby town with her daughters and bought them stylish clothes and got them to cut their hair short. When they returned home, Joe questioned Emily for having cut their hair so short and he complained they looked like boys. She did not pay attention to his displeasure and continued every two or three months cutting their hair in the same style. She herself, did the same later; a short haircut that gave her a rebellious appearance.

Emily dedicated herself to her daughters, spent more time with them, reviewing school assignments and helping them complete projects as well as attending school activities such as theater presentations and art exhibitions. Sarah belonged to the theater group that had embarked on the adventure of mounting the play 'Hamlet'.

They rehearsed the dialogues between Hamlet and Ophelia in the afternoons when Emily returned from the tailor-shop. She read Hamlet's lines while Sarah memorized Ophelia's. Emily made her repeat the dialogues until her daughter managed to recite them with the musical tone that Shakespeare imprinted on his plays. Then came the rehearsals in the theater. Emily actively participated, either revising dialogues or recommending changes to improve the presentation of the play as a whole; and she also played the piano in the background.

The play was a success, and Sarah showed a talent for acting. The next morning, Camille congratulated Emily on the play.

"What I saw last night makes me forget I live in a town like this," Camille said. She saw people were happy and smiling when leaving the theater and she had also heard many flattering comments, except for one that bothered her a lot: somebody had called Emily 'the woman of the cats' killer'.

"It's true," Emily said, "I'm the wife of the cats' killer."

"It may be interesting to have a husband who kills cats," Camille said.

"He is available if you want to know how interesting it is," she replied sarcastically.

Both women laughed. Her own comment scared her a lot. For a moment she had a vision of how far her lack of love for Joe had come. She no longer cared comments like that were of public knowledge, not to mention having offered him to Camille like this, so openly. And she was more surprised at herself when she realized that she really meant it, just as a woman offers the husband to her best friend to help her survive a night of solitude.

On one occasion, upon returning home, Emily noticed a branch from one of the oaks had again fallen down and had damaged some tiles. An autumnal wind, strange at that time of the year, lifted tiles, tumbled trees and played havoc with signs on Broadway Street. The damage wasn't serious and it didn't worry her as much as the thought that it would lend itself to communication with Joe. So, to avoid talking to him about the problem, she would assume the repair herself without his help.

But Joe had already taken over the repair. When she picked up the phone to call a construction and repair company, a truck arrived with workers. They removed the branch and cut it into pieces at Joe's request and then piled the wood up in the corner of the backyard. The repair was quick. After covering the hole that had been opened by the branch, the house looked as if nothing had happened. Joe paid the workers with a check, and they removed the rubble and left.

They did not speak a single word after that event, but days later, Emily found defects in the repair. Defects that in a practical sense were minimal; for example, she did not like the fact that the color of one of the crystals of the skylight-circle of the wall was not the same as the original design, and the same with the new tiles in the corner of the house. She could see the patch from afar and couldn't hide her displeasure. The pile of firewood in the corner of the patio was also a source of disgust for Emily.

"There is no need to accumulate firewood on the patio when the fireplace is never used," she argued.

"This Winter is going to be cold," Joe replied.

That simple and humble response from her husband irritated her so much that she treated him as an imbecile. She raised her voice loudly and proclaimed it was a mediocre repair and she would have hired a more reputable service company and would have achieved a better repair. Joe, as on other occasions, kept silent and avoided confronting her, an attitude that made her even angrier.

Chapter 14

There was a parade in the town whose nature was strange because it was unannounced, and on a very cold day in December. Very few people attended the show and those who witnessed it, wondered how and why that parade came so suddenly with no apparent motives. The parade was an allegory of something nobody could figure out: old cars and horses that pulled ramshackle carts full of melons and oranges that, when passing over the street holes, fell to the pavement.

In addition to the floats, vehicles with the name of the owners on the windshield joined the parade. Joe stopped his Cadillac at the intersection of Pine Street in the 200 block of Broadway and got out of the vehicle to see the parade. He saw a float that was luxurious and had women elegantly dressed in fashionable, colorful costumes. Sitting in the last row was a woman dressed in black; she wore gloves and a hat that made her look like Greta Garbo. It was Rose. Joe recognized her immediately. While the other women on the float laughed and raised their hands, beckoning to the people who applauded them, Rose looked very sad and hopeless.

Joe, who had not been to Colton since his return from war, went there that same night straight to her room. He gave the three knocks as the watchword, the last one a few seconds after the second, as he did in the old days. He waited for a moment and was going to knock again when he heard a tap on the other side of the door. With that, he knew it was her and not another person.

"Damn bastard," she opened the door. "All these years waiting for you." She threw herself into his arms for a moment and then asked him to leave.

"My wife kicked me out of her room, and I'm not going to let you do the same."

It had been more than ten years since that last night when they had plans to kill the Mayor and escape to California. She had hoped, for a few years, that one day he would return; but without hearing from him, she thought he was dead. She assumed the Mayor had figured out about their plans and killed him. She lived all those years with the fear that Ben Crompton the Third, knowing she was Joe's accomplice, would kill her too. She lived in constant fear, more so lately when the Mayor showed up at her door with an offer. He wanted to see her naked whenever he desired and offered to pay a lot of money for that. She rejected it, and he came back the next evening with the same offer, and again she rejected the proposal. Rose's refusal made the Mayor obsessive. He persisted every day, and everyone at Colton had knowledge of his intentions. But Rose felt as though the Mayor was planning her death. The problem reached the level at which La Mama, (the owner of the Brothel) and the prostitutes got involved. They offered to satisfy his wishes, but Crompton wanted her, the woman who had plenty of elegance, the untouchable, the doll that walked through the corridors and impregnated the nights with the essence of desire that made men dream. The one that printed a bit of cache to the brothel. All the desired attributes in a single woman. The Mayor took his obsession to the less unexpected limits because he had confessed to his comrades that he was going to kidnap her if she did not give in to his wishes. One of the prostitutes came to alert La Mama who immediately hid her in the brothel for several months, which made the Mayor believe that Rose had returned to Ukraine.

When La Mama saw that the danger had passed, Rose returned to her room.

She had another admirer, a millionaire from Chicago who came on weekends to Colton in a luxurious limousine with a group of bodyguards and employees who took care of him. Less obsessive, but more imaginative than the Mayor, the millionaire had a psychological fixation on women's feet, a pleasure that consisted of admiring and touching them, toe by toe, kissing them as though it was his only pleasure. If the woman allowed it, he paid more money. That fetish cost him a fortune because he had gone all over the world looking for the most beautiful prostitutes to indulge his unusual behavior.

Rose confessed to Joe that she was in love with someone from Arkansas, a high-ranked military man who came to the brothel, secretly. She fell in love with him because he did not see her as a prostitute, nor did she see him as a client. He planned to marry her, so adamant was he of his intentions that he had given her an engagement ring. After several months, he left with the promise to return. One year went by, and she still kept hoping, but at the same time she began to think he had lied to her. La Mama couldn't stand her sadness and did a search for his whereabouts. After a long search, La Mama found his parents who lived in St. Petersburg, Florida. They told her that he was killed in an ambush by an Iranian patrol and his body had been buried in the military cemetery of Fort Smith in Arkansas. The military man had been truthful, and was in love with her, La Mama told her, because his parents knew about his fiancé, Rose, and he planned to take her to Florida to meet them.

"Despite the bad news, I felt happy because someone had loved me," she said.

Joe contained his anger, which was a mixture of jealousy, frustration, and disappointment. Seeing her touching the engagement ring made his jealousy even worse. Joe came home that night very late. On the dining table, he saw the ashtray with cigarette butts that had the marks of Emily's red lips. He went out into the front yard with the ashtray and smashed it against the wall of the house across the street, the same one both occupied after their marriage. When he came in the house, he saw the cats crowding into the living room. Joe put a barrier on the stairs so they couldn't escape and captured them one-by-one, silently, preventing any noise, closing their mouths with one hand and with the other squeezed their necks until they stopped kicking. He put them in a plastic bag and when it was full, he took it to the trunk of the Cadillac. He drove down Oak Street to a dusty road, in a distant forest, he threw the dead animals in a pond.

He returned to Colton some days later and gave the password at Rose's door, and heard her saying, "*I have a visitor.*"

That terrible sentence was as though she was saying '*I do not belong to you anymore,*' which made Joe very angry. He cursed and pushed the door open. Sitting on a chair, Rose had her feet on the shoulders of the millionaire who had come back, sucking her toes in a trance. Lost to his hedonism, the man drooled like a sea lion without hearing the noise at the door or seeing Joe with the gun that was pointed at his forehead. The millionaire instead kept licking Rose's toes. Only when she moved her foot did the man wake up from his trance. The man screamed like a pig and when he realized that his bodyguards were not guarding the door, started shouting their names.

There could have been a tragedy in Colton that night, but the events turned into a comedy act, because the millionaire, almost naked and showing his enormous belly, ran from one place to another looking for his bodyguards, who had come out of the bedrooms rubbing their eyes. In addition to the cries of the millionaire and the laughter that aroused his curses, nothing happened. The millionaire did not return to Colton.

Joe came to see Rose every night, and things went back to the ordinary as it was in the beginning. They dreamt as before, thought about traveling to distant places, escapades that for her were a way out of Colton's realm, for him a getaway from Emily. They remembered their plan for revenge against the Mayor but now that time had passed, it seemed ridiculous, not the revenge itself, but for the ways they thought to carry it out. Since then, Joe had made, many times over, the money the Mayor owed him but he hadn't forgotten the incident.

Chapter 15

One Friday afternoon, Joe was getting ready to go to Colton when he heard a knock on the door. There, standing in the doorway, three strange men were staring at him in silence. He would not have recognized them if it were not for one of them saying, *'from Vietnam with love,'* their watchword in the war. At that moment, he recognized his friends.

Rick, Korn, and Ron had changed in those years after their return from Vietnam. They had been looking for him and now they had found him. He could tell his friends had troubles. They got in the Cadillac and went to a bar that Joe used to go before he went to Colton.

They had all met in the same battalion and they became inseparable friends in their three years of service. They went to brothels in Hanoi until Joe started going to the barracks to play Russian roulette. They never questioned his activities but they believed they were illegal because he showed up with lots of money after a night out away from them. For them, Joe was their older brother, counselor, and protector.

They all finished their service the same day and boarded a Hercules plane that brought them to the airport in New York. The four of them spent time in the waiting room of the airport, realizing everything was behind them as they were about to begin a less dangerous but more complex life. It was then they also realized they needed each other, as much as when they were in Vietnam; more so for his three friends. Rick, Korn, and Ron who wanted to stay together because, for them, the return home was like coming to another Vietnam, where surviving needed skills they had already lost or forgotten. It was not danger or the risk of an imminent ambush that awaited them in their homeland, it was a society reluctant to recognize its soldiers and eager to forget the war. Sitting on the bench Joe realized it would take them time for these three friends of his united by the same tragedy to wake up to reality. They didn't know what to do or where to go or how to start living a normal civilian life again. They needed each other to navigate the jungle of normal society.

"I must return to my family," said Joe, "I have a wife and two daughters waiting for me."

His three friends looked at him with desolation. He had no words of comfort for his friends.

"Go together, live together, do not separate, go to California," Joe said. He gave them his address in case they needed something and put them on the plane to San Francisco. It was smart advice, a command they followed until the sun of that Friday afternoon when he saw them in his driveway.

Joe suspected something bad was going on in their lives and he was right. They had fled from a gang of outlaws who would pay a large sum of money for their heads. Without having a safe place to hide, they thought about their good friend who would protect them.

The traumas caused by the war were compounded by the ravages of a dissipated life; drugs, mental and physical stress, sleepless nights and alcohol. A life without control that was most evident in Rick, who became bald on top and let his hair grow long around his ears, making him look like an old man. A little hunchbacked with thick glasses that made him look like a bitter poet, Rick couldn't keep still while talking. Korn, the youngest, had the strange habit of constantly holding the fly of his pants. He was the quietest and hardly spoke, but he stared at Joe with such insistence that Rick punched him with his elbow.

Of the three, Ron was the most mentally sound, although he had undergone changes that made him unrecognizable. After a few minutes, Ron told Joe his name was not Ron anymore, but Ronnie. Ron was in the process of transitioning to become a woman. He still had a long way to achieve a total transformation. Ronnie never had a precedent that put in doubt his masculinity while in Vietnam, just the contrary. A good soldier who was commissioned to those missions that only the most prepared, skillful and virile gifted males were able to perform.

'Ronnie' had a history, but he managed to hide his gender identity conflict, and kept it to himself during his childhood, adolescence and then in Vietnam. Born into a very conservative Catholic family, with a father who read the Bible every day and a dominant mother, Ron was their only son. Nothing was in his favor, neither the family nor the environment where he lived, a small town lost in one of the most conservative states of the Union. Tormented by his father because he didn't have any female friend during his adolescence, he confessed to them his situation.

The father and mother couldn't accept that their only son had deviations and subjected him to sessions of psychoanalysis, and had in mind to execute an exorcism on him because they attributed his behavior to a demon. So, to satisfy his parents he was a man and by mandate of his father, he went to war to reinforce his masculinity. That was why when he got off the plane in San Francisco, he confessed to Rick and Korn that he wanted to be a woman. His past was a closed chapter. Going to California couldn't have been better and it was the first thing Ronnie thanked Joe for after telling him his real name. But Ronnie was the problem. He was the reason the band of outlaws was after them. They were pursuing him.

After owning an office of private detectives in Los Angeles that was a disaster and after having been bodyguards for some Hollywood celebrities, they toured the country from north to south and from east to west on Harley motorcycles. That was how they met the band that turned out to be a group of outlaws with racist and openly homophobic views. And above all the problems was the fact that without knowing it, they got involved in their criminal life that became almost impossible for the three friends to escape. The gang had a long list of bank robberies, assaults, drug trafficking and harassment of blacks, Jews, Latinos, and homosexuals. They were also in the business of micro-trafficking, selling cheap crack in big cities.

Ronnie, although his transformation was advanced and it was almost impossible not to be discovered, camouflaged himself in the group with the help of Rick and Korn. He did not speak because, unlike all the other traits that he could hide, his voice betrayed him, so he passed himself off as though he was mute, and thus was safe for some time. One day the lack of strength in some of his attitudes put him in the eyes of the bandits who forced him to talk and so, they discovered his voice was not that of a man. It was then the beginning of his ordeal and hell for Rick and Korn, his friends who never abandoned him.

On one occasion, Russell, the leader of the band, forced Ronnie to kiss the svastika on his arm in front of the whole group. That was how it all started: boos, harassment, laughter, mockery, denigrating appeals, blows, kicks, spits; everything and all the trash directed towards Ronnie. On another occasion, Russell cracked two of Ronnie's teeth because he had woken up with a bad temper. Rick and Korn witnessed all the humiliation, in silence and with frustration, until 'the incident' that overflowed the cup: Russell was going to kill Ronnie. And that was the reason why they came looking for Joe's protection.

"You are safe here, but who knows?" Said Joe. "Not many people come to this bar but be careful if you want to have a beer. The owner is my friend."

The bar was in the outskirts of the town on a secluded street. Before they left, Joe asked the owner to call him if his friends got in any trouble then left his friends to themselves.

***

Joe who went to the flea market on weekends, had a shack in the backyard full of furniture and objects of different kinds, from kitchen utensils to living room and bedroom furniture; enough to equip another house. Foreseeing that the bandits would come for his friends, Joe bought weapons of different sizes, and power on the black market in Chicago.

"If they come, we will receive them as in the old days," he said.

He kept giving his friends more recommendations such as not to socialize with people of the town as that might put them in danger. It was imperative to avoid comments on their past with others, as well as avoid their questions. Nobody had to know who they were or where they came from and lived or what they were doing in the town. They also had to avoid confrontations, liquor, and most of all making friends. All that was prohibited, and he did not mention Colton to prevent any desire to visit the brothel.

A few blocks from Emily's house, on Oak Street, there was another house that was empty. The house couldn't be seen from the street and was perfect for hiding his friends. He bought the house and went on weekends to help them clean it and put things in place, but after realizing that it was an arduous and fruitless task since his friends couldn't keep it clean, Joe only came from time to time.

The three friends started to frequent the bar. Visited by the same customers, every night at 11 o'clock the owner of the bar played *Sweet Caroline* that was like the national anthem because all the customers sang it with great enthusiasm. For the newcomers, the owner adapted a corner away from the other costumers, with seats on the floor and a table next to the window that opened onto a view of the lonely street. The bar had a TV that was always on and sometimes the news was about the war in Vietnam.

Chapter 16

The news that a soldier born in town was killed in the Vietnam War didn't affect Emily as much as it did Joe. She heard the news in the tailor-shop and it was as though it was an ordinary event. When she returned home, she had a big surprise. Joe and his three friends were in the living room talking about the soldiers. The surprise was even bigger when she saw her three daughters listening to their conversation. She went straight up to the second floor and called her daughters.

"You are not supposed to be with strangers." Emily scorned.

"They were talking about the dead soldier." Said Sarah.

"I don't care," Emily replied back. "Even if they are with your dad." She lowered her voice.

When Joe's friends left, Emily went to talk to him.

"Who are they?" She asked him.

"My friends." Joe answered.

"I don't care if they are your friends."

"Then, why did you ask me."

"You know what I am talking about."

"I have no idea what your concern is," Joe shrugged.

His words upset her even more. "I don't want them in my house." Emily replied.

"Ah, your house?"

"And I don't want my daughters to have any kind of interaction with your friends," she yelled at him.

"They are my daughters too."

Emily turned around and disappeared in the kitchen.

Joe went to Colton and stayed the night with Rose. He couldn't forget Emily's words and that night he didn't make love to Rose. In the middle of the night he woke her up and asked her to move in with him to another place.

"Where?" She asked.

"I have an old house that needs some repair."

"I will move in with you on the condition that once we are out of Colton, you will be faithful."

"I will." Joe smiled and reached for her.

***

70

The next day he went to see his friends. All were concerned that nobody in the town was in charge of the burial of the soldier. Joe had gone to the municipal building in search of information, but he had forgotten that he lived in No-town, where there were no regulations and no funeral homes, and matters related to burials, were '*dig the hole and bury the dead yourself*'. Joe made some inquiries where he worked. He found out the soldier was orphaned from his father and was an only child who had lived with his mother before he enrolled in the army. Joe managed to find the address where the soldier's mother lived and went to see her.

The house was behind a forest of oak trees. Joe took a moment to look around and could see the trail that led to the patio was in bad conditions. He got out of his Cadillac and walked to the house and rapped on the door. An elderly woman opened it and Joe introduced himself.

"I've been expecting this moment," the woman said. "I've been through the whole town asking for help but to no avail. The only thing I know is that his body arrives in two days."

"I am afraid nobody is in charge of the burial," Joe said.

"I have no idea what to do. I don't know where or even how to bury him." The woman started to cry inconsolably.

"I will help you," Joe said reaching for her hand to comfort her.

When Joe was about to leave, she handed Joe a hundred-dollar bill. "It's the only money I have," she said.

"I have everything under control, you don't need to worry about anything." Joe refused the bill and told her he would be in touch.

The first thing Joe did was find a spot in the cemetery to bury the soldier. The cemetery was located to the south and was abandoned. The tombs, although mostly elegant and made of marble were almost lost in the grass and bushes. He saw a little hill almost at the center of the cemetery. The hill had a grave that stood out of the grass. The tomb was rectangular and had no name. It seemed like one of those nobody visited and the first impression, given its location, on the top of a hill and the fact that it was seen from a distance, was that it might belong to someone important. The white paint had given way to the moss and lichen and the edges of the tomb had lost pieces of cement. Joe discovered traces of tools with which someone had scratched trying to erase the name.

He walked around the grave when he heard a metallic sound under his shoes. With his feet he separated the grass and found the letter "L" in yellow metal. He kept searching and found an "N" the same color and size as the "L", then a "G", bigger than these two. He found more, a total of nine. The largest letters "G", "D" and "J" were the initials of the name of whoever was buried in the tomb, he concluded. He made some combinations but couldn't figure any name or surname. Later, with his friends, Joe tried to come up with a possible name but couldn't make any sense of the combinations they tried.

In the morning, the day the coffin was to arrive, the four of them went to the cemetery. After digging the soldier's grave next to the white tomb, they started to cut the grass and as they were gathering the grass cuttings, they found numbers, two "9"s, one "0", one "8", one "4", and three "1"s, all smaller than the letters. They put the numbers on the white tomb and found several combinations, but 1890 and 1914 or 1941 were the ones that they thought were the dates of birth and death of whoever was buried in the white tomb. But who was buried there was a mystery because the letters sculpted in the tomb had been deliberately erased.

Once the grave was open, the four friends went to the mother's house and waited for the coffin.

One hour later, they saw the funeral coach approaching. One soldier stepped from the car and inspected the trail to the house. When he realized they couldn't drive the car to the patio, he gave the order to unload the coffin. The funeral ceremony for her son was held on the patio after which the soldiers left.

The four friends and the woman took the coffin to the cemetery and buried the soldier next to the mysterious tomb.

Chapter 17

Joe went to his room one afternoon and found his daughters playing with the letters he had found around the white tomb. His daughters had the letters lined up in the word GENERAL. It was perfect. Joe hugged his daughters, and his effusiveness was such that it caught Emily's attention in the kitchen.

"What is that noise?" She asked.

"Nothing." Joe answered and before she could ask any more questions, he left to meet his friends to tell them of this finding.

Emily knew through her daughters about the letters, and she found it upsetting. But her distress was not because of the story behind the letters, it was because her daughters had more communication with their father than she had. She couldn't accept that situation and from that day on, she spent more time with her daughters. She played in the backyard with them and took long trips with them to St. Louis and other cities on some weekends. She started to call them after they came back from school. She asked them normal everyday questions but sometimes she couldn't help asking the "is your dad around" question and if they answered yes, she found a reason to ask them to go to their room. She wanted to prevent as much communication between her daughters and their father as she possibly could. And she succeeded.

The day of his birthday arrived and it was a sunny Saturday. Joe wanted to celebrate it with his daughters. As he did on his last anniversaries, he asked them to sit on the couch in the living room and wait for him, then he went to his bedroom. He dressed in the same clothes, a white shirt with red circles, green pants, a yellow hat and red tie, all of these pieces were gifts from his daughters. He took a fake Dracula's denture from the nightstand and put it in his mouth and then looked at himself in the mirror to practice the gestures that made them laugh. He suddenly opened the door and expecting that they were in the living room waiting for him, he jumped like a chimpanzee, but they were not there. The house was quiet and he realized they were gone. He prepared coffee and sat down at the dinner table. He had never felt so lonely.

"I lost you, but I am not going to lose my daughters," he said quietly in an almost inaudible whisper.

Joe spent the rest of the day in the library searching for information about the General. He wanted to find the answers to his questions. What was his origin, and how, and where had he died? Did he die at home or in a war? If he died in a war, the dates 1914 and 1941 matched time frames of both the First and Second World Wars. The General might've been a hero who died in the battlefield, and as time went by, Joe's curiosity had grown. He felt relieved to know he buried the soldier in a perfect place, and he had decided from that day on all the dead soldiers of the town must be buried in that spot; around the General's tomb.

At four in the afternoon when the librarian was closing the library, Joe had already searched in the book section and hadn't found any information on the General. He did, however, learn some facts he didn't know about the town. For example, its original name was Little York and not No-town. He didn't find much information in the archives, except that Little York was founded by prosperous immigrants and some of the names of the families included Emily's ancestors.

When he left the library he drove to Oak Street on the east side of town. The last house on the right was his father-in-law's and he decided to pay him a visit. The conversation was amicable at first, but then suddenly turned into an argumentative dialogue when his father-in law started to ask questions about Joe's failing marriage.

"I am so sorry John," Joe said, "I've been a good father, but not a good husband."

"If I'd known things would turn out like this, I would have most certainly have opposed to this marriage." His father-in-law glared.

Joe fidgeted uncomfortably, "I was going to celebrate my birthday today with my daughters, but my wife made sure that wasn't going to happen."

John sighed and said resignedly "I am not blaming only you Joe. I know she can be very difficult at times."

"Difficult? Hah!"

They were quiet for a long moment before John spoke.

"Above all, I adore my granddaughters and I don't give a damn about your problems. God, I love those girls!" John beamed. "They told me about the letters you found around that tombstone at the cemetery. They said you are in charge of funerals for dead soldiers. What a nice thing son-in-law."

"Thanks John. We buried the first one close to a general's tomb just the other day."

"What general?" asked John quizzically.

"A general," answered Joe. "Maybe you might know something about him."

"Well, there were many soldiers in the county, but none were generals, not even in town. I remember older kids called someone, a strange man, 'the Brave General' or 'the Bat' because he slept during the day and did his work at night."

"So, he did his work at night, huh?"

"That's all I remember. I was too young to recall any other details." John looked out the window. Wait a second, I remember they called him General Doug too."

Joe left his father-in-law's house with some answers but even more questions to think about. Joe thought then the letter "D" was Doug or Douglas which might have been the General's first name or maybe his surname. He started calling *him* General Doug or General Douglas from that moment on.

It was still early and Joe had time to think about his life with Emily. Now he was certain his wife didn't love him. He felt it was even more than lack of love; it was hate. He was also certain now more than ever he wanted to start his life anew.

He went to see Rose and let her know he was going to reconstruct the house where he was planning to take her.

"It is going to be our castle" he said. Joe thought his love for Rose was going to save him.

***

Joe started rebuilding the house across the street in the afternoons after work. His friends came to help him dressed in work clothes and carrying tools. They started with the roof which they removed totally, conserving the chimney and its foundations. They knocked down the walls, reinforced columns and placed new beams. In two months, the house was rebuilt as new and painted white. The grass was very high so they cut it. When they took down the bushes and overgrowth in one of the corners of the patio, they discovered an old car. They removed the rubble from the reconstruction area, but left the old car in its place, a black Chevy 49 coupe that had a "for sale" sign in the window.

Emily hardly noticed the activity on the other side of the street, but one afternoon, a limousine that suddenly appeared parked in front of the house caught her attention. The driver, all dressed in black opened the door and a beautiful woman got out of the car. The woman walked to the house and before going inside, stopped to look around. She was tall and by looking at her dress, Emily, who by then had become knowledgeable about women's fashion, realized the exquisite style, taste, and posture of the woman. She was that type of woman who whatever she had on, looked perfect. The driver unloaded suitcases and took them inside the house.

Later that night a scream woke Emily and everybody in the family up. The cry came from the house across the street. Joe put on his work overalls and took the gun. When he was about to leave, she stopped him.

"Is she?" Emily asked.

"Yes, she is." Joe answered.

"If you leave now, you better stay with her for the rest of your life."

Joe entered the other house abruptly with the gun. Speechless, Rose pointed to the makeup vanity table. Attached to one of the legs was an opossum with its offspring hanging from its tail. Joe placed a bucket close to the animal and shot at its head. The opossum fell into the bucket with its young. In the kitchen he filled the bucket with water and drowned the little marsupials.

***

The next morning, Joe moved his things to the other house including his guns and all the weapons he had bought in the black marked in Chicago. When Emily came back from the tailor-shop, she went to his room and found the closet empty. The bed did not have sheets and the curtains had been taken down. She had, for a moment, a sense of emptiness and then closed the room immediately. When her daughters asked her, she told them the truth that their father lived with another woman. But her daughters, especially the oldest one, asked many questions and it took a long time before the three of them adapted to the absence of their father.

Sometimes when Emily came back from work, she would find them playing in the front yard and she feared they would cross the street to the other house. Her worries reached the point that she flatly forbade them to visit their father. If he wanted to see them, it had to be in their house, not in that woman's house. That was the mandate, and they obeyed her. On one occasion, Joe came for something that he did not find among the things he moved to the other house. Emily took the opportunity to tell him about her decisions and Joe accepted them.

One afternoon, several months after the other woman moved into the house, Emily saw Joe climbing to the roof to clean the leaves from the canals. She remembered that afternoon when she saw Joe on the roof cutting the oak's branch. It was the same image; the only difference, Joe was older now. She saw him go up with the safety ropes and tie them to the fireplace and then roll them to his waist. Joe had taken the time to adjust the knots and check the rings that allowed him to move without any risk. Emily saw everything, unable to get rid of her evil desire to see him fall, as though she had the power to undo the knots without touching them or pushing him into the void. Suddenly she saw him falling off in a free fall and landing on his back. Unable to explain how it happened, her desires for his fall were so strong she couldn't take her eyes off the image. Her daughters hurried to help him while she continued staring through the window.

The immeasurable pleasure she felt when she was wishing Joe would fall, almost immediately turned to anger, and it was not against Joe. The anger was against the other woman. There on the ground without being able to get up was the man who protected that woman from all danger, the man who made the house habitable and who warmed her bed on the cold nights, and the woman did not come out to help him. That caused her a lot of anger. She crossed the street and went to help him.

Emily felt jealousy when she saw the other house in the nights, with all the lights on as though it was a ship adrift. Unable to sleep, she went to bed after her daughters were asleep and listened to the cats matting on the roof. The bustle descended into the courtyard and disappeared at times. Thoughts drifted in and out of her mind; she wondered if the other woman was more creative in bed than she was.

It was true because Rose was indeed more imaginative. She was that kind of woman who set aside all the household obligations and dedicated herself to pleasing her man. She was meant to satisfy a man's needs. She waited for Joe in bed, naked on those summer days. She avoided the heat by turning off the lights and like a ritual that started early, she set the bathtub to fill with water, then she spread some drops of sandalwood in the water.

Before she laid naked on the bed with the little window open to the sunlight, she turned on the record player and old melodies from her nation's folklore drifted through the air. When Joe opened the door returning from work, the perfume drew him in through the darkness to her bedroom. Rose didn't demand anything, never left the house because she didn't need to and didn't want to. Rose didn't care about the town's events and was happy without worrying about being at peace with God. And so, time passed by and Joe believed he was happy.

Joe did not have any worries either. They had been left behind in Emily's house and he knew, in a town where women covered themselves up to their necks to prevent any temptation from men, a naked woman in the afternoon was like a blessing from God.

***

It was Ronnie who asked him in a low voice, "Joe, what is happening in your house?"

"Which one, the big or the little one?"

"The little one," Ronnie replied. "I've seen boys looking through windows."

Rose, deaf to the noise the boys made in the window, entered the room naked and laid down on the bed, then turned off the light; it was only a moment, but it was the most vivid memory for all the teenagers who missed school just to see her.

Joe took action on the window incident. Without forbidding her to lie naked in bed, or covering the window with curtains, he decided to hang up a warning sign next to it that said *'Danger, anaconda inside,'* with an arrow pointing towards the window.

Chapter 18

Those afternoons of passion were interrupted by Rose's pregnancy. Except for the occasional mild discomfort, the pregnancy seemed to be uncomplicated. Her stable temperament was just that, stable; without a tendency to depression or the euphoria some women feel when they are about to become a mother. It was so normal that Joe wondered if she was fine or if something was wrong.

One day as he arrived from work, he went to the kitchen to put his lunchbox in place for the next day. He looked out the window and saw cats in his backyard. As many as in Emily's yard. The cats came out of the oak forest and stretched out on the grass, taking a sunbath. The fear they would enter the house was such that Joe checked doors, windows, roof, the whole house, and covered gaps, cracks, slits, by which they could possibly enter the house. In the days of strong winds, he climbed to the roof and replaced the broken tiles. Fearing they still may get in through the chimney, he plugged the external hole and put a mesh in the fireplace.

He did not use the gun because the shooting would disturb Rose's sleep, so he used the same traps he used at Emily's house and drowned the dead cats in the lake. At night, when Rose was sleeping soundly, he'd get up, and finding the cats in the traps he'd strangle them. The solution was effective for a short time only because they soon came back. He didn't lose his patience however, he continued the hunt and the fact the cats couldn't enter the house reassured him, but on one occasion when he returned from visiting his friends, he found two cats on the couch. He asked Rose if she had let them in and she said, *"I have always seen them on the couch."* That was when he lost his patience and intensified the massacre that he extended to Emily's backyard.

In one of those massacres, he had a face-to-face encounter with Emily, who, armed with a baseball bat said, *"One more dead cat and I open your head with this."* Emily had on a red lace-and-mesh baby doll outfit that in no way resembled the old lady's pajamas she wore when they slept together. Despite the darkness, the surprise of seeing her dressed in the nightgown that highlighted her cleavage and legs, was greater than the threat that loomed over him.

"I've never seen you dressed like that," he said.

"Go home," she replied.

Joe searched for the cats everywhere in the house; under the furniture, up in the attic and although he did not run into them, he found their fresh and pestilent feces under the couch and bed. The fact that he did not see them but found their prints almost everywhere, altered his temperament. Rose paid little attention to his worrisome recommendations such as staying several meters away from the cats; he was determined that under no circumstances, would he let them pass their parasite to her womb.

He had received by mistake a magazine of *Parasitology* from the Public Library of Chicago. The magazine came with the books in which he had ordered to find information on the life of the General. The magazine was a bonus special issue dedicated to the parasite *Toxoplasma gondii*, a strange name he never forgot because it reminded him of the children of Hanoi. The magazine included all the investigations carried out on that parasite. It also included information about the infection, who suffered from it, how people get infected, and how to prevent from getting it. The information was accurate and corroborated what doctors in Vietnam had told him. But he read in one of the articles in the same issue about a Cornell postdoctoral research that suggested that the spore found in fecal matter of cats could be transported by air. The information was supremely scientific and technical and was different in part from what he knew. To be sure that he understood its content, Joe wrote a letter to the researcher. A letter in which he asked the desperate question, *"Do pregnant women become infected by breathing air with spores?"* He sent the letter by express mail, and the answer arrived two weeks later. The scientist's response was yes. This in addition to not clarifying his doubts, increased his paranoia.

Joe had to prevent Rose from breathing air contaminated with the protozoan spores. He put filters everywhere to clean the air in the house. The paranoia ended when he took her to the hospital with contractions. The delivery was without complications the new baby was a healthy boy. Joe finally felt some relief and had never been so happy.

Sarah, Linda, and Rosario went every day after doing their homework to visit their brother. On weekends, they did not leave Rose's house. Shane Romano was his full name and sometimes to show him affection, they called him Little Shaney.

***

Emily, who had suspected Rose was pregnant the night she found him killing the cats in her backyard, couldn't stop her daughters from going to her enemy's house. When her daughters told her their brother's name was Shane, Emily became quiet and went to her room.

Emily continued to nurture her vanity. She went to the tailor-shop where she socialized with Camille and the other employees. The days at the tailor-shop became normal. She had developed great skill using the pedal of the sewing machine, and she sometimes helped Camille when she complained about having pain in her calves. Putting on buttons and waistbands was a tedious job, but she liked it more than the housework she left aside for the most part. Part of her job was to randomly choose a pair of trousers and confirm the measurements were correct according to the protocols: model and size. To do this, Camille and Emily used a mannequin that was on a platform in the center of the room. The measurements needed to be written in a notebook with an assigned code, date, time and size, following the strict commands the owner himself had invented. The process was tedious for the two women and part of the quality control of the tailoring. It was the last thing they did before the end of the day.

"We have to measure him up," Camille reminded Emily, jokingly pointing to the mannequin half an hour before five.

Emily got irritated by Camille's bland comments, and trivial conversations that did nothing to strengthen the friendship. Sometimes her attitudes and conversation were strange and out of place, but Emily didn't pay attention to her friend's bad moments. Once Camille hugged the mannequin before starting the measurements, "It would be more fun to take the measures if you were real," she said.

"What do you mean?" Emily asked.

"If it were a real man, do you not think it would be exciting?"

"You're crazy," Emily said. Emily did not pay attention to what her friend was trying to say.

Camille also complained about everything. She complained because it was raining or because it was sunny. She claimed the pain in her calves was because the room was cold and because of the layer of moss on the walls. She had asked the owner to install a heater in the room and he bought an electric heater that she used even on the hottest days of summer. She spoke dirty like a mechanic and said bad things about men, but at the same time complained because she didn't have male company lately. She boasted of her love conquests but, was unable to keep any relationship with her lovers.

"Life has been nice to me, no complaints."

"How many?" Emily asked. Camille, without any hesitation opened and closed her hands several times.

"Twenty?" Ventured Emily.

"More," she said.

"Thirty?"

"Multiply it by two," she answered.

"Camille!" Exclaimed Emily surprised.

"I'm not exaggerating."

"You haven't lost count?"

"Woman, are you sanctimonious or are you pretending so," she said, "the difference between men and women is that we never lose count."

"I've only been with one," Emily said.

"How boring you are."

"I'm not kidding, only one."

"You have to sleep with many to know how good it is with some and how lackluster it is with others. And then there's what people say about it."

"What?"

"All of those myths."

"Myths?"

"Yes, those myths of the American blondes, you know, that crap."

"What myth are you talking about?"

"The myth of once you go black, you never go back, it's just a myth."

"So, you've been with black men?"

"Yes, and black men are not different."

"I've only heard the myth of the Latin Lover."

"That one is not a myth at all. Once you go Latin, you never go Viking is as true as knowing that I exist," Camille said with a loud laugh.

"So, you've been with Latins..."

"Of course, they are *candela*." She whispered.

Camille had a bad habit of talking too much in addition to lowering her voice when someone came into the room, an attitude that bothered all the employees who never stopped commenting on her bad manners. She did not greet anyone except Emily and Sir von Wagner. One day, she extracted from her purse several containers of pills. She took one from each jar and put them in a handkerchief on the sewing machine. Emily curiously asked her about the pills, and she named them all, what they were used for and the side effects of each one.

"The red," she said, "is for the pain in my back, the blue, for my cholesterol, the yellow for my migraines, green for depression, purple for headaches, orange for the pain in my feet, and the pink for this stupid urinary incontinence."

It was apparent from all those problems the only disease that seemed to be real was the urinary incontinence. She told Emily about it, an illness with variable symptoms that had affected her urinary bladder for a long time. Doctors had diagnosed a muscular distension in the bladder that had lost the ability to contain urine. What was worse was not the disease itself, but the frequent visits to the bathroom. It was a problem for her because the toilet was next to the men's restroom in one of the workrooms of the tailor-shop.

Without a physical separation that would give her a little privacy, the workers in that room knew when she went, how many times a day, and how long she stayed in the restroom. And to complete the problem, to get to the restroom, she had to go through a sort of platform across rooms full of male workers. That whole scenario of getting to and from the toilet was in itself an annoyance and this voluntary incontinence she had just aggravated her situation. She had asked the owner to build one restroom in the room where she worked, but he didn't.

"These Germans have no scruples," she said frustrated.

One morning, Emily saw what she later called 'the fall of Camille Cadwell.' It was not a real fall as she went through the platform; it was a strange fall in which bad luck played a role.

"The employees are in a good mood today," she said and when she turned around to go to her workplace, Emily, who was threading the needles, looked at her back and saw it.

"Camille, holy heaven!" She exclaimed. "Your skirt."

Camille had her skirt inside her panties exposing her buttocks. Speechless, she sat in her chair in silence and couldn't put her feet on the pedal of the machine. She cried in silence.

"I never expected something like this. I am so embarrassed," she said in a choked voice. Camille didn't return to the tailor-shop.

Chapter 19

Joe opened the door when he returned from the factory, and as always, the lights were off. Careful not to make any noise, he walked on tiptoes in his work boots to the kitchen. There was a tray of pears in the dining room, the scent of the fruits invaded the house. For a moment, Joe missed the perfume Rose wore before her body started to change during her pregnancy. He took a pear and bit into it. For some reason the fruit scent was much more real in his mouth, like the taste when he kissed Rose on those hot afternoons. He felt the desire to make love to her and went to the bedroom, but at the door he saw she was breastfeeding his son.

He took a nap in the other room and when he woke up, the taste of the fruit was still in his mouth. He went to the kitchen and got a beer, room temperature as he had learned from the German soldiers sent by the Red Cross to Vietnam. He sat down with the newspaper and put the bottle on the small table next to his recliner. He heard the sound of motorcycles approaching, and he felt a hunch. The sound was the motorcyclists who had come for his friends. He was sure of it. During all of those years in No-town, he had never heard nor seen motorcycles. He went out into the front yard and then heard the noise coming up from Broadway. He put on his pants, his shirt, and his shoes, and rushed to his car. On Broadway, the motorcyclists crowded in front of the Municipal Palace.

He then went to his friends' house, but they were not there. He searched the entire town and didn't find any trace of them. At three o'clock, he passed again by the Municipal Building and the motorcycles were still there but this time he counted them. There were seven men and three women.

From one of the windows of the Municipal Building, a woman started shouting curses against the gangsters.

"You're all bitches, whores, cunts, and white trash go to hell!" She yelled.

"Fuck you!" Answered the women from the street.

"Fuck you back!" The woman yelled from above.

The scene attracted Joe's attention. He stopped for a moment and one of the motorcyclists approached and gave some hard punches to his car.

"You better leave," the man said.

"Who are you talking to?" Joe got out of the car and looked around.

The question made the man angry and he replied, "go away."

"It's my town, and I have the right to do what I want," Joe said.

"Fuck off!!! You do not have any business here."

Joe recognized the man. It was Russell, the man who harassed Ronnie. He had a svastika on his arm, as his friends had described him.

Joe backed off and went straight to his house. His daughters played in the patio, and he told them to get in the house, warning them to stay away from the windows. Rose, who was preparing for her nap, asked him for the reason for his warning.

"My friends are in trouble," he said.

"What trouble?"

Joe didn't answer. He had many questions and his mind was in another world. What worried him the most was the fact he didn't know where his friends were. Did they know their enemies were in town? Were they safe? What would he do if his friends came asking for help? He was sure the man who asked him to leave was the leader of the band and his attitude wasn't that of a man who gives up easily on his criminal intentions. He sat down in his chair. On the little table by his side, was the beer that he didn't finish before he left to find out about his friends' enemies. He drank the rest of the beer and suddenly, he remembered the only place he didn't search for his friends was the bar. He rushed to get the car keys and when he was about to leave, the phone rang. He answered it.

"Joe, this is bad." Joe recognized the voice of the owner of the bar.

"What happened?"

"Ronnie is dead."

"Goddamn!" There was a long silence. "How did it happen?"

"They killed him."

"Who?"

"The motorcyclists."

"And Rick and Korn?"

"They may be at their house. I don't know, they may already be dead."

Joe hung up the phone and went to the garage to get his machine gun. As he was loading the weapon in his car, he heard the distant sound of the motorcycles. Hoping that Rick and Korn were still alive, he rushed to his friends' house some blocks down on Oak Street. The door was half open and Joe lifted the machine gun, aiming straight ahead ready to shoot, he hit the door with the barrel and entered abruptly. The noise woke Rick and Korn who were sleeping in the living room.

"What is going on." Asked Korn.

"They killed Ronnie."

"What?"

"Get the damn guns and be on alert." Joe yelled at them. He opened the window and heard the sound of the motorcycles approaching down Broadway.

"They may turn and come up on Oak Street soon," Joe said from the window. "Korn, go upstairs." Korn ran upstairs with a machine gun on his shoulder. Joe and Ricky stayed down guarding the first floor. "Don't shoot before I do." Joe said aloud, so Korn could hear him. He heard Korn crying. "There will be time for crying later Korn," said Joe.

Twenty-one feet away on the other window that also faced Oak Street, was Ricky. Joe saw him wiping his eyes with a handkerchief, and then he leaned his head trying to hear the motorcycles.

"Just like in Vietnam," said Joe and Ricky nodded. The motorcycles passed on Broadway and they got in position with their arms. The sound of the motorcycles faded in the distance. Joe calculated that in thirty seconds the sound of the motorcycles would appear again on Oak Street, about seven blocks down. He counted the seconds.

Forty seconds went by and Joe said, "hold on up there."

When they didn't hear any sound of the motorcycles, Korn let his cry out and started to curse, "Motherfuckers come back. I want to kill you." He kept saying that until Joe and Ricky came up to calm him.

Joe didn't know what his feelings were a few minutes after he didn't hear the motorcycles returning on Oak Street. It was a sort of relief and frustration combined. He wanted to avenge Ronnie's death as well, but above all, he felt guilty. They waited for a few more minutes before they went to the bar.

The scene in the bar couldn't be more desolate. The owner was alone, the light bulbs had been destroyed by the gangsters and in the corner where Rick and Korn had sat down one hour ago, was Ronnie's body. The owner had put a blanket over his body.

Joe tried to listen to the owner of the bar who was a nervous wreck and about to collapse. What Joe managed to understand, was that his friends came earlier than usual that day and as always, sat down in the same corner. They were happy because Ronnie's transformation was going well, without the devastating effects he had expected. It was twenty minutes past three when Ronnie, who was sober decided to take Ricky and Korn back to their house because they were drunk. Ten minutes after they left, the gangsters came to the bar. Because it was early, the bar was empty and the gangsters were the only costumers. They were already drunk, boisterous and ready to pick up a fight with anybody. They sat down and ordered liquor. One of them who seemed to be the leader came to the counter. He saw the emptied bottles on the table in the corner where Ronnie and his friends had sat down and asked the owner,

"Who was drinking there?"

The owner answered, "some bad guys from Kansas City."

Then, he asked some questions about Rick, Ronnie and Korn. The fact that he mentioned their names made the owner very suspicious so he didn't answer the questions. The gangster, frustrated because he wasn't getting any information, sat down with his comrades. The owner remembered that Joe had asked him to call if his friends got in trouble, and a few minutes later, he went to his office. He got his notebook where he had all the phone numbers. While he was searching for Joe's number, he heard a scary scream. He went back to the bar area. It was quiet and dark. When his eyes adapted to the dim light, he realized then the gangsters had left and he saw Ronnie, lifeless in the corner.

How did it happen? The circumstances were much more confused now after Joe heard what the owner told him. Why did Ronnie come back to the bar after he left Rick and Korn at the house? They had no clear answers for those questions. They said that Ronnie might've come back because he forgot to pay for the liquor they had consumed that afternoon. But that answer didn't convince the owner because it was not the first time they had left without paying.

Korn, who had gone to the restroom to wet his face with cold water, returned, suddenly.

"Here is the reason," Korn said, "I found it in the restroom." He had in his hand a purple purse. Ronnie used it to carry his hormones and other supplement medicines and for the last five months, he had started carrying a small gun.

They buried Ronnie by the tomb of the General Doug.

Chapter 20

The afternoon Ronnie was killed, Emily had heard, in the tailor-shop, that a band of motorcyclists on Broadway Street got into a vociferous swearing contest with one of the Mayor's employees, and that the bandits had come to settle an old debt with some enemies. There were other unimportant comments Emily paid little attention to. She was concerned about the owner of the tailor-shop whom she had not seen for several days. She heard a rumor that he was sick. It was not the only rumor; it was also hinted that he had gone on vacation to a Caribbean Island with a young prostitute from Colton. None of the rumors were true; Sir von Wagner was in Germany. He had received a letter from his mother in which he was informed about the decision to disinherit him from the fortune left by his father who had passed away. His mom was following the instructions her husband had left in the will, something that required Sir von Wagner's immediate attention.

The fortune consisted of several buildings located in an industrial zone in West Berlin in addition to a factory of outfits for ladies and gentlemen that was not enough to supply the demand of all Berlin so it was in the process of expansion. There were also other minor properties he never knew about. According to the will, everything was inherited by his twin sister, Petra von Wagner. He had not received a penny from a fortune that, among other things, he had helped forge in his youth before emigrating to America.

The instructions, which in the will were clear and difficult to dispute in legal terms, derived from the hatred that his father had for the Americans for having overthrown Germany in the Second World War. He was angry his son had gone to America seeking his dreams when he had everything in Germany, a motive that also justified his decision. But behind the decision was his sister, who claimed she was in charge of the business while he, Sir von Wagner, the pilgrim brother, the adventurer, was on another continent.

Sir von Wagner never accepted his sister, given her personality and displeasure with her parents. He always treated her at a distance, as though he had no family ties with her. Most of all, he never accepted that his sister received a monthly allowance as an executive salary that she spent on parties and taking to bed, every time the opportunity allowed her, a different male, mostly young, who were thirsty for adventures with an older wealthy woman.

Sir Von Wagner came to hate his sister to the point of not recognizing her as such. He suspected that she, in revenge, had pulled strings on the bed of their dying father and had succeeded. He had hired the services of a great lawyer, who told him there was very little he could do. Sir von Wagner, who had counted on his part of the fortune, had planned to invest in the tailor-shop and expand his business to other towns in the county of Williamson. After he realized he had lost the fight against his sister, he swore never to return to Germany; and he stuck to his word.

Upon his return, Sir von Wagner, who had left without leaving anyone in charge of his business nor had he given specific instructions during his absence and what was stranger, without informing anyone of his departure, found the tailoring working perfectly, as if he had been present all the time. Nobody gave him negative news, the orders placed by the clients had been dispatched on time, the collection of money was as usual in a cashing machine that was easy to manipulate, the whole operation of the tailoring was up to date.

He checked the cash receipts, which after making an inventory, the accounts matched perfectly. The statements in the bank were up to date as well; satisfied with what he had found, he decided to reward his employees. He promised them long vacations for the approaching Christmas and cash bonuses. Emily got a raise and heard from the owner that he had a surprise for her.

The next morning Emily entered her workplace, and the shock was such that she couldn't suppress a scream. A man was sleeping at Camille's sewing machine. The man was strange, with long, dirty hair tied back into a ponytail, and the room was impregnated with the smell of musk. The man woke, and stood up, apologizing with a heavy accent in barely understandable English. His eyes were red from sleep, his lower lip was busted almost bleeding, and he removed the blood with a dirty handkerchief. The man looked homeless.

"Get out!" she screamed, terrified, and wishing she had a gun in her purse to shoot him.

The man who was as scared as she was, refused to leave, and she, taking courage from where she did not have it, approached her machine and looked in the drawer as if she was looking for a weapon. When she turned around, the man was pale, speechless and with his hands up in a stage of resignation. At that moment Sir von Wagner came in.

"Emily," he said. "He is the new employee."

"What?"

"The employee I promised you, the one to replace Camille."

He wore khaki trousers that were very worn, a long-sleeved shirt, with flowers, pulled up to his wrists and old sandals that showed his dirty feet. A bandage covered the big toe of his left foot; the man tried to hide the bandaged left toe by putting it behind the right one.

"But he's a beggar," exclaimed Emily.

"He is not a beggar."

"So, what is he?"

"He asked me if I had a job, beggars don't ask for a job, they ask for money."

"I do not think he is a potential worker," she said, looking squarely and defiantly at the man.

"I think he is," the tailor insisted

The man took a plastic bag from his pocket in which he kept a piece of bread and started to eat it avidly.

"Does he speak English?"

"I do not think he speaks it well."

"Then how did he ask you for a job?"

"A Samaritan did the translation."

"I insist that this is a waste of time. He has to take a shower because he smells bad," said Emily, covering her nose.

Sir von Wagner approached her and said it in a low voice, "I have faith that this one is a good worker. When I found him in the street, the first thing I did was to see if he was drunk, but he was sober, tired and hurt. Apparently, he had been attacked by vagabonds said the person who had translated the conversation between us."

The man sat down at the machine and began pedaling with difficulty. The machine produced a loud noise, and Emily asked him to lubricate the pedal, a communication with signs that the man caught on to immediately. He approached a table in a corner and looked in the drawers. He took out tools of all kinds. He disassembled the sewing machine and spread out the pieces on a table. Then, he cleaned each piece with a cloth impregnated with lubricating oil and put them back where they belonged. The whole machine was reassembled and looked clean and new. He did the same with the pedal; Emily observed the entire process, a meticulous operation that took him all morning and then, making sure what he had done was right, he sat down and pedaled for a moment, paying attention to the sound produced by the machine, the noise that bothered Emily had disappeared completely.

The cold temperature began to sneak through the cracks in the window the next morning and forced Emily to put on another coat. The cold had formed a layer of ice on the wall and condensed in the spider web forming long tears of water. The cold did not affect the man, who pedaled continuously in front of her at a slow pace, with the old sandals that showed his dirty feet and the big toe with the band-aid. He had broad shoulders that reminded her for an instant of the first time she saw Joe in the doorway. But, he had more elegant features than Joe, although he had not shaved or taken a shower in several days. The man hardly noticed she was looking at him. He did not know how to pedal, burst thread and broke needles. But all that trouble did not alter his temper, she did not see a single grimace of disgust, neither impatience nor despair.

In the afternoon, he began to clean the room. Compared with the other rooms, it was practically uninhabitable, judging by the mess because it seemed more like a compost or the back porch of a house. The room had accumulated dust and had large spider webs that covered almost the entire ceiling and were threatening to collapse at any moment. Pieces of paint fell from the ceiling and a lot of insect shells to which the spiders had sucked the lymph crumbled down. Every day when it was not the sneezing that affected Emily's temperament, it was the spiders that came down suspended on their invisible threads. Sometimes the skeleton of a cicada dropped right on her machine. The spiders, the dust, and all the mess entirely disappeared at five in the afternoon when the employees left for their homes.

The man limped out to the street completely unprotected, without a coat and avoided slipping in the ice. *"Poor soul"*, she exclaimed when he disappeared at the corner. The second day had passed without even knowing his name. The third day arrived and he had bathed and shaved but had the same clothes of the days before. His sandals were still on and the big toe bandage had been changed. He was sewing pieces to the pants but she could see he did not know where they needed to be attached.

"The tucks go here and not in the waistband," she said.
She taught him to sew buttons, to apply zippers and to open buttonholes. He learned fast and she stopped missing Camille, whom she had thought was irreplaceable. When she did buttons, he checked buttonholes; when he stuck up tucks, she did zips, or he took the

measurements to the pants on the mannequin and recited them in his rudimentary English to Emily who recorded them in the notebook.

A few weeks later, he had become an expert at the pedal and in the art of sewing. By then she knew his name was Antonio and part of his past. By then, she also realized that Antonio did more than he was asked to do; he was a good worker and an intelligent man. She began to wonder where he came from, what he did, how he ended up in town, questions she was eager to know the answers as days passed. And, very deep in her thoughts, Emily was curious about his private life, questions such as who his loved ones were, if he had a wife, a girlfriend or lover and where they were.

Chapter 21

After some time passed, Antonio told her he was a painter, one of those artists who take time to develop their talent, the type people often call "late bloomers." He had a few canvases he carried in a dirty bag. Antonio was an illegal immigrant and was fleeing from his country's police.

In summary, Emily understood that Antonio had escaped from an imminent death in his native Venezuela. A country that was plunging into the abyss, where human rights were compromised. A country where torture and forced disappearances of people who opposed the system of corruption were usual.

It all started with his master's degree dissertation in fine arts, a comprehensive work of 300 pages that gave him an honorable mention and problems. His thesis was in 'street art' with an emphasis on the history of the recently born art of graffiti in his country. It was the time when 'the anonymous', as the graffiti artists used to call themselves, took over the streets at night and wrote phrases, advertisements, and messages on the walls. It was just phrases, no pictorial art nor the actual graffiti like that of New York and other capitals in the United States.

He dared to call it 'pseudo-graffiti' in his thesis, a name that gave him problems with his advisors, but he had excellent arguments to support that designation. It was, yes, a means of expression but nothing avant-garde to attract the attention of anyone. It was a shy art form that only used comic phrases alluding to love, infidelity, sexual excitement. It was common, for example, to read phrases such as "I masturbate; therefore, I exist" and some that gave a shy opinion on religious faith, said "I am an atheist... Thank, God".

Another example he included in his thesis devoted a whole chapter to the phrase: "Pope Pius XII, the Naziest of the Nazis," It was the most aggressive. According to his thesis that was the beginning of the street art with a purpose. Although the circumstances were appropriate to protest the state of things in the country, the graffiti artists or better yet, the anonymous ones, were far from using that against the government and stayed away from pictorial graffiti.

Then, came an event that marked the history of the nation. A bomb that put an end to all the social stoicism of the mid '70s, exploded in the residence of one of the youngest and most beloved leaders of the nation. A young man with a vertiginous political ascent, lost his life at the door of his house when he was leaving for a public demonstration that would launch him as the number one leader against drug traffickers and political mismanagement.

The young politician was an activist by nature and had been a student leader, city council member and congressman; a successful political career full of debates and speeches that made the majority of the Congress unhappy. He had opposed a bill to increase the salaries of congressmen and he'd managed to erase it from the agenda along with other projects that in no way favored the public, such as tax increases.

He had enemies in the political elite, and the gang of drug traffickers who joined the Congress wanted to kill the young man, eliminating him from the map with his family and close friends. His death was essential, and they had to accomplish it before he gained more political power because, in the squares where he appeared seeking votes for his plans to get the office of the presidency, the youth were his primary support.

The next day after the death of the young politician, the phrase: 'the ship is sinking, and nothing happens' appeared on a wall. The expression was fulminating and a journalist, careless of the facts and could've been killed, took a picture of the statement and published it in the newspaper. This pseudo-graffiti appeared on a wall of the National Capitol, who dared? On the wall of the National Capitol? People wondered and also said that the artist had balls to challenge the guards. The phrase awoke the restlessness of people in the capital city and whoever wrote it, woke up his anonymous comrades who, since then scattered throughout the city and filled the walls with bloody statements and real graffiti, denouncing, and threatening. It was a chain reaction that spread to the other cities of the nation, a calibrated action beside the official forces that tightened their vigilance and spying in all corners of the country.

One afternoon Antonio returned to his apartment and was intercepted by a mysterious man who spoke in a low voice:

"We know about your thesis and the problems it has caused, you would be better off if you had not written it," the man said.

Antonio didn't get scare. With jars of spray paint, he went out that same night looking for a wall on which to paint a new graffiti, a real one, an aggressive pictorial work like those in New York like the kind he included in his thesis. He wanted to express his disgust, anger and his manifesto against all the corruption of the state on a virgin and solitary wall of a central suburb. He understood why anonymous people were called anonymous and why they lived an anonymous life, the feeling of breaking the rules, the dark side of art, the eruption of ideas against the system and finally labeling a wall that had been untouched until then; all were running rampant through his being.

Antonio imagined, while detailing his work on the wall, it was like having a woman in bloom. At midday of that slow and hot Saturday, after sleeping for a few hours, he went back to the place and to his surprise there were many people crowded in front of the graffiti, shocked, perhaps by both the artistic talent behind it and the irreverent attitude that challenged the secret police of the government.

There was his *Guernica*, the first graffiti *per se* in his homeland, the one that spat flames, hid copulas in the shadows, shouted, cried in silence, opened wounds, tore off viscera, cut dreams, the chaos of chaos, the total entropy, the anonymous and tragic *Guernica*, the one that predicted what was hovering in the sky of his impoverished homeland. The revolution of graffiti and the uprising of the people began. A man was confronting the workers who had come with big brushes ready to put a coat of paint on top of the graffiti.

A helpless human being, but with the power conferred by his enthusiasm and love for art and encouraged by the spectators opposed to the workers. That man offered them money if they did not cover the graffiti with paint. Then he came later with a crane, mechanical levers, ropes, a chainsaw and a group of men in a truck. They managed to cut the wall with the graffiti and raised it to the truck and left. The first thing Antonio thought was that his work was going to be anonymous forever.

The truth was, by then, the secret agents knew who the author of the graffiti was. It was a mistake, a careless act because he had left the spray cans next to the wall with his fingerprints.

Upon his return, he saw from the street that his apartment had all the lights on and suspicious men at the entrance of the building. He knew they had come for him.

Antonio fled to the United States. He entered through *El Hueco* on the border with Mexico and walked for days in the desert, later arriving in Austin, Texas, where he applied for political asylum. They rejected his request. He filed his documents again for the second time, and still, they denied his request for asylum, but now he was listed for deportation. He left and headed to the north. He stopped in Memphis, where one night a few vagabonds almost lynched him because he had no crack or alcohol for them. Panicked, he run away from those barbarians, lost a shoe and after when he felt safe, his foot hurt and his lower lip was bleeding. He wrapped the wound by making a strip with a canvas cloth. Without money and only one shoe that he took off and kept in a bag, he walked the streets of Memphis barefoot for some time. He learned later from another illegal immigrant that the immigration police in Chicago were less fearsome or drastic and that was why he had started the trip to Illinois. It was in Williamson County where he stopped because the foot wound hurt and that was how he encountered the owner of the tailor-shop.

It was a sad story that made Emily sob at some moments, and at the end, she went to the toilet and cried. She felt compassion, and deep inside, even more than that: Emily cared about him very much.

She was worried about his foot. Unable to put on shoes, the wound was exposed to snow, and pedaling on the sewing machine did not help. The injury was infected, with an inflammation that if it was not treated immediately could turn into gangrene. The next day, she took him to the hospital to get his toe checked by a doctor. After applying local anesthesia, the doctor removed the infected tissue, stitched the wound and prescribed antibiotics for several days. He had to avoid any movement in his foot, so she asked him to check seams in the pants, a job that did not need much exercise. She brought him the crutches that her father had used, and in the afternoon, she gave him a ride home.

She had purchased, at the drugstore, mercury chromium, iodine, hydrogen peroxide, gauze and bandages that she kept in the drawers of her sewing machine, and in the mornings before anybody arrived at the tailor-shop, she cleaned his wound the way she had learned from watching the doctor that had tended to Antonio's wound.

Eleven thirty

She glanced at Joe's room. Her daughters had uncovered his feet and they started to cut his toe's nails. She could hear the sound of the nail clipper from where she sat at the window. She remembered how Antonio had feet like those of the Greek statues. If someone had asked her, she would have responded that she began to love him by his feet in those mornings cleaning the wound on his big toe...

Chapter 22

...It was one of the coldest winters and despite the bad weather approaching, it was going to be different. She started to play the piano after many years of it laying silent. She played her favorite one day after work and the melody sounded different. The keys responded with the same impetus conferred by her fingers and when she finished, she took a deep breath. Those moments of satisfaction were not because she was playing with the same mastery as she did, it was because her days started to be different.

She looked up at the clouds and expected soon the snow would fall for many days. Afraid that Antonio wasn't prepared for the bad weather, she searched upstairs in her uncle's closet. Like her aunts, Katherine, Jennifer and Lisa, Mark had spent lots of money on clothes he never wore and they remained in the closet long after he left for Philadelphia. Some of the pieces were new and still had the labels from the store on them. Without removing them, she put the coats in a carboard box. She put the box at his sewing machine the next day.

She was afraid the tailor-shop would have a break due to the inclement weather as in all the previous winters, and she did not want that to happen this winter. One morning it started snowing, and the phone rang at six in the morning. On the other side of the line she heard the school was closed because of the bad weather. She knew that the tailor-shop would be closed too and for the first time she regretted she couldn't go to work. She went outside to clean the snow at the entrance of the house. Her daughters also came out with a sled they found in the attic and started playing, throwing snowballs to each other. She looked at them and saw that Sarah had on red lipstick.

"He is different," her daughter replied when Emily asked her questions. "His name is Alfredo; he likes math and is fifteen years old like me." Her daughter also made the confession that Alfredo had kissed her on the lips.

* * *

On Monday, a clear and bright sun rose, but it was still freezing. Emily served breakfast and walked her daughters to the door. Sarah had a twinkle in her eyes. Emily went to the bathroom and looked herself in the mirror and noticed her eyes were also shining. She took the lipstick and put some in her lips.

Someone had left a window open at the tailor-shop and it was cold inside. From a corner, a bird that might've entered the room through the open window, rose and flew over her head and she tried to get it out with a broom, but the bird hid behind some cardboard boxes. Emily sat at her machine and started working.

She saw Antonio approaching, pulled a mirror out of her purse and quickly fixed her hair.

They greeted each other and spoke of what they had done during the recess. Antonio had suffered the bad weather because his apartment had no heater. It had a fireplace, but due to the snow, he couldn't get out to buy firewood. He told her he put on all his shirts and pants, and on top the coats that she had given him. So, he managed to survive during those four days. He planned to buy firewood and take it to the apartment before nightfall, but Emily gave him another idea. She suggested that he buy a heater that he could use anywhere in the apartment, and place it near his bed at night.

* * *

They worked in such perfect synchrony and sometimes they even had the same thoughts. One afternoon, the employees were gone and they were alone. They needed to check the measurements of one of the pants, but they realized the mannequin had been sent to be repaired. Neither she nor he thought about what they were doing next because she handed the pants to him and without saying anything, he went to the dressing room, and put them on. There was not a single noise in the tailor-shop, except the one Antonio made in the dressing room. She heard everything: when he closed the curtain, when he took off his shoes and when he unzipped his pants and took them off, and then the sound when he zipped up the other pants.

When she laid down on the bed that night, she remembered what had happened in the tailor-shop. It was something she couldn't explain because everything, the sounds and what she felt deep inside, had another dimension. It was the awakening of her desires, perhaps a transgression of her emotions, but above all, she liked what had happened that afternoon. She remembered when Antonio got on the platform of the mannequin it was like the rise of a god to its pedestal. She began to take the measurements of the right cuff and the left one, slow, with no hurry, then the knee, thigh, the measurements around his hips and waist and finally his fly. It was just that, measures that she took of a garment, so far from his skin and at the same time so close she could feel the consistency of his muscles. Coming out of the tailor-shop, they closed the door and with the snow falling in the street, they wished each other a good night and sweet dreams holding their hands. Lying in her bed that night she remembered each event again.

* * *

In those days, Sarah carried a kitten, white as snow, in her book bag. She said it was the amulet of both, her and Alfredo. She had stolen the little cat from one of the female cats that gave birth to ten kittens under her bed. Sarah took care of it with such dedication; she fed it warmed milk in a bottle as if it were a baby. She had named it *'Alfredito'* and told her mom that Alfredo liked the idea of calling the kitten by his name. Alfredo had suggested that diminutive, as it was what his aunts used to call him in Lima, Peru.

When Emily saw that tiny feline as though it was a puppet in her daughter's bag, she suspected there had been much more than just a kiss. She stopped Sarah by her arm with the intention of asking her what was going on but remembered that she had a fantasy every afternoon at the tailor-shop. Like her daughter, she was in the same boat and her eyes had the same glow.

One day, Sarah came in agitated from running to tell her that Shane had been diagnosed with severe autism. It was Sarah who, in the yard of Rose's house, playing with her sisters saw that her three-year old brother Shane did not answer when they called him, nor did he respond when they threw snowballs at him. Shane also had a movement that was the flexion of his torso up and down, a movement

99

without interruption despite the cold and the calls of his sisters. Besides not responding to his name, his gaze remained fixed at a point in the snow.

Joe had taken Shane into the living room and sat him on the couch and father and sisters got on their knees trying to have eye contact with him, but he didn't respond. After several unsuccessful attempts to get him focused, the reaction of Joe was that of a defeated man, total silence. It was as if the world collapsed before his eyes; a long exclamation without a voice, an endless 'noooooooooooooo' followed by a cry also without sound, Sarah, Linda and Rosario cried as well.

In the midst of the sadness, they noticed Rose was looking at them leaning against the doorframe, as perplexed, terrified and desolate as they were. The truth was she had been keeping the secret for a long time, she knew it, but couldn't face the harsh reality either.

Joe got into the Cadillac with his son, followed by his daughters, and went to the hospital. He had thought his son had mental retardation but the specialist told him no, that the child had a mental impairment.

"To be exact, it's a spectrum disorder," said the doctor.

"Talk to me in English," Joe insisted impatiently.

"Your son is autistic." The doctor patted Shane's head and looked at him gravely.

In silence, the doctor disappeared to return a few moments later with another doctor, a tall woman who took off her glasses and looked at Shane. She asked if they had seen any aggressive attitude.

"No," Joe replied.

"Yes," said Sarah. The female doctor fixed her eyes on Sarah, waiting for more information. Sarah pulled up the sleeve of her blouse and let them see the bites that Shane had given her on her arm.

"We can do tests, but I think they are unnecessary and costly," said the professional.

Upon returning from the doctor's office, Joe couldn't hide his frustration. He got his son out of the car, locked the door without realizing that his daughters were coming behind. He sat Shane in the chair and looked at him for a long moment. He looked for his toys all over the house, and when he returned, Shane was still in the same place, with his gaze fixed on the mat and with the same movement of his torso.

Joe scattered the toys on the floor; "Shaney" he called to him. That was when he lost all hope. He had no memory that there had been autistic people in his family, but he blamed himself. He went to Rose's room. Rose was lying on the bed, with her back facing the door.

"My Shaney is defective," he cried.

"I expected it," Rose said in a barely audible voice.

"So, you knew about it?"

"Yes," she said. "How didn't you notice? It was the most obvious thing. Every day he sits in the same corner with the same movement," she paused, "but how would you know. You are always busy with your friends and trying to find out about the life of that damn General. How would you know?"

Joe lost his patience and took her by the neck.

"Kill me if you want, I was expecting this to happen," she repeated without any sign of struggle to release herself from his hands that were squeezing her neck to the point that she was losing her voice. She confessed that her ancestors from her father side had all been autistic. One of her brothers was autistic and lived in an institution back in Ukraine.

"If I had known about it!" He scowled.

"You wanted a child, and I wanted to be a mother."

Joe took the glass with water from the night table and threw it against the wall and wept quietly.

***

Since then, Rose was not the woman she was before. She had a nap every day, but now they were longer and she took refuge in her dreams as well. While he was trying to save his son; the history books in which he was searching for the life of General Douglas had now been replaced with books of psychology and psychopedagogy. He read the books eagerly, with a dictionary to find the definitions of those terms he did not understand. None of the books matched the description of his son's mental problem, and he felt a deep sadness when he found that autism was very similar to Asperger's syndrome. The word syndrome scared him and he took note of the symptoms, both of his son's illness and of Asperger's syndrome, and compared them. The two problems had the common characteristic of repetitive acts like movements, recurring phrases, difficulty in establishing verbal communication and no signs of gregarious behavior, that is to say, the impossibility of developing friendship bonds with others.

The differences were not many, they were more conceptual; in other words, the same problem with a different name. At most the same cause with different effects or manifestations, he concluded. That conclusion was not the end of his search, as he continued reading and re-reading the books, hoping to understand the problem of his son better while subjecting him to a strict and constant observation. As the days passed, his son's autism was more evident and his frustration increased, so much so that reading psychology and psychiatry books had become an obsessive pursuit of consolation. Consolation that he would find where he least expected it.

"Einstein, Newton, Joyce and stop counting, were autistic," Rick consoled him.

The phrase was magical, it made him forget his torment for some time. With the relief he felt at the hope that his son would recover, he thought of building a park in the courtyard. He thought by building a park with attractions of different types and colors, his child could be a normal child. It had to be designed for his age so he could play with his sisters, and he could change it or adapt or fix it when necessary, depending on the progress of his son. In other words, a park with all the necessary attractions.

He included in the design materials that would reduce the risks of his son getting hurt from slips, falls, blows and traumas. It would have a long tunnel that would descend in a quadrilateral area of sand; a swing in a corner where he visualized a wooden tunnel with a hanging labyrinth and in the other corner a rotating wheel, and finally a carousel in the center of the patio of multicolored horses that would adorn the small park. It was a park designed by a desperate father who wanted to save his son. He had the design in pencil on a sheet of pink cardboard.

"Look what I'm going to build for you, Shaney," he said, showing him the design and explaining what the park was going to have and how it was going to be. He went out to the patio with the design, gave a glance imagining the playground. He saw the old car covered with grass and thought it could be part of the design. The construction of the park merited all his attention and was urgent.

The park was inaugurated on a hot spring afternoon. Maybe it was the excitement Sarah, Linda, and Rosario had at the inauguration that scared Shane, who started crying and looking for shelter in his father's legs. That day, which Joe had waited for with all the enthusiasm and optimism to see a positive reaction from his son, was the saddest day of his life. Shane clung to his legs helpless, trembling and in a state of panic Joe had never seen in another human.

Chapter 23

Emily did not notice the noise of the construction of the park, nor the colors of the attractions that stood out on Oak Street. She had barely noticed that children from the neighborhood had joined the bustle of the afternoon. The bustle began at four o'clock and ended at six. It was the silence that caught her attention that afternoon when she looked out the window and saw the park. The sun that filtered through the oaks shone on the carousel, and she put her hand to her forehead to prevent the glare.

"Wow, at last he did something good" she exclaimed surprised.

***

In the tailor-shop, at five o'clock in the afternoon, Emily and Antonio heard the voices of the employees saying goodbye and the metallic noise of the main door as it closed. Antonio took the pants and went to the dressing room. Emily took the notebook and the meter and waited for him.

When Sir von Wagner brought the mannequin, he put it on the platform, and they looked at each other and smiled. The mannequin smiled at them from its pedestal too; it had been varnished and looked brand-new.

Days later, Sir von Wagner realized that the mannequin was getting dusty and asked Emily if she was using it. She couldn't hide her blush when she answered yes, but it was a lie. Nobody suspected anything; the mannequin was the only witness when both began to measure the pants that, for both, had become their secret ritual. There had been neither a confession nor a physical approach beyond the measurements of the pants.

After finishing each day, both left the tailor-shop and said goodbye to each other. Emily got into her car and watched Antonio crossing the street in the dim lights, and then put the vehicle in motion when he entered the old building. In her mind, she thought about putting on one of the suits for women and asking him to take the measurements.

One Friday when she arrived home, Emily saw that her daughters were playing in the park with Shane and other children from the neighborhood. She when to the kitchen to prepare dinner. When her daughters came in she served the meal and sat with them asking about their brother. They told her Shane had made progress and was no longer afraid of the carousel, but he couldn't go through the tunnel by himself if Sarah wasn't with him.

They sat in the living room to watch television and played monopoly and dominoes later. When it was ten o'clock, Emily took them to their rooms to sleep.

She went to the kitchen and opened the refrigerator, searched without knowing what she was looking for, grabbed a bottle of whiskey and took a long sip that went down burning her throat, and she felt a twist in her stomach. She turned off all the lights in the house and waited at the threshold of her room for her eyes to adjust to the darkness. She saw the moon thinning brightly and illuminating her bed. She took another sip of whiskey that did not go down as harsh as the first one, put the bottle on the table next to the bed and unbuttoned her blouse slowly, then unzipped her skirt, took off her bra and the lace stockings she had recently started wearing.

She laid down on the bed, naked, and thought about Antonio. When the moon left the room, she put on the same clothes, except the stockings, searched in the dark in the drawers of the closet and took out a scarf to put around the neck. She went out into the courtyard, closing the front door quietly, and got into the car. With the lights off, she went up Oak Street. When she was a few blocks away from her house, she turned on the lights and drove along the street to the tailor-shop. She stopped a hundred meters away from the old building. All the windows had no lights on except one and she figured that was where Antonio lived.

She reckoned it was twelve o'clock at night and realized there was still activity on Broadway. The employees of the Mayor's office were placing barriers in the streets and changing the streetlamps. She walked toward the old building and saw silhouettes of men struggling to take something up the terrace above the door of Antonio's building. As she moved closer she could see the men were trying to take a pair of large horns up to the terrace. Someone was directing them from below with a voice that seemed like a murmur.

Although it was dark, the man insisted on directing them with signs. Emily recognized the man who was directing the others was the Mayor. The Mayor had exaggeratedly gained weight since she had played the piano to celebrate his first year as Mayor.

She began to walk on tiptoes to avoid the noise of her heels as she crossed the street heading toward the door of the old building. She noticed the Mayor and the men stopped to look at her as if they were going to ask her something. That attitude held her for a moment, and she thought to go back to her car, but just then she saw a woman's silhouette in the only window that was lit. The woman was slender, had short hair and seemed to be sad, and she was smoking. Suddenly, the woman covered her face with her hands as if she was crying. Emily felt jealous; so, she hurried to get to the door. At the door, the Mayor stopped her.

"You cannot enter," he said.

The Mayor stood massive at the entrance, his large body left no room for her to sneak inside. She heard a melody drifting downstairs. The music was strangely sensual and made her even more jealous, so Emily became more insistent on entering, but the Mayor took her to the street. The Mayor came back to the door, and she tried again to get in the building. This time the Mayor put his whole body against hers and the wall.

His strength was such that she couldn't breathe, so she shouted: *"Shitty Mayor"*, the same phrase she had shouted that day when he put his hands on her breasts. The music went off, and there was silence. The Mayor closed the door and calling his men, disappeared down the street until they turned the corner of Broadway and disappeared into the night.

Sitting on the sidewalk recovering from her struggle against the Mayor, Emily looked at the window and saw the silhouette of the woman again. The woman smoked and moved from one place to another. Emily went to the door, but it was locked. Frustrated, she got in her car and waited until the light from the window went out. It was then one o'clock in the morning, and she inclined her head on the wheel and wept bitterly.

***

When she opened the door of the house, the lights suddenly went on. Sarah was waiting for her.

"Whore," she called her mother. "You're a whore, like the whores in Colton." Emily had inadvertently lost the buttons of her blouse in the struggle with the Mayor and had her breasts exposed. Her daughter went upstairs to her room and slammed the door. How many times would she hear the same expression from those innocent lips?

Emily cried until dawn; she couldn't forget the image of the woman in the window. That weekend, like her sorrow, was endless.

Chapter 24

On Monday, when Emily entered the tailor-shop, she heard the employees talking about the horns in the old building. She went straight to the workroom she shared with Antonio, anxious and at the same time jealous. She wanted to ask him about the woman in the window. That Monday was one of those days when nothing worked out; much less when there is something bothering the heart deep down.

First of all, Sir von Wagner, for some inexplicable reason, spent the day in the room taking measurements to the pants on the mannequin. Something he had never done before and both Emily and Antonio wondered if it was a sign of suspicion regarding their afternoons lately. Both, however, were certain nobody had seen them. At that point nothing had happened between them either, although to tell the truth, Emily had gone much further in her imagination.

So, with the presence of Sir von Wagner, they couldn't ask each other anything, nor could they even say a word all day. When she went to the restroom, she heard the employees again talking about the horns on the terrace of the old building. Most of the employees had passed the old building on the street of for many years, but seeing the horns at its entrance, was the strangest thing. They made comments, some serious, but mostly jokes saying they were cow horns, or bull horns. They asked the recurring question of who had put them there and the reasons. Everyone made fun of the event, but among the employees, there was an old man who was more reserved and who near the end of the afternoon changed the direction of the comments to serious and in a certain way worrying.

"I do not know, but I have the bad feeling those are the same horns of year 32." The old man referred to the massacre of miners in 1932. "I was a child, but aware of what had happened, and I remember it as if it was just yesterday. I think we are in a circle with no way out and those horns are a bad sign."

Emily heard the conversation, but she didn't pay much attention. In the afternoon she saw Antonio was leaving early and her jealousy was such that she wanted to follow him, but Sir von Wagner was still in the room. She left at five o'clock and went to the old building. The window where she saw the woman's silhouette was open and she could hear the same music.

Down, above the door's terrace were the horns and, on the threshold, the number 201 hung upside down and it reminded her of the struggle she'd had the last weekend with the Mayor. She went up to the second floor and looked around. She went up to the third floor and headed to a green door that was ajar. She looked inside. It was an empty room without a single piece of furniture, except for a table in the center with a solitary brush with drained paint. She had no doubt it was Antonio's apartment. The floor was dusty and had marks of the shoes she had given him. She took off her high-heels.

"Don't take them off," she heard Antonio say from another room.

"I don't want to open holes in the floor with my high heels."

"It does not matter, put them back on."

"Why is the door opened?" A question determined not by curiosity but her jealousy.

"I was waiting for you."

"How did you know I was coming?"

"I realized it this morning."

"How?" She asked.

"Well, the truth is, I've always been waiting for you," he said. She heard him scraping something, and then he gave light blows with his mouth as though he was blowing air over something.

"Who is she?" Emily asked directly. "Short hair, smokes, listens to music at full volume and also cries."

"A desperate woman waiting for her lover," he replied.

"Is she your lover?"

"No. I do not have a lover."

"Poor woman," she said with some sense of relief.

"I heard the same music every Friday." He left the room with his hands full of paint.

"I came looking for you Friday night." She told him what she saw that night and what happened with the Mayor and the horns in the terrace at the entrance of the building.

"Strange," said Antonio.

"Yes, it's strange, that's what they say in the tailor-shop."

It was about seven in the evening when she left Antonio's apartment. The sun reflected in the windows of the front building and filled the corridors. She fixed her skirt and made sure her blouse was buttoned. Next to the window, through which the sunlight came in, she pulled out a mirror and looked at her face. The makeup she'd worn in the morning and touched up in the afternoon before leaving the tailor-shop had disappeared. She applied some lipstick, smoothed her hair and started to come downstairs. She left the building with the anticipation the next day, at the same time, she would come to see him and they would make love again. She went home happy and warm inside.

* * *

When she reached the patio at home, she saw the gardenias she had planted a few days ago had opened their petals. She pulled one off and went into the bathroom and drew a bath while she savored its aroma. Emily picked up her razor and trimmed the hair around her sex. She liked the feeling of lightness so much that she looked herself in the mirror for a long moment and then scattered the petals of the gardenia onto the bathtub water and put in a few drops of aromatic oil and mixed it with her foot. She lingered and relaxed in the tub for quite a while then stepped out of the tub when she heard in the distance the children playing in Joe's park:

"The children are happy, the swallows are happy, the cats are happy," she said. "I am happy, *I have a lover*," she exclaimed, repeating the same words as Emma Bovary. She opened the bathroom door, and saw Joe, looking serious and stupefied, watching her from the living room with some books under his arm.

"You made yourself the Hitler's mustache," he exclaimed. Disgusted, she closed the door violently.

With the books that had been mistakenly sent to Emily's house, Joe got into his Cadillac and went to the bar to visit his friends he had not seen since the construction of the park. While driving to the bar, he remembered his naked wife. He felt sadness and a huge void. He realized she had completely forgotten him, and his presence in the room with the books under his arm was strange for her. She saw him as an intruder who did not cause any harm, but who caused her some repulsion. At that moment, he felt a thorn in his chest; she was much more beautiful than those years when he lived with her, and he sensed her vitality and beauty were not the results of the natural course of time. He had the suspicion she had a lover and it was a terrible thought. Now he had to avoid jealousy, frustration, and anger but he did not know how to do it.

The bar was crowded that evening. The owner of the bar greeted Joe and brought him a cushion like the ones Korn and Rick had. Since Ronnie died, the owner was more diligent with them, and sometimes he called them brothers.

"I have the anchovies you like so much," he said.

"Bring them please," Joe replied.

"They are aged because I bought them a long time ago." the owner said jokingly.

Joe, without saying a word, put the books on the table, stretched his feet under it, and let out a long sigh.

"I want to say something, Joe," said Korn who was drunk.

"What is it?"

"You have been our protector for all of these years, and we haven't paid you back."

"Yes, you have."

"When? How?"

"You helped me build the park for my son."

"Bah, that's nothing."

"And rebuilding my house, too."

"I meant *paying you back*, like saving you from danger as you have with us," said Korn.

"I didn't save Ronnie," said Joe.

Both kept silent. Across the table sat Rick, who was silent all the time and when Joe and Korn gave him a look, he took a long sip of beer and made a gesture of dislike.

"The more I try, the less I get any flavor from this shit. It tastes horrible and smells like sheep urine," said Ricky. His friends didn't pay attention. Korn, thinking about Ronnie, said.

"Ronnie always sat down there. He was on alert in case Russell came. He kept the gun in his purse, just in case. It's been almost three years, and I am not sleeping well, Joe. His death is haunting me every night, always thinking that Rick and I left him alone, unprotected that day." Korn started to cry.

"I am more guilty than you are, Korn." Joe said patting Korn's back. "I should've come to the bar before I searched everywhere for you. My lack of common sense and bad memory killed Ronnie."

Ricky said he was going out to smoke a cigarette and left.

"Joe, I don't know what's going on in his head," Korn paused, "Ricky disappears for days, and the last thing I know is that he turns up back at home making that noise."

"What noise?"

"I've heard him bleating like a goat and when he sleeps, he calls out all of these women's names. He is crazy, Joe. I think he needs to get laid."

"It's okay Korn." Said Joe.

"I've been laid and now I feel better."

"How is the chick? Is she beautiful?" Asked Joe.

"Oh, my goodness, Romina is *bellissima*! She has made me taste her waters," he said. Joe did not understand him but nodded. "Joe, take care of Ricky, would you?"

"Why?"

"Romina and I are planning to live in Florida and Rick will be alone."

That was the last time Joe saw him. He learned through Rick that Korn met Romina in Colton.

Chapter 25

One afternoon Sarah came to give Joe news. She was much more agitated than the first time when she discovered her brother's autism. Sarah could only tell her dad to follow her. They went straight to the library. Shane was sitting there reading the book "*A Thousand-and One-Nights*".

"My brother is normal," she said. Sarah had the task to teach Shaney how to read, using the same mechanisms her teacher did. After several sessions in the library, her brother took flight like a bird to which the cage had been opened. Shaney learned to read in just one month when her sisters and she took several months, and yet, that wasn't the only surprise. She had also discovered the genius in her bother because he had a prodigious memory. He could recite from memory what he had read, line after line, without skipping a punctuation mark.

Joe felt happy and some relief; he stopped the search for information related to his child's autism and returned the books on psychology to the libraries. Now, he continued looking for information on the General. He went back to the yard-sales and flea markets in the nearby towns where he bought many books. The books, all of history, some written by academics and others of dubious authorship, contained information on the central and southern region of the country. The collection included compendiums and chronicles of exploratory journeys by pioneers such as Lewis and Clark to the Missouri River, the displacement of indigenous tribes, and the establishment of colonies in the region.

He divided his free time reading books of history and fixing an old and abandoned house as a pavilion for the funerals of the soldiers. Just as it happened the first time, Joe witnessed the human agony when a loved one dies. With the first soldier, he was aware of the loneliness of a mother and with the second the loneliness, the tragedy, the anguish and the despair of a wife. He prepared the same ceremony and witnessed the saddest burial of his life and swore never to take charge of the reception of dead soldiers again.

He would take care of their graves and that would be the only thing he would do to honor them, but he did not remember that he lived in a town whose history was the darkest of all the towns in the county and of the entire nation. The second soldier's body had not cooled down in the grave yet when the third arrived, and with the intention of avoiding that terrible job, he wanted to ask his friend Rick to take that part over but Rick was not home.

Alone and abandoned, the house had deteriorated in recent months. The last storms had knocked down a tree that was reclining heavily in the back and needed immediate attention. Joe, as a good friend, contracted the services to tear down the tree and turn it into firewood. The damage the tree had caused to the house was of little consideration given the size and strength with which it could have fallen onto the roof. He oversaw the whole operation without seeing or hearing from his friend.

Joe buried the third soldier and several months had passed by when one afternoon, Sarah, as always, woke him up from his nap.

"It's not Shane," she said to reassure him, "but you must go to the cemetery and see with your own eyes."

From a distance, he saw a herd of goats eating the flowers he had planted around the graves of the General, the soldiers, and Ronnie. He parked the Cadillac and went to chase them away, but the goats did not disperse nor were they scared, they insisted on staying in the cemetery that offered them fresh and abundant grass. Docile as if someone had trained them, the goats headed up the road towards the town and Joe followed behind them in the car. So tame were they that without making any noise, they continued straight to Elm Street, then two blocks later turned to the left on Oak Street. If one of the goats stopped, the entire herd did. The herd passed Joe's and Emily's house and continued down the street. Although the sound of their feet on the gravel of the street and the occasional bleat was enough to attract attention, the parade of the goats was not noticed by the neighbors. Only one person looked out the window and saw the passage of the herd without being surprised.

And then the big surprise, the goats entered the backyard of Rick's house. The one leading the group pushed the door with its head, and the whole herd entered the house as if they were used to going in and out like humans. Once inside the house, the goats began to eat the leaves of the oak trees that were close to the windows.

The smell was unbearable when Joe entered the house. The goats had taken over and there was not a single trace of human presence. One goat was in the fireplace, another had climbed on the sofa, and others had taken over specific places in the house as if those positions belonged to them in their own right. Everything inside was

114

chaotic, the walls had holes where you could see that the goats were licking the concrete or lashing out with their horns. The furniture he had bought for his friends at the flea market was gnawed and torn to pieces. The Louis XV-style table had the legs also gnawed on and the goat that was on it defended its territory fiercely with its horns. The paintings whose frames were of good quality had suffered the onslaught of the goats, and it was evident that the canvases had been licked with their scratchy tongue. Joe broke through the goats and went upstairs where the animals were as well. On the second floor, the walls had been collapsed, and the chaos was worse than the first floor. He found cans with rotten food, an alcohol oven, old blankets, in other words, objects typical of a street dweller. Joe heard a sudden noisy blow in the door downstairs, then, he identified his friend's voice calling the goats. Joe came down to the first floor and saw him dressed like a beggar. His beard was long and he had no shoes.

"Where is Catalina?" His friend asked.

"Who is Catalina?" Joe asked him, thinking that it was a woman but Rick didn't answer. Instead, he searched around as if looking for something special.

"Where is Catalina?" He shouted again and went out to the patio. He came back into the house and locked the door.

Joe called to a mental hospital from a nearby town and made sure the officials were aware of his friend's condition and should be in charge of his friend's health and welfare.

Eleven thirty-five

She saw the door was open and watched Sarah go into the other house. Emily remembered that she needed to call the funeral home again so her daughters could take charge of his funeral. She also considered that the ceremony had to be in the pavilion of the fallen soldiers. The decision of his daughters to tell the other woman about his death caused Emily to feel disgust, but that feeling disappeared when she remembered Antonio ...

Chapter 26

... When she opened the window, the morning was cold, and the wind came in from her patio with the resin scent of the oaks. She realized it was January 25th, and recalled it was on that day, one year ago that she saw Antonio for the first time, but for her, it was the first anniversary of being his lover.

She thought about some details for the celebration of the first anniversary. She took two glasses from her great-grandmother's glassware collection, wrapped them in paper and put them in her travel bag. She also put, in the travel bag, a corkscrew and a white tablecloth.

After her daughters left for school, she sat down at the dressing table. At ten minutes before nine she was elegantly dressed in a new skirt of red flowers above her knees and high-heel shoes. When she arrived at the tailor-shop, Sir von Wagner was waiting for her.

"Your husband must be the happiest man in the world," he greeted her. Emily felt a flush on her face and did not know what to answer. He continued, "I was waiting for you to ask about the new employee. It's been almost a year since he arrived. I've heard he spends most of his time lubricating the machine and works very little."

"Neither is true, he is a good worker," she said and continued on her way to the workroom. She knew those comments were lies and had a slight suspicion they were only an invention by the owner. The comment seemed unfair, and she would've put her hands on fire to defend him if necessary but her answer did not seem to satisfy Sir von Wagner, who turned and went into his office.

With the excitement of celebrating a year of being lovers, she forgot the owner's remark and also forgot how abruptly he approached her to ask the question, in the most inappropriate place and with the most blatant attitude. It was when she was passing the central platform and in front of all the employees. The way he asked the question was not to find out if Antonio was really a good worker. It was very obvious he had other intentions. Maybe the owner suspected her relationship with Antonio.

She greeted Antonio "good morning" and he, raising his eyes from the garment greeted back "good morning Emily." But so much dissimulation was impossible to believe, there was something in that greeting, a distinctive sound that if someone were present, would conclude the man who was strange to her a year ago, was no longer a stranger to her now.

She thought the only way to remind him of the anniversary, without giving anyone reasons to be suspicious, was messages on little balls made of paper that she would throw at him.

"Do you know what day it is today?" She asked in the first little message ball.

"Yes," he answered in another.

"What do you want to do to celebrate it?"

"Make love to you all night," he replied.

"My daughters are waiting for me," she replied. And so, little balls came and went for some time, preventing neither getting caught by anybody in the tailor-shop. One of his messages said he had a surprise for her.

"What is it?"

"It's no surprise if I tell you," he answered.

Antonio left before she did. At ten after five Emily accentuated the shadows of her eyebrows and put on some lipstick before leaving. She went through the workers' room and reached the door when Sir von Wagner appeared, coming out of his office.

"Give my regards to your husband," he said.

She went to the liquor store bought a bottle of wine. She, then, went to his apartment.

"Are we going to celebrate with coffee or wine?" she asked from the doorway.

"We'll have coffee and then wine," he replied from the other room.

She put the bottle on the table and went to close the window that let in the cold wind. The wind moved a framed photograph on the wall she hadn't seen before. Strange to her, a black and white photograph of a bullfighter facing a bull with pointed horns. She looked at the photograph carefully and coincidentally, looked out the window and saw the buffalo horn on the terrace. Both, the bull's horns in the photograph and those of the buffalo horns were equally large, and for a moment she had a strange thought. She imagined that Antonio was dressed like the bullfighter in the picture, and there was something in that view that made her feel fear.

"It's a very dangerous art," he said behind her back. She did not know he was behind her and it scared her. "It's the art of bullfighting." He filled the glasses with wine, and after a long moment, he explained what bullfighting was.

"We call it *tauromaquia*, in Spanish," he said. She had never heard of such art, or word, and it seemed strange that people had fun watching a man challenging a bull in a ring.

"It seems a primitive and inhuman act," she frowned.

Antonio had a large canvas on the tripod ready to be painted on. The painting was rectangular and already had the outlines of Emily's face with her hair down and her arms under her head. It was so real that she asked him how he had achieved it without any photograph. It was the surprise he had mentioned in the little paper balls.

She undressed and then lay down on the bed as if she had read his mind. With the arms under the head, just like in the sketch, it looked like those paintings of Renaissance times. Antonio gave a final touch to the contours of the face and continued his work. Outside the wind knocked on the window and slipped through the room moving the photograph of the bullfighter on the wall.

"I'm scared," she said.

"Scared of what?"

"I don't know, but I'm scared."

They did not speak for a long time. The sun came in and filled the room with light. The tripod, the canvas, and Antonio formed a long, amorphous shadow on the floor. The shadow of his hand moved like an extension of the canvas.

"I sense they suspect us," she said.

"Ha! Does it matter that they suspect?" Said Antonio without taking his eyes off the canvas.

"I'm a married woman."

Antonio abandoned the pencil next to the tripod and made love to her. Then he went back to the canvas, and she put her arms under her head as she did before.

"If I work every afternoon for four months, I'll finish it."

"It's going to be a big painting," said Emily.

"As big as if it were two Emilys." They laughed for a moment. Antonio went to make more coffee, and she followed him into the kitchen. It was eight o'clock, the sun had hidden behind the front building . After they finished their coffee Emily stood up to leave.

At the door of the building, she looked both ways, to the left and right. The street was lonely. One of the streetlights was flashing down at the corner of Broadway, and as always, she made sure her blouse was buttoned. When she reached her car, she turned around and looked at the building for a moment. The intermittent light from the lamp post made the buffalo horns much more prominent than normal, and she turned away.

She had heard from her aunts that a genuine woman is a lady in the parlor and a vixen in bed. Now those words made more sense, much more so after she read the *Kamasutra*. She had accidentally found the book in the old family library. She, who was frugal in intimacy with Joe was imaginative and playful with Antonio to such an extent that she recreated the images of the *Kamasutra*. She had imagined signs, attitudes and poses to surprise him. Although none of these ideas materialized, because they were just fantasies, she once thought of surprising him by putting her panties in the drawer of his machine. And so, it was, the preparation of the surprise took some time because she had a fear of being discovered in the tailor-shop. She wanted to spread a perfume on the panties, so she ordered a brand found in the catalogues.

The day the perfume arrived, she had problems with Sarah. She found a small luxury box with an untied pink ribbon on the dining table, and Sarah was waiting for her.

"My father at least does what he does in the eyes of everyone!" Her daughter yelled at her.

"It's just perfume."

"I'm not blind!" Sarah shouted.

Emily took the box and went to the bedroom. After impregnating the panties with perfume, she hid them in her purse.

She came early to the tailor-shop, long before all the employees, and went to Antonio's machine. She put the panties in the drawer perfectly folded and she went back to her machine when she saw Sir von Wagner.

He was at the entrance of the room in such a state of stupefaction that he couldn't move. Scared, she started pedaling without realizing that the machine had no thread, no needle or a garment to sew. The owner broke the silence looking towards Antonio's machine.

"It's a very evocative perfume," he said. There was malice, anger, disgust in those words and even perhaps jealousy. From that day on Sir von Wagner changed his attitude toward her. He closed his office when he saw her and if for some reason, he needed to ask her something related to work, he would look at her cleavage. He started to watch her with a certain brazenness because he would lean into the room or appear suddenly with a malicious smile on his face. And that's how the days went by until it happened; what she had never expected.

It started in the lowest and most degrading way. One morning, Emily saw on Antonio's machine the carcass of a bird. It was the same bird she sometimes saw in the room. Whoever had put it on Antonio's machine, took the trouble to collect all the remains of the animal, feathers, bones and dry skin, along with all the dust of its decomposition and placed all of that on a sheet of paper with an obvious intention.

Emily felt a horrible chill run through her body, felt anger and a desire to run away, and yet she tried to put the carcass in the trash when Antonio arrived.

Antonio looked at the carcass and then at her. That look ended up tormenting her because she saw his state of helplessness and humiliation. The intention was well served. There was no doubt for her that the one who did it was Sir von Wagner. It was then that, without caring if anybody saw her, she approached Antonio and took his hand. She picked up the bird and threw it in the trash.

Several days after that incident, in the same place where the owner had put the carcass, there was an envelope. With Antonio's name on it. Claiming inefficiency at work, the envelope contained a memorandum informing him of a considerable reduction in his salary. It was another humiliation. Emily, with the paper in her hand, went to the owner's office.

"What motivates you to defend him?" He asked before she spoke.

"Many things."

"You are a married woman."

"We are not talking about my private life."

"I can fire him whenever I want to."

"It is illegal to reduce a worker's salary."

"He is illegal. Remember also that I can turn him in to the Immigration Office."

Emily from that moment, was afraid that the tailor would follow up on his threats.

***

Antonio had to work on weekends in a carpentry shop located in another town not too far away. Everything went on as before, but they were afraid that one day, the immigration officers would show up at his door. On weekdays after work, she came to his apartment before him and prepared coffee, and sometimes would wait with a bottle of wine on the table. When she listened to his steps coming upstairs, she filled the glasses with wine or filled the cups with coffee and unlocked the door. Now that they didn't have time to see each other during the weekends, a new element was added to their days, the anticipation that on Monday, they were going to be together.

Emily had many fears that started at the moment she saw the Mayor with his men raising buffalo horns at the entrance of the building. Moreover, there was a strange coincidence between the portrait of the bullfighter and the horns on the terrace. She believed sometimes the building was possessed by the devil. The comments she heard in the tailor-shop about the horns seemed to her as though the Mayor was telling something to the passersby. But what was that?

One day, she asked the old man in the tailor-shop who was concerned about the horns the day after they appeared above the door of the building.

"Oh Emily!" he said. "It's a long story. Those horns have been around since 1932 when Ben Crompton the First put them on the door of the building to show people how proud he was of his acts."

"What acts?"

"Crompton the First was, perhaps more bloodthirsty than his son and grandson. He ordered the death of the leaders of the Union because they had called the miners to strike. Ten men who lived in the building with their families, all of them killed in one of the most horrifying nights in the history of the town. I still remember that fatidic midnight when a flurry of gunfire awakened us and oh, oh the terrifying voices of women and children. Then, a few days later, the horns appeared on the terrace at the entrance of the building. At that time, people asked themselves, just as we do now, why those horns were placed there. People then, had different answers, many ended up believing that Crompton the First was crazy. Although somebody took down the horns, the building was already stigmatized. and now that I see them again after many years, I believe that stigma is still there."

"Why did his grandson put them back there?" Emily asked.

"I don't know, but just remember that Crompton the Third is as crazy as his grandfather. Who knows what his intentions are with those horns, but I believe they are sinister."

Emily now was worried and more afraid than before. Anytime she went to see Antonio, she saw the horns and she wanted to take them down. She felt the same chill every time she passed underneath the terrace, a cold wave that reached her bones but disappeared when she entered his apartment.

She had also proposed to him that they move together to a big city where she could forget about her fears. She saw that her daughters spent more time at their father's house and concluded that she had lost them, that her job as a mother had ended and that she was, therefore, free of responsibilities. Moving to a big city where she could go to concerts of classical music, and now that she was in love, seemed a perfect life in a real city. But Antonio did not listen to her. She approached him when he was painting her portrait, but it was as if she spoke to him in a strange language.

He worked on the portrait every afternoon and did not give up the brush until he completed a fundamental touch or felt he had advanced so far he could afford a break during which he made love to her intensely. In those moments, time didn't exist, nor did prayers; recommendations, and fears vanished as the sun went down; the afternoons expired, and she got out of bed and dressed, straightening her hair, smoothing her skirt. She said goodbye at the door, sometimes, she'd think, *'you should think before taking the brush, better think about it tonight, think as you sleep, look, this building has secrets that I hear as voices from beyond the graves.'* and yet he just needed to look into her eyes to make her fears fade away.

Once, frustrated, she got up from the bed where she was posing, got dressed, and left for home without saying goodbye. The next afternoon, regretful, she returned and waited naked in the bed for him to continue painting the portrait, and so time continued to pass.

The portrait was almost finished and perfect with her left arm under her head, Emily wondered if the joy on her face was real. While Antonio prepared the brushes, she took a mirror out of her purse and looked at her face next to the portrait. Her smile was similar to that on portrait with the difference that hers was a smile of desire and pleasure.

Chapter 27

Joe was promoted to machinery operator in the factory. The promotion did not mean a substantial increase in his salary even though he had workers under his command.

He kept the surplus money he made under the mattress with the money left over from the construction of the park. The new job represented less physical activity since he sat all day in front of a panel with different colored buttons that controlled the machines of the plant. He started to gain weight and lose his hair.

He kept mowing the lawn near the graves of the General, Ronnie, and the soldiers. And some months later he noticed the General's tomb had been the target of attacks; shots and scrapes with a high-caliber hammer that had marred its edges. It was as though someone had a feud with the General not settled before his death. Joe now had to discover who was destroying this grave and the reason for so much hatred. He thought about watching the tomb at night.

***

Joe had so many books that he decided to build a library. In the afternoons, while his daughters played in the park with their brother and children from the neighborhood. He assembled the library with sheets of polished pine he ordered from Canada. The library encompassed two walls from floor to ceiling and he began to put the books in an order very much depending on their subject or titles. He had looked at the books one-by-one and page by page in the last months.

The fact that he had not found any information on the General's life did not cause disappointment; on the contrary, when he finished looking through all the books, he felt a much higher interest than before, and wondering about the shots against the General's grave. Hoping that one day he would come to know everything about the General's life, he continued to order books from public libraries. He sent requests for titles which in most cases were so rare that his letters were returned with a *non-existent* response or *title under review*. Neither the negative responses of the academics nor the returned requests from the libraries discouraged him from his quest.

By then, he had buried nine soldiers around the General's tomb, who looked as if they were guarding his grave. But the deterioration of the General's tomb was such that he thought of rebuilding it with reinforced concrete. Every time he mowed the grass, he found the casings of bullets around his tomb. He accumulated them in the garage until one day realizing the pile was very big he thought about melting them and making a bust of the General. But he had first to know what his face was like and he did not even have a photograph. He thought by the time he found his picture in a book, the pile of projectiles was going to be big enough to make a bust of the General that could be seen from a distance.

Although he repaired it frequently, the shots continued opening large holes that were sometimes difficult to cover with concrete. But he did not give up. It was a war against who wanted to destroy it and he who wanted to protect it. Given the number of shots, he had the conviction that several shooters were raging against the tomb of the General.

One night after a few shots of whiskey at his friend's bar, he went to the cemetery, parked his car behind a massive tomb with the headlights pointed straight at the General's tomb and then turned them off. The road climbed from the south side of the cemetery and went up to a hill, where it became a white line further up that was crossed by the lights of cars that passed. He suddenly saw a car coming from the south turned into the cemetery and slowed down. It then came straight to the little hill of the General's grave. The driver got out, lit a cigarette, and sat on the hood of the car until he finished it. Joe could see all the movements of the man, even his gestures as the night was clear with a large moon shining above. The driver put out his cigarette with his foot on the gravel, then went to the General's grave, and jumped up on top. Joe turned on the lights of his car and saw the intruder pull down his pants and defecate on the General's grave.

"Unpatriotic!" Joe yelled at him. Closing the car door violently, he walked towards the man. "What do you think you're doing?"

"I'm shitting," the man replied.

"Do you not know that this tomb is sacred?"

"Might it be the tomb of Jesus Christ?"

By the voice Joe could determine the man was young, maybe a teenager.

"Go shit elsewhere."

"No, I can't," the boy replied.

Joe pulled out his gun. "Let's see if this makes you respect the General as sacrosanct, you son-of-a-bitch."

"The act of shitting is as sacred to me as this grave, so leave me alone," the boy said. "For some reason, the trigger of my gun did not work tonight, and I decided to shit on the tomb."

"Why?" Asked Joe, giving up.

"Because I feel a deep relief." With the headlights of the car straight at his face, the boy couldn't see Joe's frustration. He pulled up his pants and went to his car. "Is he your family?" he asked.

"No, but it is the tomb of an honored man."

"My old man doesn't think the same. In fact, I am doing this for him."

Before starting the car, the boy told Joe that his grandfather knew the history of the grave. Joe asked the boy to take him to see his grandfather.

"If you want to know, follow me."

Joe followed the young man on the road that later became dusty and narrow.

It was nine o'clock when they arrived at the house. It had all the lights on and a television at full volume. The house was sparse, not a painting on the walls nor an object of decoration that made it more habitable. It did have a large couch and a recliner that were probably the beds of its only inhabitants, the grandfather and the teenager.

"Mr. Rupert," the young man called to his grandpa, who was in front of the television, in the recliner with its back facing the entrance. Rupert raised his hand as a sign he was still awake.

"How many?" Apparently, the grandfather asked the young man the same question upon his return every night.

"None," the young man replied. "I decided to shit on his grave." The grandfather let out a loud laugh and then he said:

"Watch out, the Mayor believes Jesus is buried in that grave."

"Well, somebody caught me," the young man said.

"Who?"

"This gentleman."

The grandpa stood up quickly from the recliner as if he were in his thirties. He was tall, friendly and of lucid mind even though he looked to be over 70. His face turned serious and looked at the floor when the boy told him Joe was taking care of the tomb. He wanted to say something, but he had to think about it first. By looking at his countenance, one could tell he'd had tough years. A large scar on his left cheek eclipsed his smile. His name was Rupert.

"Well, I don't know what to say. It's hard to say I am sorry." Rupert kept silent for a moment. "It's a bad baseball season, I've never seen batters that bad," he said, referring to the summary of the baseball games on the television. "The KC Royals may get the title this year."

"I wouldn't be so optimistic, they still have to face the Cardinals," Joe said, "but it's not baseball I came to talk about."

"To what, then, do I owe the honor of your visit?" He asked.

Joe looked at the young man, "I found him shitting on the General's grave."

"General?" The old man scratched his forehead, "he was not a general, and I didn't know anyone other than the Cromptons had so much respect for that outlaw. Stay for supper, I know things that may interest you," said the old man who went to the kitchen.

The young man, who until then was concentrated on the results of the baseball competition, disappeared into the basement.

"My grandfather had direct contact with your General," the boy shouted from the basement. "You will know lots later when supper is served."

By the smell that began to waft through the house, Joe determined that the grandfather was pan searing cow's liver. He tried it as a child when his mother, in a time of economic upheaval cooked liver for dinner. He did not remember the taste but, despite his hunger, the piece of raw liver on the plate looked horrible. His mother, seeing the reaction of her only child, let out a cry of grief, and he ate the liver containing the urge to vomit just to console his mom.

The aroma of cilantro and onion hit his sense of smell and he thought the herbs were a good buffer of bad food, and a few minutes later, the grandpa appeared with a large pan that sizzled grease and flames. The grandfather put the pan on the table and invited him to sit down after his grandson brought the plates and silverware, and a bottle of red wine. The old man put a slice of bread on his plate, and a strip of the liver on top sprinkled with cilantro and onion, then he squeezed lemon on it. His grandson did the same.

"Bon Appetit," he said.

Joe imitated them by squeezing all the lemon on the liver. After tasting the first bite Joe realized the liver was exquisite and did not look anything like the one he had tried when he was a boy.

"It's a calf," Rupert said, "a young animal, fresher and healthier. It tastes less like shit. I am referring to all those hormones farmers give cattle so they grow and mature before their time." And then he cut the line of conversation, "so you're the one who is taking care of the tomb?"

"Yes," Joe replied.

"Do you know who is buried there?"

"Of course, I know, it's a general, an honorable and good man."

"I wondered if you really knew who was actually buried there," the grandfather smiled without losing his calm, "he was neither a general nor a good man," he said, filling the glasses with more wine. After a pause, he covered his face with his hands. The right hand had lost three fingers and left, uncovered, part of his face. He looked like the unfinished painting of an apprentice painter. "Doug Wade," he exclaimed.

Chapter 28

Rupert was 20 years old when he saw Doug Wade; it was during the massacre in 1932. Like everybody else, he worked in the mine and was an active member of the Union. An avid reader of treatises on economics and sociology, he had read the *Communist Manifesto* of Lenin and the *Capital* of Marx and other related books out of which he extracted statements, ideas, opinions or recited fragments that left the other workers speechless. He memorized dates and read the news about the Bolshevik Revolution, the ones that were filtered by the capitalist media of America, reluctant to admit what was happening in Russia.

He was also a good observer, with a restless aptitude and charisma that he could have used to his comfort and in his favor to convince or manipulate if he wished. But Rupert was modest and intelligent despite his youth. His humility was also his strength. All the workers liked him for that quality more than for his intelligence. The leaders of the Union had him in their sights as a potential member who could give the organization a bit of power and innovation. After a short period as a regular worker, he was elected secretary of the Union. Rupert convinced the Union to go on strike but let it be known up front that he was opposed to any violent acts. Then came that fatal event and neither his eloquent speeches nor charisma could stop the massacre.

Days after the massacre, the counterpart in retaliation executed a secret and violent persecution against the leaders of the Union. At that moment, Doug Wade, an active member of a KKK faction in the state of Mississippi, was in town at a secret clan convention. Lucas Green, the owner of the mine and the new Mayor, Crompton the First, grandfather of Ben Crompton the Third, hired Doug Wade to control the situation they presumed was going to become chaos. The desire to control the situation was only a euphemism that basically meant eliminating the cause of the problem. Crompton the First had not yet been inaugurated as Mayor after a very strange election, when the owner of the mine came to his office with Doug.

The owner of the mine closed the door of the office and immediately presented the man.

"He is the solution," he said, and Doug, without losing any time, outlined the plan to them.

"In just a few days the mine will be open and working at full speed," he promised.

"Just one problem," the Mayor said. "How much?"

"Only a voluntary contribution to help the cause," Doug said and that was it.

To help in his task, and without Doug Wade asking, Crompton put the police at his service; that was, in other words, to turn a blind eye when someone came to announce that a dead man had been found in a ditch, or in an abandoned garage. Safeguarding the streets meant less vigilance at night and recommendations not to leave the houses which were not recommendations but a curfew, prohibition of walking through the streets at night. Thus, they prepared the way for Doug Wade, making the night dark, lonely and without anyone seeing him who slept in the day and lived in the night, which reminded Joe what he had heard from his father-in-law. Doug had a Doberman that some speculated was fed with the blood of his victims. The dog had scabrous eyes that caused fear in those close by.

When the first of the dead appeared with a shot in the head, under the occipital bone, as a personal seal and indication that his work was for real, Rupert, the leader of the workers knew he was in danger. He armed himself with a pistol and even though he didn't know how to use a gun, he, had determination and balls to wait for the killer. Because that was what his comrades did, wait for the assassin, helpless in a state of stoicism. He would wait yes, but he would defend himself.

It was fifteen days of terror. The leaders of the Union fell one-by-one. The cleaning was as effective as the owner of the mine and the Mayor said when they met in the office now and then to evaluate the results. Upon seeing the success, Crompton the First, in a moment of euphoria, promised to erect a monument to Doug Wade.

Rupert took a deep breath and scratched again his forehead, an act that he repeated automatically as he was telling Joe the story.

"I have this habit since those nights when I waited for Doug." He stopped talking for a moment. "I could have fled, but I hated that man. Now that I see the facts from the distance of time, I believe that some men are born with fear for death and others with the courage to face it. I had the nerves to look for it, that is, to face who was going to be my assassin. It was during those days that I clung to my guardian angel. There is nothing wrong with having a guardian angel, religion, you see... It is good because it gives power, even if it is to do evil. Bad because I had the desire to kill Doug. The more I entrusted my angel, the stronger was the desire to kill him. It was like those assassins in Medellin, the city of Pablo Escobar, who kiss the image of the sacred Virgin Mary when they are going to kill, you know?" He stopped talking for a moment. "Do you believe in God?" He asked.

"No," Joe answered.

"That is the negative thing of the communists," he said. "I like communism, but that is the negative point," he looked at the small library where a large, brightly lit bible stood out among the few books. "I do not know how many times I've read it." And then, jumping from one subject to another, he said "it was time to face the enemy and he came when I least expected, to my house, with the dog that obeyed him faithfully. I was the last one of the leaders and it was my turn. He was not as I had imagined him, tall or corpulent, with a serious and threatening look. I always saw myself in those fifteen days of nightmare facing a giant, as though it was a fight between David and Goliath. Of course, I looked like young David, and yet the Goliath I had imagined was rather short in stature, lean to the point of giving the impression that he was weak. That gave me a little confidence when I stood up and saw he did not exceed my shoulders. But immediately I reconsidered that a murderer like him was not going to take part in a physical confrontation. A killer like him shoots, period. So, before he shot me, I shot him in the face. It was an accurate shot. Not bad for someone who had never fired a gun, for someone who had barely seen one. Doug fell on his knees and then collapsed on the floor, on top of the dog that stood up and sniffed his master."

He noticed that Joe looked at the hand that had missing fingers.

"It was the dog," he said. "It was that damned animal, as intelligent as a human that when his master was dead, as if it understood that, it came at me without giving me time to shoot him. It bit off my fingers and flew out the window. When Doug didn't show up, Crompton and his partner knew it was me who killed him. I hid in a place so close to the Mayor's office and so obvious that they looked for me everywhere except in that place from where I could see the Mayor and his friend tearing at their beards in anger and frustration. I waited until that afternoon. Sitting by the window, I had Crompton the First in the sight of an old rifle. What I should have done then was to flee and be safe away from this miserable town. I had the Mayor in the rifle sight. I just had to pull the trigger and go out the back door, walking unhurriedly down the narrow street and get close to the train-rail, hiding behind the trees until the train passed at midnight. But something so strange happened at that moment. As if he sensed he was being watched, he turned his head and looked right where I was. Instead of throwing himself to the ground before being killed from a shot, he smiled at me, and with his finger, pointed to his forehead, as if saying put it here. That reaction gave me a lot of fear, fear that I had not felt until then. That was Crompton the First, the grandfather of our Mayor, very macho and very courageous. He did not move his eyes off my rifle, and I knew at that moment he was giving orders. That afternoon I fled on the train that came from New Orleans as I had planned."

Rupert served another glass of wine and continued, "Crompton the First had paid Doug a generous sum of money for his services, and Doug in return gave the Mayor a pair of buffalo horns. Doug had bought the horns in a Sioux reservation next to a town in South Dakota on the banks of the Missouri River."

"Horns?" Interrupted Joe.

"Yes, the same ones Crompton the Third has put on the terrace of a building in the downtown area."

"What building?" Asked Joe.

"The one on the corner of Elm Street, left hand as you go west on Broadway."

"I promise that I won't shit on the General's tomb anymore," said the young man when Joe was about to leave.

Joe did not believe the story of the horns and couldn't accept the General was a criminal. He thought Rupert's story was that of another man, perhaps the same one his father-in-law referred to, a killer who had managed to insert his name in the memory of the children in No-town and at the same time had eclipsed that of the General's. Since that night, Joe had two people to think about; the good and the bad. Of both he had only pieces of information; but he would not quit his search until he knew the life of the good one.

It was eleven o'clock, and there was a full moon when he left Rupert's house. Maybe the old man realized his disbelief because when he waved him goodbye at the door, he told him to take a walk down the street where the building was with the horns so he could see with his own eyes that he was not lying. It was the first time Joe heard of the horns and the building. Joe slowed down until he stopped at the intersection of Broadway and Elm Street. The traffic light was flashing red for a few seconds and then green, Joe looked to one side and then to the other. On the left Elm Street was dark, and to the right lit all the way to the north. He turned left and a few meters further down, he recognized the horns on the door's terrace of the building.

'Rupert was not lying', he thought. He stopped the Cadillac one block away and looked at the horns with more curiosity. Ben Crompton the Third, like his grandfather, had contempt for the inhabitants of the building. If he had known before, he would have taken them down and burned them. He got out of the car and walked to the building and climbed on the terrace above the door. Three iron straps fastened the horns to the terrace and were impossible to be removed. The screws were rusted and he didn't have any tools. He was going to get down off the terrace when he heard someone coming downstairs. Whoever it was stopped under the terrace and then passed into the street. The steps were those of a woman, and Joe raised his head to look and recognized her immediately. Next, to her car, Emily turned around and looked up. In the windows of the front building Joe saw a man raise his hand and wave goodbye to Emily. She got in the car and left.

Until then, Joe had a suspicion that Emily had a lover. However, the idea itself was so remote that he couldn't believe it. He felt the urge to go up and kill the man, throwing him out of the window. That night he arrived home, turned on the light in the hall and opened the door of the bedroom. He saw Rose's face, the perfect line of her hips, naked shoulders and her hair on the pillow. He undressed and slid between her legs and penetrated her with rage. It was a simple ejaculation, without a shudder nor deep breath that altered her dreams.

Chapter 29

One afternoon he stopped in a bar close to the building of the horns. Before he went in, he saw the horns in the terrace of the entrance. They appeared much bigger and they seemed to intimidate the passersby that hot afternoon.

Joe ordered a cold beer and sat by the bar counter and exchanged some words with the bartender. The conversation switched from the late news to the horns. For the bartender, a man in his mid-forties who just had seen the horns the day before, they were nothing but an amulet for the building's tenants.

"Horns in my land are good luck," he said. Suddenly, a crowd cheering came from the street. "There we go, talking about horns," said the bartender.

The tenants came out of the building and had taken down the horns from the terrace. People in a circle were cheering two men who were simulating a bullfight with the horns. One of them had the horns and charged the other who teased him with a red blanket. For Joe, who had never heard about bullfighting, the spectacle was strange. But what called him to attention was the scarf one of the men had on his neck. It was Emily's scarf.

Joe paid for the beer and left. He drove the streets of the town with no direction and then later he went to visit the General's tomb. He couldn't forget the man's face. He was probably Emily's age, young, strong and good looking. He had a mix of feelings.

Later that night, Joe went to Colton. '*Perhaps some sips of whiskey would help him forget what he saw and forget Emily too, once and for all*', he thought as he got in his old Cadillac. There was a lot of movement in the parking lot, the luxury cars with license plates from Illinois and other states from far away in perfect alignment gave the brothel a certain air of importance. Although it was going to be stormy and windy, the cars continued to crowd in the parking lot. The perfectly dressed prostitutes, in elegant suits that made them look like respectable ladies, waited for the customers at the door. The door that night was adorned with wreaths and garlands. Colored lights that went on and off were camouflaged in the front garden. Joe was received by a young woman with a glass of whiskey on the rocks who walked him in. There was an air of sophistication in the living halls, bars, and rooms as well. The young prostitute sat down by his side, so close that he could smell her perfume and her fresh breath. Her gracious smile changed suddenly, a sad and tragic face that surprised Joe.

"Something wrong?" He asked.

"I heard that Crompton is upset, but that's not the problem, he is going to kill a man tonight."

"Why?"

"I don't know."

"Do you know the man?"

"No." She said sobbing. "But I am just wondering. He may be an innocent man, a good husband, or a good lover."

Joe took a long sip of whiskey. The woman's last words made him remember Emily's lover.

"Well, who knows." Joe put his glass of whiskey down.

She excused herself and went to the ladies' room. Joe thought about the events that happened in the last days, the story Rupert told him about the General, Emily's affair. But it was difficult to forget that someone was going to be killed that night. For some strange reason he thought the innocent man the prostitute had mentioned was Emily's lover.

"I can't stand this sensation," said the woman when she returned. "I don't know, and what upsets me more, all of these people may know about it and nobody does anything." She was about to cry "I don't know what, but I must do something." She held his hands with such force that Joe, moved, was almost ready to promise her whatever she asked him to do, even if it was to kill the mayor. "Promise me you'll do something. I know that you wouldn't, but lie to me, make me believe that you would do something to stop it. Just make me believe that."

"I promise," Joe stood up and left.

Eleven thirty-eight

Rosario came with something wrapped in an old fabric. The wrap was the same since she recovered the portrait at the photographer shop. Emily began crying.

"I know everything," her daughter said softly, keeping Linda from listening. Rosario wiped her mother's tears. "Once, a long time ago, I saw the portrait, and then I understood everything" ...

Chapter 30

...A hunch woke her up. Certain she had heard his voice, she got up immediately and thought about going to his apartment. It was raining intensely; she tried several times to open the door, but the storm would not let her. The wind was so strong that it seemed to have blocked it from the outside. She returned to her bed but couldn't fall asleep.

It was still raining when the alarm clock struck at five in the morning. She went to the kitchen to prepare the coffee, poured some in a cup, and then put in some unrefined sugar as she had learned from Antonio. Emily prepared breakfast for her daughters. Put their backpacks on the small table by the entrance, and before leaving for the tailor-shop, she reminded them to clean the mess they had made celebrating their younger sister's birthday.

The tailor-shop was empty even though it was eight o'clock. She prepared her machine and sat down to sew. Half an hour later, the employees came in one-by-one and by nine all had arrived except Antonio. There was a pair of pants on his machine that he had left unfinished the previous afternoon, and she remembered he had said when she was last evening with him that he would give the last touches to her portrait. He was happy because the painting had artistic value and he thought it could belong to an art collection. He had enthusiastically said, *'I think I am reaching maturity and my own style'*.

She looked at the clock again, it was ten o'clock, and Antonio had not arrived. She thought he may be sick and told herself she would go at noon to see him. She also remembered, while working, that before leaving his apartment the last night, she saw him thoughtful, pale like in a dream, and she had asked him if he was sick, '*I have never felt better*', he had answered.

And that morning, without being able to concentrate on her work, she also remembered that she had seen the horns in his apartment. She asked him how they had ended up there, and what he said made no sense. She said she was going to burn the horns on her patio. For the first time he had asked her to divorce her husband so they wouldn't need to hide their love.

At twelve o'clock she went to his apartment. The door was open, and she went in. She was shocked when she saw Sir von Wagner sitting down on the sofa.

"I was waiting for you," the tailor said.

"What are you doing here?" She asked. Emily went to Antonio's bedroom. The bed was empty and the blankets on the floor. The painting that Antonio had on the tripod was on the floor, too.

"It's an excellent painting," the tailor said when he saw her picking it up. The containers where Antonio mixed the paints and brushes were on the floor as well. One brush was on his bench where he sat to paint and distilled a thread of fine and long paint that almost reached the floor. Something had happened and Antonio maybe had fled, she thought. Perhaps they came from immigration and had deported him. However, she asked the tailor again and he said, "I am sorry to give you the news."

"What happened to Antonio."

"Antonio was killed."

"It's not true!" Emily yelled. The pigeons that piled on top of the building in the front took off. It seemed that time had never run its course, that neither that morning nor the stormy and fatal night had ever existed, that she had not heard the tailor saying those terrible words, that he was lying and that she was as happy as she was every afternoon. And all that denial vanished suddenly, like the pigeons that took off and disappeared. She wanted to die, to be taken to the grave with him. She went down to the street. The clouds had fallen, and it was dark. It started raining again. The wind whistled on the cornices of the buildings as she walked to her car without feeling the rain. She rested her head on the steering wheel, blank mind and pain in her chest. It was not physical pain, it was a mortal pain, it was the end, the end of the end, the end of everything.

Eleven Forty-Two

Mother and daughter remained silent. Rosario tried to untie the red ribbon around the wrap, but her mother snatched it from her hands.
"You loved him so much, didn't you?" She asked.
"I loved him with all my soul."
"All these years I tried to ask you what happened."
"I also tried to know everything, how it happened and why they killed him."
"Did Dad know you loved another man?" Rosario asked, looking at her father's room.
"Yes," Emily looked out the window, and the daughter looked at the mother expecting her to say something else.
"What else do you know?" She asked.
"He took to the grave a secret that he never confessed to me."
"What do you mean, Mother?"
"Your Dad was one of the murderers..."

Chapter 31

... Three years had passed since that day she saw Antonio for the first time to the day she took him to his grave. Everything reminded her of Antonio, the autumns, the summers, and even the snow. She had made the promise at his grave that she was going to tear apart the world until she found his murderers.

She lived with the sense of guilt, and she continued with the same bitterness and sadness. One night, she went up to the attic where she found a long, thick chain. She dragged it to Joe's park without making the slightest noise and then tied it to the bases of the swing, the spinning wheel, and the carousel. She parked the car in front of the park and tied the other end to the rear bumper adjusted it and then started the engine running, with all its power, she went down the street with the long tail of wood, cans, and logs behind leaving a trail of sparks and smoke. The dogs of the town were the only ones who woke up to the noise. She drove straight down Broadway and went on aimlessly. Later, when the queue was reduced to the chain because Joe's park was scattered along the road in pieces, she parked in front of the building. She looked at the window where Antonio used to say *good night my sweet love.*

It was very early in the morning when she returned home, laid down but wasn't able to sleep. While outside the autumn winds shook the leaves off the trees, she recalled all the moments she with Antonio. She had questions, doubts, and suspicions. Suspicions that, after thinking so much about them, she ended up believing were unfounded. Like the suspicion that Joe had killed him. She also suspected the tailor killed Antonio. His presence in his apartment was inexplicable. What was stranger was his attitude, as if he was satisfied with the outcome of the events. She did not have a point to start her inquiries, and she even thought about giving up.

She had never wondered what would have happened if fate had not taken her down that tragic path. She avoided that question, just as she avoided asking what would have happened if her life with Antonio had been different. She saw the signs of the tragedy before it happened, his talks, an attitude that made it seem like he did not belong to this world, and then having heard his voice in her dreams.

***

One afternoon, after so much thinking and concluding Antonio's death was going to remain a mystery, somebody knocked on her door. Someone she had not seen for a long time. Camille Cadwell was not the same woman from the time they worked in the tailor-shop. She had lost some weight and the years had given her a touch of importance. Dressed elegantly in a trendy pink suit that fitted her very well, Camille looked like a princess. She took off her hat and gloves immediately as the door was opened. Camille looked like a woman of nobility from some European country.

It was an emotional encounter. Camille told her what had happened to her in all the time since she left the tailor-shop. Camille wandered through some states and for some time settled in Detroit, where she worked as a waitress with a salary that was not enough to cover her needs. She then moved to Canada, where she worked in a nursing home in a suburb of Toronto and later in a private detective firm, where she applied her skills learned long before her time in the tailor-shop. None of those jobs were enough to cover her needs and so she finally returned to No-town.

"And here begins the other part of my life that is difficult to explain and that I wouldn't tell anybody else," she said.

Despite the fact that she didn't have a job or any desire to return to the tailor-shop, she went to Colton. She started at the bottom, cleaning rooms that smelled like copula, the raw smell of males and females, musk and vomit, alcohol and menstruation, that of female's fluids and semen. In short, all the human filth, more despicable than that of a hospital. The salary allowed her to subsist thanks to the benefits provided by the brothel, which paid a percentage of food and a private room that was not bad compared to those in Detroit. After doing calculations, she could save a few dollars under the mattress. She felt admiration for La Mama, the owner of the brothel. Then the owner offered her a promotion, earning more money as a prostitute. She thought about the offer for many nights, and after doing many more calculations, she imagined a comfortable life after retiring if she was smart and saved money. She accepted the offer and her first client, she said, was Sir von Wagner.

"As you hear it, the tailor."

She, who once told Emily that even if she were lonely in a solitary island and horny, with no men around but the tailor, that even then she would have preferred to masturbate thinking about Paul Newman. She confessed now that she slept with the tailor for the money he paid her.

The tailor never recognized her and still didn't until the sun of that day. He paid high for a night that surprised the owner of the brothel, who said the pay was exaggerated. A woman with no experience in bed did not deserve so much, a statement that to some extent was not true because Camille was, as she defined herself, a lady in the parlor and a whore in bed.

The owner of the Brothel received the money, took a percentage, and the rest was for Camille. Then he came with the proposal to make her his exclusively every night, whenever he wanted her. She had to be at his service when he called her, even in the least expected moments. For example, if at noon he wanted her, he only had to show up in her bedroom without announcing himself in advance. Finally, the services became more exclusive. Paying a surcharge, the tailor wanted her at his house. And so she ended up with him, full time, becoming his lover and to some extent his wife.

Without realizing it, she ended up caring about the tailor and was afraid that she might be in love. That was the reason for her visit.

Of that infatuation she had a jealousy that she couldn't put away from her daily routine, because lately, the tailor who, at the beginning, devoted all his attention to her, had begun to wake up every night with nightmares and headaches, and in his uneasy sleep he exclaimed a woman's name that was not hers. That name was Emily. The tailor had clarified all her doubts, and after a few weeks, when everything seemed calm, the tailor woke up at midnight calling out *'Emily'* again. She turned on the lamp and discovered the face of a tormented man who did not know who he was or where he was. The tailor, in addition to his bad health, suffered from a love sickness. That night he told her the truth: his feelings were for another woman. It was a terrible confession for Camille who was always sure the love of the tailor was indivisible. That confession had hurt her self-esteem. So, more out of pride than out of love for the tailor, she had come to Emily to ask her if she loved him.

"Never," Emily replied. "My love is dead."

In a few words, Emily told her friend about her life from the moment that Camille left the tailor-shop until the last day: how she met Antonio, the love she felt for him, and about his murder. Camille took a handkerchief from her purse, passed it over her eyes and then sighed deeply. She pulled, out of her purse, a shiny, silver-colored luxury case with her name in gold letters and a heart pierced by a sword and took out a cigarette and lit it. Camille's manners had undergone a transformation that did not do her any harm. The vocabulary of a sailor she used some times when she was at tailor-shop was replaced with a more elegant one, even though one could see that Camille was not sophisticated and cultured by nature, and her attitude had a dose of pretension. The hypochondriac woman addicted to pain killer pills was in the past. Calmed after listening to what Emily had said, Camille's face had an instant metamorphosis because the features that anger, jealousy, and disappointment had masked, now stood out with a fresh air that made her look much younger. She began with a happy and cheerful tone to talk about her life with the tailor.

Sir Von Wagner brought a new dress every night, designed exclusively for her. In all that time, he never brought the same design nor repeated an outfit.

"What else could one ask in this life, in these times of recession when being a prostitute is a reasonable and, in most cases, a desirable option," she said.

She had accumulated a good amount of money, enough to get out of the brothel and hold on for a while until she found an honorable job but she did not leave. Life in Colton had much attraction. Everything in her relationship with the tailor had reached the level of perfection, from romance to the most insignificant details he provided to her. He surprised her sometimes with a jewel that she never was in doubt of its quality or its high price. Yet something was missing that she had managed to get accustomed to and to a certain extent accept more out of habit than out of tolerance.

What was missing was the most important of all, the sexual act in which Sir von Wagner failed with the same lamentation with which he excused his imperfection, the misfortune and the tragedy of a weak and dysfunctional virility. The tailor cursed, damned his mother, his father and his sister, the great whore of Berlin as he called her, against whom he discharged all his rage because he thought what he lacked, was taken by his twin sister, the whore who slept with all the young Berliners, and did the most terrible damage to his life in the womb of their mother absorbing all the hormones that belonged to him by biological right.

That was the curse he always cast, word for word, point by point, when he saw his fundamental organ disappear, getting dwarfed, hiding without leaving the slightest trace in the pelvis of a diminished male. Camille comforted him by patting him on the back, sweet kisses on the cheek, on the forehead and finally the good night kiss.

After imparting all these happenings in her life, as if she were an artist capable of hiding her emotions, Camille's face changed from joyful to profoundly sad when she told her of that night, the night of the confession. In addition to jealousy, she was afraid, because she glimpsed in the face of the tailor a man capable of anything, even of killing to achieve the love of the woman he loved.

Emily was sure Camille kept secret other confessions maybe, out of fear, that she did not want to tell her. Definitely, Camille was afraid. Camille ended the visit abruptly and before leaving she promised to come and visit her more often.

"Better not," Emily exclaimed.

"Why?"

"It's not a good idea."

"Do you think he killed Antonio to get him out of the way?"

"Yes."

Camille didn't care about Emily's warning and came back again. In one of the conversations, they talked about Emily's portrait. The tailor snatched it from Emily's hands that day when she heard about Antonio's death. He took the portrait to his house and kept it in a secured room. As much as he knew about art, he appreciated the portrait, but at the same time wanted to destroy it. Camille was ignorant about the existence of the portrait until days ago when she saw him loading, into his truck. what she thought was a painting. She didn't dare ask him but suspected he was taking it to the workshop for restoration.

* * *

Several days later, after she had thought about it many times, Emily went to the workshop. She approached the only man in the place and talked to him, whispering as if there were people around. The truth was she was scared and wanted to prevent any encounter with the tailor, who she had not seen since that fatal day of Antonio's death. Hesitant on how to ask the man, she looked around and saw the portrait on a table and moved closer. The portrait was extended to its full dimensions on the table and secured at the corners by brick-like blocks of metal. The man followed Emily and stood on the other side of the table.

In what appeared to be an instant act of rage, the tailor had scratched Emily's face until it disappeared and had done the same in other areas too.

"Strange," the man said, "the tailor wants it framed and no restoration at all." He leaned into the portrait until his nose touched one the areas that were scratched, "That son-of-a-bitch used kerosene, to remove what gave the portrait identity." And the man was right because the tailor's idea was to frame and exhibit it in his living room for his own appreciation, as a grotesque image of Emily to laugh at whenever he wanted and at the same time get rid of the sensation of failure in his affairs of love.

"I was the model for that portrait," she said.

"I was wondering," the man said.

"It's a long story, but that painting belongs to me."

"He paid me quite a considerable amount of money for the framing and..."

Emily interrupted the man, "I know there is nothing I can do to recover it, but I have the hope that one day I will," Emily said and left the workshop.

Chapter 32

Many days passed and Sir von Wagner died suddenly of an untreated brain aneurysm that caused a massive spill in the parietal region of his head. His death was known throughout the town because of the importance of Sir von Wagner, who died in his bed under the care of Camille and a nurse who was at his side all the time. The burial was attended by Ben Crompton the Third, with his cabinet and henchmen, the employees of the tailor-shop, friends, and people who did not know him but came out of curiosity. Emily was also present because Camille asked her to attend the funeral.

Camille, who was very sad, had on a mourning dress, a black hat, dark glasses and gloves of the same color. Her elegance contrasted with the crowd that came to the funeral. The minister who officiated the ceremony opened with the New Testament; Saint John 11: 38-44 and began to read the resurrection of Lazarus.

"I know you always hear me; but I am speaking more loudly because of the crowd here today." The reverend noticed the crowd's attention was diverted by a dark limousine that approached slowly and parked close. The doors automatically opened and a group of beautiful and elegantly dressed women in black got out of the vehicle. The women came to where Camille was and one-by-one gave her their condolences. Then, as if they had rehearsed the movements, with a certain formal touch, they stood at her side ready to attend the ceremony.

The ceremony did not end as expected because a woman, apparently jealous, acknowledged that the newcomers were the prostitutes from Colton. The woman left the funeral, almost dragging her husband while she shouted expletives at the prostitutes. Then all the women who attended the funeral did the same then left, and the funeral ended up being a solitary burial.

The same day after the tailor's burial, Emily went back to the workshop. The portrait was on the table and still unframed. The man, apologetic, said that he didn't know what to do now that the tailor was dead. "But, if you want, I can restore the damaged areas."

"Don't do anything," Emily replied. "I am taking it as it is."
She had a problem with the portrait. Because of its size, she was afraid that her daughters, especially Sarah, would discover it. The man brought a white cloth and wrapped the portrait with a red ribbon

knotted in the middle. She was lucky because her daughters were not there when she arrived home. She hastily unloaded it from the car and kept it in the place she thought was the safest in the house, under her bed.

***

And many days later after the tailor's burial, Camille came back and said to Emily,

"I know who killed Antonio." With the death of the tailor, she was free to tell everything, and she felt it was her responsibility to let Emily know what she knew about Antonio's death. She proceeded to tell all to Emily.

On the fatal night when Antonio was killed, at ten o'clock the tailor asked the nurse to go home, that he no longer needed her as if he sensed his imminent death. The nurse objected, saying she couldn't abandon him in that state. Obeying her oath and professional principles meant she had to take care of him. The truth was he was too ill to dismiss the nurse in that way: but he respectfully insisted, and the nurse took the stethoscope, the thermometer and a pack of hypodermic syringes in a bag and left. It was raining and the wind was strong. The tailor cursed and mumbled a few words. He regretted the bad weather. He got up dragging his feet, put on the gown, from the bedside table took out the gun that he examined to see if he had bullets, and then leaned against the back of the bed. Later the doorbell rang, and Camille asked him who could it be at that time?

He said; *"Someone I'm waiting to discuss an issue with, stay here and do not come down. It is men's business."*

She heard voices that she couldn't understand because of the storm, the conversation did not last more than a minute, and then she heard the door close. Sir von Wagner came up the stairs slowly because she heard him stop to catch his breath. She waited for him in bed.

Thoughtful and tormented like someone who has to do something he does not want to do, he went straight to the bar and filled a glass with whiskey.

"Not with the pills," she said, but he ignored her and looked at the clock. She glimpsed then, that he had something in mind, something dark. Slowly he dressed in an outfit as if he were going hunting and then told her he was going to kill the lover of the woman he loved. He said that, as though he were telling her that he was going to kill a deer. At that time, Camille had no knowledge of who the woman was.

Confused, she took the bottle of liquor and drank until she lost consciousness. The next day when she woke up, the tailor slept beside her. She had never seen him so restless. It was as if he had a nightmare. She felt jealous because she thought he was dreaming of the woman. She saw the gun beside the night table and thought about killing him and then taking her own life, but she lacked the resolve.

"I wonder," she said as she wiped away her tears, "what would have happened if he had recognized me and realized I was once his employee at the shop." The day the tailor was going to die, perhaps in the act of repentance, he confessed that the plan to kill the man was determined in Colton that same night of the killing.

"The tailor was not alone," concluded Emily.

"No, he was not alone."

"Did he tell you who else was in on the plan?"

"Crompton. He was the man who came to visit the night of the killing. But there were more people involved."

Camille proposed Emily find out who the other murderers were. She wanted to start at the tailor's house now that he was dead. They could search the entire house without any problem. Camille knew the tailor kept secrets, though puzzling, would be a good place to start.

Camille had taken, from all corners of the tailor's house, boxes, files, drawers, and small cabinets that she piled up in the living room on the first floor. They started searching but did not know what they were looking for, maybe something that could at least illuminate a way to solve the mystery; any evidence no matter how inconclusive would help them start.

The question they had was, if they came to know the others who were in on the plan, what would be the next step? In a town like No-town, where justice never existed, accusing someone of murder even with indisputable evidence beyond a reasonable doubt was above all, a risk.

Nevertheless, they started searching, opening cardboard boxes whose contents they emptied onto the floor. They found bizarre things, such as a collection of commercial posters all of them original from a gallery in Aspen, Colorado; one of which was a poster for Coca-Cola, with an attached receipt that had a value of $150,000. Letters to suppliers and buyers, receipts from banks, bank statements, transactions, and so on, nothing that raised a suspicion.

They found a little sealed box with several diaries, meticulously written like reports of scientific data on expeditions to remote places. It seemed that day after day, the tailor had recorded part of his life. In one of the diaries, they found messages in the format of letters to his family, sister, and love letters addressed to Emily in which he dared to give her nights of love. He confessed his hatred for Antonio in one letter whom he referred to as "the Latino," "the illegal," "My Enemy," "the Spaniard," "the Moor." And the last one without an address, nor addressee, warning about the existence of a lady whose name he would let that mysterious person know when he was sure about their relationship with the target. The letter ended by saying; "that women do not represent a potential danger, but who knows?" They didn't have doubts that the tailor was referring to Emily and the target was Antonio.

"Son-of-a-bitch, he was just taking his time," exclaimed Camille. "He was not alone, and the case gets more complicated."

Chapter 33

One morning Emily opened the door and on the steps of the entrance were the horns with a note: '

Do whatever you want, burn them, cut them in tiny pieces, and burn the pieces to ashes and the ashes to sublimation, because I hate those damn horns as much as you, as much as I hate him, so much that I have decided to solve the puzzle.

Emily put the horns in one of the corners of the patio and thought to burn them in the afternoon in a big pile of wood, but she forgot because another anniversary of Antonio's death was approaching and her mind was elsewhere.

On the day of the anniversary, she parked away from his grave and headed down the cobblestone path with a bouquet of red roses. Suddenly she looked back; she felt someone was following her.

"Where are you going with those roses?" Joe asked her. He came a few meters behind with tools and dressed in work clothes.

"I'm going to visit a grave."

"Your father's?"

"Yes," she lied.

"Your father's grave is that way," he pointed in the opposite direction.

Both disappeared through the graves, Joe went to clean the General's tombstone. Besides repairing the General's grave and mowing the lawn, he needed to find a place to bury another soldier whose body would arrive the next day. The soldier had been killed in an ambush in Afghanistan, on a desert road. For the first time he had received a soldier's biography that, surprisingly, was summarized in three sentences and complemented with an extensive report on where and what commando did the ambush. Information that he thought was unnecessary because it explained the protocols for mobilizing patrols in war that were as strict as those in the streets of Kabul. Descriptive narrations of what happened to surviving soldiers whose bodies were ruthlessly shopped by nomads with knives and daggers.

As for this soldier, in particular, the description was detailed and disgusting; he had lost half of his body, from the hips down, pulverized by the explosion. Joe did not read the seven or more pages because the information reminded him of dismembered bodies in the Vietnam War and because it was like a report intended for legal work and not for a funeral. They had not allowed the mother to see her son in the coffin either.

That day, the soldier's father, who introduced himself as Reverend Thomas Johnson, officiated the ceremony, and his two daughters sang a sad aria that made the reverend cry and the few people who came to the funeral cried too. When the Reverend finished, he came to tell Joe, close to his ear that he would want to bury his son somewhere else.

"There's no place in the graveyard more appropriate than here," Joe consoled him.

"I do not need to tell you that my son is a black soldier," the Reverend said.

"He will be buried close to the General, who will be happy to have more company."

"I only pray that my son rests in peace."

"So, it will be, believe me."

But the Reverend, a very wise man, had his doubts very well founded because that same day, after the funeral, Joe did not quite get out of his car, when he heard the abrupt braking of a vehicle on Oak Street in front of his house. Who got out of the car was Ben Crompton the Third.

"Someone like you would be remembered by the whole world!" the Mayor shouted. "And it's not because of the cats. I am looking for you for two reasons: the first one is that I did not like that you buried the last soldier by Doug's grave."

"I do not understand," Joe said.

"You know what I mean; some people got upset."

"You in particular?" Joe asked.

"You have to exhume the body of that soldier and bury it with its people."

"That's going to be very difficult."

"And the second issue is the horns."

"What horns?"

"Those," the Mayor pointed to the old car in the patio. "I've been searching for them and thank God, I found them where I least expected."

The horns on top of the old car in the park made it look like an animal. His daughters had found them in the backyard of the house and placed them on the roof of car, fastened with a chain. They had painted the car in such a way that it looked like a prehistoric mammal, and depending on where one looked at it, it could have been a strange hybrid between a dinosaur and reptile, or a buffalo with horns and from the back it looked like a gigantic turtle. It seemed, in short, a creature out of the Cretaceous era. The horns above the car gave it a comic touch, so funny for anybody else but not so for the Mayor who was visibly upset.

Without more to say, he walked to remove the horns, but they were firmly tied to the roof so he couldn't lift them in the first attempt. The noise was enough to attract the attention of the neighborhood, Joe's daughters and Emily.

Sarah left home running and cursed at the Mayor. Then came her sisters, who joined her in the shouting, Shane, who was then 10 years old, also showed up. The Mayor was infuriated because Joe did not reprimand his daughter and all the bustle attracted the attention of some neighbors who came to the park.

With the Mayor's weight on top of the car, the roof collapsed. Only then could the Mayor untie the horns. For Joe, seeing the destroyed car that was part of his children's fun was humiliating, so he went into his house and armed himself with a two-barreled rifle and came out threatening the Mayor, who took the buffalo horns and left. The car, which was the only thing left after Emily's rage, was reduced to a pile of rusty trash.

The neighborhood kids did not return, nor did his daughters. Shane, who had learned to hold logical conversations most of the time, kept looking continuously at the car. He asked his dad the same question, *"Where is the T-rex, where is the T-rex Joseph?"*

A few days later Joe brought another car, hanging on a crane. His daughters came when they saw it and painted it with the same colors as the other car. Life would soon be good again.

Chapter 34

There was a poor circus visiting the town that had neither elephants nor lions nor bears and the saddest of all, it had no clowns. The circus didn't have tightrope walkers nor a colorful tent that could be seen from a distance, because the one that it had was old and made in bits and pieces; it was held in the center by a beam with a flag that the wind had torn into fringes. The only performance was a dialogue between a ventriloquist and a doll that he took out of a cage. The doll was dressed as a sailor, with a hat that had a long parrot feather; the sun rays that escaped through the holes of the tent produced iridescent flashes on it. Joe hired the ventriloquist to celebrate Shane's birthday. The ventriloquist arrived with his cage, sat on the grass of the patio with the children, (his kids and those in the neighborhood) who formed a circle around him. He began to spread the little sailor's parts in the cage, shoes, hands with the gloves, torso with the vest, the head with shiny hair and the beret.

Rosario asked the ventriloquist what he did with the doll; "*We both talk a lot,*" he replied.

"How?" She asked, and the doll looked at her with his eyes wide open.

"Like this," the doll spoke to her with a hoarse and very strange voice. The boys let out their laughter.

"What's your name?" Rosario asked the doll.

"Matias and yours?"

"Rosario." Then the ventriloquist sat with the doll on his knee and it looked around at the children.

"Little sailor, little sailor, you who go around the world, tell me what you see in distant lands?" Asked the ventriloquist. The doll looked at him thoughtfully. He ducked his head and then replied,

"Large and small cities." His husky, slow voice vanished with a much rougher cough; he put his hands to his mouth to hide his missing teeth.

"Why do you cover your mouth?" The ventriloquist asked the little sailor.

"My teeth! Ohhhhh, ohhhhhh don't ask those questions, sir! The salt of the sea." A cough became a loud noise and then a high-pitched whistle that made everyone laugh again. The doll looked at Shane and said, "happy birthday boy," and Shane said, "thank you."

The fun was just beginning when the Mayor arrived. He came with his men who stopped right in the circle of children and trampled the objects that the ventriloquist had scattered on the grass. One of the men put on a gorilla mask which scared the kids. Rosario started to cry, Linda was scared, and Sarah got upset. Shane saw the horns on the roof of the Mayor's car and shouted, "my T-rex, Joseph, my T-rex is here". Shane tried to run to the car, but Sarah stopped him.

"Cat killer," shouted the Mayor calling on Joe.

Joe was in the kitchen cutting the cake and filling cups with the punch for the kids when he heard the Mayor. The Mayor came to tell him that he was going to exhume the black soldier and demanded that Joe needed to find another grave. He did not even allow him to open his mouth, because he turned his back on Joe and went to his car followed by his men.

Joe looked at the mess in the park with distaste and asked the ventriloquist to keep the kids entertained. An hour later, when he saw that the fun was over, he helped the ventriloquist pack the doll. The Mayor's men had destroyed part of the objects he used in his circus. The ventriloquist, a small man who wore clothes from another era, striped pants, a long coat and a tall top hat that made him look like those characters in the cartoons, did not lament the damage. He received the payment, happy and very grateful.

***

Joe, who was still not convinced by Rupert's story, went to mow the lawn around the soldiers' and the General's graves. He saw from a distance the Generals grave now had the horns. He knew it was the Mayor who had bolted them to the grave in the same way as on the building's terrace. For Joe to see the horns on the General's grave was a desecration. He returned home and armed himself with a giant metal cutter and a saw to cut the iron screws, and a wedge to lift the bolts. He came back to the tombstone and in a few minutes the horns were untied, and he threw them on the grass. Three days later the horns were again in the same position, with the same ties, only that this time there was a warning written on a metal plate, also attached to the tomb:

"One year in prison for anyone apprehended tearing the horns from this grave." The warning was signed by the Mayor.

153

Joe tore off the plate, cut it into pieces and separated the horns again. The Mayor put them back again and increased the punishment to two years. And so, this back and forth lasted until the horns broke into several pieces. It was like an adolescent's confrontation in which neither of them would give in.

Chapter 35

Camille came dressed in a very insinuating attire, and Emily guessed that her friend had come from the brothel. Camille told Emily she had come to know, from a very reliable source, part of the story of Antonio's death.

She had met Trevor, a young man who was charming and after some glasses of whiskey, they ended up in bed. The young man confessed to her that he had witnessed the killing of a man some years ago. Curious, Camille asked him about it.

Trevor was involved in the death of Antonio without knowing it. The night that the tailor received the stranger in his house, he left for the brothel. But first he had to make a stop in a place to get marijuana which he had started taking to help alleviate his pain.

There was Trevor, naïve and scared because it was the first time he had smuggled marijuana. They made the exchange, money for the weed, but before putting the car in gear, the tailor invited him to an adventurous hunt that night.

"We can hunt a deer or if we are lucky, some illegal hidden in the forest," the tailor had said mockingly; that's what the young man recalled. Trevor saw the tailor dressed in camouflage and accepted the invitation. It was also the first time he participated in a hunt and was very curious. After a time, driving through a curvy and muddy road because it was raining intensely, they arrived at an open field judging by what the headlights of the car uncovered before the tailor turned them off.

The field was surrounded by a forest several meters down. What caught Trevor's attention was a wooden shack that the tailor told him was where they hid during the day, but they would climb onto a platform on a tree that night. They stay in the car, and waited. The tailor said his head hurt a lot so he was going to prepare a cigarette of marijuana because he needed his five senses alert for the hunt. The effects of the cigarette were immediate because the tailor became more talkative.

"We will kill a big deer," he repeated constantly.

Then, the events happened so fast for Trevor. He saw the reflection of approaching lights and heard the tailor saying with a very confident voice; "there come the others."

The cars parked at a distance and the tailor lowered the window. One of the men in the vehicles shouted something that Trevor did not understand.

"They are saying the deer is in the shack," said the tailor to the young man and raised the glass of the window and prepared the gun.

"I thought we were going to use a carabine," said Trevor.

"It's easy prey, the rain forced him to seek refuge in the shack."

"Easy hunting is not hunting," said Trevor.

"Easy hunting is perfect for apprentices. Do you want to have the experience of killing a deer?" The tailor asked.

Trevor took the gun, got out of the car and walked to the shack. One of the cars had the headlights pointed to the line of the forest, but he could see the shack clearly. He came closer and figured out there was no deer inside, nor did he hear any noise, only the rain that hit the tin roof. Then below on wooden boards he saw the hand of a person. The person was still alive and he saw the hand trembling. Trevor thought for a moment to go back to the car, but he heard, from the cars, people shouting, 'kill him, kill him, kill that illegal, kill that Spaniard'.

Trevor couldn't shoot, not because he couldn't but because he did not want to commit homicide and he didn't want to be a murderer. Somebody, a man got off from one of the other cars and came straight to him. The man, who had his face covered with a rag, snatched the gun from Trevor's hand. He wrapped the gun with a piece of cloth to muffle the sound and shot at Antonio. Then, the man went back to his car and left.

Trevor did not think of anything but to run to the forest thankful for the darkness, as the cars started to go. He heard the tailor calling him from his car. Trevor disappeared, crawling on the grass and a minute later he heard shots. Those shots were from the tailor's carabine, and his intentions were clear. He also wanted to kill him and thus eliminate the witness.

Trevor disappeared until he heard the tailor had died, as he was the only one who could recognize him as one of the killers.

"Who snatched the gun from Trevor?" Asked Emily.

"Trevor said the man who snatched the gun from his hand was not fat like the Mayor. We know the Mayor and Wagner were present. But whoever that man was, is a mystery," said Camille.

Emily cried, and hesitant reminded Camille about the risks that sometimes she considered unnecessary because she had thought that justice, although blind, takes its time, but when it works, it does with all its power.

"It is bullshit, just bullshit here in this town," replied Camille, her languid gaze was that of a woman in love. She told Emily without further details that she had fallen in love with Trevor.

"I am 30 years older than him; he could be my son." That visit was very short, barely past the threshold of the door. "Just came to let you now that I, more than anybody, understand the loneliness of a woman like you." Camille started to cry and Emily invited her to come inside the house, but she said Trevor was waiting for her and she was anxious to be with him.

* * *

That was the last time Emily saw her. One morning she picked up the newspaper at the door and saw the news on the front page: a young man had been poisoned by a prostitute in Colton who killed herself after the homicide. She did not need to read the article to figure it was Camille and Trevor.

Both Camille's and the young man's burials were the same day, distant from each other, separated by a street that divided the cemetery, on the right where the tombstones were tall and had colorful legends, and on the left they were small and lost in the grass. The young man was buried on the right by a small group of people, and Camille on the left. All the prostitutes of Colton came to her burial. Emily went down the road to join the women when from the neighboring forest appeared another group of people shouting and yelling curses at the prostitutes. Stones, pieces of brick, sticks, all that they found on their path were thrown at the women who ran to the limousines except one that confronted the crowd.

"Bunch of hypocrites!" Shouted the woman.

"You are the daughters of evil, whores, prostitutes, destroyers of marriages, pedophiles, murderers, you will see what we are going to do to you," shouted the crowd and in the bustle, some shots were heard. Emily parked the car in the middle of the confrontation to help the woman who was wounded.

"Don't take me to the hospital," the woman said. "Take me to Colton."

"I am going to take you to my house."

The woman had bleeding wounds on her head, bruises in the back, and her nose was bleeding as well. Emily put cloths on the bruises with salty water and sulfur and asked her to lie down on the couch then went to prepare coffee. When she came from the kitchen with two cups of coffee, the woman slept soundly, and she put a blanket over her. In the afternoon when her daughters came from school, the woman was still sleeping. They went up to their rooms and from time to time, came down to the living room and looked at the woman who slept until midmorning of the next day.

Her name was Lucrecia. She was petite, eyes that shone when she talked but behind her cheerful gaze was sadness. She had a slight tremor in her hands that she confessed was fear. Her story was also full of sadness and tragedies.

With the promise of a job that would represent a stable future, she embarked in Manila with other women who had the same characteristics, young, beautiful, and naive with dreams. The promise was a lie, and they were victims of a network of pimps who masqueraded as owners of a New York modeling firm looking for talented women. In Chicago they had locked her in a dark room with other women. The room had no windows and the overcrowded conditions made her sick. The captors withheld her passport and the money she had and took her to the hospital. When she recovered, they took her to Colton.

She told Emily that the poisoning thing was a fake story that concealed the truth. Lucrecia saw the bodies of Camille and the young man; both had been shot in the forehead. People didn't believe the poison story but said the truth would never be revealed like many of the crimes in No-town.

Lucrecia looked in her little purse tied to her shoulder even while she slept on the couch and it was always protected as if she had something of incalculable value in it.

"Mrs. Emily, can you take me to Colton please," she asked after making sure her passport was in the purse.

"You're not going anywhere," Emily said.

"What do you mean?"

"You stay here. The killers and captors from the Philippines... ...You are in danger; you stay here with me."

Emily immediately determined some measures to protect her. She couldn't leave the house, nor be close to the windows. These measures would be for a period that she couldn't know at this point in time. When Emily was sure all the measures were set, she asked Lucrecia to call her family in the Philippines. Lucrecia had not heard anything about her parents and two siblings, a sister, and brother for more than three years.

The bustle on the other side of the phone was of joy and sadness. All believed she was dead. In that lapse of time, there had been many changes, her mother had cancer in her breast, her father had lost almost all the family fortune in lawyers, detectives, trips to the United States, bribes here and there, visiting women who had suffered the same fate as their daughter, but who'd had the luck to return alive to the Philippines. All her family's fortune had dissipated in a race against time looking for her. They thanked God she was alive and well.

Lucrecia adapted well to her new home. Emily's daughters accepted her as if she was their older sister, a role that pleased her. They respected her and to some extent, she was the model sister. She wore Sarah's clothes, though they were big and she slept in Grandma Maggie's room. Later, she was put in charge of the kitchen. Emily then had more time to play the piano and found a job in a chain drugstore. When Emily arrived home from her job at the drugstore, she found the house clean, the dinner ready, and her daughters' homework done.

The youngest, Rosario, often fell asleep on Lucrecia's lap and then she took her to her bedroom. Lucrecia woke them up in the mornings, with the breakfast prepared and the books in their backpacks ready on the small table in the entrance. Emily reminded her every day the recommendations and repeated them: *do not get close to the windows, do not get out of the house even if you have the urgent desire to get some sunlight.*

Time passed by and summer passed by, and then autumn approached; and one evening they were all at the table eating dinner when the door opened abruptly. Joe appeared with a load on his shoulders that he wanted to keep in the attic. Joe passed the living room and went upstairs without paying attention to Emily's displeasure at entering unannounced. Emily was also opposed to keeping that load in her house, which whatever it was, produced a sharp and unpleasant noise that hurt her ears.

"Whatever it is, he has no right to break the privacy of the house," Emily said when Joe left.

"It's not that bad, Mother, it's our father after all," Sarah reassured her.

Lucrecia, who, before Joe's interruption, was telling stories that made them laugh, was silent and thoughtful after he left. Emily, who noticed it asked her daughters to go to their rooms, and then sat down on the couch with Lucrecia.

"You became quiet when Joe came in." Emily said.

"I feel like the dirtiest woman in the world." Lucrecia said.

"Did you sleep with him?"

"Yes. I am so sorry."

"He is not part of my life anymore." Emily reassured her.

Chapter 36

The cold autumn wind arrived removing the yellow leaves from the trees. It dragged them down the street, onto the patio, and piled them at the base of the house. Lucrecia, who had never disobeyed the rules Emily had given her from the beginning, went out into the yard with the rake and began to pile up the leaves. Before venturing out, she put on Sarah's trousers, a coat, booties, a hat that fell to her ears and dark glasses. She looked like one of those boys who earned a few dollars collecting the leaves in the fall. She piled them in the center of the yard and set them on fire, then sat closer until the fire consumed all the leaves. She saw the postman leaving the mail in the box and she went to pick it up. She had never peaked at Emily's correspondence, but this time she was curious and reviewed it.

An envelope caught her attention. It was not the sender since it had none listed, nor any other characteristic that caught her attention. It was the cursive, elegant, perfect and unmistakable handwriting of the owner of the brothel. La Mama wrote on the envelope Emily's name and address. Lucrecia checked the address just to make sure it was not mail mistakenly placed by the postman. She was curious to open it but put it on top of the other envelopes and waited for Emily. When Emily came, she handed her the envelope.

"Open it," Emily said.

Lucrecia took out a sheet of yellow paper that had a soft perfume that reminded her of the corridors of the brothel. Lucrecia made a gesture of passing the sheet of paper to Emily, but she insisted Lucrecia read it.

Dear Emily,

We haven't met in person, You haven't seen me, neither have I seen you. How I came to know about you is a secondary matter compared to the one that concerns us both. When I no longer had the hope of knowing the fate of Lucrecia; it came to my knowledge that she is hiding in your house. The source that provided me this information is not relevant either, but it's secret. During all these months in which I came to think she was dead or if at best she was alive, but suffering, I kept thinking about her and my fear was unbearable when I came to know that they were looking for her. Those who are behind her are not the traffickers or the pimps (those who brought her from Manila), because I paid them after they promised me to leave her alone. As you can see, my brothel is a refuge in spite of everything here, my women are free to do what is best for them. Some make money and settle elsewhere as respected women and others stay here and still have their space until they die. I still regret what happened to Camille and young Trevor and I'm afraid the same thing will happen to Lucrecia. It is a fear that does not leave me alone because my intuition and the sixth sense of an older woman, experienced in the affairs of bed and life, tells me that those who want her dead already know where to find her. Maybe you already know the reasons and the names of those who are after her and if you do not, you at least suspect. For my part, I am looking for more information that could help in some way. If you asked me about any recommendation, I would say that what you have done up to now is the best, although it would be convenient for Lucrecia and your own family's safety to hide her somewhere else. I'll be waiting for better news.

Sincerely,
La Mama

What La Mama said in the letter was very serious, and she had to hide Lucrecia somewhere else and soon, but she did not know where. She thought her Uncle Mark in Philadelphia might be able to help, but she had not heard from him for such a long time that she considered it a remote possibility if not an impossibility. Maybe he was already dead. So, without a place, she decided to hide Lucrecia in her own house. She lowered the curtains of all the windows and made sure her daughters kept them down all the time. This time the recommendations were not simple recommendations, they were orders, and her daughters were forbidden from mentioning Lucrecia in any comment in the school. But then she thought that having the curtains down all day could be suspicious so they would be open during the day, as always, like all the houses in the neighborhood, giving the feeling of normality to whoever passed the street. She thought later that the most recondite place in the house was the attic.

When Sarah saw her mom worried, she told her that she knew about one hiding place in the house that she and her sisters had found some time ago. It was behind the dresser in the room of her Aunt Lisa, a small window that looked like a skylight that gave way to narrow stairs between the walls of her room and that of her Aunt Katherine. The stairs went down to a subway that extended a few meters to a door, and this finally led to the shack in the courtyard. Emily never knew about that place with all its secret subway, even though it was part of her house. It was a secret passageway that served the function of who knows what activities but which would now be Lucrecia's hiding place. It was perfect because she could live there in the house comfortably and if there was a need to hide, they could make her disappear. The only measures left were monitoring the street permanently and identifying suspicious movements of cars and people.

Lucrecia and Sarah went down to clean the tunnel, to take out the cats and clean their feces. Before they lit the old light bulbs that a curious mind would have wondered how many acts, movements, or voices those lights would have seen or witnessed in all that time. And it was Emily who, one night, as she went to bed, had a thought that didn't let her fall asleep. It was something she had never thought about before. She could now tie so many loose pieces from her childhood, together and it was only then that she had the clues clear. Her Aunt Lisa's noisy laughter and desire for old men, and most of all, Emily wondered why the voices in her Aunt's room resembled that of her father's. How was that possible, while her sick mother slept in the most remote room of the house. She remembered her father disappearing after, arguing then saying he was going to the bar to have a beer. But then she heard his voice in the room next to hers. In all that time, thirty-two years to be exact, she had respected and revered her father to the extent that she believed he was a saint. Until now she had thought that John Michael Fletcher, her father, was never unfaithful to her mother and to prove it, remembering his disappearances, she asked him once if he visited the brothel and his answer was a resounding no. The image of the faithful and good father vanished that day.

Although that discovery bothered her, she was worried about Lucrecia's safety. She had something else in mind, an alarm. But she didn't want to buy one or have technicians setting it up at the house to prevent any suspicion. So, she decided to create her own alarm to have the house a full 24 hours under surveillance. She went up to the attic with Sarah and Lucrecia to find everything that could be used; cables, copper wire, and nails. Sarah accidentally touched, with her foot, the load her father had brought some months ago and they heard the strange and sharp noise. It was what she wanted, something that would produce a noise that would not only awaken them, but also scare the intruders by causing them an excruciating pain in their ears.

It is almost impossible to describe what Emily invented because the whole apparatus looked more like a school project created by a fifth-grade child, but when she did the first test the metal pieces from the load came off a container and fell into a glass capsule hanging from the ceiling producing a noise even more unpleasant than before. In the test, the cats came out of their hiding places running desperately seeking to escape the noise. Emily extended cables at strategic points to the entrance of the driveway and in the yard. But this alarm only guaranteed Lucrecia's security at night. If an assault happened, the alarm would wake them up and Lucrecia had to hide in the tunnel. If necessary, she would go out into the yard through the shack and from there on she would be on her own. That possibility tormented Emily because nothing guaranteed that beyond the confines of the courtyard, Lucrecia could be safe.

With luck, albeit bad luck, she would arrive in another town where the police would hand her over to the immigration agents who in turn would report her as illegal and deportation would put her in the hands of the same pimps in the immigration offices of Manila. And then, they could sell her again as a prostitute. So, Lucrecia's future was at stake.

Several months passed in which nothing happened, and the state of alert relaxed a bit. In those months, the alarm went off a few nights, and it was the cats that got in the container with metal balls or pulled the cables in the yard. But this problem stopped after some time because the cats learned how to avoid the noise.

One night all of them went to sleep and when Emily turned off the lights of the house she saw through the curtains the reflection of the moon on a car parked in the driveway. Emily saw the silhouettes of two men at the entrance of the driveway. She went up the second floor and asked Lucrecia to hide in the tunnel. She turned on all the lights in the house, and the men got in the car and left. They came back three nights later at the same time and parked the car in her driveway for a few minutes and then left again. They did the same the following nights.

The presence of intruders in her driveway coincided with another message that she received from La Mama. In short, La Mama was concerned about the latest moves and comments of the Mayor that, according to her, had his men already on the streets of No-town searching for Lucrecia: "He won't rest until he finds her, because he literally said: '*that little whore knows too much.*' Emily had thought to report the intruders to the police but gave up on the idea. She asked Lucrecia to never get out of hiding.

Then one afternoon after returning from the drugstore, the car was in front of her house. Emily parked hers in the garage and went to confront the men, who then put the car in motion and left. They were now coming every afternoon. They did not get out of the car but looked towards the house. Emily started suffering from nerves, feared for her daughters and herself, for Lucrecia, to whom the confinement was already affecting her because she did not talk and ate very little. The weakness in her body was so evident that she could hardly stand up. Under the circumstances, Emily had courage because once she came out with a baseball bat and broke the windows of the car: "*The next time I see you, I will kill you,*" she shouted. And the next day they returned in another vehicle.

Emily, desperate, thought about asking Joe for help. She sent Sarah with the message that she needed to talk to him urgently.

Joe did not come, so she decided to see him personally. It never had crossed her mind that one day she would need to ask him for his protection. She went to his door, knocked several times, but nobody showed up. She returned home defeated, sat on the couch, and shed some tears. Then a few afternoons passed and Joe came to see her. She told him everything but did not mention the existence of Lucrecia in the house.

The conversation did not go in the direction she wanted, nor did Joe seem worried. The conversation turned into a discussion in which he, reluctant to believe what Emily was saying, asked her things she didn't know the answers to. One of the questions was about the reasons why Sarah was in the cemetery the day she found the goats eating the flowers from the General's grave.

"And what do you think she was doing?" She asked him.

"She was not visiting the grave of her grandparents, or was she?"

"So, what do you think?"

"Maybe she was doing the same as her mother did every afternoon until well into the night."

"You are a scoundrel."

"And you are cunt and whore!" He shouted.

"And I still wonder where Sarah learns those words."

165

"Maybe your daughter is right."

"You have no right to judge me?"

"Well yes, I do. My daughters live with a mother of questionable reputation."

"And who is the father of my daughters, is not he the one who went to bed with prostitutes? What are you talking about?"

"Whatever the reasons that move these men to come to your patio are not my concern, it's your problem."

"Your daughters are in danger," she said as a last resort.

"Take that woman out of the house and the problem is solved," he said.

The situation couldn't be more complicated; her daughters, especially Rosario and Linda complained because they couldn't go out to the playground to play. They couldn't go to her father's park, and the worst thing was that Lucrecia had become so weak they had to help her to the bathroom to shower. Emily gave her vitamin supplements, whey powder, dehydrated amino acids in pills, lecithin and lysine and other compounds of current use at that time, that is, everything that could vitalize her. The stillness and lack of light, the confinement and loneliness had weakened her body and her spirits so much that she had become tiny, of the same weight as Rosario. They couldn't take her to the doctor because she would be at risk of being turned over to the police after recovering.

One morning an old lady entered the drugstore. The woman came straight to the counter and handed Emily a list of medications. She went to the depots, and when she gave the medicines to the old woman, Emily recognized her. Miss Rita Carter, perhaps in her eighties, still had the vitality and smile of those years when she taught her piano techniques.

"Miss Carter," Emily said.

Rita stared at her and after a pause exclaimed, "Emily Fletcher, where have you been all these years!" In those days, coincidentally, the teacher had remembered her favorite student and wondered what her fate had been.

"I'm a frustrated pianist," Emily said.

"But you are happy?"

"No" Emily replied. "I need to talk to you."

Emily took Miss Carter by the arm and both went to an office. Emily closed the door and told her the whole story, that she had Lucrecia in her house who need to be in a different place before she died. Emily said to her, in a voice cut short, that she needed her help, a place to hide her. Rita offered her house, and they planned to move Lucrecia the next day, in the daylight to prevent suspicion. If necessary, Rita would take Lucrecia to her sister who lived in Cincinnati, where she could recover and to some extent move freely.

Chapter 37

Joe went to the bar and took a look at the corner where he sat with his friends. The table and the seats on the floor were as they had been before, except for a large lamp with Asian motifs that dropped down to about fifty centimeters above the surface. The bar was busy, but nobody was seated in the corner. Joe went straight there and sat in the same seat he used to sit in with his friends. The owner of the bar came with a Dutch beer and a saucer of pastry, the same ones he had served him so many times before.

"Where are Rick and Korn?" Asked the owner.

"Korn is in Florida, but I have not seen Rick for a long time," he replied.

"For some reason that I don't know, nobody sits at this table," the owner said.

"Maybe it's Ronnie's ghost," Joe said jokingly.

"It's so strange, it seems like it's reserved for life."

"If you change the table and seats, people will probably sit down here," Joe suggested.

"I haven't thought about it, nor will I change anything; the bar would lose character." They laughed loudly.

Joe drank the first beer at once, and the owner brought another one without hesitation.

"Someone wants to say hello," the owner said.

From the last bench next to the tall table of the bar was a familiar face. Rupert smiled at him and waved his hand. Joe invited him for a beer. They talked for a long time of different things, about the new war the nation had embarked on, of the dead soldiers, of the General for Joe, and Wade for Rupert. Joe kept abreast of the latest facts related to the General's grave. Joe told Rupert of his problems with the Mayor over the matter of the horns. From the investigation of the General's life, Joe told Rupert that as soon as he retired from the factory, he would devote full-time to the search. Rupert insisted he was wasting his time and he should give up the idea that the General was a good man.

"The man in that grave had been so bad that the last events that happened in the town were ultimately determined by the wickedness of that man and the Cromptons, all of them, from the first to the last one," said Rupert, referring to the death of the prostitute and the young man.

"The young man was my grandson." Rupert sobbed.

"What?"

"Yes, the same young man you met, and now they want me to believe that the prostitute poisoned my boy."

He had gone to the police to open the case and begin an investigation to clarify the motives of the crime and find the murderers. He had gone to an office in the police station, where they gave him some hope that the case could be opened. From that office, they asked him to go to a second office where they informed him that in another office, he could communicate the crime and in the third, he was asked to complete some documents. And from this last office they asked him to bring the documents to another one that turned out to be the first one. There, they told him that the case couldn't proceed. After discovering that they played with him, stupefied and disgusted, he reminded them that an hour ago he was told in the first office that the case could be opened, and one of the policemen who played with a white mouse on his desk, without raising his head shouted, *the case is closed, period.*" He asked them who had closed the case, and the policeman pointed to the ceiling. He understood when he pointed to the office above, that it was, the Mayor's.

"How did I forget I was in a town like this?" Said Rupert.

When they said goodbye, Joe recommended that he desist from his attempts to find out who had killed his grandson. And Rupert recommended Joe stop believing the General was a good man.

Joe went back to his house when he saw in the street, in front of Emily's the car for the first time. He realized she was not lying, nor exaggerating. Without hesitation and not even noticing how many men were in the car, Joe went to confront them, directly, unarmed just with the strength that gave him the wounded pride and honor sullied by the Mayor because he knew very well that he was behind the harassment.

"It's not your problem," said the man who was the driver.

"My daughters live in that house."

"Did you hear what he says?" The man asked the other in the passenger seat. There was a third man in the back of the car. All with that cold look of those with a criminal background. The driver stuck out his tongue and made a noisy gesture as if he were practicing cunnilingus on a woman. If Joe had his gun, he would have blown the skull off the man who dared to insult his daughters.

"You have five minutes to leave; the time I need to go inside and bring you a pleasant surprise if you are still here," he said calmly and sarcastically.

He turned around and went to his house. Some minutes later he came out with a machinegun, a rifle on his back, a bazooka spear and as if that were not enough, he wore on the overalls of the factory a metal frame as bright as those of the knights of the middle ages. He approached the car from behind, and about five meters removed the safety of the machinegun that made a metallic tic-tac. With the barrel he broke the glass of the driver's window and put it on his forehead.

"If you don't take back the insult against my daughters, I will kill you." The man, scared, started the car and then drove off. They did not return.

Emily, who never found out, the reason why the men stopped coming back, was relieved. Rita reassured her on the last visit to the drugstore that everything was fine, Lucrecia had recovered.

Chapter 38

From long before its celebration, the actual parade carried out every fourth of July that some with much optimism called "the festival," was the biggest news in the town.

In the factory, the workers also talked about the parade, with less enthusiasm because it was known that the organizer, the Mayor, had announced he was going to close the factory because he considered it a cave of communists. Joe went to Broadway, which was adorned with garlands and parades. The only time he attended a similar parade was when he saw Rose in the car with the prostitutes from Colton.

He strolled up Pine Street, reached Broadway and stopped at a corner. Like always, the parade was the same, very few people attended. The same cars, with a mediocre decoration and allegorical representations, the twenty floats, one-by-one, a hundred steps away, left behind fragments of decoration, pieces of paper, giant cougars made of cardboard, cans and an occasional mummy's heads.

Joe continued down the street and a few meters up he was struck by the music that came out of an opening that looked like a patio. The music attracted some people that came from the parade, and rushing, invaded the place then sat on benches. Joe joined the crowd and also sat down. Suddenly the lights came on. Joe was also struck by an individual who impersonated Elvis Presley on a smaller platform lower than the stage where children were lined up. The bright blue costume the impersonator wore was a small size for his body, dirty, and covered in sequins. He had an old guitar without strings that also was small. The music and the laughter that the imitator provoked in the people who shouted, was deafening. The individual was so focused on dancing that he did not hear the laughter and mockery of the people. Someone threw a firecracker at the impersonator, who scratched his ears, and the wig fell off. It was then when Joe recognized him. He was Shane, his son.

When he brought home his son, Sarah told him what had happened. The Mayor had passed by in his pickup-truck with other children and saw Shane in the park. The Mayor forced Shane to get in the truck with the other kids and then he left.

That night, he laid next to Rose. He was furious and told her what had happened, a humiliation that would not have happened if they both had carried out the plans against the Mayor that rainy night, and he regretted the fact that they hadn't. She barely moved her shoulders as if to say she didn't care that nothing mattered at all.

He went to the kitchen to make coffee, then went to close the windows and when he got ready to go to bed, he heard a murmur in the living room. Shane with the repetitive movement he had as a child had beside him a book with the title *The Life of S. John Douglas*. Joe felt a sharp twinge in his chest. It was the book he had searched for through so many years; the book was the biography of the General.

"Where did you find it?"

"I do not know, Joe, I do not know."

The book, whose author was anonymous, was divided into three parts; the first about his origin, childhood, and youth. The second part when he emigrated to the south, his life as a finance manager, and the third, his fall. The third part included stories in an anecdotal tone of his life as a hitman. Joe read the book that same night and well into the dawn concluded that Rupert was right; the General was not a general, nor was he a military, nor was he a good man. The book had at the beginning the warning that said; *'It is not the intent of this book to glorify or to ennoble an individual of dubious qualities and intentions.'*

Among the facts that Rupert had not told him were that his real name was Seth John Douglas Wade, that he had been born in Kansas on August 18, 1890, that he lived a low-profile life to the point that he had no friends and those who were close described him as a man of few words, whose slow voice was only heard when necessary. The biography of Seth John Douglas Wade, narrated with great emphasis a case that was very popular in the social elites of New Orleans.

It happened on the eve of a cold Christmas when a white woman left a store with packages of gifts in one hand and her little daughter on the other. The streets were muddy, and there was snow everywhere. The woman slipped, fell and dropped all the packages that scattered in the mud. At that moment, a young black man who passed by helped her to get up. When the woman realized that the person helping her was black, she started screaming. People came out from all the stores to chase the young man, but he disappeared by the art of magic. The rumor spread that the woman had been raped by the black man.

Seth John Douglas Wade, who was already known in the secret circles of the New Orleans mafia, without being asked, chased the young black man until he found him near Memphis and killed him. That act gave him status in the circle and many advantages, money and adventures, but more than that was the fame that spread everywhere. From the south, he emigrated to No-town, where he was hired by the Mayor at that time, Ben Crompton the First, a story that he already knew from Rupert. Of his death, the book mentioned that he had been killed by a leader of the Union, and nothing else. It did not specify who killed him, nor did it say whether the murderer was captured.

"The hero of all this odyssey is Rupert," Joe exclaimed after reading the entire book.

Now that the General's mysterious identity was resolved, Joe thought about the dead soldiers. The man from Kansas, as he began to call him, was evil and Joe couldn't keep burying soldiers by his grave. He now had the dilemma of where to bury them. He had buried many soldiers by that tomb and had lost count. This caused him some discomfort. Rupert gave him an idea that he thought was the best solution to the problem. The idea was to pulverize the Kansas man's grave, in other words, blow it up with dynamite. He thought about that possibility but, it occurred to both, it would be better to use a drill rather than dynamite that would unbury the soldiers' corpses. They made plans to do it at night to prevent the curiosity of passersby.

$$***$$

"I feel like I'm getting rid of a burden that weighs on heavy on my back," Rupert said.

It was twelve o'clock at night, and they had drilled almost half of the grave. Rupert pulled out large concrete pieces that Joe put in the truck.

"The Mayor will be pleased when he sees that the tomb disappeared," said Joe.

"I'd like to see his pig face when he realizes it."

"It's going to be a very sweet revenge."

"It's not what I want, but I'm satisfied," said Rupert.

"Someday he will pay his debts altogether." Joe consoled Rupert.

"The last one he did to you was horrible," he was referring to Joe's son's humiliation.

"I do not want to remember that."

It was three in the morning when they finished destroying the tomb. They filled the hole where Seth John's remains were with wood and made a giant pile on top. They spread kerosene, then, set it on fire with the idea of burning his remains until they turned to ashes and his ashes into steam. That was how they eliminated all traces that reminded them of the Kansas man. They filled the hole after the fire with concrete and they thought that one day in the future, when No-town was no longer No-town, they would raise a column like an obelisk and would print in golden letters phrases that praised the dead soldiers.

Chapter 39

Joe knew the Mayor would be coming after he realized that Seth John's grave had disappeared. He had the remote sensation that his feud with the Mayor was coming to an ending. One afternoon he went out to burn the biography of Seth John and the other books he had bought, when the Mayor arrived. Crompton parked his car at the entrance of the park, got out of it and slowly came to meet Joe, who also walked to encounter his enemy. Ten feet away from each other, both stopped. They talked as if they were talking about some business. Joe gave him reasonable explanations and Crompton's were implausible as he claimed that being the Mayor gave him the right to do whatever he wanted and that he had no obligation to present justifications to anyone or to excuse himself for his actions.

"You are a psychopath," said Joe. "You abducted my son and made him be mocked by the entire town."

"I did it because I could and wanted to." Said Crompton.

Then, Joe accused him of the death of Rupert's grandson, "I am going to bring the accusation to another court, not in the town."

"You have no evidence."

"I do."

"You will regret it."

"People are afraid of you, not me," Joe said.

"Be careful, you have daughters," Crompton said.

"If something happens to one of my daughters, I will definitely kill you, you son-of-a-bitch."

The Mayor came closer and put himself on guard to attack Joe. But before he released his first punch, Joe came up with the idea to solve the problem like the knights did in the Victorian era. Better yet, Joe said, leave everything to the fate of the Russian roulette. It was crazy. It was not a contest like those of the Middle Ages, nor a confrontation with fists like those of the Incas in the Peruvian plains that resolve their conflicts wrestling until one fall defeated. He had proposed what he knew well, something that was already familiar. The Mayor agreed and claimed the right to decide the date, time and place, and without saying another word, he left.

He sent Joe a black-and-white photograph of the old camp a few miles from town. On the back of the picture, he announced the date and time. The date was Friday, August 13 (two weeks later) at three o'clock in the afternoon in the old camp. Joe replied in a letter that his arrival would be punctual at the place, on the day and at the proposed time.

Days before the date, Joe went to see the camp. Built by the mineworkers at the beginning of the century, the camp was not far from the town, and he wanted to be sure the Mayor would not play a trick on him, an ambush for example.

The walls of the camp were covered with moss, and the vines came in through the windows at the top. The walls were thick, with very few windows located up where what appeared to be the third or fourth floor. It took him a while to find the door because it was camouflaged behind bushes and trees. He went up to the last floor and saw an immense and emptied space. The sun came in through the few windows. There was a table in the center with two chairs, arranged one in front of the other. He figured the Mayor had arranged the table and the chairs. On the floor that was dusty, he saw shoe prints that Joe examined to be sure that no one else had come with the Mayor to set the table. He looked around again trying to discover any trick or, a hole in the wall for someone to shoot at him, but he saw nothing suspicious. He looked out the windows and realized that the room was so high that it was not possible for the Mayor to have a second man, an accomplice who could kill him. Of all this, he made sure of the security of the building, of the way to escape in case the Mayor played dirty.

During the days before that date, Joe had nothing else to think about. In the barracks of Hanoi, when he played Russian roulette, he played his life for money and now it was for honor, his own and that of his daughters, son, Rose and yes, Emily.

In those years so long ago, he did not feel any fear, and now he did. He started having an almost invisible tremor in his hands and sometimes in the whole body. His fear had reached such a limit that he sometimes did not remember some routine events such as leaving the car keys in the Cadillac or turning off the coffee pot. Deep inside his thoughts, he had the sensation of living each moment as if it were the last.

Chapter 40

The Mayor, for his part, did not leave the house during those days. He gave his bodyguards a long vacation. He did not return to his office either and disconnected the telephone in his house. He feared in the days before the 13th of August he would go crazy. He thought the only way to avoid thinking about his date with the death was to take care of simple domestic chores.

A few days passed, and the waiting was killing the Mayor, it was more difficult than the encounter itself. He also thought to settle the feud with Joe without weapons, a gentlemen's pact in which he would not disrespect Joe nor his family again. A pact in which everything was forgotten, and he thought about proposing that when they saw each other in a public place, they would avoid seeing their faces. He decided to go to his opponent's house to talk about the proposal. He dressed as if he was going to his office. When he was about to leave, his wife brought him the last letter from Joe with a confirmation of the meeting. The message also confirmed the rules with a variation never carried out in the Russian roulette. The variation was that each would bring his own gun with a single bullet.

Joe thought it over very well. He explained in simple words the reasons for that variation in the letter. *If you die*, the message said, the gun will have your fingerprints, not mine and I will be free of charges. The Mayor read his opponent's proposal before the expectant look of his wife. His opponent had written: *if you die*; as though he was sure it was him that was going to die. Those words made him more scared. The Mayor realized that he couldn't stop the roulette, that everything followed its course, that there was nothing he could do at all.

"Who is it?" Asked his wife when he tore the letter into tiny pieces and threw them into the trash can.

"An old friend," he replied.

His wife was beautiful, innocent and knew nothing about his affairs and she believed he was the best husband in the world.

"Is there anything bothering you?" she asked him one night. He turned around and cried like a helpless teenager and he had to lie his wife, "I felt a sudden panic."

"You have nothing to fear," she consoled him.

Unable to fall asleep, he waited for the night, but dawn crept in and he was still awake. He put on the earphones and listened to BB

King, his favorite singer *'The thrill is gone, baby'* with that hoarse voice, it seemed the saddest, devastating and most tragic sentence. It was as if he had the certainty he was going to die.

*   *   *

And the fateful day arrived, a sunny, beautiful day, the kind that makes us believe life is great and nothing bad hovers over our heads.

Joe got up early, as usual, he couldn't remember where he'd put the coffee maker the day before so he didn't drink coffee that morning. He didn't go to work. The trembling in his hands had reached such a point that he thought of the precise moment of pulling the trigger, his forefinger would squeeze not once but twice or more in a single turn, and that meant a secure death. His fear was even higher when preparing the gun, he couldn't put the bullet in the cylinder. He went to the basement, put the barrel in a sandbag, and pulled the trigger. It was as he had feared to happen, his finger uncontrollably pulled the trigger more than twice before taking away the barrel from the sandbag. It was a serious problem that put him at a disadvantage with his enemy. He had no salvation, and the chances of dying were high.

By midday, he had tried several solutions, but none had been effective. He had taken almost a bottle of whiskey, another of brandy with milk, everything he could find in the kitchen, pepper powder, red pepper dissolved in olive oil, leaves of mallow and thyme, but none of those mixtures calmed his tremor.

He went to the emergency room of the hospital. When the doctor diagnosed a nervous breakdown caused by an excessive secretion of adrenaline that could significantly affect his kidneys to the point he'd have to be hospitalized, Joe refused categorically, arguing he had no time, and had something urgent that afternoon he couldn't postpone and he would come back the next day for the hospitalization.

"Nothing can be more urgent than your health," insisted the doctor.

"I'll be back tomorrow if it does not rain."

"You think it's going to rain tomorrow, huh?" The doctor said, leaning out of the window.

The doctor prescribed him some pills to relax his nervous system and asked him to return the next day. But the pills didn't work either. At one o'clock, he gave up and went to see his daughters. Sarah had cut Linda and Rosario's hair in, a modern cut that made them look different.

"Cut my hair too," he said as he sat down on the chair.

"You're shaking," Sarah said.

"I'm sick from my nerves."

Linda and Rosario began to wash his hair while Sarah went to the kitchen. Sarah returned with a cup of valerian infusion.

"This takes away your trembling," she said. Joe took the infusion and, in an instant, he fell into a deep sleep. He began to dream it was raining, the wind began to blow lightly, and then became a giant tornado that passed through the town and went toward the old camp and destroyed it leaving the space clean. When he woke up, Linda and Rosario were still washing his hair. Sarah took the tools from an urn and pulled the chair closer to the large mirror.

"Cut it short," he said.

Sarah shaved his head on the sides first leaving the top for later and looked at him, he had a mohawk haircut and she started laughing, Linda and Rosario laughed too.

"You look like the *'taxi driver'* from the movie," Linda said. Sarah came with the camera and took pictures, and his daughters laughed happily.

"I want you to remember me like that always, without sadness," he told them.

He did not wait for his daughter to finish cutting his hair. It was time to go to meet the Mayor. He stood with the crest uncut, kissed Linda's and Rosario's foreheads and asked Sarah to follow him to the patio. They hid behind the big oak tree. He took out of his overall pocket a small gun. He explained to her how to remove the lock before firing, how to shoot, and how to hold the gun when firing. In that short training, he realized the trembling in his hands had disappeared and he looked at his daughter's eyes and felt that she was his angel and there was no person in the world he would love more than her.

"What is this all about?" Asked his daughter holding the gun.

"Just promise me you will protect yourself and your sisters from any danger."

"You talk like you're never going to come back, like you're going to die."

"Promise me."

"I promise," his daughter answered putting the gun in her pants pocket, and he kissed her goodbye on the forehead.

"You forget something," she said.

"I have not forgotten," he said. That day Sarah was 18 years old.

"I will be waiting for you for the cake."

He gave her a happy birthday kiss and went home to get ready. He thought about promising his daughter everything, forgetting about the Mayor and celebrating his favorite daughter's birthday. He took the gun and left. He went through the streets of the town, took the road to the east. The old camp was visible from a distance, perhaps three miles away. He turned off on the road that led to a forest, parked the Cadillac in the woods. On the stairs that led up to the large room saw the Mayor's footprints as an indication he was already there.

"I know you came to visit the place," the Mayor said.

"I just came to make sure."

"I'm a man of my word," he said. "What I did or said was because you insulted the memory of a hero."

"A hero? hah! You insulted my family," Joe sat in the other chair, put the gun on the table, and the Mayor did the same. Joe examined the Mayor's gun while the Mayor observed and then the Mayor did the same with Joe's. They both looked at the guns, part by part, an examination that was carried out in silence, only the sound of the cylinder where they put almost all their attention to make sure it had the bullet. Without saying anything else, just with the movement of their heads, they told themselves everything was ready to begin. One final thing to be determined was who started first; the Mayor took a coin out of his pocket.

"Examine it," he said. Joe looked at the coin on both sides. "Face or cross?" The Mayor asked.

"Face," Joe replied.

The Mayor threw the coin into the air. The coin fell on the table and took a few turns until it fell face up, so Joe started. He spun the gun's cylinder, put the barrel on his temples and he pulled the trigger. The metallic noise vibrated in the room. Joe took a deep breath, and the Mayor's face turned pale, his hands shook when he took his gun. The sound of the trigger slipped like the first one. The turn now was for Joe who took his gun and put it on his temple and pulled the trigger. The tic sound and turns of the cylinders went for some minutes.

"This is more terrible than death itself," exclaimed the Mayor.

"You started this war," Joe replied.

The Mayor took the gun to his head. The echo of the shot slithered down the stairs and broke one of the windows, and a flock of pigeons came out of the ledges. Joe watched the pigeons fly over their heads, but he had not realized that the Mayor had tilted his own aside. The gun still in his hand pointed to the floor. Joe felt dread. He stood up and walked away. From the staircase, he gave the last look. The Mayor's face had turned white, and a trickle of blood was running down his cheek, in his hand, the gun was still pointing towards the floor.

Outside the camp, Joe closed the iron curtain that served as the door. The road back home was long. How long had it lasted, he had the feeling that nothing had happened, and yet he was incredulous that the Mayor was dead and he was alive and on his way home. It seemed like a dream, a story like the ones he accidentally read in books searching for the biography of Seth John.

He arrived home; his daughters were playing in the yard with a giant, multicolored ball. He remembered he promised to be with his daughter Sarah for her birthday, and he let out his tears.

The house, as always in silence, began to be invaded with shadows. He saw Rose in her room napping and Shane in the library absorbed in reading. It seemed he had never left the house, except his tears kept falling down his cheeks. He saw his haircut in the mirror and thought he would keep it. He stretched on the bed, put the gun on the bedside table and fell asleep.

Later the screams of his daughters came through the window and woke him up. He saw the gun on the little table. He thought about the Mayor at that moment, alone, sitting in the chair waiting for a charitable soul who would find him, and bring the news to the town. He took the gun and saw through the window a cat stretched out on the branches of an oak tree. He aimed and fired at it. The animal fell off the tree, death. That could have been him if fate had been to the contrary. He felt chills. He shook them off and went to celebrate his daughter's birthday.

Chapter 41

The Mayor's wife had seen him that day cleaning his gun, and she felt curious because it was the first time in all of those years of marriage he had done that. And she felt much more curious when she saw he loaded the gun with one single bullet. She asked him why?

"I don't know," he answered, "one bullet will be enough."

"Enough for what?"

He avoided her question. Then at two o'clock, she saw him polishing his shoes and getting dressed, the same suit with the difference that he looked much more elegant, like that day when he was going to meet a congressman who had announced a short visit to the town. She had helped him tie the red ribbon of his shirt and did not ask where he was going. Not a single doubt passed through her mind, nor premonitions at that moment. She had never asked him questions, but she asked herself if such elegance had to do with his visits to the brothel. Contrary to his public life of a deceitful and corrupt administrator, Ben Compton the Third let his wife believe he had never laid his eyes on any of the prostitutes. Even more, she had never questioned his late returns home, nor ever found a hint or smell of women's perfume on his suits, nor had it ever crossed her mind to test the fidelity of her husband. He had given her two children, a girl who was then 9 and a 7-year-old son.

She sent the kids to bed late that night, sat down with a glass of whiskey, and waited for him. She waited as usual until midnight, dressed in her nightgown went to bed. She got up the next morning to prepare breakfast; eggs, bacon, cured chorizo from Germany and black coffee imported from Central America. She served the breakfast to the kids and herself and kept a portion for her husband, knowing that sometimes he came home two or three days later.

When the morning of the fourth day came, she started wondering. And when the afternoon passed, she was worried and decided to go to Colton the morning of the fifth day, something that never before had crossed her mind.

A blonde woman who could hardly open her eyes opened the door and said that she, for the sake of discretion and safety of the clients, couldn't give her names. She did not forget that she was the Mayor's wife or that she was an honorable woman, so she asked again and received the same answer.

"No ma'am, I can't provide that information."

"Can I talk to the manager?" The prostitute went to talk to the owner of the brothel. Some minutes later La Mama came and told her the same.

"I know he comes to Colton and I don't give him troubles for that," she said to the owner.

"You know the problems if I give you that information? And you are not the first wife who comes searching for the husband."

"It's been five days since he left," she insisted.

"For the first time in all of these years that I own this place I am going to break the rules, and I hope I don't get in trouble."

"Nobody is going to know," the Mayor's wife said.

"Your husband has not come since three or so weeks."

Her search ended up in the bars of the town and then in the municipal building, where she was told that the Mayor went on vacations. She went to the police, and the search spread to nearby towns. The police had some hypothesis, the possibility of a kidnapping was the most plausible explanation.

Many days passed and then one afternoon she heard knocks on the door. A policeman brought her the news that a man was found dead by some kids in the old camp.

The policeman asked her to go with him to identify the corpse.

***

"We have to get him out before the vultures eat him," she said to the policeman. She did not know at that moment that her pain was going to be even bigger and for much longer, that she was going to curse her bad luck, the existence of the town and her husband.

Ben Crompton the Third had to feed the birds for several more days, during which, the caravans of cars stopped to see from a distance the cloud of birds entering the building.

The town had a vague memory of the old building and those who remembered the history knew of the first strike of the workers at the mine and the tragic outcome. They remembered those days, perhaps because they suffered the consequences or because history passed from generation to generation, and said, *'justice is blind and limps, takes its time but it comes.'* There, in the large room of the camp, Ben Crompton the First who rejected the rights of so many families with his signature, and later to ensure no workers dared to strike again,

183

made the decision to kill the last rebels of the mine. And there in the same place, was the last of the Crompton, dead and feeding the birds. That couldn't go unnoticed in a town, whose collective and morbid pleasure moved in the afternoons in a caravan of cars and stopped to see in the distance, the camp and the cloud of birds that fought to enter the room.

No one, not even the police nor the forensic officers wanted to stop people from enjoining the spectacle, neither had the intentions to recover the body of the Mayor despite the pleas of his wife. She went from one place to another asking to do what was needed by law, even to the most miserable. But they answered her evasively or directly with a flat "no", and some did not hesitate to say behind her back, '*He had it coming. It was well deserved.*'

She walked the streets in her black dress, in search of a pious soul to help her bury the body of her husband but could fine nobody willing to do her bidding.

Chapter 42

Emily saw the Mayor's widow at the drugstore, she was so sad but Emily couldn't promise her the impossible. It had been a confusion of feelings, the strange sense of liberation during the days that followed the disappearance of the Mayor, and her compassion with his widow. She put aside her pride to ask Joe to help the Mayor's widow recover the body of her husband. Emily sent Sarah to ask her dad to come urgently, and he came because he thought one of his daughters was sick.

"You who bury the soldiers can help her," she said.

He still had the Mohawk haircut and without saying anything, turned around, and walked away. She followed him to the entrance of his park.

Although it was more painful for Joe to see the widow suffer he would never go to retrieve the body of the Mayor. It had not crossed his mind that his wife, who had been insulted and his daughters disrespected by the Mayor, would ever ask him for a favor of such magnitude and he would deny it even if the widow came in person.

"Don't you realize that, if it had been you, I would be in the same situation?" She said.

"If you knew, the harsh reality, you would not ask for mercy for the dead, and you would be celebrating like the others," he said.

"What do you know?" She asked, taking him by the arm.

"Do not even ask," he shouted.

His silence and inability to face her confirmed everything, but she did not say anything else or dare ask him more questions. Then, the next day, early in the morning, he came to tell her everything. He asked her under oath, on the name of his daughters that they would not find out how the Mayor died, even after his death, and she promised. He told her how the Mayor had died, and that no matter how bad he was, his death made him feel deep sadness. Not for the dead himself, but for the widow.

That same afternoon the widow came, as always dressed in black, a black scarf covering her head, he saw her eyes through the opaque glasses.

"I came to ask you for help and I will thank you for the rest of my life," she said. She asked for it not as a favor but as clemency. "It's the only help I've asked in my life, and everyone has denied it to me. I expected you to have pity on him." Her voice had the fatigue of several nights without sleep. She had a handkerchief with which she wiped her tears. She had parked the car at the entrance to the park.

Joe saw the coffin in the trunk, half of it was swinging on the outside, long and wide, unadorned, but of good wood and opaque enamel, one of those coffins for someone who was owed some dignity. Joe went out to adjust the ropes that tied the coffin to the back trunk of the car. The friction of the strings had scraped the enamel. The scratches and dust were also noticeable because the widow had spent several days with the coffin, going from one place to another. Joe made sure the coffin was safe, and then they both got into the car and went out onto the main street where a caravan of cars was getting ready to go to see the old camp.

"Sons of bitches, I won't give you more pleasure," she murmured. Her voice was grave and firm, but then she broke down in tears. They continued up the street from the town. The noise of the coffin when the car passed the bumps of the road mixed with the silent cry of the widow. The vehicles stopped to see her and then continued behind.

The widow had prepared the grave close to his ancestors. The row of tombstones with the name Crompton from the first to the last generation, all stood out among the other tombs. Three generations that had taken over the history of No-town, and now that Joe was burying the last one, the story seemed to be at an end.

At that moment, the image of Benjamin Crompton the First burying Seth John Douglas Wade came to his mind. He wondered what the grandfather of Crompton the Third thought at that moment, perhaps, for a single instant he would have thought better about prolonging his hegemony and progeny, as genes passed from father to the son. Maybe his sarcastic laughter was the same as that of Ben Crompton the Third, whose intense eyes held no compassion, no pity and were filled with too much pride, then degradation as corrupted flesh surrendered to the worms, and in the end, their only enemy.

***

The party lasted several days. It started after the Mayor's funeral, after people witnessed the burial from the cars, with the windows down and a pleasant smile on their faces. September 10th was a date to remember and celebrate each year in the town as that glorious day when everything changed. The three days of celebration were noisy, a carnival in which people wore costumes, disguised in strange garb, some parodied the Mayor in his white suit.

Days after the carnival, people learned the truth about what the Mayor did or failed to do in his long term in office. Reports came to light about his murders, business with mobsters from Kansas City and Chicago, bank robberies, kidnapping young women, felonies against the treasure of the municipality, unpaid bills to suppliers that implied, as happened to Joe, shameless thefts, and many other acts. There were suspicions of even darker plans, actions, and events that were going to turn the town into the pariah of the south and extend its ostracism for more decades to come.

Emily saw the list of crimes committed by the Mayor in the local public newspaper, the names of the people he had killed or contributed to their death, either through bribery or direct participation and she did not see the names of Antonio, or Camille and Trevor.

All these acts were now in the past and seemed as if a malignant tumor had been excised and destroyed, because the town began to live. The town finally had a City Council that replaced the *ad hoc* members from the time of Crompton the First. The Municipal Building opened an office to help people and a young and educated Mayor opened the doors of the Mayor's office from day one to everyone. No-town opened to progress; the multinationals began to arrive. Walmart started to build a distribution center, one of the largest in the south, Pizza Hut opened its doors on November 11, McDonalds in December, and the list went on and on. Engineers began to build a bypass road to Highway 57.

The town finally had a festival like all the towns of the state. It was a summer festival with bands playing pop music, jazz, and even some classical music. It included a new opening parade that was lavish and the envy of festivals in the surrounding towns. The parade did not include the sad and strange floats of the past nor the one transporting the prostitutes from Colton.

Colton remained immune to the changes of the town. Rich men came from far away, but whatever happened in the brothel, did not concern the town. Colton and the town that previously coexisted in a symbiosis were now two separate entities. Yet, the existence of the brothel was questioned by the female population. It was like those appendages that become worthless or unnecessary that must be extirpated, and the sooner the better.

Everybody was expecting an event that would cause its collapse. The condemnation hanging over the brothel was imminent. The Mayor had a closing order against Colton ready on his desk, and the ladies gathered on Broadway on a Sunday morning after leaving the churches. From there they started a silent pilgrimage, with banners, slogans, all the women of the town were present, girlfriends, fiancées, wives, lovers, grandmothers. Even some sensible men and those with a dose of resignation because the vast majority of men were going to miss the brothel. The pilgrimage traveled the 4 miles to the brothel that hot morning under the shade of the oaks and pines that for all those years had guarded the night passage of men to the brothel. People arrived at Colton and crowded into the entrance. The gate opened wide, and the great antechamber of the brothel was illuminated by a high and luxurious chandelier. From inside of the brothel came a smell of perfume mixed with liquor.

The women, in silence, looked at each other until one said.

"What the hell did we come here to do?"

"Let's wait a moment," said another, then from deep inside they heard the loud voice of La Mama giving orders. At times she let out a loud and raucous laugh. The laughter then became stronger as if she was approaching the gate. The women were alerted.

"There she is," said one.

La Mama appeared with a long, green toga, a red turban that ended in a knot like a flower on the forehead, the same color as the toga, red lips, red nails, white sandals, long eyelashes and an attitude of power that could subdue anyone. La Mama looked like an Egyptian priestess, haughty despite her age, the delicacy of her gestures and the candor of her eyes contrasted with her voice. The owner of Colton also inspired respect. La Mama stood up at the entrance and contrary to what everybody expected, she greeted them very elegantly. But all the women were in shock and did not respond. La Mama looked at the crowd.

"Gee, looks like the whole town is here," she said.

"We came to close the brothel," said one woman.

"Close Colton?" La Mama said without raising her voice.

"Yes," all responded in unison.

"Colton is yours," La Mama said. "Colton belongs to you and your men."

"My man has never visited your dirty house!" Shouted one woman and several seconded her.

"How do you know?" La Mama replied.

"I know him more than I know myself," the same woman said.

"Does your man have a job?"

"Yes, of course."

"Does he have friends?"

"Yes."

"Are his friends as good as your man?"

"Shut up," a woman shouted.

"Close it! close it, close it, close it." All shouted.

At that moment, the last customers who had spent the night began to leave the brothel. The men broke through, and women opened a path for them to walk to the parking lot. Some, perhaps those who came from afar, came out with their foreheads high and a gallant smile and others combed their hair. Finally came two men who had covered their heads.

A woman recognized her husband. "Oh, damn you, so that was the business trip?"

Another woman happened to identify the second man, "so, this was the visit to your grandma? Bastard!"

Suddenly there was slapping and punching, as well as curses, lamentations, threats of divorce, crying and heartbreak. Everybody got excited, the brawl prevailed over fear, and when they began to demand with shouts to close the brothel, the Mayor arrived in his official car. Just as the women made the path for the men who left the brothel, they created one for the Mayor. The Mayor, wearing a T-shirt, blue jeans and fashionable tennis shoes looked more like a pop star than a public official. He arrived carrying an envelope in his hands and walked through the long path to meet La Mama.

"By order of the court of the municipality of Little York, the brothel must be closed from the date I transmit the message as it is in the letter."

The young Mayor handed the envelope to La Mama, and there was a single cry among the women, "Yea!!!!!!!!"

While the owner of the brothel held the envelope with the order, the women began to spit at the floor. Some walked to the door and spat inside. It seemed that in that act they freed themselves of all the hatred they had accumulated for many years. La Mama turned around in silence without saying anything and with the envelope in her hands, and with all the dignity with which she opened the door, she closed it forever.

Chapter 43

Joe walked the streets of the town without fear of seeing the Mayor. The money he stole from him, and the humiliations to his family were left behind. He had some money, remnants from playing Russian roulette, that he deposited in the bank now that he was sure nobody was going to steal it. Banks that nobody thought of now established themselves in town. Chase Manhattan, and other banks started to take over the old buildings in the downtown area.

His days were the same. His job, which didn't demand any mental effort, worried him now that he had nothing to search for in books. The factory had started a contract with a machinery company to renew the production process and had promised a better salary, given his experience. He wondered what experience the administrators were talking about as pressing the same buttons in a panel every day did not require any mental struggle nor expertise.

More than an increase in salary, Joe wanted to be promoted to a level where he could exercise his mind. That promotion was never going to happen and he was sure with the innovation everybody speculated about, the new machinery would be controlled by computers and those who controlled the computers would be people with a college degree and he would be excluded like an old machine in a corner. That would be a humiliation, as terrible as the humiliations of the Mayor, which were to his honor. But in the factory, it was going to be a humiliation to his intelligence. Fearing this was an inevitable fact, he thought about retirement.

Every afternoon he drove down Oak Street on his way home from the factory and looked at Emily's house. His daughters in the yard played with Lucrecia and in his park, Shane played with kids from the nearby homes.

His son had developed an appetite for reading and read two or three books each month, and what was more important, he had become very skilled at memorizing mathematical formulas and had learned the constant numbers such as π, e, gamma number, and so on. He surprised him by reciting paragraphs from Don Quixote, Romeo and Juliette, the Odyssey, and others, a surprise that was a blessing for Joe, who told his colleagues in the factory and people in the barbershop about his son's abilities.

Shane was an extraordinary kid, and Joe was happy to be his father. Shane was like a puppy that stumbles over everything, falls at the slightest bump in the driveway, hall, or rooms in the house, and yet he had the intelligence of all the kids who came to play in his park. Joe never punished nor raised his voice against him. When one of his daughters had the laces of the shoes loosened, he gave her a lesson on how to tie them, and when he saw her again with laces untied, he scolded her; but with Shane it was different. His son never learned to tie his shoes, and he did not care. He played with him in the park, something he did not do with his daughters. They climbed on the carousel, on the spider, got into the tunnel and fell together in the sand that cushioned their falling. There couldn't have been happier days than those.

* * *

Every once in a while, Joe would see the Mayor's widow on the street or in the supermarket. He would greet her gentlemanly, and she would always thank him for the favor of burying her husband. Dressed in mourning style, in black despite all the time that had passed, she persisted in reminding him what a good husband he was and closed the short conversation saying, *"Despite that people say otherwise."* Joe just listened to her, and when they said goodbye, the widow again thanked him.

All his hatred had been forgotten and seeing the widow was like remembering again. That's why he sometimes avoided her. And then he began to receive sporadically letters from the widow in which after thanking him again for the favor, she told him with a tone of vindication details of the Mayor's past. Each letter contained an event different from the previous one. She sent to him in the letter anecdotes, like when he was a child who cried a lot, without a cause, the poor boy, he would cry without consolation. He was weak in character, she said and in his dominant figure was hidden a helpless child, my poor little Benny. One September 10th (the anniversary of his death), Joe received a letter,

Despite his weakness, the weeping boy had explosions of strength and the boy who did not dare to kill a fly, chased wild cats that if he caught them, ended up hanging from their neck on a branch of a tree.

Joe read that phrase without being able to believe it. He did not know whether to hit the wall with his forehead or send the widow a letter asking to please stop writing him, that the last thing that interested him was to know the Mayor's follies. The last thing he needed was to know was that his enemy also killed cats. He had managed to forget and to some extent recover from his humiliations and now to know they shared the same madness, and anger, was a discomfort because it was as if his connection to the Mayor continued even after his death.

He stopped picking up the mail. Forbade himself to look at the envelopes, and when Shane or Rosario picked up the mail, he asked them to sort out the letters from the widow and put them in the trash.

Chapter 44

Joe received a letter from Korn. He was happy in a small town on the seashore on the western coast of Florida with his wife Romina. He had written Rick many letters but had not received an answer and was worried. He asked Joe to give him a visit and then let him know if Rick was okay. Korn's concern made Joe also worry about Rick and he decided he should visit him.

It was a long time since he'd seen his friend living with the goats. Joe went down to the end of Oak Street and thought he was lost because he couldn't find the house. He returned, looking again for the old house but did not see it either. He thought for a moment his memory was failing him, so he went back for the third time, driving very slowly, and then he recognized its wide windows, and the high gate at the entrance.

The house had been restored and seemed that its inhabitants, after a long process, and a large investment of money, had made it the most beautiful of all the houses on Oak Street and perhaps of the whole town. The house was, in conclusion, different from the one he had bought for his friends in that auction shortly after they arrived in town, although it conserved its eclectic design between bungalow and contemporary.

Whoever saw the house would assume the inside had also been restored. There was no sign of the goats, which he remembered had destroyed the frames of the windows and part of the walls. The front patio had a flowery frontal-garden, even though it was late winter. There were lamp posts perfectly aligned to the sides of the long entrance. On the right side was a fountain with a human-sized replica of Aphrodite, and on the left, another statue of Calliope.

Joe parked his Cadillac and walked to the door. He knocked three times hoping that whoever opened it would give him news of his friend. An elegant man opened the door. He seemed to be in his early fifties and had a stately baldness that he carried with honor. He was well kept and sported a clean and carefully trimmed beard. The gold-rimmed glasses he wore had very thin, almost transparent, lenses that afforded him the imposing look of an intellectual.

"Joe," the man said, "you don't recognize me, do you?"

Only then did Joe recognize Rick. Well dressed and wearing an expensive cologne, Rick greeted Joe warmly and both hugged. The house inside was not the dunghill or the barn stable he had seen a long time ago.

"And the goats?" Joe asked.

"I gave them their freedom, and now they dwell in the forest." All the goats were gone except one, Catalina, which stayed in the yard and whose butt was stamped in the wall. Rick had framed it with gold and had covered it with transparent enamel, and thin glass. It looked like an abstract painting without imagination.

The room had light, delicately decorated as if there was a woman who took care of the house; the room smelled of roses, the curtains tied at the center, and behind them was another transparent curtain. Lamps in the corners, pictures on the walls and vases on the shelves, and in the center the sofa with the seats and the table completed the decoration of the whole room.

His friend invited him to walk upstairs. The upper level of the house was the bedroom, with the bed in the center and large windows that let the daylight in. It was an open space that gave the feeling of freedom. The white and clean sheets and blankets on the bed, of elegant and expensive interweaving, fell reaching to the floor.

On the side, almost against one of the walls, was the bathtub, with clean towels, perfumes, oils, and aromatic soaps. Chalk of sandalwood released a thread of smoke on a table of beautiful decoration next to a window. Rick took a box of aromatic herbs and gave them to Joe to smell.

Rick had changed totally, and Joe asked his friend about the causes.

"Love," Rick replied.

Joe asked who the lucky woman was who had brought so many changes to his life, and he replied that it was a secret he wanted to keep for a while. But he told Joe he had made all the changes because he was in love and the woman would come to live with him very soon. He had plans to take the woman to Philadelphia where they would spend two weeks and he said that cities are like women who wear lipstick and dress in sexy cloths at night, a comparison that puzzled Joe, who thought his friend was still crazy. He also told Joe he was going to take her to New York, where they would also spend another two weeks visiting museums, the World Trade Center, and there, with the Big Apple under his feet, he was going to ask the woman to marry him.

"I had to explain to her the reasons why people call New York the Big Apple. She is so naïve and innocent, it is worth saying that I have never slept with her," he said, looking at the bed. "It has not come to my mind that much daring. These sheets haven't been broken-in yet, unused from the day she told me she wanted white sheets".

Joe realized, despite the indications, that his friend was not fully recovered, even though he seemed to be a happy man.

"It has been a long wait, however," Rick continued, "each change deserved her visit, or better, each visit deserved a change. First, was the arduous cleaning of poop and urine, scrubbing with a brush and soap everywhere until I recovered the original shine of the floor. Then, she came to see me here. Something still smelled bad, and she was right, the goat's urine was still there. I opened the windows and doors for many days to ventilate the smell until the ferment of urine was replaced by the soft smell of pollen and the aroma of herbs, I burned in a pot... ...And then I invited her again, and she gave her approval. She said; it needed a carpet, and I installed it throughout the floors and stairs, in the whole house. When I opened the door on her next visit, she came in with her gazelle walk. I regretted having put on carpet that muffled the sound of her heels and had only the option of imagining it. Ah female of my dreams! I fall asleep with that image. I looked like the Andean *Cock-of-the-rocks* bird which collects straws, pieces of glass, cigarette butts, beer cans, any shiny object that makes the nest more attractive to its female."

But the changes that Joe saw were not that simple. It was not just the cleaning. After a look around, Joe knew his friend had made changes that, without a large investment of money, would not have been possible. Joe asked him where he got the money.

"You will not believe me, Joe." He opened the drawer of a table and showed him a tiny transparent bag of cocaine. The crystalline powder appeared like a cloud of pureness, and one couldn't resist the temptation to lick it. The little bag had been sent to him by a friend from New York, who proposed to him a distribution business in all the states included in the Mississippi basin.

"But I have to tell you the story from the beginning, Joe."

They sat down after going through a bar that exhibited all kinds of liquors, from the most rudimentary to the finest: Peruvian Pisco and aged wine from Sicily and the stretches of Tuscany. The entire wall from bottom to top and from side to side, with shelves full of bottles of different size, shape, and color, all the liquors of the world, like a museum. He had different brands of whiskey, champagne, Bacardi rum, the list was endless. He opened a bottle of Russian vodka whose value was of the order of four digits, poured the liquor into the glasses; the flow of the liquid was so pure and the aroma transcended firm, consistent and lasting. They drank it all in one sip, and he poured more. Then they came down to the living room.

"Let's start at the beginning," he said crossing his legs, "because everything looks like those little, tiny paper strips hiding in the Chinese fortune cookies, those that people believe bring you luck: that *'you must look at the moon tonight because in three months the stars will shine on you'*, that *'your present plans will be successful tomorrow'*, you know, all that kind of crap. So, I went to New York to see my friend David...

...I did not have to look twice, nor ask to know what he was doing. He was waiting for me at the airport in a luxurious car, dressed very elegantly with gold chains around his neck and dark glasses by Dolce & Gabbana. Without further preambles, we went to his office: an old cafe that breathed a stench of tobacco, sea salt, and oysters, you can imagine the slums in New York. But his office was not in the café. We slipped deep into the darkness and walked upstairs. I do not know how many floors because there was no light and I had to stop to take a breath, you know, the ravages of a sedentary life. Suddenly, as if he had the magic of making things appear in the darkness, he opened the door. The office was a total mess, his desk had nothing, no documents, no typewriter, no duster, no books because my friend was not an academic, nor much less the administrator of a mediocre restaurant; just a Brother balance of high precision, the most modern, because it was calibrated to a millionth error. He put aside the scale and the transparent bags and while he adjusted the straps of his trousers and adjusted his bowtie and took off his vest leaving the cartridge with the gun, he looked more like those detectives that appear in those forensic movies. David looked around, and said, you can imagine the scope of the business, the west is virgin. My friend planned to distribute the drugs in Chicago, St. Louis, and the cities of the Mississippi Valley, Memphis, and New Orleans. A vast empire was opening before his eyes that shone when he mentioned the names of the large cities, and that area was going to be mine, I was going to be a millionaire in a matter of days. But the bad sometimes prevails over the good because I was almost going to say no. But I thought about her, and she seemed to be pushing me, *don't be weak, don't be a little man, do it for me*, I could hear her voice saying those words of courage, and I took the chance and did it...

...What comes next deserves another vodka, Joe. When good luck is on our side, there is no way to stop it. Time passed, my eyes adapted to the dim light and I figured out we were in an office, because things appeared, standing up in their places, the big safe-deposit box as big as one closet with its bright rudder loomed in the gloom. The door of the safe-deposit box was open, and then I was surprised by his confidence despite noticing my curiosity, there was nothing to fear, he said. Whoever wants to reach me has to know how, and he was right because we walked in the dark and he was the only one who knew how to get there or how to squeeze into the interiors of the building to get where we were."

Rick went to fill the glasses again and for a moment he stopped thoughtfully, with his eyes on Catalina's painting.

"How beautiful it is," he said. "Where we were?" Joe reminded him.

"Oh yes, my friend opened the curtain, and the office was filled with sunshine. I had then an idea of how high we were because I could see over the tops of the buildings and the sea stretched beyond, in front of Manhattan. A giant ship maneuvered its anchorage in the port of New Jersey to the south end. He looked with binoculars, then opened the drawer of his desk and took out his notebook, *there it comes*, my friend said looking again with the binoculars, *pure Colombian*...

...The bells from a church tolled, it was twelve o'clock, and David asked me if I was hungry, I said yes. 'Oyster broth or better soup of swallow's saliva, bull's root soup, or oxtail stew, whatever you want, soups for men with *cojones'* he said. He recommended the soup of swallow saliva because it was good to clear intelligence. I decided on the bull's root soup, and my friend said from the door of the office, I will bring you both, he meant the soup of swallow's saliva and the stew. As he disappeared, I got close to the safe-deposit box that had no more space to store money, Joe. He had money to buy a city or a small country in the tropics. I took a look at New York through the window, the sun hit the buildings. The twin towers of Manhattan, so slender, yet arrogant, a plane passed as close as if it went against them. I remembered I had made plans to take my love to the tower where the tourists go, the same place where men take their girlfriends to ask for their hand in marriage. There I would ask her to marry me. I went to the window and saw a very narrow staircase that came off around the wall, going round and round until it disappeared deep below, it made me dizzy just to look at it. Suddenly I heard steps coming up. My friend came in with the soup pits and behind him came some men with their submachine guns pointing at his back...

...What a bad luck! I said to myself. One of them went to the safe-deposit box that I had closed while my friend was out of the office, and I do not know why I did it, maybe to prevent myself from temptation, because, Joe, I do not know if I should tell you. It passed through my mind the dark thought of killing him or hiding a roll of those bills between my pants and my balls. I saw the face of satisfaction on my friend when he saw the door closed. He thanked me with his eyes, while I responded with mine. The thief clung to the rudder of the safe-deposit box and spun it around, but the door did not open; the others forced my friend to repeat the code, and the man tried again, but the box did not open. The thieves were nervous and whoever tried to open it was sweating and was about to cry. I could guess they were inexperienced. The thief kept trying to open the door, and his nervousness clouded his brains. Then they forced my friend to open it, and he went to the box when suddenly the office door opened again and then the shootings. Joe, I was afraid, for the first time in so long. I remember the war, we had worse times than that time in New York, but it's been so long and you forget the tricks. I hid behind the curtains, the shots lasted for two or more minutes I couldn't know and waited until everything was silent, not a voice, not a whimper, not a murmur. The curtain had a hole, and I saw through it that the office was full of smoke. I waited a while and looked out when the smoke dissipated. In one corner were the thieves who had come to rob my friend, all dead. The others, who maybe came to settle an old debt with my friend or maybe came to rob the other thieves, in the other corner, also dead. My friend was still alive and bleeding on his desk, he asked me to take him down to the cafe where a doctor could see him. Joe, I saw him without hope, and I thought before taking him on my shoulder downstairs. It had not been the first time I would do it. In the war, I did it when one of my soldiers asked for clemency after losing his legs, part of his chest and asked me to kill him. Joe that's life. And, I thought about her, my muse, my goddess, my virgin and I remembered the code of the safe-deposit box that my friend had recited so many times to the thief that I memorized it. He had the gun in his hand, carefully, I removed it, my friend did not hesitate a moment to point out the place, here in the center of his chest. I shot him...

...Now I had the safe-deposit box in front of me and the code. Joe, my hands didn't work, they had an uncontrollable tremor, the memory is not cowardly like the hands, the memory does not tremble, it works or it doesn't, I remembered the code clearly, but my hands, Joe. There was my life, inside that box. I started to turn the rudder, turned it several times and did not hear the click; my hands didn't obey my commands. I thought my friend had recited other numbers to the thief. And to complete the bad moments, I listened to the steps of someone who came up; my heart rose to my mouth and throbbed like it was going to burst. I hid behind the curtain. I heard the knocks on the door and the voice asking if there was anyone inside and since no one answered, the footsteps left. Joe, time is relative, as Einstein said, it expands, stretching, exactly like our consciousness. Just moments before, my friend asked me if I was hungry and then he was dead on his desk, and the bells of the church were tolling, announcing that it was already two o'clock. What was absolute at that moment was the image of my muse that gave me courage because I tried again to open it and nothing. I don't know how many times I tried. I decided to leave, but I couldn't go downstairs and reach the street through the café. They would notice my nervousness or may be waiting; so, I had no other way to the streets than the exterior fire-stairs, those that clung to the wall of the building. I saw the safe-deposit box again with one leg outside the window. I tried again and oh Joe, the click, the wonderful and saving sound opened the door and saved my life. So much money, I filled my pockets and a plastic bag that I put on my shoulder and started descending to the street. My nerves were gone, and I needed to get down alive...

...And here I am Joe, waiting for the right moment, so I can bring my muse to my palace."

They drank the last glass of vodka and Rick went to the bar to open another bottle. Joe said he had enough and Rick returned the bottle to its place. He had a safe-deposit box in a corner with the door opened, the rolls of bills crowded together in the three or more divisions. On the floor, scattered around the box, there were many rolls of bills. He told Joe that on the second floor he hid many more. Joe imagined for a moment the goats eating the bills.

"Now that I'm rich, I can marry my muse," Rick said approaching the window. The transparent curtain showed the bright light from the sun and the black asphalt of Oak Street. "Here she comes, Joe," he said as if he saw an apparition. Joe approached the window and recognized Lucrecia as she passed with the small basket for the store. His friend raised his hand to say goodbye. "You see how she says goodbye with her little hand?" Joe only saw that Lucrecia passed without looking and without raising her hand. "Her smile, she always carries it since she saw me."

Joe realized then that his friend was just as crazy as before and had no salvation.

Joe wrote Korn a long letter in which he told him everything, how Rick got rich, becoming the wealthiest man in town and his platonic love for an ex-prostitute whom Rick considered a woman of noble or prominent descent. The love that at first, I thought had redeemed him, is driving him crazy without turning back. That love is like that of the Knight who loved a peasant woman, believing she was a queen, he said, remembering what his son, Shane, had recited from a book. "But worse because at least that woman was a peasant, and the one whom our friend loves, is a prostitute, and I worry a lot." He finished the letter telling Korn he would keep a close watch on Rick and promised to save him from any madness that could lead to (hopefully not) making her his wife. He ended the letter stating, "You know as well as I do that Rick does not give up, he's as stubborn as a goat."

But Joe forgot the promise. He did not visit Rick again and did not care that with all the money he had, he was easy prey for the thieves and that they could even kill him.

One afternoon Joe saw that Catalina was in Emily's yard and wanted to find out how the goat got there. It happened one morning when Lucrecia came from the store with the groceries and the goat came behind sniffing the vegetables she brought in a basket. Lucrecia tried to scare her away, but the goat followed her to the gate of the house and stayed. They had named her Maggie, but they started calling her Catalina when Joe told them the story of his friend.

Lucrecia did not know she had an admirer and she wondered who he was. By the indications of Joe and the existence of Catalina, she remembered the house and vaguely associated it with the noise of the goats. Despite Emily's warnings, she kept going down the street to the grocery store.

"Watch out for that man, he may follow you to the store, and it would be scary," Emily said.

She knew from the conversations with Emily that his house was one of the most beautiful on the street, and with flowery front gardens, open garages and elegant curtains, but she had never been curious to meet her secret admirer.

On one occasion, Lucrecia looked unintentionally and saw him in the window, uncertain, with his head tilted, his face undefined in the gloom, like that of a man who was lost, with his eyes half-closed as if he had just gotten out of bed. She kept on her way and later looked behind at the window again, and the man had closed the curtains. He was different from what Emily had said about him. He was not that dreadful, nor so strange, and she thought if she had seen him face to face, she would have felt compassion, not repulsion.

Chapter 45

One afternoon Joe received an unexpected visit from Rick. He realized his friend's mental state remained the same, disoriented and making efforts to remember the reasons for his visit. The only thing that occurred to him was to take out a black and tiny box with a beautiful and expensive ring that had an embedded diamond and interwoven gold threads. The little box had the signature of the house where the ring was made, a famous jewelry store in New York called Emeralds and Diamonds Brokers. The price, Joe could guess was very high, and it was the engagement ring for Lucrecia. Joe tried to convince him that the woman did not deserve that, but Rick insisted that she was the most beautiful human specimen in the world.

"That specimen is a prostitute." Joe said.

"No, I don't think so, you're lying," he said, changing the tone of his voice.

"She escaped from Colton."

"You lie," he said, scratching his head, closing the black box and putting it in his waistcoat pocket.

"You've never seen her nor talked to her, Rick. You are my friend, and I worry about you."

"Joe, I know her for a long time and the only thing we need is to make love."

He had done everything for his friends, risked his life for them in the war and in the town. He was like an elder brother, and lately, he had tried to get Rick away from some of his follies. The time had now come when he did not even want to lift a finger for Rick. Maybe time had distanced them, perhaps he was tired and realized that after confessing Lucrecia was a prostitute, nothing was going to convince him. Yet, there was one more confession he did not want to tell him about, but he did.

"I fucked her." Joe stated.

Rick looked at Joe incredulously. His face was that of a child about to cry, overwhelmed by sadness. Rick glanced toward Emily's house. The goat was grazing in the front yard, and Rick pulled a handkerchief from his vest to wipe his tears and left.

"She is a woman who has been with many," Joe shouted.

"Enough, Joe!" He replied.

Rick went to where the goat was. He hardly passed the entrance of Emily's yard when the goat started running and rammed him, knocking him to the ground. That morning Rick was lucky because at that exact moment, Lucrecia was passing on her way back from the store and the goat went to sniff at the basket.

Lucrecia helped Rick get to his feet. After sitting him on the steps of the entrance, she went to the kitchen and brought cloths and warm water to clean the mud from his face. She recognized him. His face in the window, despite the gloom, was unforgettable. He had the sweetest look she had ever seen in her life and wondered where the reckless man was, where the crazy criminal he'd been described to her as. The descriptions that Emily had given her did not match the image of the man in front of her. He was a man who had put her on a pedestal, who had invented a fantasy like those only seen in Hollywood movies. It was love at first sight.

While she saw him looking for something in his waistcoat pocket, she thought about telling him her past but did not know where to start. She thought to confess to him that she began to love him from that moment, with deep love, innocent and pure love that eclipsed the dark part of her past. But she had to tell him the story first, with the details that hurt so much, like a confession and at the same time a repentance, which she'd had for a long time. He interrupted to tell her that he had lost the ring. He had lost it during the attack of the goat. They went together, holding hands to look for it in the mud, but they only found the empty box.

"It does not matter," she said, "I have to tell you something."

He listened to her without interruptions, within each event that she was telling him in a choked voice, his pain grew deep. Where she came from, who she was, and how she had ended up in the brothel.

"There is something else," she said. She had kept the most sinful act of all for the last.

"Then is it true?" He interrupted.

"Yes," she replied.

No one knew about that encounter, even though Emily was at home that day and her daughters were on vacation.

The days that preceded were a torment for Lucrecia because Rick didn't come back. It was a love that ached deep, intoxicating and yet enchanting. She went to the grocery store and looked at the window, hoping to see him. At least his face in the gloom like the first time, but she never thought about showing up at his door. That love was killing her because at the table, she barely tasted the food she had prepared herself. It was like those days when she had to hide, but now she was sad. Emily suspected the reasons causing Lucrecia's sadness.

"You love him," Emily said. It was a confirmation, not a question, and Lucrecia barely shook her head, nodding. "Well, then you have to go to his house, Rick is waiting for you."

"How do you know?"

"I do, it is that simple," Emily said. That love reminded her of Antonio, and Lucrecia was sort of vindication for her and the rebirth of love. "I think you must go to visit him."

"What? Showing myself at his door with no other justification than my love? No, no and no," said Lucrecia. "I was a prostitute but I still have my pride."

"We will find another justification, just wait." Emily and Sarah prepared that visit. Sarah began to do her hair, a hairstyle that Lucrecia herself wanted, one that would make her look desirable to Rick's eyes. While her daughter worked on her hair, Emily thought about another justification, other than love. Emily thought about the goat; in other words, with the justification that she was taking the goat back, Lucrecia could see him and talk. But just at the moment when she was going to tell Lucrecia about her idea, Linda came to tell them that Catalina was sick. They all went out into the courtyard. Catalina was not ill and what they saw was the natural course of life in an organism that eats, processes food, nourishes itself and throws out the useless matter, or putting it rather bluntly, defecated a green liquid and later, the ring that Rick had brought to Lucrecia.

"You wanted a justification, well there you have one," Emily said.

***

Lucrecia knocked three times on his door and felt a sudden panic when he opened the door wearing a King Kong mask.

"I have a collection of masks, and I was trying them on." He invited her to come in.

"I found the ring," she told him how she had found it, and both laughed.

"Luck is on our side," he said putting the ring on her finger, "may this ring with the special bath from Catalina's digestive juices unite us forever," and he asked her to marry him. She did not answer yes but told him that she wanted a traditional wedding, with the engagement ritual, the visit to the house of the bride and the preparation of the wedding ceremony.

"I want everything, as every woman expects that day to be the biggest day of her life. I wanted to start with the formal presentation of you to my family." Lucrecia referred to Emily and her daughters.

On the day of the groom's presentation, Emily had a tray on the table with cookies like human fingers; she had ordered them for the occasion from an Italian bakery. She told them the cookies were called "bridal fingers" and all laughed at the comment. They had the bridal fingers with champagne and all day talked about many things, about plans, remembrances, everything but sad moments.

Lucrecia came to visit Rick one night. He had all the lights on. On the walls hung paintings that she didn't see on her first visit. She saw the painting of Catalina, although she didn't know about art, that image in the wall caught her attention. She knew what it was. The small vagina and a few centimeters higher the hole and at that moment both thought about the same thing.

"The engagement ring came out of that hole," he said.

"What a coincidence," she replied. "I also thought the same."

"It was a good start," he pointed out and showed her the wide stairs that went to the second floor. "The goats used them to go to the second floor until the day I saw you. You are my redemption," he said.

"Where did they go," she asked.

"To the forest, I hear them every once in a while."

They went up to the second floor, in the middle the tall bed with clean and white lines, and the pleasant smell. She couldn't believe that all of that space was inhabited by goats, neither could she imagine that he slept on the high like-bench bed surrounded by the goats.

All that was in the past, and he did not know if those experiences were a good topic of conversation; but she would listen to him sitting on the couch or laying down in the bed feeling her petite body by his side. They told stories after they made love.

"This story," she started, "happened in the suburb of Manila where we lived. My mother and her father, that is, my grandfather are the protagonists of the story, and my father in part. She, my mother thought that my father was a bad man, although he was faithful. She had, like every woman, the hope that her father, my grandfather, had at least a little honor beside being faithful to his wife. And, indeed, she looked at my grandfather in all dimensions. She meant in everything, from honor to responsibility and fidelity. She admired him to the point that she came to believe he was a holy man, just as Emily thought of her father. By the way, my story is somewhat similar to what Emily told me about her father. My grandpa was retired from a company and spent his afternoons playing dominos in the street with his friend, every day at the same time. It was a daily routine, my grandma served him lunch at twelve o'clock, at half past one, he slept a twenty-minute nap, then a shower and at two o'clock he had his friend at the door to play dominos. They played until dinner time when they said goodbye after lifting the chairs. He ate dinner and sat on the couch to watch television. And so, time went by, just with the interruption of the holidays or a family affair that forced them to postpone the game; until one day they did not play dominos again, and my grandmother did not realize it until much later when she saw him leaving with his new clothes, bowtie, and hat, something he never did. She did not pay attention to that change in his routine the first time, neither the second. At the third time, she asked him, and my grandfather said he was going to a friend's house. Coincidentally, a neighbor told her that her husband disappeared all elegantly dressed at three in the afternoon also...

...Then later, she heard the same story from other neighbors. There was already a collective suspicion going on, but they, very discreet, did not want to create a scandal. One of them unintentionally found out where the men went and what they were doing. The story, in short, was like this: my grandfather went to see the train that passed at three o'clock with his friend and other men, all of them over 75 years old. The train passed under a bridge that had benches on the sides where they sat. When the train passed, the noise was so intense that it seemed that the bridge was going to break in pieces and the gale was such that the dry leaves rose high as in a tropical hurricane. But the show was not the train, it was a beautiful woman who happened to walk the bridge just at that moment, and the wind lifted her skirt, letting the men see her panties. The grandpas, all of them to prevent any suspicion by the woman, wore dark glasses. No one laughed, nor did they say malicious things, nor did they include the woman in their conversations. It was just watching her, the whole show. After she passed over the bridge, they went to their houses...

...When my grandmother was told about it, she did not say anything, she just laughed out loud and my mother, who had already us all, was shocked and felt a profound disappointment. That simple thing about my grandpa marked the end of the little appreciation my mom had for men. She said men were useless, worthless and made for the purpose of reproduction. That was the story, and I think it has a message if you look at it seriously. The message is that everything is so relative. What was a problem for my mother was a funny thing for my grandmother. Maybe there is no message at all, but it is conclusive."

"And what do you think?" Rick asked.

"I'm in the middle," she replied. "Sometimes I care and sometimes I don't."

"Maybe your mother's conclusion was extreme."

"Sometimes I take her side, and I think all men are man-whores."

They kept a long silence. It was 2 o'clock in the morning, and they could hear a lonely goat cry.

"I know what you're thinking about me," she said.

"I don't think anything bad, the past is the past," he consoled her.

"Your silence says something else."

"There are so many things happening tonight that I could describe them one-by-one and we would need to live many lives to finish. Yesterday, I was nobody, and this morning I discovered myself. What else can I ask to please me if I am happy."

"I would like to change all of my past," she exclaimed.

They woke up early in the morning.

"Let's go to California," he said.

"San Francisco?"

"San Francisco is fine."

"I always dreamed of living in San Francisco."

"I want to learn how to fly helicopters."

"Are you crazy?"

"Perhaps."

Chapter 46

They got married a few days later. The party started at three in the afternoon after the wedding. People came out of curiosity, some ate and left, others stayed and still others with more confidence went inside the house. Among these, were those who looked at the picture of Catalina's rear.

At twelve o'clock at night, when the party was at its peak, Joe arrived, drunk, wearing working clothes and a helmet. He went straight to the table where the containers with food were and served himself a dish and then went to sit with the spouses.

The tables were arranged in rows, adorned with tall jars that had red roses, lit by bulbs of different colors hung from wires spread over the entire backyard. A colorful carrousel gave the night a childish touch and some nostalgia, despite the noise it made. Many of the neighbors who came to the party, had thought it was a piñata. Located in the center was a stage with microphones and musical instruments.

When the musicians took a break, Ms. Rita would line up her group of children and sing a merry tune, then one that was not that happy later and then a very sad one afterwards that made those with very sensitive hearts to shed a few tears, especially Emily who had to hide in the bathroom and cry bitterly.

That night Joe felt nostalgia, but it was a different one. Drunk, Joe tried to upset Rick with questions.

"How much?" He yelled at Rick.

"What are you asking, Joe?" Rick retorted.

"How much was the cost of the party?"

"Ask Emily."

Joe made a gesture of disgust. "Slut, even in the affairs of my friends she is present."

"Joe, stop, you're drunk."

"They are all whores."

"Joe, your daughters are here."

"Where are my daughters?"

"They were the bridesmaids of the wedding."

"Damn you and your little whore."

Sarah, Linda, and Rosario had not realized that their father was present, nor did they expect him to come, given the displeasure he felt about his friend's wedding. But neither Emily nor her daughters cared about Joe's presence. What was more, they were happy that the spouses were having a great time. Mother and daughters had great admiration for the couple, and nobody was going to divert them from that perception.

For Emily, Lucrecia's marriage was her redemption of love. They were what she always had wanted, a marriage in which love was the base, and sustaining force of daily life. Lucrecia and Rick were going to be happy, and she foresaw it. When she saw Joe in front of the microphone on the musicians' stage, she guessed his intentions, and she was not going to allow him to sabotage the party nor cause the spouses a terrible disgust. So, she unplugged the wires.

Joe's displeasure was such that when he saw himself talking, and no one was paying attention, he went to stop the carousel with a metal bar that he stuck on one of the wheels. Then he came straight toward Rick to fight him, and that was when he found himself face to face with Sarah. It was only a moment, without words, the mere glance of his daughter that made his drunkenness dissipate and his mind went blank. He also felt a deep regret when he saw the carrousel stopped and the children waiting in a long line in silence and suspense. Joe removed the bar from the wheel and the carousel turned again with its noise.

Joe adjusted his helmet and left quietly, continued up the street, then stopped and looked back at the glow of the party down Oak Street. He felt a deep loneliness, he was overcome with the feeling that everything he had done in his life had made no sense. That night, looking at the glow of the party, he said in a small whisper, *"It's a great party my friend, be happy."*

He kept walking the five blocks to his house and at the entrance of his little park, he stopped,

"This life is shit," he said in exasperation..

Eleven forty-eight

Sarah's visit to the woman was long. Whatever they were talking about would be important. Whatever it was, the center of that conversation had to be Joe, his life between two houses and two women who had barely seen each other. They would talk about his illness and maybe about facts Rose knew and after his death, she feels free to tell her stepdaughter. Secrets, perhaps obscure mysterious acts like the death of Antonio and other people. Secrets she knew or had some clues of the actual circumstances. She came to believe Camille knew the truth and suspected Lucrecia did also; but like Camille, for some reason that had puzzled her through all those years, Lucrecia didn't dare to tell her...

Chapter 47

...When Lucrecia came to say goodbye, Emily asked her to write, "if for some reason you forgot some detail, just let me know." She felt with Lucrecia's departure she had lost in a certain way the hope of learning the real truth about Antonio's death. Lucrecia seemed to want to turn the farewell conversation onto other matters.

"I owe you my life," she said and gave Emily a white envelope, "don't open it until after two weeks of my departure." Emily put the envelope on the piano and forgot about it. Several months later, looking for the notes of one piece that she wanted to play, she saw the envelope and opened it. It was a handwritten letter that asked Emily to go the bank and meet Mr. McNeal, the manager. The letter has the single sentence that said: *tell him that you come on behalf of Rick and Lucrecia Carpenter.*

Emily went to the bank in the afternoon, and a woman took her to Mr. McNeal's office.

"You must be Ms. Fletcher?"

"Yes," Emily replied.

"I've waited for you." He pulled out a folder with documents from his desk. "You know what it is?

"No."

"Well, I'm glad to give you the news, the Carpenters opened an account in your name."

"How much?" Emily asked.

"Find out yourself." He handed her a sheet of paper. Emily was speechless suddenly.

"It's a lot," she said in disbelief.

"Certainly, I noticed they have a lot of appreciation for you," the banker said.

Emily saw the amount again and made some calculations of what she could do with the money. Sarah, who had finished high school, had told her with great enthusiasm that she wanted to study at the university near the town, an education career with an emphasis on preschool. That was about one year ago, and all that time she had seen her daughter sad and regretful for not being able to enroll in college.

She had told Joe of Sarah's wishes in one of those unexpected encounters and it ended in bitter arguments. She had blamed him for spending a fortune on building the park and buying books without any thought when his daughters needed resources for college.

Linda, who was in her senior year, had never told her what she was going to study, but was sure she was going to ask for money as well. It had been a torment to think her daughters were not able to go to college. She had concluded she was the mirror of the frustration of her daughters, so when she saw the amount of $500,000 that Lucrecia and Rick had deposited in the bank in her name, she felt something deep inside, a feeling of triumph and she did not know what to say to the banker.

"Is this money ..." She couldn't finish the question.

"Legal?" The banker said as if reading her mind.

"Yes."

"Are you doubting the bank's principles?" Her interlocutor asked.

"Oh, no sir, that never! Where do I have to sign?"

She left the bank with the document in her hand, thinking how to give the news to her daughters. She sat with them in the dining room at dinnertime and, as usual since Sarah finished high school the subject of the university was inevitable, but that night, strangely enough, the matter of college was not mentioned. Sarah had gone to the student registration office at the university to find out about a scholarship application and was told that the selection committee had chosen another applicant, a few years older, a single mother who lived with the support of the state. Before taking the dishes from the table, Emily asked each one of her daughters what their dreams were. She got three different answers. Sarah said going to college, Linda wanted a convertible car and Rosario a trip to Disney World. Rosario asked her mother about her dreams, and she said, "to have a lot of money so I can help make all your dreams come true, as in the children's stories," she continued: "well, we are going to Orlando very soon." She asked Sarah to go to the college and pay the tuition for her classes. "Linda," she said, "I am going to think a bit about the convertible."

"Is this a sarcasm?" Sarah asked not expecting an answer.

Sarah took it as an insult and to avoid any arguments with her mother, went to the kitchen to wash the dishes. For the first time, Emily saw herself in her eldest daughter. They both had that trait that bonded them even though they were different in temperament. Her daughter was like Joe, and on certain occasions, she was afraid of such similarity that she feared for her future. She never saw Joe as a successful man because she'd never heard him talk about his dreams.

Her daughter had dreams and was different from her father in that respect. Seeing her in the kitchen scrubbing the dishes, she saw herself. Knowing now she could tell her that her dreams were about to come true, was to some extent her redemption, her own personal triumph with which Joe had nothing to do. That was why when Sarah asked her how she got the money, she didn't respond because she wanted her daughters to think she was the only one capable of making their dreams come true, nobody else.

Linda gave some importance to the fact that her mother had little regard for her dream. She got the idea of the convertible when she saw the pictures of the queen of teenagers exhibited at the entrance of the school. The girl in the photos was about her age and in a convertible with her hand held high up, greeting the crowd during her drive along Broadway after she won the contest for the most beautiful teenager in the state.

That day seemed remote, and nobody in the school cared about the queen as Linda did. Linda wanted to be like her and thought that a good way to start was to have a luxurious car like that of her idol.

Emily, perhaps more enthusiastic than her daughter on the idea of becoming a beauty pageant queen, bought her the convertible. Emily arranged everything with the agency where she bought it to give her a great surprise. The personnel from the dealership brought the car on Friday midnight and parked it in the yard.

The morning of that unforgettable Saturday was sunny. Linda got up at nine, opened the curtains, and saw the car in the yard. She thought her mother had a visitor, but an instant later, she shouted with joy. She ran downstairs and went to her mother's room, hugged and kissed her and promised in return she would bring her the scepter of the state queen. Her other sisters, who did not know the reason for so much joy, also came into the room. That Saturday was a happy day for everyone.

While Linda and Rosario were still looking at the car, Sarah told her mother that she had won a scholarship that exempted her from paying tuition for her entire school, and she also promised her mom she would be an excellent student. The promises of her two daughters were different, and she thought about it for a moment. While Sarah wanted to pursue a teaching career; Linda, on the other hand had the selfish idea of being a queen. And Rosario...Rosario would always be a kid at heart.

Chapter 48

It had already been several months since Linda received her high school diploma after some struggling, especially in the areas of science and mathematics. Linda hated biology and algebra and was about to give up. Her final grades were low but acceptable. Linda did not hang the diploma in the room as Sarah did. She folded it as she had done with the reports of bad grades and kept it in one of the drawers of her closet. She was done with school and everything it included. It was a surprise to Emily who had waited patiently for some clues about her future and worried about it.

"What are you going to do?" She asked her daughter.

"Nothing," Linda replied.

The convertible she had bought to stimulate Linda in her plans to be a beauty pageant was after all a problem. Linda got up late and went to visit her high school friends in the convertible. All of them crowded in the car and drove the streets of the town until midnight. They explored other towns and ventured to go further, to cities they had barely heard of. They went to almost every movie, and Linda got hooked on the classics. One night she saw "Rebel without a Cause," a film she thought reflected her own life. She bought the VHS cassette and saw the movie many times in her room.

She liked James Dean, his personality, arrogant, proud, pretentious, apathetic, and above all rebellious. Dean had so much magnetism that just by saying his name she felt something like a tingling in her belly, a revolving something that made her think crazy ideas. One day she confessed to Rosario, her younger sister, that she wanted to squeeze someone's neck.

One day Linda asked her mom for some money and went to St. Louise. She bought clothes and cut her hair short. With the excitement of a teenager that explores different things, she put on the new clothing and looked at herself in the mirror. She looked like James Dean in the movie with the red jacket, jeans, boots, and short hair. It was a total change in her look; she tied the jacket to the waist to highlight her teen-in-bloom figure, and the other teenagers admired her. She was, in fact, beautiful and had a reputation in high school and was encouraged by people, including her former teachers to pursue a career in modeling

She was the kind of girl who, with some effort and not much talent, could've reached the stars. Linda was that human being who had potential for something extraordinary, but these traits were hidden and would require some direction or coaching by someone smart enough to uncover them.

Her life was about to take an unexpected direction. Her mom, frustrated after the changes in her physical appearance and afraid her personality was going to be that of a rebel child, became obsessed with the future of her daughter, an attitude that was far from helpful.

The morning Linda turned 19, without anyone seeing her, she packed some clothes in the trunk of the convertible, took a few dollars she'd saved, and made sure she had the credit card in her wallet. Then she left.

Three days later and without knowing anything about her daughter's whereabouts, Emily reported her disappearance to the police. Worried she had searched her room with the idea of finding some clue, and found nothing, just a few pieces of lingerie in one of the drawers of her closet.

Two officials, a man, and a woman came to give her some information they had received from the Colorado Springs police. They told her that Linda had stayed at a hotel and bought some sanitary towels at the Walmart store in that town.

"Your daughter is heading west, maybe to California," they informed Emily.

They couldn't bring her back home because Linda was already mature. Emily had no choice but to wait. One month had passed, and she received a letter. Her daughter was in Hollywood and told Emily she was going to become a movie star.

Sarah read the letter, nothing of what her sister said seemed new; she could oversee how far Linda could go, and it was nowhere. Linda was an intelligent young woman who wasted her potential in dreams she would never achieve. Her sister suffered from something so strange, but so prevalent in the youth of her generation, and that was mental inertia.

Rosario also read the letter and, contrary to her oldest sister, was pleased that someone in the family ventured forward on their own thinking about reaching the stars. Rosario went to tell the news to her father. He read the letter.

"I figured it already." He had the intention of tearing the letter to pieces, but Rosario grabbed it from his hands.

He did not have very fond memories of Linda, who in the last couple of months had started to ask questions, such as why did you go to Colton? As she became an adolescent, Linda was confrontational with him for almost any reason. Her attitude was sometimes direct in which her intentions were to show him her irreverence. He avoided her when she came to visit her brother and avoided her questions by saying, "your sisters never dared ask those questions." This response annoyed her greatly and contributed to the deterioration of their relationship.

One late night, long before she left, Joe saw the convertible parked in his park. He approached the car and opened the door. His daughter was almost naked with a man. Maybe Joe would have gotten furious or may have just said a few words and nothing more, but he discovered in the darkness that the man was much older than her. Joe forced her to get out of the car.

"You're a whore," he whispered in her ear and then screamed at the man, "if I see you again, I will kill you!" The man got out of the car and left without saying anything.

"You are the most despicable father of the world." She yelled at her father.

"You are just like your mom." He rebuked.

That night he lost his daughter. That hit him directly in his heart. He would have preferred a catastrophe than to have seen his daughter semi-naked and possessed by an older man. He felt that his daughter, in addition to disrespecting him was somehow challenging him.

Rosario kept him informed of Linda's happenings and was happy to hear her sister was going to become a famous actress. Joe knew that was an illusion but didn't want to disappoint his youngest daughter. He thought someday, Linda would come back loaded with problems.

Chapter 49

Joe was worried that Shane, almost seventeen, did not know how to tie his shoes, and thought about hiring an instructor. His daughters had taught him some skills, and some personal hygiene. Teaching him the sense of independence and other aspects such as social skills, was challenging, but his daughters were very persistent, and his son achieved a level of understanding where he did things like every young man his age.

Yet, Shaney was careless about his appearance; although he cleaned himself every day, he wore his pants without tying the belt, most of the time he would skip some buttonholes, or tuck his shirt inside leaving part of it outside, his hair uncombed, and the shoes always with the laces loose. It was incredible since Shane could effortlessly solve the most complex of puzzles. Everybody was aware that Shane disassembled the Cadillac's engine and put each piece back into place without hesitation and yet, at the same time, was unable to tie his shoes or carry out the simplest functions.

Joe had seen his son reading the books upside down and doubts assailed him. He wondered if his son read the other way around too. That behavior worried him a lot and he decided then to hire a specialist in reading problems to modify that habit. He put a notice in the local newspaper.

The announcement said: *A reading specialist needed, she should be compassionate and patient.* The next day, a woman came; her name was Tatum McGee and she was the only candidate for the job. She showed Joe a very brief resume and a diploma from the school of psychopedagogy from the University of Michigan.

Tatum McGee was his neighbor at the other side of the park. She had lost her husband in the Gulf War and wore a black suit that made her looked older. She didn't have children, and it was not because she didn't want them. She tried unsuccessfully during her husband's trips back and forth between home and the Gulf. Desperate, and in a way blaming him for infertility, she imagined all sorts of reasons; stress due to her husband's profession as a soldier, but nothing convinced her otherwise. Strangely, in all that time until the death of her husband, she didn't think about visiting a doctor.

Dedicated to her profession during the years she had attained experience with children suffering from mental retardation, autism and other mentally challenged kids, Tatum saw her patients, or better her students, as if they were her own children.

* * *

Tatum began to organize the books by topics, with the help of Shane; those of natural sciences that included biology, evolution and the publications by Darwin, from the *Origin of the Species* to the *Voyage in the Beagle*; math and physics; all these books in the highest part of the library. Then the social sciences, history, geography and humanities and finally the literature books occupied the three lower shelves.

Tatum noticed a large book with gold letters on the highest shelf. This was *Don Quixote de la Mancha*; the book was thick, a deluxe and illustrated version in English. She had read it several times and concluded that every human being should read it at least three times; the first during adolescence, the second in youth and lastly in old age.

Joe saw the library door open when he returned from work. He went to take a nap and listened to the distant and unsettled voices of his son and his instructor. At times, Mrs. McGee's soft and elegant laughter woke him up. Sometimes as he was leaving for the factory, he asked her about his son.

"He is very receptive," she answered.

He found the poems of an American poet of the last century in luxury edition; the book was new and priced at $1.50. He purchased the book and at home, he put a thank you note to Mrs. McGee in the book and left it at the entrance to the library.

On one occasion he returned from work and found the library door closed. He put his head to the door but didn't hear anything. He went straight to his room where on the little table by the bed was an envelope. It was letter from the factory announcing the exact date of his retirement. He had 120 days left, and all the worries about being ignored, diminished, relegated, and confined to the most secluded room of the factory faded suddenly, and yet other problems came to his mind: "*I do not want to die of inertia;*" he murmured. He was 60 years old and he still felt young. The Vietnam War had not driven him crazy like his friends, but he had nightmares from time to time, all fears about something he couldn't figure out.

He wanted to think about some plans besides feeling anxious, other than buying useless things at yard sales. He contemplated the possibility of finding out about his Italian roots. He had never gone to Italy but had that sense of familiarity with the Italian landscape as if the geography where his ancestors dwelled was passed on through his genes. He wanted to be with his son, take him on long trips, and be part of his life.

He took the almanac from the wall and set circles around the days of the second week of September 1998. He marked that date as his first day of retirement. He wrote next to each day in tiny print: "Monday, day of getting up late," "Tuesday, the same," "Wednesday the same," "Thursday beginning of Friday," "Friday, make Emily's life bitter," "Saturday, scape from her reach and count the money to spend it in the Sunday yard sale," "Sunday, disappear all day."

Why did he write Emily and not Rose? It was one of those moments when he used to call Rose, Emily.

The almanac made Sarah curious one day when she came to visit Shane. She took it home with the idea of showing it to her mother. But something distracted her, and the almanac ended up in a closet drawer until Linda and Rosario found it the day of his death.

Eleven and forty-nine

He had his problems like every human being. One has the right to have his own follies as long as they do not affect others. But Joe did what he did to all of us, you, me, your sisters. She looked at Joe's house; *and she, and you have in your hands the proof of his madness, Emily said pointing at the calendar from the year 1998 that Rosario was holding...*

Chapter 50

... The night before his last day at the factory, Joe sat down to watch the baseball game between the Red Sox and the Yankees. Still, his mind was on other matters. At 60 years old, he was healthy, had never had a sign of pain, just a minor discomfort in the lower part of his back, and above all, he had the energy of a man in his thirties. Most importantly, his libido was at its highest, but like everything else in life, something was missing. Since he started his life with Rose, she had confined him to a regime of abstinence, and he lamented that.

When the baseball game was over, it was eleven o'clock at night, and Joe had barely paid attention to the score: the New York Yankees lost for the first time in their own stadium. That night, two beautiful women dressed as cheerleaders came out to entertain the crowd and Joe watched the show, strange for a baseball game. When the cheerleaders finished their presentation, Joe turned off the television and went to his room. As he walked down the hall, he felt that his sex was erect. Rather than going to his room, he went to Rose's. He did not remember the last time he had made love to her, but he recalled that moment very well. It was the dumbest copulation of his life. That night (the eve of his retirement,) he lay down beside her, breathing hard, but nothing happened either, not a sigh, not even the contraction of one of her muscles.

He did not blame her, he blamed himself. What was missing? Was his presence so terrible that his lover did not respond. He wondered if Rose was simply telling him with her silence that he was far from being a good lover.

He laid down on his bed, covering himself with blankets from head to toe, but he was unable to sleep because the pulsation in his penis was such that it merited masturbation. In the morning he woke up without remembering it would be his last day at work.

He prepared coffee and then breakfast. He opened the door to Mrs. McGee, who was very elegant that morning, and he let her know how beautiful she looked. She thanked him and felt a little flush on her cheeks. If he had been twenty years younger, Mrs. McGee would be his lover, he was sure about that. Mrs. McGee had a beautiful smile; she had short hair dyed red which highlighted her freckles. She was desirable and perfect for those afternoons of loneliness and abstinence. Every morning he had a present for her; a book or a thank-you postcard. He had forgotten the present that morning as he was leaving, but he let her also know how thankful he was for her being his son's instructor.

There was an emergency upon his arrival at the factory. A thick cloud of smoke that did not allow him to see the machines, nor the workers, although he heard voices, shouts going from one place to another, curses and urgent calls to evacuate the plant.

The alarm that had remained silent for many years sounded aloud that morning, a sign that whatever was going on was terrible. A minor alarm had happened once, but nothing as disturbing as that day. The engineers at the time had said the problem was temperature gradients with rapid condensation of the air. But then, he realized by the smell that the pipe of the ammonia was broken somewhere and the oxygen's could also be damaged by the high temperature. There was fear that a potential chain reaction would blow the factory into pieces. He had to close the valves of the pipes and shut off the engines before a disaster occurred. Joe went through the smoke to the panel with all the controls of the plant, and in the dark, pressed the bottoms that were the most critical. Then, he closed gas valves and turned off the engines and the whole factory.

After opening the floodgates of the plant to evacuate the smoke, Joe went to the emergency room. At the meeting table, the engineers tried to define the causes of the problem.

"The problem is under control but needs an immediate solution," Joe interrupted.

"Who is this motherfucker?" One of the engineers asked.

"Joe Romano," he introduced himself.

"How do you know?"

"I have 30 years of experience that end today," he said.

He knew the cause of the problems since a long time ago and had written reports and made verbal recommendations. All of these reports were archived in the offices of the managers, engineers, and supervisors. He had stated in the reports that it was imperative to change the pipes for a larger caliber because the flow of fluids had increased with the concomitant increase in pressure. He did not know about concepts like fluid viscosity, matter expansion, nor did he understand algorithms, but he had the intelligence to identify the problems in the plant. It was not his responsibility, but he had all the experience.

His reports, perhaps because they came from a low-level operator, were paid no attention by anyone. In one of the reports he said if the pipes were not changed, the consequences would be devastating, such as chain explosions, fires, uncontrolled valves, fluid leaks. In other words, as he had said: a Chernobyl at a local scale, a catastrophe that would ultimately pollute the air and the small creeks of the region.

That morning, after he realized the engineers were not going to pay attention to his concerns, he left with the feeling that he had saved the plant. He walked to his Cadillac satisfied and yet at the same time with a deep sensation of emptiness.

Joe went straight to the hospital, where he had an appointment with the doctor. Nothing serious, just an ailment in the lower back that he thought was sciatica. The doctor, after an auscultation to his back with the stethoscope, neither confirmed nor contradicted what he believed. The doctor told him he needed to do some tests and gave him another appointment for a week later. The doctor prescribed him an analgesic. He stopped by a liquor store, bought a pack of twelve cold beers and went to celebrate his first day of retirement with Rupert.

Whenever they talked, the death of Rupert's grandson took over the conversation and the other deaths that happened before. It was difficult to avoid that topic. But that day, Joe told him about the events of that morning at the plant and about the discomfort in the lower part of his back.

They sat on the porch, and each had a beer. In the yard, towards the center was the trunk remains of what was once an oak tree that a strong wind had tilted towards the house and Rupert had taken down. The trunk was thick and tall, and Rupert thought to sculpt an image in honor of his dead grandson. He had been working on the project for many days and did not know what he was going to get out of it. He thought about sculpting his grandson's face, but judging from what it looked like, it was a large tusk and looked nothing like his grandson.

"It looks like an Indian's nose," Joe said.

"It's a good guess," said Rupert.

"One of those Indians from North Dakota."

"The truth is that I do not know what I want from that trunk," he said. "Maybe an Indian, or a brontosaurus tusk. Whatever it is, it's going to be a good sculpture and my grandson (he looked up at the sky) will be proud of me."

Joe thought for a moment. He realized Rupert had been working on this project for a long time. He asked him when he would finish it.

"Before I die," he replied with a smile.

He was 86 and in good health. There was no medicine in his house, no medical prescriptions and he ate anything and everything.

The secret, he confessed, "is just refusing to die. It's here," he said, pointing at his temple. He took a sip of beer and looked at the trunk.

"I think it's going to take me a long time."

Rupert went every other week to the cemetery to cut the grass around the obelisk and also took care of the grass around the soldiers' tombs and his grandson's grave.

"To some extent, having burned Doug's bones is like having burned a bad memory," he said. "It's as if I had not killed anyone. There is not a gravestone in the cemetery that reminds me of that."

"I have one," Joe said.

"Just one?" Rupert asked. Joe avoided the question and went to get another beer.

"The Mayor's?" Rupert insisted.

Joe Nodded, "Yes."

"Then you killed him."

"Not exactly, but it's like that."

"Bastard," he said with an open laugh.

"He owed me money and a few insults to my family."

"And what did you get with that, a widow who keeps bringing flowers to his grave?" Rupert's words cut off the conversation for a long moment. "But your revenge is as if it were mine as well. I have the conviction that he killed my grandson. If he did not, he gave the order."

Joe felt uncomfortable talking about the past and much more now that he wanted to live his retirement in peace.

"I feel like everything starts anew today," Joe said.

"Going to the cemetery is like keeping the ties with the past."

"You don't need to get yourself into that," Joe insisted. "I want to forget what happened and how it happened."

"I can't," Rupert said. "My grandson was the only thing I had." They kept silent for a moment. "I see the Mayor's widow every time in the cemetery," Rupert continued. "I see her with a bouquet of flowers, but she is not alone. Like her, another woman all dressed in red goes to the cemetery, and I can tell they share the same loneliness. Whoever sees them could guess their thoughts. The one in black, we know, is the Mayor's widow and the one of red, I do not know. But judging by her attitude, she comes to visit the tomb of her lover. You can tell the difference as well, yes, they are different. The one in black covers her head with a black shawl and the other with a red one. And how they walk to the graves, even in that, they are different. The widow walks as if carrying a burden on her shoulders and visits the grave because it is a duty. The one in red walks to the grave with desire, Joe."

Joe put his hands to his face. Although he desired to cover his ears, he was about to ask Rupert to stop, but Rupert continued. "Both are sad, but the one in red... ...How her lover died, who knows? Trying to tie things up, my grandson was killed because he was with the woman who was searching for the killers of a stranger, and I wonder if that is the man buried in the tomb."

Joe stood up and said he should leave. Rupert, surprised, insisted that he stay for dinner, told him that he had some veal chops marinated with garlic and pepper from the previous night, but Joe declined.

The bitter taste in his mouth was not that of the beers. Having visited old Rupert was a bad idea and the dozen beers they had consumed, instead of being the panacea of oblivion, had brought back memories he thought he had already forgotten.

***

It was seven in the evening. He heard the echo of the piano in Emily's house and went to her door. The melody she played was sad. He perceived in it the eternal sadness of the woman in red as described by Rupert. Emily hit the keys angrily, perhaps she suspected his approach and tried to blame him for something. It was not the romantic melody of that distant afternoon when he came to her house for the first time.

The tune reached deep inside him, remorseful like a dark thought. He gave three knocks. The piano stopped and he heard firm footsteps on the floor, the firm steps that his old friend described. The door opened, and there she appeared, suddenly, devilishly beautiful, dressed in red and with the scarf of flowers on her head, the only missing thing was the bouquet of flowers. But it was enough for him to look inside, surreptitiously to see on the dining table the bouquet with red roses. A lock of her hair fell and eclipsed her fury, and the blouse with the first button undone showed the cleavage of her breasts, like two moons that refuse to wane, celebrating her loneliness and triumph at the same time. Emily looked into the distance. Although he was there in front of her, she closed the door as if she had not seen him.

Chapter 51

Tuesday was his first day as a retiree. He woke up early and brought coffee to Rose. It was perhaps the only interaction he was allowed. That morning, she opened her eyes when he put the cup of coffee on the bedside table. The room was lit by the cold autumn sun as it filtered through the shutter. She had never allowed him to look at her at that time of the morning, but at that moment there was certain vehemence in her face.

"Are you happy?" He asked.

"Yes," she answered, staring blankly at an unfixed point somewhere in the room.

He sat down at the dining table and drank his coffee slowly. What was he going to do that day? Maybe he would go to the barber or the supermarket to buy some groceries. The feeling of having nothing to do made him a little nervous. Maybe over time he would get used to it. He prepared breakfast, fried eggs in oil, toast with a layer of jam and butter and black coffee.

The first thing a man with all the time of the world thinks of is how to survive the possible boredom of the hours.

He wrote a check to pay Mrs. McGee's salary, and as he was leaving for the barber, he saw she had hung up a notice on the door that said, "Do not interrupt." Curious, Joe leaned his head close to the door, but did not hear Mrs. McGee's sharp laugh. He thought perhaps she had not come that day and opened the door.

He would always remember that morning: Mrs. McGee, naked, had her hair disheveled, her eyes almost closed and she was on the edge of exhaling a deep scream that she tried to silence with her hand, but the scream escaped. Mrs. McGee, on top of Shane covered her face with his shirt.

Joe closed the door. Later when Mrs. McGee left, smoothing her skirt, Joe gave her the check for her services. There was not a single word spoken. She understood that her services were terminated.

***

Rupert was at the barbershop when Joe walked in.

"Happy Tuesday," he said.

"Not very happy," said Joe.

"I already thought about it," he said. "If we have two options; be happy or miserable, surely the second one is the most probable."

Rupert's statement made sense and fit well that morning. That sentence was so correct. *"Damn, Rupert, you just guessed what happened and what will happen in my unhappy life,"* he said to himself. That phrase suited him perfectly; the bad versus its opposite, the eternal tendency of everything including our emotions toward chaos of which he was a perfect example. Wasn't it the weird word of entropy that Shane, his son, the boy, the innocent young man he found that morning making love to his teacher, had mentioned? In conclusion, he thought, as Rupert was getting his hair cut, that he was condemned to the ineffable, infallible, unfathomable, inscrutable and, above all, inevitable misfortune.

For a moment, while the barber was preparing more foam for the last touch to his mustache, Rupert showed Joe the photographs of the beautiful women on the wall.

"That's the most beautiful," said Rupert pointing to Marilyn Monroe.

"One of my clients comes to cut his hair every Tuesday, and I get the feeling it's just an excuse to see her picture," the barber said.

Joe and Rupert left together and went to a florist shop, where Rupert bought a bunch of red roses.

"It's not what you are thinking," he said. "I do not have a dead spouse to bring these roses to as the two women do." It seemed that Rupert insisted on reminding him of the two women. "The flowers are for a woman that I want you to meet."

Joe followed Rupert to a house several blocks away. Rupert knocked on the door, a woman in her seventies, opened it. Rupert gave the roses to the woman, and she, without saying anything, put them in a jar full of water. It seemed that she had that jar ready for the roses, as if she was always expecting them from Rupert. They went to the dining table where there were two plates with cake and two glasses of milk. Rupert and Joe sat down, and the woman went to the kitchen to get a plate for Joe.

"She prepares the best cake in Williamson County," Rupert relaxed in his chair.

On the wall of the living room, she had all the prizes she had won in competitions for the best apple cakes of the region. Apple cakes were not her only specialty. She prepared cakes of other flavors and texture like peach, pumpkin and had presented a modified recipe from the Caribbean region based on ripe plantain. The presentation of her new recipe was a disaster because people refused to try it. She had drawn the conclusion from that bad experience that Americans are not very adventurous when it comes to exotic foods. That experience marked the end of her success in the contest.

Rupert took a sheet of paper from the pocket of his shirt.

"Today we have plantain cake." Every day that he went to visit, she had a different cake, on Monday apple cake, Tuesday plantain, Wednesday pumpkin, Thursday orange and Friday, it was pineapple.

That Tuesday the cake was fresh out of the oven and looked delicious.

Rupert had met her during those dark days after his grandson's death when she exhibited her new creation. Rupert was the only one who tried it, and he liked it so much that he asked her for the recipe. Instead of giving him the recipe, she invited him to her house. She was then 65 years old, and nothing happened that day neither the following ones that they remembered, neither a kiss nor a caress, none of that, even though they had talked about getting intimate. In addition to the question that she asked him on every visit: if he had brought condoms, she asked if he was wearing boxer underwear. She asked him those questions maliciously at the door, but it was just to spice up their time together. That was about 10 years ago, and they continued doing the same since then. Nothing that a couple, regardless of age, would have done, at least the audacity to take a nap together. She liked only that, to provoke and push him to the edge of the abyss with the promise that one day it would come to be; time passed, and Rupert was still waiting for that moment at his 86th.

Rupert wondered why she did that to him. Incapable of asking her, he wasn't ready to give up, and yet he had surrendered to his stoicism, waiting until she gave herself up to him. Only that night, with his friend present, Rupert heard the answer to his question.

"Rupert" she called him sweetly as she cut more pieces of cake and put them in the plates, "I have loved you all of these years."

She had been the happiest woman since he had entered her life; happier than when she lived with her deceased husband. She confessed without any hesitation that once she managed to feel an orgasm just thinking about him. It was the most intense orgasm of her life, without intercourse. She was ready for him, in any way, any moment, without the materialization of the act. She said that she was like the wife who reads romance novels and sees the neighbor's husband and dreams of making love with him.

"That's how it happened in those first days after I met you," she said. She had heard his car approaching and looked through the door's holes, and as Rupert walked to the house, she felt the *momentum*, a contraction between her legs, like the overflow of a river without control.

"Just seeing you," she said, "one of those memories that nobody wants to compare, nor repeat, because of the fear of disappointment, frustration and above all forgetfulness. That's the reason and I had preferred to live off that reminiscence."

It was almost midnight, and she went to the kitchen for more plantain cake. Meanwhile, Rupert told Joe that he felt like the happiest man in the world.

"I gave her an orgasm without touching her, what else could a man ask for?" He asked rhetorically.

Chapter 52

It was a clear night with a full moon. Joe regretted that Colton did not exist anymore, it would have been the perfect place to end what was left of the night. He felt the desire to sit next to a beautiful prostitute, even if it was only to admire her from head to toe, desire her, just as Rupert had desired his woman, and that would've been enough at that moment when the moon mysteriously calls with an irresistible magnetism to intimacy.

He once said to himself that the death of Ben Crompton the Third was a great relief for the town, but it eliminated the brothel and he regretted that. In all the years of its existence, Colton had been the place for men to deflower a desire and sometimes for women (with their faces hidden under a mask) to satisfy their curiosity. In Colton, even if it was regarded as the most hated place in the town, utopias were straightened, forgotten loves were resurrected, contradictions resolved, enmity was reversed and, above all, equilibrium was established, for the most part, all of these perceived by those who gave themselves to lust and perdition.

That was part of the benefits of its existence, but also the opposite to a large extent. What would've become of the town if it had never had the brothel? Deep inside he believed that if nothing else, the brothel was one of those things that, although undesirable, was necessary.

It was almost three in the morning when Joe arrived at his house. The pain in the lower part of his back was intense. He attributed it to the long time sitting in the house of Rupert's friend. He went to his room and looked in the drawer of the table next to the bed for the jar of painkillers and took two pills. Nothing, neither the pain itself nor the pills, reminded him that the doctor was emphatic in giving him another appointment and that it was mandatory.

In the morning, he sat down to have his coffee. A copy of *National Geographic* was on the dining table that his son had left there. He opened the magazine right where Shane had folded a page, maybe like a sign to resume his reading later. Joe read the title that his son was presumably reading on the evolution of the human species. He settled himself in the chair ready to read it. An introductory paragraph gave an idea of what the article was about and hooked him. It was a profound article that demanded all his concentration, although he did not understand it and the back pain was still there. The article caught Joe's attention, not because of the content, but because as he progressed in reading, he understood less and admired more his son's intelligence. He read the entire article, and the only thing he could summarize was that he had not understood anything. He put the magazine on the table and poured himself another cup of coffee.

It seemed to him that his son called him from the library, a voice that did not sound like his: it was sad, there was something more than that, bitterness, maybe nostalgia. He looked out the library door. Shane was sitting by the window, looking toward the house where Mrs. McGee lived. Joe saw the changes she had made in his son.

When she first came, Shane was the boy who had no direction. Only ten months had passed, and the changes were surprising, changes not only in his behavior but also in his physical appearance. It is impossible to believe that people can alter the looks of others, but it happens, and his son was an example of that process. He also learned to bathe and shave, had his shoes with the laces tied correctly, his hair combed and dressed impeccably. In other words, his son was different.

But all the admiration he felt at that moment was eclipsed by the sadness of Shane. Joe suspected his son was waiting for Mrs. McGee, and it was not the waiting of a student for the teacher, but that of a boy in love. Joe changed his clothes and went to see Mrs. McGee. She opened the door and only showed her face with the traces of a bad night of sleep.

Joe got to the point. "I've come to propose a deal. My son needs you, we both know your method is effective, I see the changes." It was a pledge that rather than convincing, made Mrs. McGee suspicious of his thoughts.

"I do not understand," she said.

"You know what I mean."

"Mr. Romano," she said, "are you talking about yesterday?"

"Not precisely, although the results ..."

"What happened between your son and me only happens once in a lifetime," she interrupted. She had thought about what had happened and made the decision that there was no turning back.

"Just come back, I'm asking you like a desperate father."

"No," she said. "And I'm very sorry for what happened."

"No regrets. Just come back and let things take their course."

"Mr. Romano, it's impossible."

Joe offered her three times the salary he had paid her before in addition to doing repairs to the house, but Mrs. McGee said no.

"Think about it," Joe said, "I'll be back tomorrow."

When he was about to leave, she said, "wait, I have something."

The wind opened the door a bit, and he could see her walking away until she disappeared behind a blue fabric division that separated her room from what perhaps was the kitchen and dining room. That image of Mrs. McGee, wearing a purple satin baby doll outfit that clung to her body, made him forget the low back pain. He thought about his son. He couldn't define what he felt at the door of the woman who had given everything to his son. He did not know if he was happy or worried about Shane, but he did feel a little envious.

Through the division of cloth curtain with indefinite figures, Joe saw Mrs. McGee going from one place to the other and then she stopped to change her clothes: the sensual purple satin baby doll for her everyday cloths. He also saw that she stopped to think for a moment. Maybe she was thinking about changing her mind. I wish, he said to himself, she would be good for my son.

She came back with a large folder with thick lids and rings that secured a large number of sheets of paper. She invited him to sit on the couch close to her. Mrs. McGee opened the folder.

"This is the report of Shane's advances," she said. Each sheet of paper, systematically prepared, contained information about the activities, day by day, the changes in his learning abilities, one attitude replaced by a more advanced one, a behavior that the previous day had not been able to modify or reverse or had been in the process of transformation for a long time. For example, tying his shoes, everything was recorded. The achievements in the learning of concepts, simple and complex, many of which were abstract that she did not understand, but that had enough knowledge to determine how difficult they were. She had written almost two hundred pages, on both sides, a clear and concise description of her contribution to Shane's evolution.

"Call it the natural history of your son or whatever you want," she said. The last pages were written in a conclusive tone, in which she provided recommendations and suggestions such as enrolling Shane in a university and attached a list of those Colleges that could accept him. Large universities, with special programs for exceptional students, one of which had an autistic student with the same characteristics as

Shane. Days before, she had requested information from that university and sent an inquiry for a test and interview, which she said was coming.

"I spent the night writing the last pages," she said. She closed the report and gave it to Joe. It was a sad moment, some tears to fell down her cheek.

Joe insisted again, and she told him that Shane did not need her anymore. She said she had taught him many things and she had nothing else to teach him.

***

He left the report on the dining table with the idea of reading it later. He poured himself a cup of cold coffee without sugar. He took the first sip. The coffee he had bought in the store lately was the best, it seemed the owner had changed the supplier. That coffee had a different flavor, it was black and robust and it tasted even better with a bit of brown sugar and a cake from the same store. The shopkeeper was his friend, younger, maybe in his late forties, and it was fun listening to his stories. Stories he repeated at times and that gave Joe the certainty they were true. Joe also told him his stories when he stopped by the store for a cup of coffee before going to the factory and now that he was retired, he would come to visit his friend more often.

The container was almost empty and he had to buy coffee, so now he had an excuse to go visit him.

"I was waiting for you," the shopkeeper said. He went to the coffee machine and poured him a coffee. "It arrived yesterday and is considered the best in the world."

"This is real coffee," Joe nodded. "Where does it come from?"

"It's from a country that I do not remember its name, from the northern part of South America."

"Give me two pounds," Joe said, "I think I'm going to need a lot of coffee these days."

"Do you have visits."

"Nah, it's my son." He lied; the coffee was to pass the night awake as he studied the report of Mrs. McGee. He ended up telling the shopkeeper everything, what happened during the previous morning, and the refusal of Mrs. McGee.

"That's an adventure," said the shopkeeper after he heard the story of Shane, "I would be proud."

"I do not know if I'm proud to know he's a man."

"Well, what a coincidence, I have another story, different, but they seem alike after all," the shopkeeper said, changing his face, from happy to sad and then disgusted. "My daughter, my princess, who is everything to me and for whom I work and keep this business, forgot her little purse before getting on the school bus this morning. I curiously opened it, and guess what I found?"

"A lipstick?" Joe said.

"I wish. It was a box of condoms." The shopkeeper wiped his eyes with his baker's hat and looked at the purse next to the register, a tiny red one with a patterned rose that was almost faded. "But the story does not end there. As soon as I learned about the condoms, my wife confessed that last weekend when I went to Chicago to buy merchandise to stock the business, my daughter said she wanted to sleep with her boyfriend and managed to talk her mother into taking her to the boy's house. What a disaster, and now I feel something, but I do not know what it is exactly."

"Neither jealousy nor anger," said Joe "It's a strange feeling, and you are not alone, my friend, because your daughter's story is like my daughter Linda's." He told him that story too.

"What you did for your son is what I would have done, besides being proud."

The situations of his son and the shopkeeper's daughter were different and yet somewhat similar. His reaction was as contradictory as hatred and love, rejection and acceptance; because he never forgave his daughter but gave his son support and admiration to the point of humiliating himself trying to convince Mrs. McGee to come back.

Chapter 53

When Emily came from work, she opened the door and was hit by loneliness. Her daughters were gone and the house looked empty and too big. First to leave was Sarah, then Linda and finally Rosario, who had finished high school and was in a university in Chicago. Sarah had finished her career and was working in another county to the northeast of the state, in a small town on the banks of the Ohio River. Linda had written her a long letter, almost 20 pages in which she told her in detail of her adventures in Hollywood. It was strange that Linda wrote her because her daughter was not known for such subtlety, but it was her. And Emily read the letter many times. Of her three daughters, Linda had everything, beauty and intelligence, two traits in a young girl like her that could delineate the road to success or disaster. And in that letter, she oversaw the second thing. In a few lines she summarized her appreciation for Hollywood, she said, "Hollywood is a woman with a sensual but sad smile, it depresses me."

Linda lived alone in a studio in the downtown of Hollywood. She did not like it, but it was the only thing she found and was enough to sleep in the free time after a day of hard work. The price was not that high even though it was in downtown. The studio had certain advantages besides the price, for example, it was close to the luxury stores, and she could feel that she was in Hollywood and see the Hollywood stars every day, sometimes from the window if she used the binoculars that she had bought for that purpose. It is fascinating to see them, she said. It's as if life, nature, something intrinsic gave them the privilege that we all lack, to be attractive by the way they walk or dress and the way they associate with the world and to be admired and desired no matter how bad or mediocre they are as actors or actresses. "Besides", she continued, "they are made to be admired, that's all." However, she stated when she saw Hollywood for the first time, she felt a tremendous disappointment.

She worked all the time in different jobs, as a waitress in restaurants, as cashier in a theater, nanny for a young couple, computer transcriber for an old man who claimed to be a writer, and other jobs that helped her pay the rent, fill the tank of the convertible, buy food, and from time to time buy an expensive garment like those used by the stars.

"Don't answer me," she said in the postscript of the letter. It was not the refusal to receive her response, nor was it that she avoided witnessing her mother's grief for the absent daughter who might have troubled her heart. It was much more; it was plain and simple that she wanted to break all the bonds with her family. She vowed never to return, no matter what, whether it was the sad news of the death of her mother or one of her sisters.

That was Linda, her daughter who wrote those hard phrases that closed the long letter and further down from the postscript, she asked her for money. Linda carried her name very well, for all the characteristics except compassion, kindness and all the other synonyms applicable to the list.

And that was the only time Linda wrote to her mother. She had withheld other stories that, if she had told them, she was sure her mother would have done everything possible to come and take her back home. Nothing in the letter hinted things were not going very well in Hollywood, but she underestimated her mother who already had suspected it.

***

One afternoon Linda went to a gas station to pump gas. She slid the credit card in the machine, typed in her code and the message "no funds" popped up in the screen. With the idea that maybe it was a mistake, she tried again and the message was the same. She tried several times, only hoping that a miracle would happen for her to fill the tank to go to work. She leaned against the car, worried and ready to cry, when someone appeared as if fallen from the sky, a man with a thick mustache, dressed as a cowboy, a big hat and a friendly smile.

"The gas stations in Oklahoma City have television," he said. "I saw the last minutes of the Warriors against the Salt Lake Jazz while filling the tank," he continued and then, as if he had guessed her anguish, "some problem, young lady?" He asked.

"I do not have money to fill the tank," she answered. The man pulled out a $100 bill.

"Here," he said.

"I only need 20," she said.

"It's yours, take it," he commanded.

"Then give me your address to pay you back."

The man got in his car, a red Hammer. "We'll see each other later," he said closing the window, and left.

When she was paid her salary, she reserved a $100 bill with the idea of paying if she ever saw him. A few days later she found him on a busy street. They spoke for a moment, and when she pulled the bill out of the purse, he refused to take it. Instead, he said that he would be more than rewarded if she accepted an invitation to have a drink.

They went to a moderately elegant bar, one of those that abound in Hollywood, filled with tourists every night, bars that present a seedy show, with artists who, for multiple reasons, including bad luck, didn't make it to the summit.

The man, somewhat elegant in his manners, had neither a college degree nor a real job; but he was charming. He had been a gigolo in his younger years, a vagabond in the streets of New York and Los Angeles. He was always accompanied by beautiful women and a few low ranked actresses. He was doing business with a guy called Harry. The business operations were varied, all illegal of course, including mainly the distribution of 100% pure cocaine to the women who were with him, a business that represented a good income. Part of the business included the traffic of beautiful women, and Harry was in charge of that part, with the promise of turning them into Hollywood stars.

Reuben, as he was called, had no place or address where he could be found. From time to time he had the idea of becoming a pastor of a church with no denomination and he had the means, besides some money. He had also the power of conviction and a repertoire of stories and anecdotes that dazzled poor Linda. At times he threw a promise that warmed Linda's ears and made her excited. Linda was not ambitious, but his promises inflated her ego. Among them, the promise of a prosperous horizon: a minor role in a film in which he was the producer that would open the doors of Hollywood. Other promises were money and a more spacious apartment. In other words, the culmination of the dreams of any young woman with a minimum dose of ambition and good luck. Finally, after a few words and a few sips of a sweet and delicious liquor to her palate that tasted like glory gave her a taste of Hollywood, as if the way to enter that universe was restricted for all her senses except her palate. They ended up in a motel, and that's where the story started.

After the first night in the motel, there were others. It became a habit since he came to visit her twice a week. Sex and liquor in abundance, sometimes a dose of cocaine, an insipid conversation, a story that he repeated many times but nothing of the initial promises.

All this should have seemed suspicious, but Linda was perhaps naïve or cared little for how much Hollywood offered her.

One day, he said he had a surprise; a role in a short film. He didn't tell her more, nor was she curious to know what it was.

"You just have to show up at this address."

"That simple?" She said.

"Yes, very simple, tell the director you know me."

"What name?" She asked.

"Who?"

"Director."

"His name is Harry."

Finding the address took her almost half a day. She imagined a central location in the downtown of L.A., a somewhat modern building with a striking sign, something like Harry's Productions or Contemporary Acting & Co; in short, a firm that, although perhaps not famous, was in the running to be so. But it was not like that. She found herself at the front of a tall facade without any sign that anyone would imagine was an acting school, with cameras and lights and voices. Nothing of the sort, just a rusty plate with the address that Reuben had given her.

And what struck her most was that the place was very far from Hollywood in an almost rural area. In the parking lot were some cars, and she hesitated for a moment after she got out of her convertible, but curiosity pushed her to go to the door.

"What would my mother say if she saw me here?" She exclaimed as she pressed the doorbell.

A short man opened the door, and his eyes went straight to her cleavage.

"Damn Reuben, he got a good one now," he said.

He was broad-shouldered, with a fat neck and a large head, disproportionate to his short stature. He was grotesque from head to toe, one of those individuals who even the flies would not land on.

"Come in," he said.

There was nothing inside that impressed except for a stage, rooms with no door and boxes stacked in the corners that almost touched the ceiling. On the stage, a man and a woman were acting. They were young and good looking and remained with their hands in an unfinished gesture or expression, and their eyes fixed somewhere. Perhaps her intrusion interrupted the scene, and both were waiting for an order.

"Who the hell told you to stop," the man shouted at the young couple.

"The lights are out!" Shouted the young man on the stage.

The man ran upstairs where a large lamp threatened to go out. The man hit it hard and the bulb lit up. He then climbed another narrow staircase with a mop to reach a lamp located high up. The stage was now lit, red and blue. He came back to the door to talk to Linda.

"So, you want to be an actress, do you?" He asked her.

"Yes, I do," she answered.

"You will become a star here," the man said with a loud giggle.

"Where's Harry?" Linda asked.

"Harry!" the man shouted, beckoning with his hands as if Harry were far away. "This damn animal does not come when I call him."

The actors on the stage disappeared, and Linda heard the noise of a car leaving. The man also disappeared and then a minute later, "miss, come to the last room, Harry is here," he called to her.

By then, she should've left, got in her car, and disappeared as well. But she did not. She did not even think about it. Maybe it was curiosity. She went to the room from where the man's voice came from.

Sitting in an armchair naked with his erect penis and a smile on his face he was waiting for her. His arms were held high, in one hand he had something that looked like a booklet and in the other his underwear.

"Do you want to be a Hollywood star?" He asked.

Linda ran to the front door and went to the parking lot. When she put the car in gear, the man came out naked, with a mop and started to hit the car. She accelerated and hit the man who flew a few meters. Linda looked through the mirror. The man looked dead.

She got to her apartment nervous, packed what she could in her suitcase and when she was about to leave, Reuben arrived.

"What happened?" He asked.

"He is dead," she replied.

"What?"

"I killed him."

"We're in trouble," he said.

They fled to a small and remote town in Utah and settled there for some time.

Linda returned home by autumn when the wind whistled in the pines and took the leaves from the oaks. She saw her mother picking up the leaves and hastily piling them up in the corner of the yard.

Eleven fifty

Linda cried and left her father's room. Rosario came behind her, and both went upstairs. Rosario tried to comfort her sister whose crying was not because of her father's death, it was a sorrowful cry, like someone who had lost hope. Emily, like her daughter, cried in silence. How could love be so durable and at the same time be a torment? She looked at his room. Her daughters had left the door ajar and she saw Joe. For some reason, her daughters had covered his face with a handkerchief. It was inevitable that vision and the feeling everything was coming to an end, and the conviction she had to live without knowing if he was the third man in the killing of Antonio.

"Mother," said Linda "I have to confess many things, things that happened after my return from Hollywood." At that moment they saw Sarah leaving the other house and turned their attention to the park where she stopped. Shane came behind Sarah, who held his hand; then both sat on one of the benches in the little park ...

Chapter 54

... Emily heard somebody talking to her and thought the wind was playing a joke on her because it was whistling in the eaves of the house. It sounded like the voice of a woman, and the noise of the dry leaves had prevented her from listening clearly. The voice spoke again, then she looked behind and saw a woman next to the oak. Her loose skirt reached the grass and the long fringes like those of a kite rose in the air. The woman seemed so strange that Emily thought for a moment she was one of her aunts, but it couldn't be, because she thought they had been gone so long and might've been dead already.

The woman was young in appearance, tall and white. Emily looked at her face and recognized her daughter's unmistakable smile. She had the small lift of her upper lip that, in her adolescence, when Linda wanted to be a beauty queen, she wanted to correct. That imperfection remained intact despite the years. Now her daughter had other features that made her different, and almost unrecognizable. The beautiful teenager had undergone a total metamorphosis. The long and slender neck was gone too, and Emily felt a small sadness creep over her. "My poor daughter" she said to herself, looking at the ground because she did not want Linda to see her disappointment. She recalled the old days when Linda had the idea of becoming a beauty pageant queen. Those days were gone and Emily looked at her almost not believing she was her daughter. Time had been cruel to Linda.

After a long hug and a few tears, they were able to talk. Linda introduced Reuben and explained to her mom that he was her savior. She told her some things about Hollywood, how she met Reuben and part of their life in Utah. It was important for her to vindicate herself with her mother, to let her know she had grown up and had changed. While Reuben inspected the piano and looked at the photographs on the wall, Emily and Linda went into the kitchen with the excuse of making coffee, and there she cried and told her mom everything. She regretted all the wasted time, mourned for having left without saying goodbye, for not having gone to college like her sisters. It had been ten lost years in which she did nothing. She said she came back because she wanted to start over, to make up for the lost time by dedicating herself entirely to a noble cause. She told her mom briefly, almost whispering that the noble cause was to build a church. Emily, who was still surprised by the transformation of her daughter, couldn't hide her frustration.

"What? A church? How?" She asked.

"With your help we will," she said.

"What help are you talking about?"

"We need resources."

"It would be the last thing I would do in my life, give you money to build a church!"

"I'm asking you for a loan."

"How are you going to pay me?"

"God will provide," she said. It was the end of the visit. Emily could see her daughter was eager to start a new episode in her life.

Emily did not see her again for some time, during which she wondered where she was, what she was doing, and how she was going to build the church. As an answer to all these questions, Emily kept telling herself that her daughter was crazy. She attributed the idea of the church to the man whom she thought was a pimp. She had observed him during the time he had been in the living room. She was sure he was twice her daughter's age. That age difference disgusted her. Once, as a child, she heard from her aunt Lisa saying 'when a woman falls in love with older men is because she does not have a father'. So, she drew another conclusion: that her daughter saw in Reuben, not the man, but the figure of a father. That idea tormented her as well.

During that time, she also had some conversations with Joe. Despite her concern, she never told him about her daughter's return. Joe asked at some point about the fat woman next to the oak tree, and she lied to him, saying she was a friend of Sarah's.

"I have a hunch she's going to come back with nothing good on her hands," he told her.

That phrase not only surprised her but made her worry more and solidified her decision to keep their daughter's return a secret.

***

Emily received a letter from the bank stating her account balance was at zero. She never suspected her daughter was capable of stealing what was left of the money she had received from the Carpenters. How Linda managed to deceive the people in the bank was a mystery, but she suspected Reuben was behind the embezzlement. She had the fear that Linda would disappear like the first time, but after a while she came back alone, without her companion. She was wearing a new suit, expensive shoes and a Halle Berry-style haircut. She sat crossing her legs with delicacy and elegance. Linda had the power of transformation from one moment to the next without much effort even despite her obesity. She could be extremely rude and then a few seconds later be the sweetest woman in the world. But her ambivalences were not just pretensions, they were part of her personality, and suited the bad side of her very well. And this time, she made a serious claim, with the threat of suing Emily for not supporting her when she was in Hollywood.

Before leaving, Linda told her mom she had already chosen the place where she would build the church, an old house on Oak Street. Linda did not give her mom more information. The farewell at the door seemed to Emily like that of a spiritual counselor, serious and poised as though she had completed a rigorous training.

Chapter 55

One morning, Joe was awakened by an unbearable noise: voices, machines, hammer blows. He got up and looked out the window on Shane's library. On the other side of the park, several workers were demolishing Mrs. McGee's house.

Joe put on his old coat, his sandals, and went out to the park, more curious to know about Tatum's life than the noise made by the workers. He saw who he thought was the boss, a somewhat elegant man with a big hat and in cowboy attire. However, the man was not the one giving the orders, because Joe heard a woman's voice somewhere, strong like that of a matron, who had everything under control. The man came closer.

"I'm sorry for the noise."

"Where did she go?" Joe asked.

"Who?"

"The owner of the house."

"My wife may know," said the man. "If you want to know about her, my wife can give you information. Come to visit us when the church is built."

"Church?" Joe asked.

"Yes," the man replied, "We needed one on this street."

"What is the name of the church?" Joe asked.

"We do not know yet."

"Hard to find names, huh?" Joe exclaimed.

"My wife is good with names, I'm sure she'll find one that will attract faithful people and keeps them happy," the man replied after a pause.

"There are not many faithful people around here," Joe said.

"We'll see."

Joe checked from time to time to see the progress in the construction of the church. In three days, the house had been demolished and the rubble lifted. Then they cut the grass and bushes, knocked down an oak tree that was in the front yard, and all the space was clean. Then, in two more days, they had almost twelve columns of concrete, and the base and the walls in 7 more days. The wall facing Joe's park had large windows. It was going to be a medium-sized church that pretended to be big, like those that had been in town for many years. They had, after many days, installed behind the whole structure a shed and on its other side what could be the residence of the man and the woman.

Joe saw the whole construction without even knowing the entire project was the idea of his daughter. He had seen her several times from his window in front of the building. Even though on many occasions they saw each other, Joe had not recognized her. The curiosity was from both sides, like an instinctive and reciprocal curiosity: hers to wonder if it her father simply ignoring her, his to wonder who that woman was.

And then, one morning when he returned from the supermarket, he heard the woman yelling inside the building and his curiosity rose even higher. Yelling orders to the workers and the orders were accompanied by profanities. Joe went out to repair the attractions of the park, only with the curiosity to listen to the woman's curses.

"Damn the mother who gave you birth!" The woman shouted. "We don't have much time and have a lot to do to finish this project."

He heard voices from the workers that he couldn't understand. Perhaps they were shocked by the woman's words and dared not protest her orders. He looked through the windows when the noise disappeared and saw the changes inside the building. They had built an altar and behind it a large cross that still had to be placed in a crypt in the wall. The windows on the opposite wall were stained glass with silhouettes from the Bible. Piles of chairs at the entrance gave an idea of how many people the church was expecting to attend but judging by the number the room was by far too small for the number of chairs. The interior was well-lit by skylights. The church did not yet have a dome, but a platform had been erected where it would be placed.

The day the dome arrived there was a lot of noise. It was towed by a large truck that took the driver some time to park in the exact place to have the crane lift it up and onto the platform. Once done, the building suddenly looked like a church; like those seen from a distance in remote parts of the United States.

With the installation of the dome, the bustle was over, the church was ready to open its doors, and Joe felt a bit of nostalgia because Mrs. McGee's house had disappeared. The house that sometimes seemed to collapse with the smallest gale had been the residence of the woman who had transformed his son, in all dimensions, including turning him into a man.

***

Joe went to the kitchen to fix dinner even though he felt the pain in his back. He prepared chicken legs browned in hot oil with potatoes and parsley; a simple meal because the pain did not allow him to stand very long. The pain wouldn't allow him to sit that night at the table with his son. He served the food for his son and called him, then put Rose's portion in the fridge and went to bed. He took several painkillers and laid down on his back. He tried to remember how long ago the doctor had seen him, it was almost 4 years.

Indeed, he received several calls, one of them was the doctor's assistant asking him to come to the doctor's office. Sometimes they left a voice message on the phone, and all were warnings of the consequences if he did not get the tests done. The last message was the doctor, who explained point by point the symptoms and the reasons why he suspected his pain was something to take seriously. Joe promised the doctor he would go the next day, but he didn't, and that was the last call.

For him, it was something simple, a muscular pain, and he thought the doctor exaggerated. In all that time, he relied on his own diagnosis and self-medicated painkillers to reduce the pain. But this time the pills did not help, and he finally was worried. It seemed like a parasite had made its way into the lower back, producing a puncturing pain as if that horrible creature was eating him slowly.

At dawn, without having been able to sleep, he got up. The pain remained the same, and in a haze with the pain and not thinking clearly, he took a handful of pills, the same ones he'd taken at bedtime and at midnight.

He sat on the edge of the bed and thought if he gave himself up to the pain, it was going to defeat him, so he felt it was best to stand up, start the day as usual. After preparing breakfast for his son and Rose, he took a hot shower, dressed up, and left in his Cadillac without knowing where he was going. He just wanted to keep his mind off the pain, not thinking about that parasite. He took Broadway and saw in the distance the sign of his friend's coffee shop and went to visit him. Maybe a simple conversation could take him away from the pain. The bakery was empty, and the baker immediately realized something was wrong with Joe, so he asked him.

"Nothing serious," Joe said.

The baker went to one of the sacks he had on display and took a handful of aromatic leaves and put them in a bowl with water. When the infusion began to give off a scent that spread throughout the bakery, he served two cups with a little lemon. They sat at a table in the far corner next to the window. The baker sat facing the door so he could see when a customer entered. He told Joe the mixture was of many aromatic herbs, lemon balm, verbena, thyme, and others that came from India.

"With this I healed Ligoria's lumbago," he said.

Joe took long sips and when he finished, the baker brought another cup for him. The conversation went from one topic to another, and in a few minutes, they were left without having anything to talk about. They remained silent for a long moment, both looking at the street, the slow traffic of the cars on Broadway, people passing by, and Joe trying not to succumb to the pain while the baker was troubled by the latest things going on in his life.

"Ligoria asked me for a divorce," the baker said. Joe shifted in the chair, looking for a position that would lessen the pain.

"I'm sorry to hear that," Joe took a long breath.

"The same reasons as always."

"What reasons?" Joe asked.

"Being honest, none," said the baker. "She says she's tired and I asked her about the reasons, and she replied that she's just tired. I'm saving money to take her to the Caribbean on a long vacation. Maybe that idea of divorce will fade away."

"I do not want to discourage you, but it's a serious issue when a woman asks for a divorce without a motive," Joe said.

The baker opened his eyes wide. For months, his wife had been talking to another woman, whom, at that moment, the baker only remembered she was big but very well proportioned and beautiful.

"I wish I had a few years less to approach her when she comes, the sound of her heels excites me."

"That's the reason," Joe interrupted. "Your wife suspects you like that woman."

"No," said the baker, "that woman is a pastor and is building a church."

"What?"

"Yes, she is a pastor and the first day she came, she asked me for money to build the church."

"And did you give her money?"

"No, but Ligoria did."

The truth, he said, was that this woman and his wife Ligoria talked a lot and in a shallow voice so he would not listen to them.

Ligoria called those conversations, "counseling sessions" and during that time, the baker suspected, that the shepherdess had transformed his wife, so much that now she wanted to divorce him. Ligoria spoke of the shepherdess as if she were her saving angel, with such admiration that the baker had begun to be jealous.

"Lately she talks about joining the club the shepherdess wants to create after she's built the church," he continued.

"A Club?" Asked Joe.

"Yes, a Club, I don't know what kind, but my wife is very excited. Although the idea of the club gives me bad feelings, I am not going to prohibit Ligoria to talk to the woman. Oh God! She is one of those women that come to this world to do evil and to drive this world crazy: men, and women, all." The baker gave a malicious laugh.

Just at that moment when the two were talking about the female pastor, they heard footsteps coming from the sidewalk.

"It's her," said the baker. "She will enter the bakery shouting my wife's name and when Ligoria comes out, they will kiss. Then my wife will give the woman a check who in return will put her hand on Ligoria's head. And my wife will shake as if she had received an electric shock." And that was what happened, just as the baker described it. The shepherdess entered the bakery and went straight to the shelf without realizing that the two were present.

The shepherdess' voice caused Joe a great shock because it was similar to that of his daughter Linda. Joe looked at her, but the woman was too big to be his daughter. The resemblance of the voice was just coincidence. The fright was such that he forgot his back pain.

"Take care of your bank account," Joe recommended the baker when the shepherdess left the bakery.

Chapter 56

The owners of the church had put a marble plaque on the side of the door with an inscription in golden letters, not so large they could be seen from the cars nor so small that it did not attract attention. The legend was intended to attract people and that morning when he returned from visiting the baker, he saw many cars parked and people crowded in front of the marble plate. Joe had a hard time understanding the legend. It seemed to him to be the description of a philosophical system.

Days passed by and the movement on Oak Street increased. Old, young and children, women and men, got out of their cars to read the sign. The shepherdess and the man invited people to come into the church. It seemed everything was ready, but the days kept passing, and the date of the grand opening was not announced. The delay had an apparent intention. The longer they delayed the opening, the more curious and enthusiastic people would be. It was evident the woman and the man intended the existence of the church should be known in every corner of the town and the county of Williamson.

Joe also was in expectation of that day; the day the church would open to the public, but his curiosity was not the same as that of the people. He had never gone to church and if someone had asked him about the state of his faith, he would not have had much to say. He wanted to see, up close, how people could believe all the lies the shepherdess had reserved for them. His opinion of religious matters was somewhat critical, although Joe never made that position known to anyone. He had accidentally read in a book 'it was not God who created us, but us who created God', in our image and likeness. He remembered that statement because the person who sold the book, (also a pastor), had it on the list of texts that should be banned in the United States. The title he did not recall but the pastor, at the time, said it caused him anxiety, uncontrollable anger, and a desire to spit in the author's face, who was a professor at Cambridge. Joe remembered the pastor's expression that was an indication of how far humans can go in their beliefs.

Joe anxiously waited for that day also because he had the curiosity of the neighbors' reaction to the noise and the presences of strange people in the street. For Joe, the presence of the church, and the woman and the man on the other side of his patio, were much worse than just the presence of a bad neighbor. He did not stop thinking about disasters, a tornado to destroy the church or any event that would not allow that woman to open it. But in the midst of his thoughts, he told his son who, from time to time, watched the revolution on the street.

"They will open the doors and people will come to listen to a trashy sermon, which everyone would buy as if it was their daily food." Joe frowned.

Time continued to pass and it seemed Joe would never know the owner of the church was his daughter. Emily had told her other two daughters to keep it secret and told him lies. For example, that Linda was still in Hollywood and had vowed never to return to the town. As always, when Linda was the center of their conversations, he told Emily the same thing, the same phrase he said many years ago that Linda would come to no good. Emily had come to accept it as right. She saw it, just across the street every day when she woke up. She knew everything, that her daughter had deceived many people in the town with promises of different kinds and like Joe, she foresaw a terrible ending. Even then, she would never tell him the truth.

Nor did their daughter Sarah dare to tell him either. Her reasons for keeping the secret from her father were different from those of her mother. For Sarah, the act of telling him required courage, and she who was the favorite daughter was not in a position to assume that responsibility, because it was as difficult as announcing to someone the death of a loved one. Rosario was far away, and the distance justified the silence surrounding the return of her sister.

And Linda, the despised daughter, the daughter who would have received damnation from the father, would not tell him anything, nor would she knock on his door to identify herself as the lavish daughter who'd returned repentant. Linda thought less and less about her father. Even more, it had not yet occurred to her to ask herself what he thought, nor did she suspect her father was totally ignorant that she had returned and was the pastor of the church. She saw him lean out the windows, something she disliked because she couldn't have a single intimate moment with Reuben for fear that he would see them. Not even in one of those moments in which their eyes met did she have the remotest intention of telling him. It was perhaps much more real to say that for Linda, her father was dead, just as she was dead to him.

At the barbershop, Joe heard that one of the reasons why the church was taking so long to open was because it didn't have air conditioning and the owners were waiting for the temperatures to drop a little. Another rumor was that there were disagreements between the couple, disagreements on how they were going to distribute the earnings from the services. He also heard that the conflicts were related to the intimacy of the couple, as it was rumored that the woman and the man had not slept together for a long time and the woman was unfaithful, screwing around with a young man who lived very close to the church. But there was another rumor Joe was unaware of and that, if he had heard it, he would have realized the woman was Linda. The rumor was: the shepherdess was the daughter of a man that was once called the cat-killer.

Then autumn came with its chilly days, the leaves began to fall from the trees. Oak Street continued just as turbulent as before, and there was so much expectation that another rumor was already running through the town. It was said that people were tired of waiting for the church to open and enthusiasm was diminishing with the passing of the days.

It was perhaps that rumor, in itself, that forced the woman to open the church. It was scheduled to open on the first Sunday of the fall season.

Chapter 57

On Saturday night, the eve of the first service, Joe went to his room tired from making some repairs in the park and cleaning the roof channels. The pain had returned with the same intensity. For the first time he thought to be prepared for the worst that could happen, and it was not just to accept that his days were numbered, it was that he thought about his son and Rose. He sat on the bed and opened the drawer of the night table and took out a folder. He checked document after document, slowly. For a long time, overseeing those days, he had bought an insurance for his son and Rose. According to his calculations, the insurance would provide a secure future. He just had to leave the signed documents in the hands of a serious lawyer, something he thought he would do the morning of the following Monday. He took the pills, this time it was a dose three times bigger than usual and hoping to have some relief, he covered himself from head to toe with the blankets and closed his eyes. It was a terrible night because he was awakened by voices and hammer blows in the church that lasted almost until dawn. At seven o'clock in the morning he heard a piano, an out-of-tune violin, clapping of hands and voices singing psalms; the church had opened its doors and celebrated its first service.

Joe put on a robe and went to the window. His son also looked at the people who gathered outside because the church was too small. Some had even gathered in his park.

"The only thing that will destroy this country is not the terrorists, nor a war with other powers; it's this fanaticism," he said to his son.

Since then, a crowd of people that was bigger every Sunday came to the church. Many of the attendees invaded the small park, and some sat on the steps at the entrance of his house. In other times, he would have made a great uproar, with a gun in his hand, as he did when the boys crowded in the window to see Rose; but these days he did not have the energy.

After some Sundays, he noticed that three men and two women always sat on the stairwell at the entrance of his house to listen to the sermon. The same people always, as if the stairwell was reserved for them. Joe, surmised, after listening to their conversations, that they came to church because maybe they had nothing to do on Sunday mornings. The men talked about everything while the two women listened. When the conversation became a little unpleasant and not acceptable to the ears of decent ladies, the women read the Bible. The men were friendly, and Joe sometimes talked to them. One of them, named Deddie, was black and the others were white: Mike, who was short, didn't have a Bible as did Ben who was tall.

It seemed that the three men lived together because they referred to the home as our home, our car, our kitchen as if they were properties shared by the three. You could also see that Deddie was taking care of the other two, who said they were adopted, brothers. It was noticeable that neither the men nor the women had the slightest idea of the denomination of the church. Joe, curious, asked them.

"The Children of God," Ben replied with confidence.

"No, it's called the Sons of God," corrected Mike, who had removed his cap and was very attentive to the piano that was playing in the church.

"It's the same," Ben replied.

"No, it's not the same."

"Neither is correct," said Deddie, "It's called the Lambs of God," and the others nodded.

"Have you heard about the Club?" Mike asked.

"The holistic Club?"

"Yes, that's what they call it, holistic, although I do not know what the hell that means."

"That Club reminds me of Colton," said Mike.

"Oh no, I hope that's not true, although I've heard things," Ben crossed himself and the others smiled with malice.

"What things have you heard?" Asked Deddie.

"I've heard things that can't be told just like that," replied Ben.

"You mean what we saw the other night? Asked Mike.

"You did not see anything that night."

"Oh, yes, I saw something."

"You were drunk."

"And you had eaten a cookie with that."

"What?" Exclaimed Deddie, disgusted, "It's not helping to prohibit these dummies to go around looking for trouble."

"Well, do you want to hear what I saw?" Asked Mike

"Tell us," said Deddie

"Well, but first I have to remember what I saw."

"Get to the point and tell the story, damn it," commanded Deddie.

"It was that night when Deddie brought his little woman, you remember Ben," said Mike.

"Who is going to tell the story, you or me?"

"You."

"Ah, well, I'll tell the story then, and you shut up. I know in detail what happened."

"Well, start."

"Shut the fuck up."

"Hell, what's wrong with these fools, it seems that everything I teach them is just trash," said Deddie angrily.

"I've heard the shepherdess is a bitch," Ben began, quietly and with some apprehension. "They say she is. They've seen her doing things."

The two women, who at the beginning were attentive, got up and went to sit far away, one of them crossed herself.

"That night when you brought the little woman, Mike, and I escaped through the window and went to buy liquor."

"You do not have to tell that," interrupted Mike.

"Damn you, let him talk."

"Making a long story short, after buying a bottle of whiskey, we went up Pine Street and then we turned onto Oak. I do not know why, but we went up Oak Street."

"You said that in the church there was a party every night."

"Did I say that?"

"Yes, you said that."

"Ah, yes, I said that, now I remember that I said that."

Deddie couldn't stand his frustration and went to sit on the last step of the entrance and leaned against the door close to Joe.

"Why doesn't the service start so these two will shout their mouth?" Deddie said.

"Do not forget to tell what you did after seeing through the window."

"What did I do?"

"You do not remember that right there you masturbated?"

"Mike!"

"Once and for all, close your mouth" Screamed Deddie. This time he was determined to give them some punches in their faces, but Mike continued.

"Show the Bible to Deddie," Mike said mischievously. Deddie snatched the Bible from Ben. It was a simulacrum, it had the appearance of a book, but when opened, it was a box in which he kept photographs of naked women. He had hundreds of photos in color and in black and white.

"And I was wondering why you're so interested in the Bible," he said to Ben in a surprised tone.

At that moment the service began in the church, and the three sat on the steps, in silence and very attentive to what was heard through the speaker installed on the side of the church.

Chapter 58

Many Sundays passed then one morning Joe was awakened by a noise. The noise was not the piano, nor the clapping of hands nor the violin. It was the owners of the church who were arguing. Joe got up quickly. The street was empty, he did not see the crowd that normally flooded Oak Street; his park was also alone and nobody was sitting on the swing bars, nor did he see the three men at the entrance of his house.

Joe went to pick up the newspaper when he saw the desperate woman who went out to the street and the man who tried to calm her down. The woman scandalized the neighborhood, clapped her hands and argued with the man. They entered the church, and the yelling got lost and then reappeared, there were door knocks and slams, steps going up and down and finally curses and threats. The woman in a moment of anger left the church again with pamphlets that she threw to the street. The wind scattered them in the neighborhood.

Life had surprised Joe so many times, but it had saved the biggest surprise for that day. A pamphlet landed on his door and he picked it up. The flyer had the announcement of that Sunday's sermon, written in cursive:

'Pastor Reuben Williams and his assistant Linda Romano will discuss the Psalms of Solomon today, Sunday, August 13, 2000.'

He looked at the pamphlet several times without believing it. He took the binoculars and looked at her through the window to be sure the woman was his daughter. He recognized the lifting of the upper lip. Even after having the certainty that the Linda Romano of the pamphlet was his daughter, he went to see Emily and she confirmed it. He asked her the reasons why she did not tell him, and she responded that the idea of secretly keeping her presence in town had not been hers but his daughter's.

"So, you know about the rumors?" He insisted.

"What are you talking about?"

"The Club, the orgies!"

"I don't know," she said, "but I've heard people talk."

Other events occurred that Sunday in addition to finding out that the shepherdess was his daughter. Almost at noon, another scandal on the street caught his attention. A woman shouted in front of the church, demanding the shepherdess show her face, while calling her *'husband stealer,' 'boyfriend stealer,'* and *'home breaker.'*

When Joe looked out the window, there were three more women who had joined the scene. And then more women appeared, they all shouted the same thing. The women threatened to take the shepherdess to court, and as the minutes passed, more joined with banners, as well as posters in which they called the church the *'church of the devil'* and *'church of the orgies'* and *'Colton number 2.'*

It seemed as if that Sunday would never end, because after the women left, someone passed by in a car shooting in the air. That night, there was a terrible gale that knocked down trees and detached cables from the poles. Joe, as always, unable to fall asleep, heard blows, like those of a whip. The pain almost did not allow him to get up, he could barely open the curtain, but as he did, he noticed the sound came from one of the electric cables that jumped, weaving in the yard. In each lash, the wire ignited fire in the grass, and the flames extended towards the door of his garage and advanced towards the church. He went to the garage, and with a shovel, put out the flames that threatened to reach the house. He looked toward the church and the flames were climbing up the walls reaching to the roof. Joe went back to his room and called the fire department. When he heard someone answering on the other end of the line, he hung up. He opened the curtain wide and looked at the fire.

Eleven fifty-five

That day, when she was able to recall all the months and that year of his agony, her sense of emptiness couldn't be more persistent. She glanced around the room as if she could remember a moment or an event that would take her away from that empty sensation. All things, the pendulum of the clock, the old sofa where Joe sat to ask her father for her hand in marriage, the family photographs, the same doors with their thresholds through which so many people had passed.

Everything as before, nothing that could alleviate that emptiness, only the canvas Antonio painted of her and Rosario had left it on the dining table to bear open witness to her misstep.

On the other side of the street, the abandoned house, with its yard and the park which in that year lost all its attractions, and the remains of the church that looked like the skeleton of an elephant. These recent relics made Oak Street much lonelier.

"Besides, I must confess something to you," Linda interrupted her thoughts. "He was the one who caused the fire."

"How do you know."

"The report of the firefighters says that the fire started at his yard as if he did it purposely."

"Amazing that you think that about your father."

"He hated me."

"He hated all of us …"

Chapter 59

Joe fell asleep despite the glow caused by the flames consuming the church. He slept as he hadn't in a long time. He slept until well into the day, and when he woke up, he saw on the other side of his patio the black frame of the church that was still standing. The highest part of the dome had collapsed and was still smoking. He picked up the newspaper and sat down to read it with a cup of coffee. On the first page, it stated the year 2000, even with its problems, was one of the most normal years in history; the world economy showed only a slight change, according to an economist nominated for the Nobel Prize. Other titles he barely read except for one about the latest results of a study on social evolution in the human species. Joe read the information. The study explained that the tendency to infidelity had a genetic basis. The study said that infidelity in men was more regular than in women, and men with larger testicles were the most unfaithful. About women, the study said there was a direct correlation between dominant character and liking for sex, between clitoral size and sexual promiscuity; that is, the study explained, that women with conspicuous clitorises were prone to having many sexual partners. When Joe read these lines, he thought of Linda.

The news of the fire was on the last page of the newspaper. The title: *Pastor Dies in the Fire of His Church*, informed that the dead man was from Los Angeles and that his assistant had suffered considerable burns. Joe recognized the two men in the pictures who were in custody as the potential suspects. They were Ben and Mike, the men who sat by his door on Sunday mornings. He went to the police and gave a statement of how the fire started and assured them the two men were innocent. He thought he could provide that information and return to his routine, but he was subjected to a thorough and exhausting interrogation.

After two hours, they asked him finally if he had called the fire department, and he answered no. They also asked him if he had tried, as a good citizen, to save the lives of the occupants of the building, and he said no. He explained that he had to stop the flames that were advancing towards his house and when he did stop those flames, it was too late.

***

Despite the events, Joe had never felt so calm and relaxed. It's strange that in the midst of a tragedy, sometimes the mind leans to the opposite like buffering our sufferings, like that saying from old times, *'every cloud has a silver lining.'* The low back pain suddenly disappeared, he felt fine and thought his good health had returned, so he started the mower and went out into the backyard. He thought to repair the park, but he realized it needed too much work and then gave up. He picked up fragments of trees, rocks, concrete blocks and burned sticks from the fire and piled them up in a corner of the yard. He saw the small staircase by the window, the same one the boys had used to see Rose on those long-ago afternoons. He climbed it and saw Rose, naked and taking her nap as usual. He looked at her for a long moment. Her door that was always closed, was opened. He walked around the house and went inside to her room. He laid down and made love to her.

As if he wanted to make up for lost time, he returned at midnight and made love to her until dawn.

"Come back tonight," she said when he got up to make coffee.

As a lover who wants to please his beloved, from that day on, he surprised her with a different detail every day: a postcard, perfumes, an elegant dress, black gloves, booties, a bracelet and so many other gifts. And so, every afternoon at three o'clock he made love to her. Sometimes, he found an excuse to climb the little staircase just to see her. Nothing was going to prevent him from those afternoons of pleasure, not now that he didn't have pain, felt vital once again, and had all the time in the world.

One morning, Joe heard knocks on the door. One of the policemen who did the interrogation came with a notice of appearance from the court. Joe felt a deep stab when he read that he was accused of arson.

"Son-of-a-bitch." He said, "my daughter is crazy."

He had to appear in court that same day at two in the afternoon for another interrogation.

"Just do what the notice says," the policeman smiled.

"Do you see that?" Joe pointed to the loose wire on the pole, "That motherfucker screwed everything."

The policeman went to check the wire and looked up the pole.

"That night was windy and the wire was spreading flames in the whole yard," Joe said.

"If I were you, I would get a lawyer," the policeman advised before he left.

Arson! It was a terrible accusation and he damned his daughter and wished she had died in the fire. What upset him most wasn't the accusation itself; it was the fact that he knew the truth. But it seemed he couldn't prove it.

At noon, he sat down at the table to have lunch.

"Who knocked on the door this morning?" Rose asked.

"It was a policeman asking questions about the fire." He lied.

Rose was excited. She had a glow on her face that made her even more beautiful.

"Three o'clock?" She smiled.

Like any of the words they said to each other every afternoon, it didn't require an answer nor an explanation, just the certainty that he showed up at her room at three o'clock and made love to her. Joe, at that moment, was ready to promise her anything so he didn't remember his appointment with the court.

So, he answered, "three o'clock."

He thought, as he did every day before three, to take a recovering nap, then a shower, shave, and wear some men's cologne like a ritual before he appeared at her door.

It was one o'clock when he went to his room. He laid down and fell asleep. He woke up and saw the clock on the little table, it was twenty minutes passed two.

When he was in bed with Rose, he heard knocks on his door.

"Sons of bitches!" He shouted, "you couldn't come at another time?"

The policemen came heavily armed and brought an arrest warrant for not coming to the interrogation. They read him his rights and without giving him time to get dressed, they proceeded to put the handcuffs on him, as Joe objected. They took him out of the house by force and had a fight with him in the courtyard. One of the policemen punched him in the abdomen and knocked him to the ground. The officers handcuffed him: "Sir, you are under arrest." When they tried to pick him up, they realized he was unconscious. But that was not the only thing that happened to Joe, a thread of slimy water was coming out of his nostrils, and his breathing was very weak. The agents took him to the hospital.

An hour later, the doctor told the policemen, "this man is dying and we have to hospitalize him."

After a few days, the policemen went back to the hospital and the doctor came with the bad news: Joe had mesothelioma, a cancer of the lungs, with no cure or treatment to prolong his life. Science was still incipient in that field at the time, and chemotherapy treatments instead of alleviating the disease aggravated it and, therefore, the doctors ruled not to apply them. The disease was so advanced that it had metastasized into adjacent organs and tissues: the esophagus, lymphoid tissue of the large intestine and larynx. They had to connect a probe in each lung to evacuate the fluid from the alveolar sinuses, the doctor explained. The doctor did not say how much longer he would live, maybe months. The doctor assigned a nurse who would go to his house twice a week to evacuate the fluid that accumulated in his lungs. Joe heard all and shed some tears in front of the policemen who left the hospital.

The nurse who came in the ambulance told Rose about the recommendations. She handed to Rose her planned visits and gave her a succinct explanation about the possibilities of some decision-making procedures, such as taking him to a nursing home where he could be on observation as needed.

"He needs lots of rest, no solid food and dim-room light," the nurse said and left.

Joe heard the recommendations in silence. "I think all this shit is killing me more than the illness," he said.

"We need to follow what she said." Rose advised.

"Those stupid protocols, those personalized visiting-plans." He looked at the package Rose received from the nurse, "that scares me."

He took off the hospital gown and took a long bath with hot water and soap and scrubbed his skin as if trying to eliminate the smell of medicine from his body. Then, he put on his pajamas and laid down in Rose's bed.

Rose came later with a bowl of soup. She sat down by the bed.

"I don't know how many days I have left," he said. He heard she was crying.

At midnight he woke up and went to his room. He wrote Rose a long letter telling her about his decision to pass his last days in a nursing home. He explained the reasons for his decision 'the deterioration of my body scares me and would scare you and my son.' Between the lines, one could guess that he was sorry for not having gone to the doctor, but he said it was unnecessary because he had the certainty he was going to die. Then he wrote about his past. In some lines, he justified his actions and repented in others. He wondered if life would have been less difficult for her if she had not known him. "Maybe," he wrote, "you would have returned to Ukraine, and you would not have such loneliness. Perhaps you would have found a good husband who might've given you children and happiness, but fate is sometimes inherent to our actions. If we had the ability to glimpse the future, we would change events, some deliberate, others unconscious and even those, products of our pride; then perhaps our destiny would be less cruel, and more bearable." He wrote to her that during the years they had lived together, she in her room away from reality and he without the ability to understand her silence, through all those years he had never stopped loving her.

"Now I remember everything," he wrote, "like a movie, like an album made of remembrances, an album that someone was compiling without losing a single detail. The most distant facts now appear so recent. I remember the night of your heartrending scream as if someone had come to kill you. I remember how without thinking twice, I took the gun and left willing to die if necessary, to save you. I remember very well the terror you had because of the horrendous creature that hung from the parallels of the dressing table. Now that I do not know how much life I have left, I can glimpse the events: that night, your silence took over your life and confined you to your room and the cause of all of that, who would it be if not me? I never thought I was the source of your fear. And you were right, yes, you were right: shots in the yard, killing cats, screams in my nightmares, my favorite game Russian roulette, confessions of deaths, revenges, tribulations and so many other facts that would have reduced to silence and perhaps madness even the strongest woman in the world."

He asked Rose for forgiveness for what he did to her, and for what he could've corrected but didn't, knowing that he himself was falling into the abyss and in that plunging, he was taking her as well.

He wrote at the end that she would not see him agonize because it would be too painful, 'remember me with the best memory you have of me, like those days in Colton, like those nights when you barely imagined what life had reserved for you.'

It was five in the morning when he finished the letter. He put it on the little table by his bed, and then he called his daughter Sarah to let her know about his decision to die in a nursing home.

***

When he opened the door, he felt cold even though it was a hot summer morning. He put on a coat and a hat and left. In the yard, the Swifts made a loud shout in the oaks. He did not say goodbye to his son. He thought that confessing to him that he was dying was more traumatic than leaving without saying goodbye. He also felt in moments like that it is better to separate oneself from the beloved ones without explaining the causes of the departure, and without promising a return that would never be.

He remembered he had still one responsibility to complete before going to the nursing home. He got in his Cadillac. He started the engine and drove up Oak Street. He pushed hard to give the engine more gas, but his muscles didn't respond. He made sure it was the right time to show up at the court office and submit to what the judges had decided about his accusation. He parked his car and rested for a moment.

It took him a long time to walk from the parking lot to the Courthouse. He stopped before he climbed the steps to reach the entrance of the building. Holding the handrail, he started to walk when a policeman who was coming down approached him, "Where are you going, Sir?"

"I came for an interrogation." Joe answered.

"You can't attend an interrogation like that, Sir."

"My daughter accused me of setting her church on fire."

"Oh, the church?" Said the policeman.

"Yes, the church! I am innocent." Said Joe.

"Well, the accusation has been dropped."

Joe kept climbing the stairs and the police, said, "You don't need to do anything. I personally attended your daughter who came a couple of days ago to drop the accusation."

"Well, in that case bring me the notice to the nursing home."

"I will, Sir."

Chapter 60

When Sarah heard about her father's decision, she called her mother and they had a long conversation. After some discussions and agreements in which Rosario was also involved, they decided to bring their dad to Emily's house.

Some days had passed after the conversation and despite the fact that she still had her doubts, Emily agreed to take care of Joe. But she had personal motives to bring him to her house, so she went to the nursing home.

"Why?" He asked.

"Because your daughters want you to die at my house," she said.

"Why?" He asked her again. She understood he was asking for her motives.

"I don't know." She kept a long silence and then she said. "You are dying Joe; don't you think this is the moment to confess the truth? I just want to make sure that my suspicion is wrong?"

"You have a suspicion, what else do you want from me?"

"Just the truth."

"Your damn suspicion and your damn interrogation. I just get out of one and you are thinking...who knows what. If I go to die at your house, you will subject me to another interrogation. Am I going to die in peace?"

"I am taking you to my house, no matter what." Emily pushed the wheelchair to her car and behind came the nurse to help her.

As they drove away from the nursing home, Joe thought about that distant afternoon when Benjamin Crompton the Third died. Perhaps the Mayor then sensed his death as he had the certainty of his own at this moment.

The first thing Joe did after Emily put him in bed was to check his finances. In the short moments that the pain allowed him, he wrote a letter to his lawyer giving him the power over his savings. He explained in the letter, as he had done on other occasions, how these resources should be distributed for the daily support and well-being of his son and Rose. "Do as I have determined... forever," he concluded the letter. He signed it and put it in an envelope. He tried to get up and take the letter to the mailbox, but Emily did it for him. That was his only conscious activity in all that year. He avoided any conversation with Emily, and if he needed something, he knocked on the wall.

***

And so, one year went by. She went to his room that morning and held his hand. Joe was cold. She realized the end was very near. The hours passed, and she did not hear a single knock on the wall, not even the louder one with which he asked her to come and keep him company; neither the three blows to let her know he needed to go the bathroom. She sat down to play the piano and without thinking she played a piano movement by Beethoven, a slow and sad melody that a few minutes later was interrupted by the nurse who came to evacuate the fluid from his lungs. The nurse came earlier than usual, and as always, she followed the regular procedure: she took his temperature and pulse, touched his forehead, "he is cold," she exclaimed and asked Emily for another blanket. Then she opened the two catheters connected to the lungs, and the fluid began to flow into the container, and without further words, the nurse put away the thermometer and stethoscope and prepared to leave.

Emily followed her to the patio. She wanted to hear the nurse's verdict, who switched the conversation to the latest research advances in the cancer that Joe suffered. There were many foundations created suddenly to raise funds to support a hundred investigations that promised outstanding results in the understanding of the causes and cure of the disease. It was expected that, in less than two years, there would be a treatment that, if not a cure, would at least prolong the life of patients with mesothelioma, giving them hope until a definitive cure was developed. There was research underway at many institutions, such as John Hopkins Hospital and the University of California at Berkeley among others, not counting institutions in Europe and Asia. The nurse told Emily she had heard all that information from doctors in meetings. "The future is promising," she said and lamented that Joe's illness had been untimely.

"If it had happened a year or two later, we may have saved him," she said.

That night, before going to bed, Emily went to his room. Unlike every other night, the room was cold. She set the thermostat at 75 degrees as the doctor had recommended. She left the door open to alert her to any noise coming from his room and read until late. She fell asleep with the light on and the book on her chest.

It was an uneasy sleep, with shocks in which she woke up with the sensation that Joe was talking to her. It was as if he wanted to confess something, but she fell asleep again. And at five in the morning, she heard the three knocks on the wall.

Noon

The big clock in the living room announced that it was twelve o'clock with twelve strokes that were interrupted by a distant siren. Emily called on her daughters to be ready because the ambulance from the funeral home was coming. For her it was as though the day turned another direction because when Sarah came back, she let her know that Rose wanted to see her.

"It is urgent," Sarah said.

Emily had opposed in the morning to tell Rose the news of his death, and now her daughter brought the message that she wanted to see her.

"That never will happen," said Emily.

"It is urgent." Sarah insisted.

"Never, ever would I go," she said from the chair where she had been all that morning.

"It's important." Sarah kept going on. "She knows things you want to know."

After thinking for a moment, Emily went to her room and put on her best dress, wore makeup as she did when she visited Antonio. When she came out all dressed up, she surprised her daughters.

"I do not want her to see me sad," she said and left for the other house.

Chapter 61

The door was open, so she went in. It was dark inside, she heard Shane's voice somewhere and kept walking. She raised her hand to orient herself in the darkness. She saw a faint glow of light and went toward it. She pushed the ajar door open and it was almost as dark inside that room. She waited, and then the image of Rose emerged, sitting on the bed with her hands on her knees.

She had never seen her face to face. The only time was when Joe fell off the roof and she saw her through the glass of the door. She seemed younger than then, dressed in black and her hair tucked at the back of her head.

Emily sat on a bench by the wall.

"He always sat on that bench," she said in her soft and sad voice. "I'm not your enemy." She kept silent for a long pause, a ray of sunlight entered through the tiny window and lit the room. "I never was," she said, turning her gaze to the window. Emily was surprised by the beauty of her profile.

There was not a single painting or photograph on the walls. Emily had an image of the interior of the house that did not coincide with the reality, but Rose was as she had imagined. Emily felt her hatred of so many years fading away. After seeing her sadness, Emily realized her resentment was not jealousy, but the fallout of all that had happened. Sitting in front of Rose while listening to her, she felt the desire to hold her hands and let her know she did not hate her either.

Emily understood Rose had the same remorse as well, both marked by the same pain and loneliness, joined by the same man who was the creator of their sorrows.

Suddenly they heard a slow beat coming from the library. The blows were not violent but were as if they would never end.

"It's Shane, it's his way to show his sadness," Rose said. "I forgave Joe everything except that he forgot his son."

"He was sick," Emily said. "He couldn't walk."

"He was his son."

"You could've brought him to see his dad."

Rose kept silent. She stood up, lit the bedside lamp, and then took the curtains of the tiny window down. Emily could see that she was taller than she had thought.

"I told Sarah I wanted to see you because I know things I'm sure you've wanted to know all of these years. I'm sure you always wondered if Joe was involved in Antonio's death. You have to remember that Joe had several dead on his shoulders."

"It was the war," Emily interrupted.

"Yes, it was the war and don't forget the Mayor."

"The Mayor committed suicide." Emily knew everything about the Mayor's death and tried to defend Joe against the accusations of Rose.

"No, it was a game that looked like suicide, but let me tell you the story of Antonio's death. That afternoon, on the eve of his death, Joe was in a bar, in front of the building where Antonio lived. He was alone by the bar counter. The bar was almost empty, just a few people. A sudden bustle was heard in the street, and people stood up to watch. Joe did the same, taking his beer. The street was crowded with people in front of the building. Joe could see the reason for the bustle was the simulacrum of a bullfight, in the middle of the street and in the daylight.

Can you imagine that? A simulation of something that has never been seen in the entire nation, much less in a town like this. Doesn't it seem strange to you? People without knowing what was going on kept coming out of the building and the ones that passed by the street joined the crowd. They had formed a circle around the two men who played at bullfighting. One as the bullfighter and the other as the bull. Whoever played the bull held the large horns, the same ones that were at the entrance of the building. The bullfighter, a dark and tall man, teased the bull with a red sheet. You may already know the history of the horns, Joe also told me about them...

...The bustle was heard all over the street, cheers, and 'ole, ole' from those who knew about bullfighting. Joe paid for his beer and left with the intention of returning home, but he was struck by the bullfighter. It was intuition, suspicion, jealousy, call it whatever you want. He looked at him very carefully, and that's when he saw around his neck the blue scarf with red and white circles, the same one he had seen on your head on many occasions. He confessed to me that he had felt a twinge in his chest. But at that time, Joe did not know the Mayor was also present watching the simulation, nor did he know the Mayor was going to kill the bullfighter for dishonoring the memory represented by the horns. It was incredible what was going on in the scene and outside of it, in addition to the events that were going to happen that night...

...Two elements put Antonio in danger, two objects that had nothing in common and yet determined his death; the horns and the scarf put him before the eyes of two men who, being enemies, had something in common: the same enemy. What a strange coincidence. But a third element needed to be added; the love that the tailor had for you. Remember that the tailor-shop was only a few steps away from where the simulation of the bullfight happened. I also came to know that the tailor was very jealous of Antonio. What a strange coincidence, I wonder if the tailor also saw the simulation through the window...

...Joe came home that afternoon and then left for Colton almost at eleven o'clock that night. He had kissed my forehead before leaving, which was strange because when he left, he always kissed me on the lips. He returned at dawn with a strong smell of gunpowder on his clothes and the flannel he had wrapped around his hand where he hid the gun. I've had it since that night, wrapped in the same flannel that he had used to muffle the sound of the shots...

...I remember Joe crying inconsolably, sitting in that same seat where you are."

She had kept the gun wrapped in the flannel in the drawer of the table and had made sure Joe never found it.

"This is the gun that killed the love of the two of us; the one who killed your lover and killed the love I had for Joe," she said. "A woman can love a murderer, but never someone who kills the love of another, even if that woman is her enemy." She reached for the flannel that, despite the passage of time retained the smell of gunpowder. The shots had left dark spots and a large hole. Rose showed it to her against the light and handed the gun to Emily who refused to hold it. Rose insisted. When Emily took it, she felt a burn on her hands.

"Joe killed him, there's no doubt about that," Rose said. "Joe snatched the gun from the young man and then shot the man who was in a shack. By then, he didn't know that man was Antonio." It was the same story she had heard from Camille.

For many years Emily had tried to get the truth out of Joe, from the moment she learned about Antonio's death, she suspected that Joe was involved and now that Rose confirmed it, she didn't want to believe it.

"If you still do not believe it, here is his confession, the letter he wrote to me the day he left to die at the nursing home."

Emily read: *"If I do not dare to confess her the truth, you who know all, tell her that I killed Antonio."*

"He left me that responsibility, but he never knew that keeping the secret hurt me so much that all my disdain and silence was for that reason because he killed an innocent man."

The two women cried for a long moment, and their weeping was interrupted only by Shane's blows in the library.

"He keeps throwing books on the floor," sighed Rose and there was a long pause before Emily asked if Joe told her about the events before the murder and how he came to know that the dead man was Antonio.

"Joe was with a prostitute that night and had learned through her that the Mayor was going to kill a man he referred to as *the stranger*. The prostitute got scared after she heard that. She asked Joe to save the man and she in return, (he told me,) would be his lover whenever he wanted. Joe, drunk, promised her, although he wouldn't have done anything. His promise was just to comfort her. However, he left with the idea of making her believe that he went to save the man who at that moment he did not know was Antonio. I am more than sure if he knew, he would've saved him, Joe was a bad man but not so bad that he wouldn't have done something to save an innocent person...

...Joe walked to the main door of the brothel and thought to go to the parking lot for a stroll. At the door, Joe met an acquaintance who, like him, had been drinking for several hours. They talked for a few minutes when they saw the Mayor getting into his car with his men and other cars followed behind. The acquaintance told Joe that there was a big hunt that night and that the deer was the Mayor. Joe in the middle of his drunkenness said to him that he had been told that the deer was not the Mayor but another man...

...The acquaintance said no that the death of the Mayor had been planned for a long time and that night was his last. He told me when he heard that, he had a mixture of joy and fear. Joe joined the caravan, convinced they were going to kill the Mayor. He followed the group of cars from a distance but lost sight of them when he mistakenly took another road. But after a while, he managed to see the glare of the lights of the cars and after a few laps, he arrived at the site...

...There were many cars, all with the headlights on, some pointing to a fixed place, a dilapidated shack, others to the forest. Joe parked somewhat far away, opened the window and heard voices: *shoot him, shoot him*, amid the noise and the raining, he also heard some shots and somebody shouted at a young man who had a gun: "He is the Mayor, shoot him." The young man looked behind at the lights and was scared...

...Joe got out of the car, covering his face from the nose down and walked toward the young man, snatched his gun and fired towards the shack. He returned to Colton and told the prostitute that who was going to be killed that night was not a stranger but the Mayor. Joe was thrilled and had some drinks with the prostitute to celebrate the Mayor's death. An hour later, he was doubtful and went to the place, and found that the dead man was Antonio. He recognized him because he had your scarf on his neck. Joe came back home and sat down on that bench and cried. Even though he knew Antonio was your lover, he was sad he had killed him and hated the Mayor more than ever and swore to kill him."

***

Emily left Rose's house and stopped in the park for a moment. People from the funeral home were leaving her house with Joe's body.

She waited until they put him in the ambulance. Her daughters were at the window, crying.

Emily went up Oak Street, a few blocks later she turned onto Pine Street. She drove two more blocks and parked in front of the building where Antonio once lived. Everything was as before, the old buildings were the same, only now they were taken over by business and the street was crowded.

The building where Antonio had lived was still intact with the gate open but without the horns, and his window was open. She walked upstairs to his place. From somewhere, a melody came down like those afternoons when she walked upstairs to see him.

Emily arrived at his door mumbling the song, *Yester-me...yester-you... yesterday...*

Author Profile

Uriel Buitrago, a native of Colombia, is a professor at the Oklahoma State University (Department of Integrative Biology) and has taught at multiple colleges and major universities in the United States and abroad. Uriel has published short stories, poems, and several scientific articles in international journals. He is also active editing in the field of natural sciences for publishers McGraw-Hill and Pearson, and national and international journals.

Every year, in May, Uriel travels to the Amazonian Rainforest to work with high-school students and natural sciences instructors. Part of his project in the Amazon is to equip high-school laboratories with microscopes, charts, and biological preparations. For Uriel, being in the Amazonian Rainforest has been inspirational for his creative writing as he is now working on his second novel which is about the adventures of a boy in a remote village in the Rainforest.

Uriel is a longtime member of a Chicago writing group and a member of the Oklahoma Writers' Federation. He currently has three more novels in the state of embryogenesis.

CPSIA information can be obtained
at www.ICGtesting.com
Printed in the USA
BVHW090337130822
644509BV00007B/109